All Summer with you

BETH GOOD

Quercus

First published in Great Britain in 2019 by

Quercus Editions Ltd
Carmelite House
50 Victoria Embankment
London EC4Y 0DZ

An Hachette UK company

A CIP catalogue record for this book is available
from the British Library

PAPERBACK ISBN 978 1 78747 741 4
EBOOK ISBN 978 1 78747 742 1

10 9 8 7 6 5 4 3 2 1

Typeset by Jouve (UK) Milton Keynes

Printed and bound in Great Britain by Clays Ltd, Elcograf S.p.A.

All Summer with you

CHAPTER ONE

Jennifer had been sobbing for hours. She felt ragged, raw, and had lost all sense of time. She was lying face down on her bed, ignoring occasional notification chimes from her mobile, when the bleating of a goat brought her upright.

She knew it was a goat, and not a sheep, because her friend Rekha had once kept three goats at her beachside Cornish home. Three very vocal goats, named after three Hindu gods: Shiva, the Destroyer, whose key skill had turned out to be precisely that; Ganesha, the Elephant God, due to the odd shape of his head; and Durga Devi, the Invincible Goddess, known for knocking over and rummaging among the dustbins, no matter how securely their lids had been fastened. Only Rekha had moved away to Devon years ago, taking her goats with her, so this couldn't be one of hers.

Jennifer grabbed the box of tissues from her bedside table, blew her nose, dabbed ineffectually at her eyes and swung herself off the bed.

Her reflection mocked her from the mirror on the wardrobe door: long, dark, tangled hair, red-rimmed eyes and a complexion as mottled as a halloumi and beetroot salad. Her oldest, baggiest pair of jeans were speckled with paint from redecorating the living room, and her vest top had ridden up her midriff almost to her chest, making her look decidedly louche. She had lost weight, too. She wasn't quite as flat-chested as she had been in her teenage years, but boyish would not be an inaccurate description of her figure.

Was it any wonder Raphael Tregar had preferred the curvy, well-endowed Hannah Clitheroe to her? Her chin started to wobble precariously.

'Forget him,' she thought out loud, and wagged a cross finger at herself in the mirror. 'Raphael Tregar is not worth it. He's just a man. But you're a woman, and women can do anything they set their minds on. Anything at all. You hear that? You're a *woman*.' Having established this important distinction, she wandered to the window and gazed down curiously into the small front garden. 'And you, my friend,' she continued, finding a pair of slanted eyes looking back up at her, 'are a goat.'

She had moved into Pixie Cottage a week ago, and had been working on her keynote speech for the Pethporro Folklore Festival for most of that time, barely venturing out except to purchase fresh milk and the occasional cheese sandwich.

She was already feeling lonely out here, in the middle of nowhere; she could not deny it. Lonely and a little depressed.

But wasn't that why she had moved here in the first place? To escape the demands of the outside world, and wallow, and write her book?

It seemed the world was not done with her yet.

This was her first encounter with a local.

'But whose goat are you? That's the real question. It's not like I have many neighbours all the way out here.'

She lifted her gaze to the vast Porro Park estate that bordered the cottage, her neighbour's house invisible behind thick woodland. Not just her neighbour, in fact, but her landlord. Pixie Cottage belonged to the estate, and was formerly home to a gamekeeper, apparently. Now it was a rental property, and she was its latest tenant. Apart from Porro Park, there was no other human habitation for several miles in any direction. So unless the goat was living wild in the woods …

Losing interest in her shocked expression, her visitor lowered its head to graze the herb bed, and Jennifer heard the faint jingle of a bell.

She leant closer to the window, staring. The animal was wearing a collar under its fine grey goatee beard. A thick collar, with a bell attached to it. Perhaps this goat had a reputation for wandering, she thought grimly, watching it chomp a second generous mouthful of flat-leaved parsley. A collar and bell meant it was no wild Cornish goat, to be chased away at will, but a domesticated animal with an owner.

An owner who was almost certainly aware of its absence by now and quite possibly frantic with worry.

'Okay, you pest. That's enough of my parsley.'

Jennifer pushed her feet into her sandals and hurried downstairs before the wretched animal could spot the runner bean climbers wreathed lavishly about a bamboo frame just ten feet from the herb bed. She hadn't sown any of the plants at Pixie Cottage herself, of course, but she hoped to be the one who would reap their harvest later that summer – not this nameless goatee-sporting thief.

The cottage was not difficult to negotiate in a hurry. One-bedroomed, it boasted an open-plan kitchen and living room downstairs, with a tiny bathroom on the first floor, next door to her bedroom. The living room had a glass-fronted log burner for winter months, and thick walls to ensure the place stayed cool on hot summer days, according to the agent who had let her the property. Most of the windows downstairs were narrow and festooned with ivy; daylight had a delicate green tint, as if the cottage were underwater. But Jennifer rather liked that. She had felt for so many months as though she were drowning. The greenish light seemed to confirm it.

The place had been bland magnolia throughout when she moved in, a colour she despised. She had redone it in white downstairs, and the living room smelt bracingly of fresh paint.

The local paper was still lying below the log burner where she had thrown it earlier in a fit of temper. She didn't so much as glance at it on the way out. But her nerves prickled.

That bloody photograph!

There was still no sign of Ripper, she noticed. Since installing a cat flap, her Siamese cat had been vanishing at regular intervals in search of voles and other hapless prey. At least there didn't appear to be any corpse trophies lying around this morning.

Meanwhile, the goat was demolishing brightly coloured nasturtiums, both front hooves sunk in the flower bed, head down as it munched busily.

There was an old length of rope in the shed. Jennifer shook off the spiderwebs, looped the rope over her arm and approached the goat in a firm but non-threatening manner. The goat looked up and stopped chewing. Nasturtiums trailing from its mouth, it eyed her warily.

Now, what was it Rekha had said about the best way to catch goats?

CHAPTER TWO

'Come on, goaty-goat. Time to go home.'

The goat bobbed its head, unimpressed by the rope. It bleated and complained all the way along the shady woodland path that lay between her cottage and Porro Park, as they walked in the direction of the house. But Jennifer did not relent, clicking her tongue at the reluctant animal and tugging gently on the rope she had knotted to its collar whenever it showed signs of trying to bolt.

'Not far now,' she said in a reassuring tone.

She knew her way through the woods, having explored this path a few times already, curious to see where film star Alex Delgardo lived. Not that he actually lived here, of course. The great house at Porro Park was a second home for the celebrity actor, who spent most of the year in some multimillion-pound London pad, according to the letting agent.

He had strict rules for any tenants of the former game-keeper's cottage, too. Her background had been vetted, and on moving-in day, Jennifer had been made to sign an agreement. She was not permitted to pass beyond the woods, or take any photographs of the main house or its occupants, or allow any guests to enter the grounds via her premises, which was inside the grounds of the park. The whole estate, including her little cottage, was concealed behind a huge wall topped with broken glass and razor wire.

For privacy, she had her own side entrance by road to the estate, with a gate operated by a key code: a complete faff to manage in the pouring rain, as she had already discovered, jumping out of her car once to enter the code, then leaping back in, utterly drenched.

Abruptly, the path ended at an eight-foot-high red-brick wall. Beyond it she could see nothing but rhododendron bushes, huge and glossy-leaved.

There was an arched doorway in the wall, and in it an iron-studded wooden door.

The door stood slightly ajar.

'Your escape route, no doubt,' she said to the goat in a disapproving voice.

The goat spotted the doorway and abandoned all pretence of not knowing the way. It bleated merrily and trotted ahead of her towards the wall, looking almost eager to get home. Jennifer walked behind, still keeping hold of the rope, just in case. But it was clear the greedy runaway knew where it was going.

She followed the goat through the arched doorway onto a charming rhododendron walk, a gravel path edged with massive bushes that still bore a few red and pink blooms from their spring flowering.

'This is odd,' she muttered. 'Who on earth do you belong to? Not Alex Delgardo, that's for sure.'

Her new neighbour was known for playing tough military men in blockbuster movies. She and her stepsister Caroline had watched a few of his films together on their occasional girls' nights in. His most famous role was as Cheetham, an ex-SAS officer on a quest to clear his name, a quest that continued relentlessly from film to film, giving him ample opportunity to blow things up.

She chuckled. 'Somehow I can't see a big film star owning a goat.'

The goat replied with a non-committal '*meh*'.

Though Delgardo hadn't made any new films recently. There'd been some kind of incident during the making of his last one – a terrorist attack, that was it. People had been killed, others wounded.

Alex Delgardo himself had been injured in the attack, though not seriously. She vaguely recalled an interview he'd given a few days later from his hospital bed. He had looked shocked and gaunt on camera, his chest bandaged, his face scratched and burnt. But he'd sounded perfectly calm. The show must go on, et cetera.

However, since the attack, Alex Delgardo hadn't been much in the public eye. Now that she thought about it, she couldn't remember if he was even making films any more. Maybe his wounds had been more serious than the reports claimed. Maybe he'd started a hippy commune down here in Cornwall and was working as a goatherd.

Laughing at that mental image, Jennifer found she was almost trotting herself, trying to keep up with the goat. Then the powerful animal gave a sudden jerk and broke free, running off with the rope trailing after it.

'Damn,' she said breathlessly. 'Hey, come back!'

The annoying creature rounded a corner ahead of her and she hurried after it, stopping dead at the sight of a man.

A man she recognised from a thousand internet memes.

A man bending to stroke the goat's ears as it happily mehed and headbutted his legs. Bare, muscular legs clad in army fatigue shorts.

Alex Delgardo.

On-screen, his designer stubble was always perfect, his short, dark hair impeccably cut and under control even during chase scenes. Today, he had the faint stirrings of a beard where he had not shaved in a while and his hair was messy, standing up in places as though he had been running impatient hands through it. Apart from that, Delgardo looked essentially the same as he did in his films. He was thirty-one, she seemed to recall. Two years older than her and in the prime of life. He certainly looked uber-fit. His broad shoulders were almost bursting out of the sandy camouflage t-shirt he was wearing, his tattooed biceps rippling impressively as he reached down to untie the rope fixed to the goat's collar.

'What's this?' he was saying in a deep, gravelly voice that was so familiar it made the hairs rise on the back of her neck. 'Who tied you up, baby?'

Baby?

Maybe he really was into goats.

'That's disturbing,' she said under her breath.

Alex Delgardo looked up and saw her. He straightened to his full height, which had to be well over six foot, and his dark eyes narrowed on her.

Sexy, she thought.

'Hello.' Again, that voice stirred all sorts of deep-buried instincts inside her. 'And who the hell are you?'

Rude, too.

She didn't reply immediately, recalling the iron-clad tenancy agreement she had signed only a week ago promising never to enter her neighbour's premises, and wondering if a stray goat could be construed as an emergency.

His gaze moved slowly up and down her body, returning to her face with as much suspicion as the goat had shown earlier.

Like goat, like master.

'And what were you doing with Baby?'

'I . . .'

Before Jennifer could come up with a coherent response, an old lady in a long white dress appeared from the shrubbery behind him.

With a shock of voluminous white hair, and a lopsided daisy chain hanging around her neck, the old woman came pushing out from between the gigantic rhododendron bushes as though she lived in them, had always lived there and was now emerging in order to utter some life-changing prophecy.

Jennifer stared, amazed.

Behind the woman came a gaggle of goats: maybe half a dozen skinny, raw-boned goats with mad, staring eyes and bells jingling from collars identical to the one her stray goat wore, closely following their leader as though she were the goat version of the Pied Piper.

This vision in white spotted the goat on a rope and gave a shriek, clapping her hands in delight. 'Baby!' she exclaimed, and Jennifer realised this must be the animal's name and not a term of endearment.

The other goats *meh*ed loudly, crowding round their lost compadre with excitement, some even chewing on its trailing rope.

'How lovely,' the elderly woman said in a sing-song Cornish accent, studying the goat first and then Jennifer. 'Of course, it had to be *you*. And here you are at last.' She beamed at her. 'We've been waiting for you.'

CHAPTER THREE

'I asked who you were,' Alex Delgardo said curtly, ignoring the old lady.

Jennifer dragged her gaze away from the white-haired woman and looked reluctantly at Delgardo instead.

Instinctively she drew herself up, determined not to be overawed by his celebrity status. She might not be six foot, but she was tall for a woman, and she didn't like the way the film star was frowning at her.

'I'm your tenant at Pixie Cottage,' she said. 'This goat came into my garden. I thought I'd better bring her back before she strayed onto the main road. You really ought to take better care of your livestock.'

Delgardo's eyebrows rose at her tone. Clearly he wasn't used to people talking back to him like that.

'Name?' he demanded, sounding tough and terse, rather like his military character, Cheetham.

'You don't know your own tenant's name?'

'My PA will know. He takes care of all that.'

Of course he does, she thought.

Jennifer put out her hand. 'In that case, I'm Jennifer Bolitho.'

She waited, but Alex Delgardo didn't shake her hand or reply. He merely looked her up and down again, plainly indifferent to what he saw.

A mobile phone rang, loud in the peace of the gardens.

'Mr Delgardo,' she began, but he stuck his right hand in the air, palm out, as though directing traffic, and she stopped.

Delgardo fished a mobile out of his pocket with his left hand and took a few steps away to take the call. He didn't say much but listened, head bent, his right hand still stuck in the air.

After a minute or so he muttered, 'I'll be right there,' and ended the call as abruptly as he'd begun it. He turned back. 'It was good of you to bring Baby back to us, Miss Bolitho,' he said, finally lowering his hand. 'But you need to go home now. We're busy today.'

Jennifer stared at him, astonished.

'Nana?' He glanced round at the old lady and her goats, his voice suddenly gruff. 'That's enough walking for today. You'd better come back with me to the house.'

'In a moment, Alex.' She smiled benignly, playing with the daisy chain around her neck. 'I need to speak to Miss Bolitho first.'

Alex Delgardo hesitated, looking frustrated.

'Run along,' the old lady insisted.

The film star shot Jennifer a quelling glance, said, 'Five minutes,' in an ominous tone, and then set off back along the rhododendron path at a near run.

The old lady watched until he was out of sight, then turned back to her. 'Don't mind my grandson. He's had some, um, bad news. That always puts him in an awful mood.' She did not elaborate on what kind of bad news he'd received. The goat pushed its nose into the old lady's dress, and she patted the animal on the head. 'Yes, yes, I know. Poor Baby. Did you wander off again and get yourself lost?' She tutted. 'I expect you're starving.'

'Not the way she's been tucking into my flower bed. Especially the nasturtiums.'

'Greedy little thing, isn't she? Though I don't blame her. Nasturtiums are so tasty.' She beamed at Jennifer. 'But how marvellous to meet you, finally. I've been expecting you for days, my dear. Would you like some cake?'

Her eyes widened even further. *I've been expecting you for days.* 'Cake?'

'It's never a bad time for cake, is it?'

'I'm not sure Mr Delgardo would like that.'

'I expect he'll be livid.' The old lady laughed. 'But who cares about that?' She shook her head. 'Men. Sometimes you have to put your foot down and just say no.'

Baffled, Jennifer allowed the woman to take her hand. 'I'm Jennifer Bolitho,' she said again, thinking maybe the old lady had mistaken her identity, 'from Pixie Cottage.'

'And I'm Nelly.'

The old lady patted her hand just as she had patted the goat's head, then began to croon a song in Cornish, smiling into her face. Jennifer's Cornish was extremely rusty, so she wasn't sure what the song was about. But afterwards, Nelly nodded with satisfaction as though she had been casting a spell. Which perhaps she had been.

'There, there,' Nelly said soothingly, and released her hand with a sigh. 'It'll be all right now. You'll see.'

If only that could be true, Jennifer thought bitterly. Her memory flashed back to the newspaper she'd hurled violently across the room that morning. The photograph of the smiling, happy couple ...

But she nodded and said nothing, humouring the old lady.

They walked back along the rhododendron path, the goats frolicking around them, seven in number now that Baby had rejoined them, until they reached a broad green lawn. It was beautifully cared for, as were the impressive flower beds, though she noted a few sad, tattered plants here and there, and the occasional unexpected gap. The goats' preferred snacks, presumably.

Beyond the lawn stood the main house.

'Porro Park House. Do you like it?' Nelly asked, peering intently at Jennifer as though her answer would mean everything.

Jennifer was genuinely taken aback by the house. From the surrounding grounds, she had expected to see a traditional manor house, possibly several centuries old. A few barley-twist chimneys, perhaps. Faded red brick, crumbling outbuildings. But this looked like something from one of those architectural shows on television, the facade all glass and reflective steel, a contemporary design with solar panels across the roof and down the west-facing side of the building.

'It's amazing.'

Inside, at ground level, she could see a gym, with a wall of free weights and at least one treadmill overlooking the lawns. Beside the gym room was the glint of blue water, with mosaics decorating the tiled walls above. An indoor pool, she realised. Somebody was in there, swimming lengths at a relentless pace. She could see the splash of water as a tanned arm sliced through it, again and again. Front crawl, and fast too.

'That's Brodie,' Nelly told her, seeing her interest. 'Alex's friend. Such a polite young man. He goes everywhere with my grandson,' she said confidentially. 'Completely insepara-ble, those two.'

Jennifer raised her eyebrows, wondering if the film star was gay. 'Is that so?'

'Thick as thieves, they are. Brodie was in the army with him, you see. That's where they met. Basic training.'

That aroused her curiosity. 'Really? I didn't know Mr Del— I mean, I didn't know Alex was in the army.'

'Before he went into films and became such a success.' Nelly smiled indulgently. 'Have you seen any of my grand-son's films?'

Jennifer hesitated, not wanting to seem like a fan. 'Erm, one or two.'

'Too noisy for my tastes. And so violent. All those guns and car chases, and bombs constantly going off. Exploding helicopters, too.' Nelly shook her head. 'But I suppose some-one must enjoy watching them. They're always asking him to make a new one.'

Jennifer grinned.

'They came down from London together a few days ago. After ten o'clock at night, without so much as a phone call beforehand.'

'How thoughtless.'

'I was in the bath when they arrived, making a racket

with that noisy helicopter. Silly boys. I thought they were burglars. Hearing someone in the house nearly gave me a heart attack.'

'I can imagine.'

Nelly leant towards her, lowering her voice as though afraid they might be overheard. 'Alex is in some kind of trouble. He thinks I don't know. But I know *men*.' She tapped the side of her nose. 'It's a good thing you came over when you did, Jennifer. I was beginning to think I'd have to call you.'

'Call . . . me?'

'Who else?' The old lady obviously had her confused with someone, Jennifer decided, feeling uneasy. But Nelly beamed at her again, more like an old Cornish saint than ever in her white dress and with her mass of hair. 'Come along, time for cake.'

Nelly led her through a sliding glass door into a beautiful modern kitchen. The floor was laid with shining white tiles, and in the middle stood a wooden island counter. A double-topped red Aga was set into the wall opposite. Through the windows on the other side of the kitchen, Jennifer could see a large formal garden with several statues, stone benches and a number of topiary animals carved out of dark green neatly clipped yew.

The goats tried to follow them inside, but Nelly shooed them out. 'No, you naughty lot. You're not allowed in the house. Not while the boys are here. Brodie's orders. Now go and play,' she told the animals, adding, 'I'll bang the tin when it's lunchtime.'

The goats turned and skipped away across the lawn in an

ungainly, jostling group, as though they had understood every word.

'You have so many goats,' Jennifer said faintly, watching them go.

'Seven, at the last count. Like the seven dwarves. Which Alex says makes me Snow White. And I do dress the part sometimes, don't I?' Nelly indicated her ankle-length dress with a laugh. 'Except they have different names to the seven dwarves, because when I bought each goat I didn't know I'd end up with seven. Do you see?'

'Makes perfect sense.'

'Baby is the youngest, and she's forever running off. She's not unhappy here, you understand. She just loves to explore. I should have named her Columbus. Except she's a girl, so that would be odd.' She pointed to each of the goats in turn. 'That's Bananas. Fruitcake. Calamity, because she's always having accidents. Hoppy. Whizzer. Oh, and the one with the big ears is Toby. He's my newest acquisition.' She shut the sliding door and ushered Jennifer into the kitchen, then halted, saying in a surprised voice, 'Françoise. I forgot you were working today.'

An angular, dark-haired woman in a severe black dress stood by the sink, arranging rose stems in a tall vase. She looked round at Nelly at once. 'Am I in your way, madame?' She had a strong French accent. 'I can leave these and do the bedrooms now, if you prefer.'

'No, no.' Nelly gave the woman an uncertain smile. 'I've just brought my new friend in for some cake. This is Jennifer Bolitho.' She took a cake tin out of the cupboard and prised the lid off with hands that trembled slightly. The rich smell of chocolate filled the kitchen. 'Jennifer, this is my grandson's housekeeper, Françoise.'

'Hello,' Jennifer said.

Françoise looked her up and down with disinterest, then turned back to her flower arranging. 'I can cut the cake for you, madame.'

'I can manage.' Nelly reached into the cupboard for some side plates but Jennifer got there first, carrying them to the table for her. 'Thank you. Do you like chocolate cake? There was some delicious carrot and walnut, but the boys had the last of that last night. Over a mug of cocoa during their council of war.'

Council of war?

'Chocolate cake would be lovely, thank you.'

Alex is in some kind of trouble.

Jennifer didn't know what to make of that.

'Chocolate is my absolute favourite too.' Nelly cut a thick slice of cake with a handsome silver cake knife and slid it across onto the plate that Jennifer was holding up. 'The doctor says I shouldn't have cake. But I don't care. That's why Alex brought me here, you know. To keep an eye on me and stop me having cake,' she added darkly, and then cut herself a skinny slice of the chocolate cake, as though following doctor's orders all the same.

'I'm sure he isn't trying to stop you having cake.'

'Huh. You'll soon see what he's like. Thinks he can tell everyone what to do, even his own grandmother. I'll be ninety this summer. Ninety years old. Can you believe it? Almost a whole century I've been alive. But in here,' Nelly said, pointing to her heart, 'I'm still nineteen.'

Jennifer smiled, glanced down at her plate of chocolate cake, and then quite mysteriously dissolved into tears. Teardrops shimmered in her eyes, then spilled down her cheeks and she sobbed, her voice incoherent as she stammered, 'I'm so sorry, so sorry, I don't know what … what's come over me.'

CHAPTER FOUR

The plate was taken away, and Nelly guided her firmly to a kitchen chair.

'Sit.'

Jennifer sat, still blubbing like a five-year-old with a scraped knee, and buried her face in her hands.

'I'm sorry,' she couldn't stop herself saying.

'Oh, my dear.'

Nelly drew up a chair opposite her and put a comforting, knobbly hand on her knee. The gesture was meant to be kindly. Yet somehow it made things worse.

Whatever must the housekeeper be thinking?

But even as Jennifer glanced her way, Françoise swept up the vase of long-stemmed roses and bore it briskly out of the kitchen, not even looking at her. All very discreet, under the circumstances.

Once the kitchen door had closed behind her, Nelly produced a white handkerchief from a pocket of her dress and pressed the cool linen into her hand. 'There you are, my dear.' The old lady saw her expression. 'Don't worry about Françoise. I know she's not much of a smiler. But she won't say a word. She runs this house like clockwork, and never gives Alex any trouble.'

Jennifer had no idea what that meant.

Nelly winked at her. 'Alex kept finding the last house-keeper in his bedroom. With no clothes on. Happens to him all the time, poor boy. Being a film star, you know.'

'Oh.'

'Françoise has a girlfriend.' Nelly lowered her voice. 'Very nice French woman. Marie is her name. She makes the most delicious macaroons.'

Jennifer sucked in her breath, trying not to sob.

'Poor, poor child. Whatever is the matter?' She watched closely while Jennifer dried her face and then blew her nose. Her voice became soft as silk, soothing Jennifer's shattered nerves. 'What's his name?'

There was no point pretending. Not with this woman.

'R-Raphael,' she managed to say. 'Raphael Tregar. He and I ... We were ... He got married last week. To another woman. I saw it in the local paper this morning.' She stuffed the damp hanky against her mouth and spoke through it, her voice shaking and muffled. 'They both looked so ... so happy!' The tears came again then, hot and scalding down her cheeks, running into the corners of her mouth and drip-ping off her chin. 'Oh God, whatever am I going to do?'

'Perhaps you should start by telling me a little more about it,' Nelly suggested gently.

Jennifer nodded, and began to explain.

That morning, she had driven back from the shops with a box of provisions and the local paper, meaning to look at adverts for second-hand furniture. She had rented Pixie Cottage unfurnished, unlike her last rental property in Boscastle, which had come with everything included. Since the only furniture she owned up to that point was a bookcase, Jennifer had bought the bed and sofa online and left it at that. Which meant Pixie Cottage was spartan, which she rather liked. But maybe a little too spartan.

So she had sat down with a steaming cup of tea and flicked through the paper, idly looking for furniture ads. And what had she found instead?

A photo of a bride and groom, smiling into the camera, tiny shreds of confetti dancing above their heads and catching in the bride's lacy bodice.

Her hand had trembled, and she'd nearly dropped the cup of tea.

Then she'd peered closer, reading the caption below the photo in tiny grey print, and felt the carefully constructed cocoon she had built around her heart begin to crack and break into pieces.

Pethporro Councillor Raphael Tregar, 32, and his new bride Hannah, née Clitheroe, 28, celebrating their wedding at St Juliot's Church last Saturday in proper Cornish style.

A brief story had accompanied the picture, just one paragraph, mentioning the annual Pethporro pageant that Hannah had organised last year, and citing the vast number of tourists and locals who had visited the seaside town that day.

That damn Pethporro pageant . . .

She herself had been asked to run the pageant, and had enjoyed the challenge. Until the day Raphael had abruptly decided they needed more time apart, and sacked her. There had been more to the situation than that, of course. But that was how she remembered it. As a period of terrible upset and confusion.

'So you see,' she told Nelly, 'I'm not having a great day.'

'It doesn't sound like this Raphael Tregar was entirely honest with you.' Nelly peered at her closely. 'And don't take this the wrong way, my dear, but perhaps you weren't being entirely honest with yourself either.'

'I trusted him.'

'You should never trust men. Not until you've got this firmly in place.' Nelly waved a gold-ringed finger at Jennifer, then added conspiratorially, 'And with some men, not even then.' Her lips twitched in a wry smile. 'I'm not very good at being politically correct, am I? But that doesn't mean I'm not right. We feel so much, as women,' she finished, tapping her heart, 'and so love always gets us *here*. Where it hurts the most.'

'Yes.'

'It stands to reason we need to protect ourselves against love. Against *feeling* too much. Otherwise people are bound to take advantage of our generosity. Like this Raphael character did with you.'

Jennifer blew her nose and nodded.

'What kind of name is Raphael, anyway? Does he have a long white robe and a harp?' Jennifer shook her head, laughing through her tears. 'He sounds like an Old Testament angel.' Nelly made a face. 'Though I rather imagine he didn't behave like one.'

'Far from it.'

One minute she and Raphael Tregar had been happy together, or so she had supposed; the next he had cut her loose without any proper explanation. *To give us both space*, he had said. And while she was still smarting and planning how best to get him back, Hannah Clitheroe had moved to Pethporro and basically stolen Raphael from under Jennifer's nose. While carrying another man's child, too.

Now she was weeping into a stranger's hanky in an unfamiliar kitchen, while a tall, lean-faced man stared at them through the glass doors into the house.

To her surprise, it wasn't Alex Delgardo.

'Oh . . .' said Jennifer, and sat up straight. She rubbed her damp face one last time before crumpling the hanky into a tight ball, hating the idea that someone else had seen her crying. Someone who didn't look as sweet and forgiving as Nelly. 'Seems like you've got another . . . visitor.' She pointed shakily over the old lady's shoulder. 'Perhaps I should leave.'

Nelly turned to look. 'Oh no, that's just Brodie. Now don't look so worried, I won't tell him any of that other business. Or Alex.'

'Thank you.'

'It'll be our little secret.' Nelly jumped to her feet, astonishingly spry for a lady of her advanced years, and waved the newcomer into her kitchen. 'Don't be shy, Brodie. Did you have a good swim? Come in and meet my guest.'

The sliding door opened and the man came into the kitchen. But Jennifer could see he was reluctant to make her acquaintance. Wary, even.

So this was Brodie.

He was tall, with short blond hair slick against his head,

his broad shoulders flecked with water, a blue towel wrapped low around his hips. His blue eyes locked with Jennifer's, almost defiant now, which puzzled her. Then he came towards her, his gait a little unusual, and that was when her gaze flashed down his body and she realised that his left leg was no longer there. He had a prosthetic leg in its place, the foot end fixed snugly into a trainer.

What had Nelly said about Alex Delgardo's best friend?

Brodie was in the army with him, you see. That's where they met.

Presumably he had been wounded in action.

Brodie stuck out a hand, his smile cautious rather than welcoming. 'Pleased to meet you, Miss . . .?'

'Bolitho,' she said, a little shyly, and got to her feet. She shook his hand. 'Jennifer.'

'I'm Brodie Mattieson.'

Nelly nodded, watching all this with apparent satisfaction. 'Jennifer has come to look at the goats,' she told him, and Jennifer turned to stare at her, mystified.

'Ah.' His smile broadened, more relaxed now, and he gave her hand another encouraging squeeze before dropping it. 'That's wonderful news. I've been doing my best to manage the situation and keep track of them. But seven goats is not an easy task. And what we really need here is an expert.'

'I'm an expert,' Nelly said indignantly.

'But you can't be running about after a pack of goats all day. Not at your age.' He frowned and looked at Jennifer. 'Is it a pack? The collective noun for goats . . .?'

'Herd, I think.'

'Thank you.' He smiled at Nelly. 'You simply aren't fit enough to keep up with a herd of goats, and you know it.

They're unpredictable animals, goats. They can be very frisky.' He glanced at Jennifer again, wanting to enlist her support. 'Can't they, Jennifer?'

She thought back to the way the goat had dragged her all over the place instead of sticking to the path, and said, 'Yes, very.'

'There you go. You heard the expert.' He wagged a long finger at Nelly. 'Seven goats, and far too frisky for someone in your condition.'

'Oh, pooh,' Nelly said, and pursed her lips at Brodie. She didn't argue with him, but there was a disappointed look on her face.

In your condition.

Was Nelly unwell? Or simply a bit doddery?

Jennifer felt rather awkward, feeling she had somehow been the cause of an argument. 'I wouldn't exactly call myself an expert. In fact,' she added, 'I imagine Nelly must be more of an expert than anyone else. They're her goats, after all.'

'Isn't she modest?' Nelly smiled at her suddenly, her unhappy mood dispersing like mist in the sunshine, as though the whole goat thing had already been forgotten. 'And very fond of cake, too.'

'Frankly, who isn't? Especially your chocolate cake, Nelly.' His wink was disarming. 'It's so addictive, it's practically a drug. Ought to be illegal.' Brodie surveyed the cake still standing out on the worktop. 'I wouldn't say no to a little slice myself. May I?'

'Of course you may.' The old lady winked back at him with an air of great mischief. 'As if I could stop you, great strapping lad that you are. Here, let me get you a plate.' She turned to fetch one but Brodie put a hand on her arm.

'Sit down,' he told her softly, 'and let me do it. You know you're not supposed to be exerting yourself.'

'For goodness' sake.' She grinned at Jennifer. 'They treat me like china, these boys. It's flattering, considering I'm as tough as old boots.'

Once Nelly had sat down, Brodie located the plate stack in the cupboard, took one out, then cut some cake for himself. Everything done with smooth precision, as might be expected of a former military man. His sharp blue gaze kept flicking back to Jennifer, though, as if her presence there still puzzled him. Which didn't surprise her, as she was puzzled herself. Something told her Nelly had definitely misunderstood the reason for her visit.

Jennifer has come to look at the goats.

She decided it was time to clear up any confusion. 'I found a goat in my garden,' she said, and was embarrassed to see both turn to stare at her. 'Eating my nasturtiums. I didn't know who she belonged to. I was aware of the terms of my lease, that the park is strictly off limits for walking. But the goat wanted to come this way, so I let her lead me. And then I met Nelly and . . . and Mr Delgardo,' she finished lamely.

'She means Alex,' Nelly put in helpfully.

'I would have gone straight home,' Jennifer told him, a little defensively. 'But Nelly invited me in for cake. Insisted, actually.'

Brodie had a dry smile in his eyes. 'Yes, she has a tendency to do that.' But as he hesitated, picking up his very generous slice of chocolate cake, his brows suddenly twitched together. 'Hold on, you said . . . the terms of your lease. Where do you live?'

'Pixie Cottage.'

'The old gamekeeper's place?' When she nodded, he sank his teeth into the slice of chocolate cake, and for a moment there was silence in the kitchen. Then he added, somewhat indistinctly, 'So you're the new tenant? I thought you were a man.'

'Sorry?'

He finished his mouthful of cake. 'I'm sure the letting agent down in Pethporro told me you were a man. When she rang to say she'd arranged for a new tenant, she said your name was Jeremy.'

Instinctively, she drew back her shoulders and pushed out her chest. It was not an overly endowed chest, but it clearly belonged to a female of the species.

'As you can see, I'm not a man. Does it matter?'

'Not at all. I must have misheard Jeremy for Jennifer. She does have a thick accent.' He grinned. 'Proper Cornish, you know? A real local.'

'Better watch out. You tend to get a lot of us in Pethporro.' She finished the last few crumbs of her cake and stood up. 'Thank you so much,' she said politely to Nelly, 'I'd better get home now.'

'But you haven't examined the goats yet,' Nelly said. 'And Alex will be coming in soon for his tea. It would be a shame if you two didn't get a chance to chat properly. I'm sure Alex would be fascinated to hear what you think of his films.'

Brodie made some kind of choking noise, and both women looked round at him in alarm. Nelly hurried to pat him on the back. But he edged away, still choking noisily, and went to the sink instead, running himself a large glass of water.

The door to the garden opened.

Alex Delgardo stood on the threshold, staring at her. 'You again,' he said, seeming amazed. He looked from Nelly to Brodie, who was still choking over the sink. 'Brodie, are you okay?'

Brodie waved a hand in the air, then downed the whole glass of water at once, his throat convulsing with each swallow.

Jennifer rubbed her forehead, feeling suddenly quite overwhelmed. But she didn't want to be rude and just run away without any explanation.

'I think you must have misunderstood,' she told the old lady. 'I didn't actually come here to examine your goats. Perhaps you've confused me with someone else.'

'No, that can't be. The cards told me you were coming,' Nelly said cryptically. 'Stay and have some more cake. Oh dear, I didn't make your tea.'

'I'm not thirsty. But the cake was delicious.' Alex Delgardo moved away from the doorway, leaving her escape route clear. Quickly, Jennifer headed for the sliding door. 'You must let me have the recipe sometime.'

'I can fetch it for you now.'

'No, really, I don't . . .' But Nelly had already left the room.

Brodie put down his plate in the silence that followed her departure. The smile had died from his eyes, his gaze still fixed on Alex Delgardo.

'Alex,' he said cautiously, 'this is Miss Jennifer Bolitho. Your new tenant at Pixie Cottage. Not a man, as we were led to believe.'

'Yes, we've met.' Alex Delgardo held up a hand as his friend made to say more. 'It's okay. I'll deal with this.'

Deal with this, Jennifer repeated inside her head, finding it hard to breathe. He meant her, of course. Deal with *her*.

'It was good of you to bring the goat home,' Alex Delgardo told her politely. 'I'll make sure none of them ever wanders outside our grounds again. But Nelly hasn't been very well lately, and it's probably best if she doesn't get too excited by visitors. Especially *strangers*.'

Well, that put her in her place.

'So, if you want to leave right now,' Alex continued in the same smooth, matter-of-fact tone, not at all as though he were throwing her out on her ear, 'I'll explain when Nelly gets back that you couldn't wait any longer.' He paused. 'And that you won't be back.'

She met his eyes, which were hard and cool. Like black marble. Nothing she could say would ever make a dent in the absolute certainty of this man's reply.

Alex raised his eyebrows, waiting. 'Goodbye, then, Miss Bolitho.'

Feeling rather like a bug that had just been brushed off his shirt, Jennifer made her way back out into the garden, blinking in the strong Cornish sunshine.

She didn't say goodbye.

CHAPTER FIVE

The sun was busily climbing into a deep blue sky by the time Jennifer left the cottage a week later, still combing her hair as she walked, having spent ages getting dressed, unable to decide what to wear. In the end, she'd gone with white cotton shorts and a loose blue top that hopefully concealed the amount of weight she'd lost. In her gym bag, she had packed her special storytelling outfit for this afternoon's session at the Pethporro Celtic Centre: black leggings, a long, deep green shift-style top and her special green floor-length 'storytelling cloak' with its glittering sequins, embroidered flowers and swirly patterns.

Plus a pair of green Doc Martens to complete the image of a professional storyteller.

Not that she *was* a professional storyteller, of course. Not yet.

But today was the first step along that path.

Her stepsister Caroline had been insistent they meet for lunch, otherwise Jennifer would still be at her desk, bent over her laptop, preparing for this afternoon's debut storytelling session.

She was getting nervous now, she couldn't deny it. Butterflies in her tummy, sweaty palms, a dry throat. Which was plain silly of her. All this upset over telling a story to a small audience at a local venue. A story on which she was an acknowledged expert, as a folklorist with several books published.

How hard could it be?

Except this was more a *performance* than a simple retelling of a folk tale. She would be expected to wear an impressive outfit, like an actor in a stage play, and to walk about, use her voice properly, make dramatic gestures . . .

Yes, there were those butterflies again.

Problem was, she didn't feel properly prepared for this afternoon's performance. After meeting her new neighbours at Porro Park, she had taken refuge in research for her new book on Cornish folklore, trawling through dusty tomes and websites for obscure facts and fresh angles on the folk stories she planned to include. This new book was taking longer than usual to research. That was what she'd told her editor, who had emailed that week to check on her progress, anxious over her long silence. But the real truth was that she hadn't been able to write a word of it.

She backed into a parking space near the Pethporro Celtic Centre and left her storytelling outfit in the car, where it would be handy after lunch. She came to the centre frequently to buy books and trinkets, fascinated by everything Celtic, and for occasional tarot readings by Georgette, one of the owners of the centre.

It was Georgette who had persuaded her to take over their seasonal storytelling slot after the last storyteller moved away.

'It's easy. Just wear a big cloak and hat, and trot out a few of those old folk tales you're so fascinated by,' she'd told Jennifer earlier in the year. 'Maybe put on a few comic voices, too. Pretend to be a troll or a Cornish pisky. Tourists love that kind of thing.'

'But Georgette, I'm a folklorist. It's all books and internet forums. I've never performed a story in front of an audience in my life.'

'You've given public talks on folklore.'

'True.'

'So where's the difference?'

'Erm, putting on voices? Pretending to be a troll?' She had tipped her head to one side, her expression ironic. 'And wearing a storyteller's hat and cloak? I mean, come on!'

But Georgette had ignored her concerns and booked her for the full summer season. One storytelling session per week in the large back room at the centre, where they also put on short historical or archaeological films and a few outdoor sessions, weather permitting, on Sundays and at local festivals.

The money was quite good, surprisingly, which had encouraged Jennifer to sign the contract. After all, she needed to pay the rent.

When she reached the tapas bar, Jennifer was relieved to see her stepsister already there, waving at her in a desultory fashion from the doorway. Caroline was often late for their lunch dates, being a midwife and on call for emergencies. But today she had arrived early, looking as elegant as ever, tall and slender, her long blonde hair swept up to one side and held in place by a diamanté clip.

'You look depressed,' Caroline said, kissing her warmly on the cheek. 'What's up?'

Jennifer had already told her on the phone about her unpleasant encounter with the landlord, so she just rolled her eyes by way of an answer.

Caroline understood at once.

'Oh, forget about him. Delgardo can't stay here for ever.' Looking very cool in a green linen knee-length dress with flat leather pumps, she led Jennifer into the tapas bar and they threaded their way between the closely spaced tables towards the alcove they always reserved for their lunch dates. 'He's a celeb. They never stay anywhere for long, especially not sleepy backwaters like Pethporro.'

'I suppose you're right.' Jennifer surprised herself by shivering, and glanced up at the ceiling fan as though it was to blame. 'That's new.' She eyed the steadily whirling blades with disapproval. 'And rather draughty.'

'We can ask them to turn it off.'

'No, it's fine.' Jennifer slid along the narrow alcove bench opposite. 'Incredibly hot this summer, isn't it? Record temperatures. I'm overheated from the sun, that's all. I'll get used to it.'

The restaurant was quite busy, but it was already late June and Pethporro was crawling with tourists. Brilliant for local shops and businesses; not so great for residents simply trying to negotiate the cramped Cornish lanes and roads.

The waitress appeared with menus and a courtesy bowl of olives in garlic-infused oil, and spent a few minutes chatting about her younger sister, who was currently expecting a baby. Conversations about babies always seemed to happen whenever Caroline appeared. Though given she was a qualified midwife, that wasn't so surprising.

Jennifer waited until the waitress had gone, then leant forward and asked, 'Caro, did you really mean that? About Alex Delgardo leaving?'

'Absolutely.' Caroline smoothed out an imaginary crease in her dress with one tanned, manicured hand, her nails smooth scarlet. Out of uniform, her stepsister was always well turned out and very conscious of her appearance. 'I'm sure he'll soon head back to the big city – London or New York or Hollywood. Wherever his agent tells him to go. Then you can relax, and enjoy some peace and quiet again while you write your new book.' Caroline smiled across at her. 'How's the book coming along, by the way?'

Jennifer grimaced.

'That bad? Maybe a nice lunch will help stir your creative juices.' Caroline opened the conspicuously shiny menu. 'This place has had a serious facelift. About time too. It used to be so twee and faded when it was a bistro, don't you think? I came in last week for their grand reopening. Same owner, same staff, different chef. Look at this new tapas menu. Out with the lamb cutlets, in with the calamares and empanadillas. Isn't that amazing?'

'Talk about big city.'

'I know,' Caroline said, running a red-tipped nail down the list of tapas dishes, 'I feel almost sophisticated just reading this.' They both studied the menu in silence for a moment. Then her eyebrows rose. 'Good grief, I don't believe it. *Dolmas*. That's stuffed vine leaves. In Pethporro. Whatever next?'

Jennifer was only half listening, her gaze skimming over the list of exotic dishes without really taking them in. 'I kind of wish I hadn't gone over there . . .'

'Yes, why did you?' Caroline peered at her intently from over the top of the menu. 'You didn't explain on the phone.'

'There was a goat.'

'A goat?' Caroline lowered the menu to stare. 'Wait, don't tell me . . . Delgardo doesn't have a lawnmower.'

'Obviously not. And the lawns there are vast. They have seven of them.'

'Seven lawns?'

'Goats.'

'You're pulling my leg now.'

'I swear to God, they have *seven* goats.'

'What, like the seven dwarves?' Caroline frowned. 'Wait, they? Who's *they*?'

'Alex Delgardo and his grandmother.'

'He lives with his grandmother? You *are* joking.'

'It's true.'

'Delgardo must be devoted to his dear granny, that's all I can say. Isn't he usually surrounded by glamorous models?' Caroline thought for a moment. 'Oh yes, there was that Swedish blonde with legs so long she had them insured. She was his plus-one at the last royal wedding. Whatever happened to her?'

'No idea,' Jennifer said shortly, feeling a little annoyed. 'You clearly know more than I do about his life.'

'Don't you ever read *Hello* magazine?'

Not wanting to lie, she ignored that question and frowned at the list of tapas choices, trying to concentrate on food instead of a disturbing mental image of Alex Delgardo cavorting about the lawns of Porro Park with a bevy of scantily clad beauties.

Not long after she'd finally made her decision, the waitress came bustling over, pad in hand. They both ordered a selection of dishes with a bread basket on the side, and soft drinks rather than a glass of wine. Jennifer was driving, after all, and Caroline was apparently on a diet, though she didn't look like she needed to lose any weight.

'I don't know, maybe he had the Swedish blonde hidden away somewhere in the house,' Jennifer said once the waitress had gone. 'I only saw two women there. One was his housekeeper, who's gay, and the other was his granny. Nice old lady, if a little eccentric. She's the one with all the goats. But one goat strayed and ended up in my garden, so I took her back to them. Or rather, the bloody animal dragged me over there.'

'Into forbidden territory.'

'Exactly. And then his grandmother got the wrong end of the stick and decided I was some kind of vet.'

'A vet?'

'I didn't understand either. Somehow she got it into her head that I was a goat expert. Kept telling everyone I was there to examine the goats. Don't laugh, it wasn't funny.' Jennifer popped a juicy green olive into her mouth, musing on what she had seen at Porro Park. 'There's this other guy hanging around the place, too. Nelly – that's the grandmother – told me they're just friends. But if you ask me he's more like a bodyguard. The stern and suspicious type. Ex-military.'

'Sounds intriguing.'

Jennifer caught something in her tone, and frowned. 'I don't imagine Simon would be pleased to hear you say so.'

Caroline raised her eyebrows. 'Who cares what Simon thinks? I haven't seen *him* in weeks.'

'Have you two split up? You certainly kept that quiet. I had no idea.' Jennifer scanned her stepsister's face but saw no strong emotion there. 'Are you okay about that?'

'God, yes. Simon was beginning to bore me, anyway. Always going on about his bloody ex-wife.' Caroline shrugged delicately, resting her chin on her hand. 'Are you sure you didn't misunderstand the situation?'

'Sorry?'

'The reason Alex Delgardo is in Cornwall. In all the time since he bought that house, I've never known him come down here in person except when the renovations were being done. I thought he bought the park as some kind of investment. The grounds are huge, after all.'

'I agree, it's strange. I thought the place would be empty.'

'Except for a herd of goats? Maybe he's come here to make a film.' Caroline looked at her, lips twitching. '*Men Who Stare at Goats* meets *Little Red Riding Hood*, perhaps?'

'The house is surrounded by woods . . .'

'Which makes Delgardo the Big Bad Wolf.' Caroline reached over, poking her in the arm. 'So you must be Little Red Riding Hood.'

The mental image was so ludicrous, Jennifer couldn't help laughing too.

'Don't.'

Caroline pulled a mock-menacing face. 'Better watch out he doesn't gobble you up, little girl,' she said in a deep voice, waggling her eyebrows.

Jennifer seized her napkin and used it to stifle her giggles. 'Stop it,' she managed to say between gasps, then looked up automatically as the door to the tapas bar opened. Her laughter died at once and she straightened, horribly self-conscious. 'Oh, no.'

'What is it?'

'Whatever you do, don't turn round.'

Caroline immediately turned to look over her shoulder, eyes full of curiosity, and froze in her seat. 'Oh my goodness.' She glanced back at Jennifer. 'This should be interesting.'

It was Alex Delgardo himself, of course. Because that was just her luck at the moment. Whatever could go wrong, would go wrong. Sometimes she thought fate was laughing in her face.

'Don't you dare speak to him!'

'Spoilsport,' Caroline whispered, but didn't argue.

Bending her head, Jennifer pretended to examine the cherry-covered tablecloth with fierce attention. *These red double cherries on stalks are really quite pretty*, she thought desperately.

Maybe he wouldn't remember her.

But she had forgotten about her bad luck. The approaching feet, clad in expensive-looking black trainers, stopped beside their table a few seconds later.

'Hello again, Miss Bolitho,' a familiar male voice said, and there was no choice but to look up from the tablecloth, having been well and truly recognised.

Her gaze rose up faded blue jeans with a slight flare and a fitted black t-shirt to Alex Delgardo's face. He had Nelly on his arm, her long white hair tied back in a ponytail, her thin cheeks flushed with exertion. The old lady smiled at her happily.

'H-hello,' Jennifer replied in a stilted voice, not wanting

to talk to the nasty man but feeling it would be rude not to. She gave Nelly a deliberately friendly smile. 'Good to see *you* again, Nelly,' she said with emphasis. 'I hope you're well.'

Sounding a little breathless, Nelly said, 'I'm so glad we bumped into you. I'm worried about one of Fruitcake's front hooves. I think there may be an infection. Perhaps you could come over and look at her.'

Caroline made a snorting noise under her breath.

Jennifer bit her lip. 'Oh, erm, I have a thing this afternoon. I may not be able to . . .'

'A thing?' Alex Delgardo repeated.

'A *performance*,' Caroline said quickly, leaning forward. 'Oh, didn't you know? Jennifer is the new storyteller at the Pethporro Celtic Centre. She starts this afternoon. Half past two in the back room. It's only five pounds a ticket for adults.' She smiled up at them winningly, quite ignoring Jennifer, who was trying to kick her under the table. 'You should come and hear her perform. Both of you. It's going to be amazing.'

Jennifer finally made contact with her stepsister's elusive ankle.

Caroline yelped and fell silent, though not before shooting her an aggrieved look.

'A storyteller?' Nelly seemed delighted. 'But that's wonderful. I had no idea. I'd love to hear Jennifer telling a story. Wouldn't you, Alex?'

'Absolutely.'

Alex Delgardo was not looking at Jennifer, though. His smile was wry as he studied Caroline instead, his eyes suddenly appreciative. But then, Caroline was tall, blonde and leggy. *Ticking all his boxes*, Jennifer thought, noting with dismay the way the two of them were sizing each other up. And her stepsister looked stunning today in the figure-hugging green dress, it had to be admitted. Unlike Jennifer.

'Hello,' he said, and put out his left hand to Caroline, since he was supporting Nelly with his right. 'I'm Alex Delgardo.'

Caroline turned to him. Her smile suddenly reminded Jennifer of a crocodile. 'Please,' she said, 'I know exactly who you are, Mr Delgardo. I'm Caroline Enys.' Caroline shook his hand with just her fingertips. 'Jennifer's stepsister.'

Jennifer forced herself to interrupt, fearful of where this might be leading. Any minute now, Caroline might invite him to join them out of pure mischief, and then she would just die of embarrassment. Minutes after strangling her stepsister, of course.

'I'm sorry,' she said quickly, 'but we're just about to have lunch. And as Caroline said, I'm on a bit of a schedule. Maybe we could chat another time?'

There was a short, brutal silence.

Alex Delgardo raised his eyebrows at this stark dismissal, but nodded. 'Of course. Sorry for the interruption. Nice to meet you, Miss Enys.' He patted Nelly's arm. 'Come along, Nana. There's a good table over there. Right under the fish tank. You like tropical fish, don't you?'

'But what about the goats?' Nelly demanded, refusing to budge. 'Fruitcake's hoof?'

He stopped and looked back at Jennifer.

She felt heat bloom in her cheeks, knowing herself to have been put on the spot, and heard herself say, 'I . . . I can pop over in a day or two if you like, Nelly.'

Nelly's face came alive. 'Thank you. I'll bake something in your honour. I was going to make scones. Do you prefer cherry or cheese?'

'Either is good.'

Somehow Jennifer managed a smile to accompany this muttered response, and the two moved on, Nelly smiling and nodding. But not before she had seen a strange look in Alex's eyes. Grudging approval? Or irritation? Maybe a conflicted mixture of the two.

Whatever lay behind that expression, Alex Delgardo was obviously not keen on her visiting the house again. Even if it did make his grandmother happy.

'Well, that certainly told him.' Caroline watched him seating Nelly at the table, and winked at Jennifer. 'Though you didn't help matters by agreeing to look at their goats again. Mixed messages, don't you think?'

'She's an old lady. I didn't want to hurt her feelings.'

'Hmm.' Caroline peered at her suspiciously. 'Are you sure that's the only reason? Delgardo is quite a looker, after all.' She paused, arching one suggestive eyebrow as she added, 'In the flesh.'

CHAPTER SIX

After lunch, the two of them left the restaurant without looking over at Alex Delgardo and his grandmother, who were still eating their lunch – and causing quite a stir among tourists and locals alike. It seemed as though several dozen people had suddenly 'popped in for a coffee' just to catch a glimpse of this much-famed celebrity resident of Pethporro. Most were simply hovering in the doorway now, unable to get a table, or peering shamelessly in through the front window, camera phones poised for a quick snap of Delgardo taking a mouthful of his feta cheese salad.

The blue sky was dazzling, and it was scorching on the street outside the tapas bar. Jennifer felt flushed and hot, while Caroline looked as cool as ever in her dress.

'Will you come to hear me perform?' she asked, already knowing the answer.

'Storytelling?' Caroline made a face. 'Much as I'd love to support you, it's not really my thing. No hard feelings?'

Jennifer laughed, giving her stepsister a warm hug. 'No, it was always going to be a long shot. But look, come and see me at the cottage one evening. We can watch a trashy film and get drunk together, then you could sleep over.'

'What kind of trashy film?' Caroline said, once more raising a single mobile brow. 'One of Delgardo's action blockbusters? I've got a DVD of his latest Cheetham.'

'Ugh, no thanks.'

'Come on, Jen, this is me. I saw how you looked at the man.' Caroline paused significantly and her voice deepened as she added, 'And how he looked at you.'

'Sorry, were you in the same restaurant as me?' Flustered, Jennifer pushed her flopping hair back off her forehead. 'If anything, he was devouring *you* with his eyes.'

'*Me?*'

'Duh.' Jennifer tried to make a joke of it. 'Everyone knows Alex Delgardo only dates blondes.'

'Is that so? I thought you never read the celebrity rags?'

Jennifer shrugged, not quite sure what to say. She moved aside for a young family on holiday, the mother, a harassed expression on her face, pushing a parasol-covered buggy along the narrow Pethporro pavement.

'I probably read that online somewhere,' she said, not entirely truthfully. There was a stack of celebrity mags in a drawer back at home. Not that she wanted to admit that; Caroline would only laugh at her. 'You know how it is. You click on a Facebook link, and end up vanishing for hours down a series of rabbit holes.'

'Yeah, I know exactly how it is,' Caroline drawled. 'Clicking on celebrity eye candy when no one can see what you're up to.'

'Anyway, I do not fancy Alex Delgardo,' Jennifer said loudly, and saw the woman with the buggy turn around to stare at her, open-mouthed. She lowered her voice to hiss,

'Please, Caro, don't wind me up about this. He may be rich and famous, and yes, okay, I agree he's good-looking. The whole package.' She blew out her breath, uncomfortable under the hot sun. 'But he's not Raphael.'

'You seriously need to get over Raphael.'

'Maybe. But not with *him*,' she said, hooking her thumb back towards the tapas bar.

'Keep your knickers on, sweetie. I get it. You're not into Delgardo. I must have misread the signals, sorry.' Caroline hesitated, looking thoughtful. 'In that case, I assume you won't mind if I—'

'Don't you bloody dare. He's my landlord.'

'What's that got to do with it?' Her stepsister saw her furious expression and shrugged, taking out her phone as she muttered, 'So selfish,' under her breath. She checked her schedule. 'How about Thursday night for a girly get-together at the cottage? Something to take your mind off Raphael.'

'That's the night before the Pethporro Folklore Festival opens.'

'So?'

'I'll be working on my speech.'

'I thought it was nearly done.'

'You know me and speeches. It needs . . .'

'A complete overhaul?'

'Exactly.'

'So I'll come over and help you rewrite it. No, don't make that face. You can read it out to me. Like an after-dinner speech.' She grinned. 'I promise not to yawn.'

Jennifer's eyebrows rose. But she didn't say no. Caroline's offer was generous, given that she had no interest whatsoever in Cornish folklore. And it would be helpful to practise her speech out loud.

'Okay, brilliant. You bring the wine, I'll make dinner.'

'Nothing too fattening, please.'

Jennifer grimaced. 'Chicken salad – is that fattening?'

'Not too bad.' Caroline looked her up and down critically. 'Though you could do with putting on a few pounds, frankly. I haven't seen you this skinny since we were teenagers. Have you been eating properly?'

'Good grief, Caro. Get off my case, will you? I told you, I'm fine.' Jennifer hugged her arms around her, feeling awkward now. 'I'll see you Thursday night.'

'Should I dress up?'

She stared, bemused. 'Whatever for?'

'I don't know.' Caroline made an innocent face. 'In case a movie star should happen to drop by for a cup of sugar?'

'Oh, for goodness' sake, is that the only reason you're coming to dinner?'

'Not the *only* reason.'

'Alex Delgardo will not be there. On Thursday or any other day. He owns the cottage, he doesn't *visit* it. So if you're hoping for a second glimpse of his biceps, you can forget that right now.'

Caroline pursed her lips. 'Okay, whatever.'

Her stepsister gave her another quick peck on the cheek before disappearing into the throng of tourists crowding round the gate into Pethporro's tiny thatch-roofed museum.

Incorrigible, Jennifer thought, shaking her head.

But it would be good for the two of them to enjoy a girls' night in together. They hadn't done that in ages.

Walking slowly past Pethporro Museum, Jennifer stopped to stare.

There was some kind of open-air performance going on at the museum, which had been recently renovated for the summer season. A woman in Victorian dress and an over-large bonnet was walking about the formal gardens, singing sea shanties in a hearty manner. She waved at Jennifer in passing and continued on, smiling at the tourists as she encouraged them to join in with the chorus.

Mystified for a moment, Jennifer suddenly recognised the woman's voice and realised it was Penny Jago under that bonnet, a local expert on Cornish lore like herself.

She didn't know Penny well, since her partner Bailey was close friends with Hannah Clitheroe – she couldn't quite bring herself to think of that woman as Hannah *Tregar* – and after one particularly unpleasant encounter just before Christmas, Jennifer had decided to steer clear of Hannah and her friends. But she'd met Penny a few times at Cornish folklore conventions and was aware that she taught a Cornish language class in Pethporro as well as in a few of the surrounding towns.

Penny Jago had been involved in helping out with the Boxing Day pageant, so obviously she'd have been roped into entertaining the summer tourists at the museum as well. The pageant Jennifer ought to have been running instead of Hannah.

She put her head down and hurried on, trying to flush all thoughts of Raphael and Hannah out of her head. It wasn't exactly easy, though. She would have had more luck trying to catch rain in a colander.

*

The Celtic Centre was a low-built, unassuming shop, whose front window boasted a vast array of Celtic-design swords, helmets and chainmail vests for the re-enactment enthusiasts, its cool interior stacked with expensive tourist trinkets as well as a staggering number of books and pamphlets on a range of Celtic subjects.

It was the books she came here for, not to mention the company of Georgette, an American former university professor who'd made her home in Cornwall back in the 1980s and who now ran the Celtic Centre with her partner, Pete.

Pete, leather waistcoat straining over his generous stomach, looked up from the pamphlet he'd been reading and smiled as she rattled through the bead curtain hanging across the doorway.

'Afternoon, Jennifer. You're a bit early.' He put 'A Guide to Cornish Pirates' back on the spinner. 'Looking forward to your debut?'

'Not particularly, no.'

'Nervous, are you?' He was an eccentric dresser, but it suited his Celtic surroundings, one gold stud in his ear and a dark, grey-flecked beard tied up neatly with a jewelled cord. 'Don't worry, you'll be fine. Georgette says you're a natural.'

A natural screw-up, Jennifer thought, but smiled bravely. 'That's very kind of her. Actually, I was hoping to see Georgette before we start. Is she about?'

'In the nook.' He nodded over his shoulder towards the back of the shop. Right next to the passageway into the room where she would be performing, a curtain concealed a low doorway. 'With a client. Five minutes, yeah?'

Which, roughly translated, meant: *Georgette is doing a tarot reading in the cramped back room set aside for such arcane activities and is not to be disturbed.*

'No worries, I'll just wait out here.' Jennifer smiled at the customer now beside him, an old man in a cap, bent almost double. 'Sorry to interrupt.'

The old man paid no attention to her, intent on examining a wizard's staff with pokerwork all down the shaft, an interweaving of ivy leaves and ancient runic signs.

Pete winked at her, then turned back to the customer, painstakingly explaining what each marking on the shaft signified.

Jennifer wandered over to the book area of the Celtic Centre and began to browse the titles on the shelves marked CORNISH FOLKLORE. Most were familiar, as they didn't move much book stock outside of the summer season. But there were usually at least two or three newish books to capture her attention. Fresh in was a recently published book on countryside spells. She hooked it out of the row of books and flicked through the pages, intrigued.

So engrossed was she, the sound of Georgette saying goodbye to her client went unnoticed and suddenly Jennifer jumped at a tap on her shoulder.

'Jenny?' It was Georgette, her hair covered in a brightly coloured turban, strings of beads around her neck. 'You're early. Didn't get the time wrong, did you? We're all set up for you in the back room. It's going to be splendid, I can't wait.' Her warm American accent always sounded so welcoming. 'What's that you're reading? Bettina's new book? It's a signed copy. She comes into the shop sometimes, though not as often as she used to. Not in great shape these days.' She smiled to see Jennifer pop the book under her arm, a sure sign she intended to buy it. 'Did you come early so you could have a reading?'

She occasionally visited Georgette for a paid tarot reading, though she was not a huge fan of her choice of cards. Georgette insisted on using one of the oldest tarot decks, the cards of Marseille, rather than the pack Jennifer favoured, designed in part by Aleister Crowley, a famed and reputedly dangerous twentieth-century magician. Not only were his designs beautiful and ethereal and painted by Crowley's friend, Lady Frieda Harris, an artist, they also incorporated many fascinating symbols and lettering, which lent the cards a marvellous depth, especially when it came to meditation.

'Not this time, no.' She gave Georgette a brief hug. 'I need a favour.'

Georgette looked at her keenly. 'You'd better come through into the nook, then. So we can chat undisturbed.' She ushered Jennifer through the curtain and into the small back room where she conducted her tarot readings and the occasional seance.

The place was dim and stuffy, the single window closed, fabric blinds pulled down to block out the sunlight. Several incense sticks were smoking in a carved burner, filling the air with the creamy scent of sandalwood. The circular table in the centre of the room was laid for a reading, the cards still spread out in a typical Celtic cross formation.

Jennifer could not help glancing at the previous reading as Georgette began to tidy up. 'That doesn't look good,' she said, raising her eyebrows at The Ruined Tower card right on top, which usually spelled disaster.

'No, poor thing. I tried to soften the blow, tell her everything would work out. But as you can see . . .'

Clicking her tongue, Georgette gathered up the cards and slid them back into the pack, then wrapped the whole bundle in a square of black silk kept specially for the purpose. This she placed reverently into a wooden casket on a side table, closed the lid and locked it.

'There, all done.' She sat down at the table, reached for Jennifer's hands with a well-practised smile and turned them over to study her palms. 'Let's see . . .'

Jennifer kept still, entertained as ever by this performance, only to become alarmed when Georgette suddenly stiffened and muttered, 'Oh my goodness.'

'What is it?' Jennifer strained forward to see her own palms, which looked the same as usual. 'Have you seen something bad?'

CHAPTER SEVEN

Georgette made an odd face and released her hands. 'Oh, I'm sure it's nothing to worry about.' She cleared her throat. 'What was this favour you wanted?'

Jennifer stared at her. She liked Georgette, but the tarot reader could be infuriatingly mysterious at times. She reached into her handbag and produced a slim, tatty volume, once vellum-bound, now re-covered in plain brown paper.

'I keep running into issues deciphering this old Cornish text,' she said, pushing the book across the table. 'I was wondering if you could help me.'

'Me?'

'You know some Cornish, don't you?'

Georgette was examining the interior of the book, her eyebrows raised. 'Yes, I know a little Cornish. But this is archaic. It's a kind of spell book, isn't it? With sections on plant growing and gathering.' She eyed one page, which featured a rather curiously shaped mandrake root, with a lopsided grin. 'Goodness me.'

'I was hoping you could help me with the translation.'

'Not me, sorry.' Georgette closed the book and pushed it reluctantly back across to her. 'You need Bettina for that.

Except she's not been well, poor lady.' She hesitated. 'You could try Penny Jago's Cornish language class.'

Returning the precious book to her bag, Jennifer stiffened. 'Penny Jago?'

'She took over Bettina's class last September, don't you remember? They're held every Tuesday evening in the Pethporro town hall.'

So she'd been right. Penny Jago was still running those Cornish language classes. Jennifer pretended to look unaffected, but her heart was thudding unpleasantly fast. She felt stupid, and hated the fact that she was blushing. Over the mere mention of one of Hannah Tregar's friends . . .

Penny and Bailey didn't even live with Hannah any longer. Hannah had offered to take them in last year, after they were left homeless owing to the severe flooding of a number of Pethporro seafront properties. But the couple had moved back into their tiny cottage in early spring, once the flood damage had been repaired and the place was habitable again. Her stepsister had mentioned the move to Jennifer in passing; as Caroline had rather indiscreetly told her, Bailey had been undergoing IVF treatment in the hope of starting a family, but had put the treatment on hold until the pair could get back into their own home.

'I just saw Penny Jago,' she said faintly, 'doing some re-enactment work at the museum. Victorian sea shanties.'

'Her Cornish is excellent. Far better than mine. And I've heard great things about her classes.' Georgette's eyes sparkled. 'Apparently, the students get a cup of tea and a delicious slice of home-made hevva cake during the break. Made by Penny herself to a traditional Cornish recipe.'

Jennifer gathered her things and stood up awkwardly. She was not keen on the idea of joining Penny Jago's Cornish language class. But she did need help with this old text, and it would be ridiculous if she allowed Penny's friendship with Hannah to interfere with her work. Not when it was so important that she fully understand what she was reading; after all, it was one of the key texts she intended to reference in her new book on Cornish lore.

She was still concerned by Georgette's reaction earlier, as though she had seen something calamitous when she'd studied her palms. Not that Jennifer was totally convinced by palmistry. It seemed a bit more haphazard than most as a form of fortune telling. But she was curious.

'You sure I can't do you a quick reading?' Georgette asked.

'I'm not really in the mood, sorry.' Jennifer made a face. 'Bit nervous about the storytelling session. I'm sure I'm going to forget what I'm supposed to be saying.'

But Georgette was not fooled, seeing her instinctive glance towards the chest where the tarot cards were kept. 'Come on, sit down again,' she said comfortably, and bustled over to the carved chest and turned the key. She took out the pack, unwrapping the black silk to reveal the cards. 'This won't take long. And we both know you'll be brilliant today. Absolutely brilliant. You're a born storyteller.'

'I am?'

'Of course you are. But not much good at little white lies.' Georgette grinned up at her. 'Sorry, honey. But your face gives everything away.'

Jennifer sank down onto her seat again.

'Maybe a quick reading, then,' she muttered.

'Super-quick, I promise.'

With a few practised flicks of her wrist, Georgette shuffled the tarot pack after the last reading, then handed it reverently across to Jennifer.

'Now shuffle the cards again, thinking of nothing but your question,' she said, falling into the dreamy tone she used with her regular clients. 'Once you're ready, cut the pack wherever it feels right to you. Place the bottom half on top, and then hand the cards back to me.'

Jennifer closed her eyes and did as she had been instructed, shuffling the cards while thinking intently of . . .

Well, she had intended to think of Raphael. He was the figure who had dominated her thoughts and dreams for so many months now, after all, his dark, forbidding figure looming into her mind at every spare moment. She wanted to know how Raphael was feeling, whether he still secretly thought about her at times, despite his recent marriage to Hannah Clitheroe, and if there was any hope of her ever getting over him.

Yet for some reason, whenever she tried to picture her former lover, another face swung in the way, blocking out Raphael's image. A face with the arrogant, undeniably devastating good looks of a film star.

Alex Delgardo.

Good grief, what on earth was wrong with her?

She flicked furiously through the tarot cards, eyes shut tight, trying to return her full concentration to Raphael. How he had spoken to her on the phone last winter and told her he was seeing another woman, and it was getting serious. The agony it had caused her, how she had begged him not to make such a terrible mistake. She could still recall the hoarse note in his voice, the way he had said her name, so apologetic, so achingly different from the terse dismissal Alex Delgardo had handed out to her in his kitchen . . .

Damn that man. How did he dare speak to her like that? And today in the tapas bar he had seemed so cool and confident, his attention shifting to Caroline's blonde good looks while barely giving her a glance.

She opened her eyes and realised that Georgette was staring at her. Hurriedly, she cut the pack, put the bottom half on top, then handed the cards back to Georgette.

With a click of her beads, Georgette leant over the cards, hesitated, then raised her eyebrows at her. 'So what kind of question was it this time? Work, life or love?'

Jennifer grimaced. As if Georgette needed to ask. Every tarot reading she'd had over the past few months had covered the same basic question: Raphael, Raphael and Raphael again. That sad litany had become her whole life these days.

'Love.'

Nodding, Georgette laid out the cards in her customary Love Spread. Two cards along the top row, three below, and one below that. Face down at first. To be turned over with great ceremony as she reached each card during her analysis.

'This card represents you,' Georgette said softly, and turned over the first card on the top row, then paused and looked up at her in sudden swift sympathy.

It was Le Pendu, The Hanged Man.

Jennifer bit her lip, feeling a little shaken. Not the card she would have chosen to represent herself. But maybe it reflected the sacrifices she had been making recently. The hard work of moving home, and the solitude in which she had chosen to live, staying away from the world she found so stressful.

'And the second card?'

Georgette took hold of the second card on the top row. 'This card represents your significant other in the Love Spread.'

'Raphael.'

'If that's who you were asking about, yes.'

Jennifer understood why Georgette was so hesitant. It had become common at this stage of the reading for her to uncover some appalling card of ill omen. Death, perhaps, or The Ruined Tower, known in this pack as La Maison Dieu, both cards basically spelling destruction and the end of everything. Which Georgette always tried to interpret in gentler terms, of course, claiming the universe was telling Jennifer to move on before something worse happened to her. Though she could not imagine many worse things than the pain and grief she had been suffering since Raphael broke up with her.

She wanted to move on, she really did. To forget Raphael and do something new with her life. But whenever she tried to look forward, to open herself to life and new experiences, some tiny hidden door in her heart stoutly refused to be unlocked. Behind that door lurked the deepest of her fears. The terrible, soul-crushing fear that she had been rejected because of who she was; that, ultimately, she was unlovable.

'Here goes, then.' Gingerly, Georgette turned over the card and made a sharp noise under her breath. 'Oh my!'

Jennifer stared.

The card lying face up on the table was The Lovers.

'Well, that was unexpected.' Georgette looked from the card to Jennifer and then back again. There was confusion in her eyes. 'You were thinking about Raphael when you shuffled the pack, weren't you?'

Jennifer bit her lip. A little too late, she pushed the image of Alex Delgardo far to the back of her mind. Like an old pair of boots being shoved to the bottom of a cupboard.

'Perhaps we'd better start again,' she said guiltily.

'I'd love to.' Georgette glanced at her watch. 'Only I'm not sure you have time, honey.' Her smile flickered, teasing. 'Or have you forgotten that you're about to become Pethporro's new storyteller?'

CHAPTER EIGHT

The Merry Maidens of the Stones

Once upon a time, high on the Cornish moors, a large group of young women were on their way to church, walking together on a bright and windy Sunday morning.

One of the young women, the cleverest and lightest of foot, stopped and listened to an unexpected sound. 'Music,' she said, pointing up the next slope, where trees grew about a rough cluster of rocks, 'I hear music.'

The other women came to a halt too, listening, their faces amazed.

'What wonderful music,' the youngest said, and caught at her best friend's hand. 'Listen, Mary! It's making my feet tap. Are your feet tapping, too?'

'They are indeed!' Mary peered down at her own feet and laughed in surprise. 'Look at me, I can't seem to stop moving.'

'Nor me,' another of Mary's friends cried, and grabbed at her other hand. 'What kind of music is that? It's so marvellous.'

The eldest there called out a warning. 'Cover your ears! Don't listen! It is the music of the Little Folk, and not to be trusted.'

But it was too late.

The others were already swaying and rolling their hips, linking

hands in the dance. Their long hair blew in the breeze as they
danced and laughed, smiling at each other. They caught at the hand
of the eldest, and dragged her into the circle, too, though she pro-
tested and tried to pull away, knowing the danger they were in. But
the music soon crept into her heart and she too began dancing with
the rest, happy and laughing, alive in the sunshine . . .

Until suddenly they all stood silent and still.

Never to move again.

The back room of the Pethporro Celtic Centre was surprisingly full. Mostly with adults; the summer season wasn't in
full swing, as not all the schools had broken up yet. The
stories Jennifer would be telling at these sessions were not
always right for smaller ears, so parents had been discour-
aged from bringing any children of primary school age to
hear them. But they all seemed fascinated by the story she
had chosen to tell at her first session, and had clapped
enthusiastically when she finished.

As she'd started to tell the tale of 'The Merry Maidens of
the Stones', Alex Delgardo had slipped into the room at the
back, a smiling Nelly supported on his arm. Jennifer could
not believe it. At the sight of him, her heart had performed
an awkward little somersault in her chest and she had felt
her pulse begin to race, something that had not happened
to her outside of a gym in months.

Alex had grinned at her across the room as he sat down,
as though enjoying her discomfort. Bloody man.

If only Caroline had kept her mouth shut . . .

But her voice did not falter, thank goodness, and Jennifer
had carefully avoided glancing in their direction throughout

the rest of the story, feeling ludicrously self-conscious and not entirely sure why.

Probably that damn tarot card reading.

The Lovers, indeed!

But at least Nelly seemed to enjoy the performance, listening with rapt attention and nodding occasionally, no doubt familiar with some of the standing stones mentioned.

'Cornwall is an ancient land,' Jennifer began as the applause died away, 'as ancient as any on this earth, and on many of its remote hills and moors you will find what are known as standing stones, tall fingers pointing at the sky or leaning together, providing a magical chink for the sun's beams to glance through at the solstice.

'Some stones are arranged in a ring in a formation commonly known as a "dance". Others stand in pairs, or even alone, sentinels set in those high, dark places where a traveller might pass by and beg protection from unruly spirits. People used to believe these stones were placed there by the Druids, as part of some long-lost ritual, but their origin goes further back than that. Some stones are many thousands of years old, their rough sides pitted by weather, their markings lost to the wind and rain, totems of mystery in a mysterious land.

'On a lonely, windswept road that leads to Land's End, towards the very edge of those western islands, you will find nineteen standing stones, monuments to the past raised under a granite sky. There are eleven more in a row near Wadebridge, though there may be stones missing, and further stone circles exist in other parts of Cornwall, constructed in much the same way.

'But according to local legend,' she continued with a frown, 'these were not always stones, but women. Pretty young women, too, and unmarried, as they invariably are in these old folk tales. Young maidens on their way to church who, hearing strange music in the distance, were caught up in the thrill and excitement of a country dance. And as they danced, their bodies were suddenly and irrevocably transformed into cold, hard stone.

'So why did such a terrible thing happen to these pretty young women? It was a punishment, of course, for dancing on the Sabbath, for enjoying themselves and displaying their female bodies in defiance of holy law. Or so the old stories tell us.'

'How ridiculous,' Nelly said loudly from the back.

'I agree,' Jennifer said. 'These stones largely predate the Christian Church. So these are stories that have been imposed on ancient artefacts by the religious fervour of the day. It's much the same in Buryan, in the west of Cornwall. There, you'll find the "Dawns Myin" – the dancing or merry maidens – more stones reputed to have been young women. The story goes that one minute they were whirling about the fields in a fertility dance, under one of the gorgeous harvest moons we see here in Cornwall, and the next they were frozen to stone. These too are accused of being punished by God. But other stories claim it was the Little Folk, the fairies, who put a spell on the young women for intruding on their secret lands. Or possibly a family of rugged Cornish trolls, creatures who love to make mischief among humankind.'

'There's no such thing as trolls,' one teenage girl said,

sitting cross-legged at the front. Her solemn eyes met Jennifer's rather crossly. 'Or fairies.'

'If you say so,' Jennifer said, smiling.

'I do,' the girl said, and folded her arms, raising her chin.

'Okay.' Jennifer stalked up and down, her swirling green cloak brushing the knees of those sitting on the floor at the front. She was still avoiding Alex's ironic gaze, aware of a slight flush to her cheeks. She had known this would not be easy, and she refused to give up just because one or two of the audience members were looking at her sceptically. 'At Men-an-Tol, on the western moors of Cornwall, a strange circular stone with a hole in the middle like a ring doughnut draws visitors and locals alike.'

'A ring doughnut?' This time it was the girl's mother who had spoken, her voice sharp, disbelieving.

'That's right.' Jennifer stopped in front of the woman and her daughter. 'Visitors post photos of the stone to Instagram, gawping for ten minutes before moving on to the next Cornish site of interest. But the site has value beyond opportunities for a selfie. For centuries, possibly millennia, locals have sent their children scooting through the hole in the stone to cure sickness, while new brides have clambered through by moonlight, or even made love with their partners beside the stone, to ensure pregnancy.' She paused, rustling her cloak for effect as she walked up and down again. 'You see, the round hole in the centre of the stone, worn by weather and singing with the wind, suggests the entrance to the womb and the deep creative power of the female body.'

The girl's mother clapped both hands over her daughter's

ears and glared up at Jennifer, though the girl looked to be at least fourteen years old. Hardly too young to hear such words.

'Folklorists through the ages have studied these standing stones at length and come up with yet more tales of maidens punished for dancing on the Sabbath, and have even claimed that the three-thousand-year-old Men-an-Tol stone once guarded the passageway to a lost burial chamber for a warrior king . . .' She paused, unsure if she should continue. 'But I take a different view of the subject.'

Across the room, Nelly's smile encouraged her to go on.

'I believe,' Jennifer said firmly, 'that these peculiar and dramatic stones, far from being evidence of punishment, were raised in the ancient wilds of Cornwall to celebrate the power of women. That if the stones appear to stand or dance or give birth under moonlight and in sunshine, that's because women do those things in their everyday lives.' Reaching up, she stretched her cloaked arms wide in a theatrical gesture. 'In short, I believe these standing stones represent the beauty, strength, determination . . . and sheer witchy awesomeness of the feminine.'

Georgette started the applause, recognising the end of her prepared material, and soon everyone had joined in, including the woman and her sceptical daughter. Even Alex Delgardo was clapping his hands, though she read amusement in his face. But he was a professional actor. What had she expected?

All the same, she definitely needed to work on her presentation skills.

And stop swirling her cloak about quite so much.

'That was excellent,' Georgette said heartily, still clapping as she stepped forward, 'a truly fascinating story about our Cornish standing stones. Thank you very much, Jennifer. I've never been up to Men-an-Tol, but your talk has persuaded me to pay it a visit this summer. Though I doubt I'll be climbing through the hole in the centre of the stone any time soon. I'm not really in the market for a baby.' Everyone laughed, and she smiled benignly at the audience. 'Now, any questions for our new Pethporro storyteller?'

Several hands went up.

Georgette turned and winked at her. 'Told you so.'

CHAPTER NINE

The next morning, the goat was back.

Jennifer was staring out of her bedroom window at the animal, who appeared to have made straight for her nasturtium patch and was already busy there, head down, guzzling the prettiest and brightest blooms.

It was the same goat as last time. She would recognise that wedge-shaped face and air of cheeky nonchalance anywhere.

The timing of the goat's return could hardly be worse. She had just been meditating in the post-dawn cool, sitting cross-legged on an unbleached white rag rug, thinking calming thoughts about the universe. It had been lovely. She had been almost herself again, not the ragged, lovesick fool she'd been for too many months now.

And then the bleating had begun, disturbing her inner peace.

She'd thrown open the window and leant out, shouting, 'Oi, stop eating my nasturtiums, you hooligan!'

The thieving goat didn't even look up.

Her large hairy lips closed over a gorgeous orange bloom, wrenched hard, tugging it free from the twining climber, and the flower was gone. The goat straightened then, gazing mildly about the garden as she chewed, mouth slightly open, the orange bloom rolling round and round inside her ravening maw like a pair of colourful knickers in a front-loading washing machine.

So much for Delgardo's promise that it would never happen again.

What was the blasted animal called?

Baby.

'Hey, you! Yes, you, Baby, or whatever your name is ... Shoo!'

She glanced over at the bedside clock. Half past six, just gone. And she had a goat in her front garden. There was no way in hell that she was walking the annoying, hairy creature back to Alex Delgardo's glass palace again at this time of the morning. Especially after her reception last time. So her only chance of peace was to chase the creature away.

Baby eyed the house speculatively, throat paused mid-swallow, but failed to spot Jennifer at the window. The animal gave what looked like the goat equivalent of a shrug – a vague quiver of her broad white shoulders – and returned to her devastation of the nasturtiums, undeterred by the disembodied voice from above.

Jennifer blew out an exasperated breath and gave up any hope of returning to her early-morning meditation. She grabbed up her rope sandals and stomped downstairs in the simple leggings and vest top she'd been wearing for her meditation session.

'Oh yes,' she was muttering under her breath, 'you'll never let those bloody goats stray again.' She stopped in the open-plan kitchen to drag on her sandals, raising one foot at a time as she leant against the worktop. 'So good to know Mr Hollywood megastar Alex Delgardo keeps his promises. I won't be bothered by escapees ever again, no, *absolutely* not.'

As she crossed the living area, she spotted the rough draft of her speech on the coffee table. Her talk on Cornish folklore and magic was due to be delivered at the opening event of the Pethporro Folklore Festival, which was soon; she had nearly finished the first draft last night, wrestling with the last few paragraphs. Over a bottle of Pinot Grigio, truth be told.

The wine had improved neither her prose style nor her ability to string ideas together in a coherent fashion, but had left her happily befuddled by the time she stumbled up to bed a little after midnight.

A sudden thought struck her.

Snatching up the draft of her speech, Jennifer strode outside into the warmth of the early sunshine. Ripper, her cat, a cream sealpoint Siamese with piercing blue eyes and a dark, whisking tail, was outside too. He was crouched beneath the honeysuckle, gazing at the goat with understandable antipathy.

'Okay, goaty,' Jennifer said, perching herself on the low garden wall with her back to the woods, 'you asked for this, so don't complain if you get bored.' She glanced at the cat. 'Sorry, Ripper. I know you've heard this draft half a dozen times. But you can always slink off to catch mice. I won't be offended.'

The cat merely blinked. And stayed exactly where he was, a stone cat nestled within the fragrant shrub.

Jennifer cleared her throat and launched into an impromptu recital of her speech. 'Good evening, ladies and gentlemen,' she announced loudly, 'and welcome to the opening event of the Pethporro Folklore Festival. I'd especially like to welcome all those of you who love Cornish folklore as much as I do . . .'

The goat, who had taken a few startled steps away as she exited the cottage, stopped, turned round and stared at her in blank astonishment.

When Jennifer continued to speak to the garden in general, posing no apparent threat to her breakfast, Baby trotted over to the nasturtium patch and dived straight back in.

The cat followed it with a slitted gaze, his expression inscrutable.

Jennifer read through the entire speech aloud, occasionally pausing to rethink an overcomplicated phrase or change a verb that didn't quite fit. By the end, she was fairly sure it worked, except for the section on the traditional use of seaweed in Cornish spells, which still needed editing. It helped her to go through the talk aloud, and to an audience, even if that audience consisted of one hairy goat with her attention entirely on sweetly scented contraband and one partially hidden cat.

'I hope this has given you a taste for all things Cornish and folklore-related,' she concluded, 'and thank you so much for listening.'

She lowered the last sheet and was startled by the sound of applause.

'Great speech,' came an amused male voice from a few feet outside her garden wall. 'Do we get coffee and biscuits now?'

Jennifer stared round in horror and jumped down from the wall.

'You!' she gasped.

It was Alex Delgardo, looking cool and fresh in a loose white t-shirt and jogging bottoms. As she glared at him, he lifted his Fitbit watch to study it, still grinning.

'That run wasn't too bad. Twice round the grounds, then out through the woods.' He tapped the watch, then looked up at her. 'Though I wasn't expecting to be educated, too. I understand why you do the storytelling. That's a paying gig. But do you always come out and address your garden first thing in the morning on the topic of Celtic magic?'

Without waiting for permission, he strolled through the open garden gate and stroked Baby's head. The animal continued to munch happily, ignoring him completely as it tore a mouthful of parsley from the herb bed.

'Or perhaps you were hoping to convert my grandmother's goat to Wicca,' he continued, his voice lightly mocking. 'I must say, you're very well informed. I had no idea Cornish seaweed could be put to so many interesting uses.'

Feeling hot-cheeked, Jennifer thrust the speech behind her back and opened her mouth to say something snippy and accusatory.

But at that instant, a weird thing happened.

As their eyes met, she got the oddest sensation in her toes. A kind of tingling, and then a tugging that worked its way up her spine and shivered along the back of her neck. Her feet seemed to leave the ground, and for a few seconds it felt as though she were floating towards him, completely weightless, while at the same time Alex Delgardo came sailing towards her, both of them wrapped in a dazzle of misty light.

She blinked, baffled by this unearthly vision, and it immediately vanished. Instead, she found Delgardo staring back at her, his two feet rooted securely to the gravel path, his grandmother's goat chewing agreeably beside him.

A wave of embarrassment swept over her, and she didn't know what to say.

Behind her back, her grip loosened on her speech. Several typed sheets, annotated in red pen, fell to the ground. Jennifer half turned, scrabbling to recover them.

She was even more horrified when she straightened to find him in front of her, one errant sheet in hand.

'Please don't help,' she said, snatching the sheet from him.

But Alex was already bending to retrieve the last sheet from among the rambling sweet peas, where it had become entangled just out of her reach.

'Here,' he said, handing it over, and gave her one of those dark, intense, sidelong stares for which he was justifiably famous. 'Are you okay?'

'Meaning what?'

Good grief. What was wrong with her today? She sounded like an old-fashioned schoolmarm, all prissy and buttoned-up. But perhaps she was. Perhaps she'd spent too long alone.

Her cheeks flushed. Now where had *that* thought come from?

His brows twitched together. 'You look a little—'

'*Tired*.' She shuffled the loose papers, aiming for an air of super-fast efficiency, and prayed he wouldn't notice that the end sheet was now in the middle and her opening remarks had been relegated to the back of the pile. 'That's all. I'm just tired today. Too many late nights recently, thinking about—'

'Your speech?'

'You,' she said absently, without meaning to, and sensed rather than saw him stiffen in surprise. Her brain back-tracked. 'I mean, your goat.'

One eyebrow quirked upwards. The other remained at frown level.

'You can't sleep for thinking about my *goat*?'

'I was, erm, worried about her coming round here again. Invading my garden.' Damn it. Jennifer folded the crumpled, dog-eared sheets of paper over twice, and then tucked the whole bundle under her arm. She kept her back straight, chin up, glaring at him. 'Eating my nasturtiums.'

'*Your* nasturtiums?'

Jennifer ignored his teasing tone, still off balance after the 'floating' vision. Perhaps she really did need more sleep.

'You promised it wouldn't happen again, Mr Delgardo.'

'I'm sorry about that. I'll talk to Brodie. It seems our goat retrieval interventions have not been as comprehensive as we hoped.' Briefly, she was taken aback by the note of sincerity in his voice, before recalling that he was an actor by trade. Alex Delgardo could probably convince anyone of anything, and mesmerise his victims with those dark, smoky eyes while doing so. 'This is definitely the last time you'll be bothered by any goats, you have my word.'

Then he left her speechless by adding, as casually as though he was talking about the weather, 'May I come inside?'

CHAPTER TEN

She took a step backwards, unable to disguise her dismay.

Alex Delgardo wanted to come inside her cottage? To invade her privacy?

His smile was disarming. 'Not a landlord inspection, I promise. I just want a chat.' He hesitated. 'Though if it's a bad time, I can come back another day.'

'No, I suppose ... You'd better come in, then.'

'This will only take a few minutes,' he said smoothly, bending his head as he entered through the low doorway to the cottage. 'I'm just following up on something the letting agent said last time we spoke.'

'I see,' she said, wishing she had the nerve to say no and send him on his way again. But he was her landlord, after all. 'I'm very busy, you know.'

'Of course. There's a damp patch on the exterior wall upstairs. I'm sending someone over to get it fixed. A local man, name of Bob Relly.'

'I know Bob.'

'Unfortunately there's been a delay. Bob's doing another job at the moment. He can't come over until it's finished. So I thought I'd check it out myself.'

She looked at him suspiciously, but he had already turned away, noting the detritus on the coffee table and sofa from last night's excesses. An empty wine bottle and only one glass. A bowl that still contained a few nuts. It must be obvious that she'd been drinking alone, which made her feel even more embarrassed.

'Sorry about the mess,' she began awkwardly, then noticed her bra dangling over the back of the sofa.

Too late, she recalled removing her bra yesterday evening, to be more comfortable, without actually taking her top off – a trick she had learned in her teenage years. But he must think she'd been entertaining a man here and had thrown her underwear aside in wild abandon . . .

Her cheeks suffused with heat. She rushed forward to drag the offending wispy black bra off the back of the sofa and stuff it into a large wicker laundry basket.

'I wasn't prepared for visitors,' she muttered, not looking at him.

'Oh, don't mind me,' he said, with a ghost of a smile, and began examining a row of three glass jars displayed on the kitchen counter. 'Newt Eyes,' he read aloud, picking up the jar and gazing in apparent horror at its contents. Putting it down again gingerly, he moved along the row. 'Wolf's Bane, and . . . Devil's Dung.' His head swung towards her. 'Devil's Dung? I'm not sure I should ask . . .'

'You said something about a damp patch?'

'Right, yes.' He cleared his throat, leaving the kitchen area. 'As I was saying, I need to see your bedroom. If that's okay.'

'My bedroom?' Her voice was almost a squeak.

'That's where the damp patch is.' He raised his eyebrows at her. 'Or have I got that wrong?'

Jennifer glared at him. 'No, that's correct. I told the agent about the damp as soon as I moved in. And I know you're the landlord. But I didn't realise you'd be quite so . . .'

'Slow to respond?'

'Hands-on, I was going to say.' There was that smile again, damn him. 'I thought you'd be rather too busy to see to something so trivial yourself. Being a film star, and all.'

'My PA was supposed to deal with it. But I'm afraid it slipped his mind, and now he's busy with something else. I thought I'd better come over myself, rather than put it off any longer.' He added, 'You remember my PA? His name is Brodie. You met him at the house the other day.'

'I remember.' She paused. 'So you want to go *upstairs*?' She glanced towards the stairs, highly protective of her privacy. 'Right *now*?'

Was this some kind of dubious come-on? He was, after all, a man with a reputation. But for dating supermodels, she suspected, not wild-haired Cornish witches who kept jars of newt eyes in the kitchen.

'I promise,' he said, meeting her eyes with complete self-assurance, 'this will only take a couple of minutes. Though if you'd rather wait for Bob . . .'

He turned on his heel, heading for the still-open door of the cottage, where sunlight was pouring in across the slate floor.

'No,' she said at his departing back, and he halted, looking round at her with a supercilious expression.

Despite her misgivings, it would be ridiculous to send

him away if this inspection was only going to take five minutes. Her bedroom was her private sanctuary, it was true. And she was not unaware of how attractive she found him. But what harm could it do? It wasn't as though the attraction was mutual.

'You might as well take a quick look. Since you're here now.' She spun him a thin smile as he returned, heading for the stairs. 'Why not?'

He said nothing, proceeding upstairs at an unhurried pace, with Jennifer following behind, a little nervous now and racking her brains trying to recall whether there might be any more items of underwear strewn about in the bedroom.

He stopped at the top of the stairs. There were only two rooms upstairs in Pixie Cottage. Her bedroom, its cream door wide open, the sound of birdsong loud through its open windows. And the bathroom, its door slightly ajar, leaving a gap through which sunshine poured onto the dark polished wood of the landing.

'May I?' he said.

When she didn't protest, he pushed the bedroom door open and studied the walls, hands clasped behind his back.

She pointed out the creeping dark patch high in one corner where the exterior wall met the slope of the roof. 'There.'

'Yes, I see.' He stood beneath it for a moment, then said, 'Damp, almost certainly. There must be a leak in the roof.'

While he was checking out the damp, she surreptitiously tidied up behind his back. Her fluffy slippers, kicked off last night without ceremony, she placed neatly side by side next to the bed. With a few hurried jerks, she straightened the plain white duvet and repositioned the olive-green cushions so that they leant against the pillows instead of being scattered around on the bed.

There wasn't much she could do about the other side of the bedroom, though. Due to a lack of storage space in the cottage, she had stacked various boxes there, tea chests from her recent move still only half unpacked, some of their contents lying about . . .

'It's more widespread than I expected.' He paused. 'But you don't need to worry, Miss Bolitho. Now that I see the extent of the problem, I'll make arrangements to get the leak fixed straight away.'

'Thank you.'

'I'm afraid it will mean workmen coming into the cottage itself. They'll need access to your bedroom.'

'Understood.'

He got out his phone and took photos of the damp patch. Some close up, others taking in that entire corner of the bedroom. She waited behind him until he had finished, watching everything he did but saying nothing.

The temptation to snatch up her own phone and start taking photos of her famous landlord was strong, yet somehow she resisted it.

She could only imagine what Caroline would say if she were here. Her stepsister was intensely professional at work; cool and reserved, in fact. But out of uniform, she was very different. Noisy didn't really cover it, especially on a girls' night out. If she walked in right now and found a film star standing a few feet from Jennifer's bed, there would probably be shrieks and giggles and possibly some inappropriate comments. So it was just as well Caroline didn't know a thing about it. And better if she never did.

I have Alex Delgardo in my bedroom, Jennifer kept thinking, slightly dazed.

Surreal.

'The room will need to be redecorated after the leak has been fixed, of course.'

'Is that necessary?'

'It could cause you health issues if we don't dry out the wall and replace the wallpaper. This won't be a quick job.'

She was horrified. 'How long are we talking?'

'At least a week.' He made a face, studying the photographs on his phone. 'Maybe longer.'

'A whole week of workmen traipsing in and out of the cottage? But I've got so much work to do. I'm writing a book, and . . . well, I'm behind schedule.'

Alex Delgardo thrust his hands into the pockets of his jogging bottoms and jingled his house keys, his gaze still fixed high up on the wall.

'I can see how that might be a problem for you,' he said slowly.

'Problem? It's a bloody nightmare.'

He didn't respond immediately, and she wondered if her exclamation had come across as horribly rude. He probably wasn't used to people speaking to him like that.

Then he stirred. 'Look, I've got a proposition for you.'

'I'm sorry?'

'I need to ask a favour.' He met her gaze, then glanced hurriedly away, a dark tinge of red in his face. 'I've got a . . . a problem.'

Stunned, she gaped at him, wondering what kind of problem a movie star could have that might be solved by asking her for a favour.

'A problem,' she repeated blankly.

'Exactly.' Alex Delgardo turned and looked out of the window, his back to her. 'And I've come to the conclusion that you're the best person to help me with it.'

CHAPTER ELEVEN

For a few seconds of wild disbelief, Jennifer wondered if she had fallen asleep during her early-morning meditation and was still dreaming.

It would not be the first time that had happened.

Though, generally speaking, she didn't ordinarily dream about celebrities asking her for help. Especially grouchy, arrogant ones like Alex Delgardo.

'Me?' she half squeaked, and then recovered herself, not wanting to sound idiotic. 'Well, I'm certainly willing to listen, Mr Delgardo. What exactly is the problem?'

'It's my grandmother.'

She stopped smiling. That didn't sound good. An awful premonition nudged at her heart. 'Go on.'

'Nana's not been well recently.' Alex Delgardo paused. 'I don't want to go into details, but I'm out of my mind with worry.'

'Oh no, poor Nelly! Is it serious?'

'I wish I knew.'

She was confused. 'Pardon?'

'My grandmother is an obstinate woman, fiercely independent, and she hates hospitals and doctors. It's obvious she's not herself and needs proper medical attention, yet she refuses to discuss her illness with me.'

Jennifer could perfectly understand Nelly's desire for privacy. But equally she could see it was driving her grandson crazy, wanting to know what was wrong.

But how could she help? She wasn't sure she had anything to offer.

'On the other hand, Nana's taken quite a shine to you.' Alex Delgardo looked her up and down, then glanced around the room, eyeing her fluffy slippers and her bed with its vivid green cushions, his expression baffled. 'And you obviously like her too, or you wouldn't have offered to come round again to look at the goats. Anyway, it occurred to me that putting the two of you together for a few weeks might be a good idea.' He seemed mesmerised by her heavily stacked bookcase. She supposed there were probably a few odd book titles there that might have caught his attention. Like Beth Rae's *Hedge Witch: A Guide to Solitary Witchcraft*, or one of her new personal favourites, *Spells for Angry Women*. 'So,' he finished, 'I'd like you to stay with us at Porro Park until this job on your cottage is completed.'

Her brain stuttered. What did her landlord just say?

I'd like you to stay with us at Porro Park . . .

He had said it as though this was the most natural suggestion in the world. Which it most definitely was not. Not even close. Nor had it been a tentative suggestion. It was what he would *like*. It struck her that she was not being given much of an option except to agree.

Jennifer struggled to find a suitable response to his outlandish idea.

Was her mouth hanging open?

With barely any hesitation, he ploughed on, apparently oblivious to her shocked silence. 'To my mind, it's the logical solution to both our problems. The roof repairs can be tackled without you having to deal with workmen coming in and out all day while you're trying to write, and with you at Porro Park, I may be able to discover what Nana's medical needs are, and if I can help in any way.'

Hurriedly, she closed her mouth. Just in time, too, as Alex Delgardo chose that exact moment to look round at her.

She raised her eyebrows, to indicate astonishment but not downright rejection. His own brows rose slowly, as though to combat hers. She kept hers elevated, and was pleased to see his descend again under her querying stare.

The battle of the brows.

And it seemed she was the winner.

'Sorry,' Jennifer said uncertainly, 'but I don't completely follow your thinking. Getting me out of the cottage while the damp patch is fixed, yes. That makes sense and is very kind, thank you.' She frowned. 'But how will having me stay at Porro Park help *you* find out what's wrong with Nelly?'

The goat bleated from below.

With a frown, Alex Delgardo returned to the window to look down at the troublesome creature. The goat must have moved closer to the cottage, because he had to bend over the windowsill to study her.

His jogging bottoms tightened as he bent, and Jennifer took the opportunity of admiring his taut behind with just one swift glance before looking away again. It would not do to be caught ogling him. Besides, she had already seen his handsome rear in the flesh. On-screen, along with countless millions of other women, no doubt. Always assuming it was his own bottom.

She averted her eyes. Thank God he couldn't read minds.

'I mean,' she carried on, trying to distract herself, 'it's not like you expect me to spy on your grandmother for you, worm my way into her confidence and then secretly pass on whatever I find . . .'

She fell silent as he turned to look at her intently.

'Oh my God, that's *exactly* what you expect me to do.' She was breathless with indignation. 'You want me to spy on Nelly for you.'

He looked sheepish. ' "Spy" is a harsh word.'

'But an accurate one,' she said hotly.

'Believe me, I only have my grandmother's best interests at heart.'

'I doubt she would agree.'

'So would you rather a stubborn old lady died for lack of medical treatment, and you discovered afterwards that you could have prevented it?' His voice was equally hot.

For a few dangerous seconds, their eyes made contact.

'I accept that it's unorthodox,' he said. 'And of course you must decline if you feel it's too underhand. But surely the end justifies the means in this case?' His voice grew rough. 'It's been heartbreaking, these past months, to watch Nana struggle with her health and feel helpless to intervene. So if there's anything you can do, anything at all . . .'

He broke off, suddenly choked with emotion.

Jennifer felt awful.

She liked Nelly. But she did not want to become his spy. It

seemed horribly dishonest. And yet, in a way, he could be right. Maybe the end would justify the means, if it meant saving Nelly's life.

'Besides,' he added, clearing his throat and recovering his composure with obvious difficulty, 'you moving to the park will solve the problem of Baby visiting you every five minutes.'

'She'll still escape and eat my flowers,' she pointed out, her tone a little acidic, wishing she could find a good reason to decline the offer. She loathed the idea of noisy workmen tramping through her private writing space. But at the same time, a week or so in this man's company would probably try her patience to the limit. If only she didn't feel so jittery around him. It was really quite uncomfortable. 'The difference is I won't be here to see her.'

He shifted, moving back into her eyeline. His eyes locked with hers, disturbing in their intensity. There was something in those eyes . . . She didn't know what it was, but it made her shiver.

'I suppose Nelly likes you so much because you're a goat-whisperer.'

'A *what*, now?'

'Don't try to deny it,' he said. 'I saw the way you were with Baby. And look, she's come straight back here again, visiting you like an old friend.'

'She's visiting my flowers, not me.'

'Come on. You have some kind of mysterious affinity with goats.'

'I really haven't.'

He frowned at her. 'Will you come? To the house, I mean.'

'I don't think it's a very good idea. Spying—'

'Not spying. Making friends.'

'Spying,' she repeated stubbornly, 'on your grandmother does not seem right to me. Even with the best of intentions.'

'Is this about last time? I mean, up at the house?' He folded his arms, watching her. What he saw in her face must have convinced him, because he nodded. 'I offended you, didn't I?'

'How can you tell?'

'I'm sorry if I was a bit rude. You caught me on a bad day.'

She resisted the urge to laugh.

Ditto, she was thinking.

'Look,' he continued, 'Nana told me all about you after you'd left. How much you know about goats.' He waved a silencing hand at her protest. 'Yes, yes, I understand. You're very modest about your skills.'

'No, I'm genuinely *not* a goat expert.'

He looked taken aback. 'Oh.'

'I'm a folklorist,' she said, then added, with a touch of defiance, 'and a witch.'

'A *witch*?' His eyes widened. 'Hence those weird books over there.' She knew he'd seen them. 'And the jar of newt eyes in the kitchen. And that other stuff . . . What was it?'

'Devil's Dung.'

'That's the one. Very tasty, I'm sure.' He made a face. 'Remind me never to come around for dinner.'

She stuck her chin out, not dropping her gaze.

'But no wonder Nana likes you.' Alex grinned suddenly, showing a levity she had not seen in him before. 'The two of you have plenty in common. My grandmother is part witch,

I'm convinced of it. Always gathering herbs and performing odd rituals. I've often caught her wandering the grounds barefoot at dusk, "communing with the nature goddess", as she puts it. And you may not be an expert, but it's obvious you know your way around a goat.'

She blinked, disturbed by that mental image.

'I have to admit,' he said, glancing around the room, 'I wouldn't have guessed. Not a black cape or cauldron in sight. As a boy, I was convinced Nana had a flying broomstick. And a toad.'

'All the old clichés.'

'There's a reason they became clichés.'

'Broomsticks. Toads. Really?' She shook her head pityingly. 'Modern witchcraft is more likely to be done with an app these days. You badly need to be brought up to date.'

'Says the woman with newt eyes in her kitchen.'

She blushed at that. 'They're not real newt eyes,' she told him. 'They're just brown lentils in a watery solution. But they bob about realistically enough in a potion. It's called make-do-and-mend magic. Or kitchen magic, if that's easier to remember.'

'Come and stay with us while this work gets done,' he said persuasively, 'and maybe you can educate me.'

Jennifer almost laughed at the thought of teaching Alex Delgardo anything, then caught a knowing look on his face.

Oh God, he knows I find him attractive.

Suddenly, she was straight back there with Raphael, and that pitying look on his face when she begged him to give their relationship another chance. It had been mortifying, seeing his expression and recognising what it meant. No, worse than that. She'd experienced the most awful, cringe-making humiliation that had left her curled up in a ball for months afterwards, barely able to function. She was only now beginning to surface, and had no wish to revisit that again, wandering in the land of the rejected.

With such devastating good looks, Delgardo must know how hard it was for a woman to resist him. And as a celebrity, that effect must be doubled. Quadrupled, even.

'I shouldn't really . . .' she began, but he interrupted her.

'I think it's cancer,' he said bluntly.

She fell silent, staring.

That was not what she had expected to hear.

'I wasn't prying, believe me. My housekeeper came to see me. She'd caught my grandmother reading a book on how to deal with a cancer diagnosis. I was devastated, as you can imagine. Perhaps I should have been more tactful, but I couldn't help myself. I went straight to Nana and asked if she had cancer.' Alex held her gaze, clearly angry with himself. 'I messed up. She walked away, refused even to discuss it with me. And I haven't been able to get a word out of her since.'

Horrified, Jennifer didn't know what to say. 'I'm so sorry.'

'My grandmother took an instant liking to you, Miss Bolitho. That's a rare thing, trust me. Maybe if you were to come and stay with us for a few days, you could get to know Nelly better. Talk to her, bake cakes with her, take walks with the goats . . . She needs a friend, but more than that, she needs someone to make sure she's not exerting herself. Someone to look after her, without making it obvious.'

'A carer?'

'Nothing so arduous.' He paused. 'A companion.'

'Sounds like a full-time job.'

'I'll pay you.'

At once, she was offended. 'I wasn't angling for money. I just meant ... I still have my book to write. It's my livelihood. And I'm up against a deadline.'

'Then please accept three months' rent on the cottage,' he said. 'Not as a payment, but as a thank you. For the imposition.'

She held her breath, tempted by his offer.

Three months, rent-free.

She had been worried about making rent payments once her savings ran out. Folklore books were never big sellers. And this would certainly make her life easier.

'I can see I've offended you, and I'm sorry,' he continued. 'But I love my grandmother. Nana brought me and my sister up more or less single-handed when my mother abandoned us. Now it's my turn to look after her, and I'm willing to do whatever it takes.' Alex Delgardo looked at her keenly. 'So, what do you say? Will you come and stay with us?'

'I . . .'

'I'm begging you, Miss Bolitho.' There was a sudden wobble in his voice. 'She won't confide in me, but she likes you. Enough perhaps to open her heart.' Alex was looking at her intently. 'Look, even if you can't commit to being her companion, will you at least try to find out if my nan is dying?' His voice deepened. '*Please.*'

CHAPTER TWELVE

Arriving at Porro Park was a dangerous step into another world, like the underground caverns of the Knockers in Cornish mining folklore, a world she didn't know and wasn't sure she wanted to join. She rejected Alex's offer to drive her, and came round in her own car two days later, having packed up all the clothes and research books she thought she'd need for a stay of a week or two.

'Hello again!' Unaware of her ulterior motives for being there, Nelly greeted her enthusiastically at the front door, dressed as before in flowing white. 'My grandson says you need a place to stay while your roof is repaired. I think it's a wonderful idea. You must stay as long as you need, of course.' She peered down at the wicker cat carrier on the step. 'A pussy cat, too? How adorable. What's her name?'

'Ripper.'

Nelly's brows rose. 'Oh.'

'And she's a he.'

'Right.' Nelly watched as she carried the swaying cat carrier inside, Ripper spitting and trying to claw his way out, then added dubiously, 'Well, I'm sure he's very welcome too.'

'Don't worry, Ripper's not as bad as he likes to pretend.

He's a rescue cat, you see, and had a difficult upbringing. I can keep him in my bedroom, if you'd rather.' Jennifer hesitated. 'Though he likes kitchens best.'

'In that case, I shall ask Françoise to look after him for now. Just until you've unpacked and settled in.'

Françoise?

Jennifer was confused at first. Then she recalled the severe, unsmiling housekeeper she had met on her previous visit. Oh, yes. She and Ripper would get on just fine.

'As long as it's not too much extra work for her.'

'Of course not. Just leave the cat basket there, and I'll get Françoise to take him to the kitchen for a nice saucer of milk.' When Jennifer hesitated, unwilling to leave him, Nelly held out a hand. 'Please trust me, my dear. He'll be in good hands.'

'Thank you.'

'Not at all.' Nelly gave her a reassuring smile, then exclaimed, 'Oh no, leave your bags there,' when Jennifer tried humping her heavy suitcase inside too. 'Alex can carry them upstairs. He's very strong. You should see his muscles!'

Jennifer looked around the hall, half smiling at this description, but could not see the muscular Alex.

'I think he's on the phone,' Nelly confided, catching her curious glance. 'It's the third call from his agent this week. I haven't asked, but it could be a new film deal.' She clasped her hands together, lowering her voice. 'He never says so, of course, but I'm sure Alex has buried himself here because of me. And he and Brodie are always hanging around the house, asking how I am. As if I need to be looked after.'

Not knowing how to respond to that, Jennifer managed a wan smile.

As Nelly ushered her into the big house, she soon spotted Alex reclining on a large sofa in the living room. His phone call must have finished. From what she could see, glancing cautiously round the door, he was watching a film on his iPad, headphones on, wearing shorts and with bare feet up on the arm of the sofa, his large body relaxed.

'Now, where are my manners?' Nelly reached out and took her by the arm in a waft of lavender perfume, leading her away from the living room. 'Let me show you where everything is, my lovely. It's a great barn of a place. But you'll soon learn your way around.'

Nelly gave her a guided tour of the ground floor, oblivious to the uncertainty behind her smile. She had come here expressly to spy on Nelly. Even if it was with her best interests at heart. She could only hope that Nelly never found her out.

After a quick look around, including five minutes lingering in the tall, beautiful atrium with its potted ferns and glass ceiling, Nelly peeked into the living room again and instructed Alex to help with her bags, exactly as though he were a bellboy.

To Jennifer's surprise, he didn't argue, removing his headphones and casting aside his iPad without comment.

While he went to the door, the old lady insisted on showing Jennifer up to her bedroom, which apparently Françoise had just finished preparing for her.

It was clear, though, that Nelly was already tired. Progress was slow up the majestic flight of stairs that hugged the wall of the atrium, and Jennifer had to be careful not to climb too quickly, for fear of wearing her new friend out.

But the view through the glass walls of the atrium across the sunlit Cornish hills and fields was captivating.

'Oh, Françoise,' Nelly said breathlessly at the top, spotting the French housekeeper with an armful of freshly laundered white towels, 'there's a cat in a basket downstairs near the front door. A dear little thing called ... ah ... Ripper. Could you look after him until our guest has settled in?'

'Of course, madame.'

But Françoise did not sound impressed. She deposited a stack of towels in an adjacent airing cupboard, and then nodded to Nelly before heading downstairs without another word.

It was a lovely bedroom, bright and airy, with high-climbing blooms of clematis and white roses almost knocking on the windowpane. Jennifer could not deny how much pleasure it gave her to stand at the window and look out across the gravelled drive down a long, tree-lined avenue that stretched nearly the whole way to the main road. Leaning forward, she could see her ancient Citroën, too, which she had parked a few feet from a low-slung silver Aston Martin that probably cost more than her cottage.

No prizes for guessing who that car belonged to.

'I hope Ripper won't be naughty,' Jennifer said, turning away from the window. *Our guest*, Nelly had called her, yet Françoise had looked unconvinced. Did she know about Alex's plan? 'He can be awkward with strangers.'

'Oh, I love cats,' Nelly replied, beaming. 'I lived on a farm when I was a child, and we had cats everywhere. I'm sure he'll be no trouble.' She threw open the door to her en suite. 'Let me show you the bathroom.'

Jennifer almost fell back, blinded by gleaming white tiles and gold taps. There was a low bath sunk into the floor itself, with four taps and steps down, like a paddling pool. On closer examination, this turned out to be a Jacuzzi.

'Good grief,' she muttered.

Even the soap was posh, elderflower and jasmine, and there was a lavender-scented hand cream for afterwards, if she felt so inclined. Glancing about for a towel, she found a stack of immaculate white hand towels on a shelf above the loo. Seduced by so much luxury, she held one soft towel against her cheek for a moment and closed her eyes.

Her reverie was disturbed by a muffled *thud thud thud* from outside on the landing.

Dropping the towel, she followed Nelly back into the bedroom. Alex Delgardo appeared in the doorway, carrying a suitcase in each hand, another heavy bag tucked under one arm. He was a little flushed. 'What have you got in these bags? Rocks?'

'Alex, don't be rude,' his grandmother chided him.

'I needed to bring my research materials with me,' Jennifer told him.

'Research materials?'

'Books, papers, files. The book I'm writing is about Cornish witchcraft.'

Nelly smiled approvingly.

His mouth twitched, looking from her to his grandmother. She suspected he was remembering the esoteric books he had spotted on her bookcase in the cottage. But all he said was, 'Why do I have a vision of some ancient, dusty stack of tomes riddled with worms?'

'I have no idea,' Jennifer said through gritted teeth. 'Perhaps because you're still living in the past where witches are concerned?'

Nelly snorted, then hurriedly turned the sound into a cough when Alex glanced back at her, his eyes narrowed.

'Dear me,' the old lady said, discreetly making for the door, 'I think that was a sneeze. I must have a touch of hay fever. All this fine weather we've been enjoying, no doubt.' Nelly twiddled one of the bright yellow flowers that adorned her hair. 'Wonder if we've got any antihistamine in the kitchen cabinets?'

'I'm sure we have,' Alex said vaguely, setting the suitcases down beside the bed.

'You could show me where, Alex.'

Nelly was waiting for him in the doorway. But Alex didn't take the hint. He stood, huge and unmoving, studying the room with a frown as though still checking she had everything she needed.

'Thank you both so much,' Jennifer said, hoping to get rid of him. She was grateful that they had gone to such lengths to make sure her stay was a comfortable one. But his looming presence was beginning to unnerve her. And the last thing she wanted was for Nelly to suspect the true purpose behind her visit. 'I'd better unpack.'

Still, he didn't leave.

Nelly looked at her grandson again, then seemed to give up, slipping out of the room. 'I'll see you at dinner, Jennifer.'

Alex said nothing, awkwardly looking down at his feet as though he had something on his shoes.

As soon as his grandmother had gone, Alex strode across

the room and stopped about three inches from her face, his sudden proximity a shock.

'You will talk to her, won't you? You'll look after her and . . . find out what's wrong.' He spoke in a low voice, perhaps concerned that his grandmother was still outside the door. 'You haven't forgotten?'

'I haven't forgotten.'

'Thank you.'

'Though I'm sure you don't need all this subterfuge and skulduggery.'

His dark eyes clashed with hers. The contact between them was suddenly so intense, it was almost painful, and she had to stop herself from taking a hurried step backwards. She didn't want him to know what a powerful effect he had on her. Not when his ego was already the size of his enormous house. Or perhaps bigger.

'Nelly's as closed as an oyster as far as her illness is concerned. She'll talk about cakes and goats until . . . well, until the goats come home. But her health?' Alex shook his head. 'I went to the hospital, begging for answers. Even the local surgery. I spoke to her doctor. But everyone said the same thing. Without her permission, they aren't allowed to discuss her health with anyone. Not even me. Her body may be in trouble, but her mind is still in excellent working order, so it seems her health – or lack of it – is her own business. Not mine. As though I were a perfect stranger, not her grandson.'

'I can't say I blame her for not wanting to discuss it.' Jennifer hesitated. 'Some things are private. Even if that means keeping important things from your own family.'

He scowled at her.

This time she couldn't help herself, and took an instinctive step backwards, reminded of a scene in one of his more violent action films where his character, Cheetham, had confronted a villain about to explode a nuclear bomb, and frowned at him in exactly the same fashion. Roughly ten seconds before breaking the man's neck and leaving him in a slumped heap on the floor . . .

'What are you doing?' he demanded, his eyes narrowing.

'Nothing.'

'You edged backwards.' He raked her up and down with another of those penetrating stares. 'I saw you. Like a frightened rabbit.'

'I did no such thing,' she lied, turning away.

'Wait a minute.' He caught her elbow, and she stiffened. 'Thank you,' he said brusquely, 'for agreeing to speak to Nana for me.'

She managed another tiny shuffle backwards, pulling away from his touch.

'I need to unpack.'

Alex Delgardo glowered at her, thrust his hands into his pockets and muttered something on his way out of the door that she didn't catch.

She guessed it wasn't anything complimentary.

As soon as he was out of her room, Jennifer bent with relief to unpack her case of precious research books on Cornish magic and folklore. *Why do I have a vision of some ancient, dusty stack of tomes riddled with worms?* Not a single dusty tome in sight, she thought crossly, picking out the first few books and constructing a stack of them on her bedside chest of drawers. And as for all those horrid, wriggling little worms that often infested old books . . .

How dared he suggest that?

With difficulty, she pushed Alex Delgardo and his barbed comments out of her mind. She was only here while the damp problem at Pixie Cottage was rectified. Not to lock horns with *that man*. Though she would certainly keep a watchful eye on Nelly, as agreed, and even try to have a conversation about her illness, if that could be managed without causing offence.

Once her books were unpacked, she was irritated to find a faint powdering of book dust on her hands after all. As though he had willed it there just by the power of suggestion.

'Bloody man,' she said, reaching into her pocket for a tissue.

The roar of a fast-approaching car made her stiffen and hurry to the window.

What on earth?

A red, open-top sports car was tearing up the drive, spitting gravel everywhere. A woman was driving, a bleach blonde in reflective sunglasses so huge they dominated her face, hair flying around her head.

Jennifer caught a movement immediately below her window, and looked down to see Alex Delgardo coming out of the house. He stood on the steps, arms folded, as though waiting for his visitor to arrive. Something about his stiff body language suggested impatience. Perhaps even annoyance.

The red sports car was a Mercedes. The woman driving it wrenched the wheel round as she reached the entrance to the house and parked at an untidy angle not far from

Jennifer's dusty yellow Citroën. She jumped out, leaving the door open, and flew into Alex's waiting arms.

She was tall and statuesque, even more so thanks to the heels she was wearing. Her black dress, decorated with large red roses, hung loosely from an ample cleavage. She looked Amazonian.

The two embraced closely, then Alex went back to the car with her, the woman speaking volubly the whole time, not quite loud enough to be audible through glass.

Alex lifted several cases from the back seat of the car, accompanied by the woman, a snakeskin-effect handbag dangling from her arm. As they walked back to the house, he bent his head to murmur something in her ear. Something he presumably did not want anyone in the house to overhear.

Whatever he said, it clearly surprised his visitor.

The blonde in the black and red dress stiffened and for the first time took a few steps away from Alex. She stood still, staring up at the bedroom windows, her gaze narrowed and searching.

Flustered, Jennifer drew back at once and stood out of sight, breathing fast. But it was too late. She was certain the woman had seen her. Worse, she had spotted her watching the arrival of her sports car. Like a nosy neighbour twitching the curtains.

How embarrassing.

But at least seeing the woman had told Jennifer one very important and revealing fact.

Alex's visitor wasn't simply statuesque.

She was pregnant.

CHAPTER THIRTEEN

She wandered downstairs a couple of hours later, starving and unsure what to do about grabbing something to eat. Nelly had told her to make herself at home. But she felt awkward eating someone else's food, and had brought none of her own from home.

Also, she needed to feed Ripper.

Her Siamese always tucked into a handful of dried food at about this time, and though she had stupidly forgotten to pack his cat biscuits, she was sure Ripper wouldn't say no to a chopped-up slice of ham or a little tuna, just on this occasion. Whatever could be spared as a quick snack.

The atrium was bright and sunlit, almost dazzlingly so, thanks to the vast glass roof in place of a ceiling. Plants with lush foliage had been positioned strategically about the place, sprawling from pots or popping out of wall fittings, some even suspended from above, giving it the exotic appearance of a hothouse. Yet despite all this trailing greenery, the atrium had an oddly sterile air. Like a hospital trying to look more welcoming with the use of potted plants. There was no fragrance, and the air was still and suffocatingly warm. The floor was tiled with black-and-white-flecked marble squares, which made it hard to move silently, despite her flat-heeled sandals.

On her way to the kitchen, where she imagined Ripper was probably starting to pine for his owner, she passed an open door and heard voices inside.

Alex was talking to his visitor.

She had not come downstairs intending to pry, but she froze in the doorway, staring inside with a sudden, lively curiosity. On the blue sofa facing her, she could see the blonde perched on the arm rather than sitting comfortably on the seat, her face contorted with a mixture of despair and anger.

Somewhere out of sight, she heard Alex say in his deep voice, 'Stop worrying. It's not going to be a problem.'

'Not *your* problem, you mean.' The woman sounded distressed. 'For God's sake, Alex, this baby . . .' She put a hand to her swollen abdomen. 'I can't go on like this. I simply can't.'

Nelly drifted into view from the other side of the room, still clad in her long white robe, yellow flowers in her hair. She gave the woman a quick hug, then backed away, as though afraid she might bite.

'Calm down, my darling. You'll only make your baby upset.'

'*I'm* upset. Why shouldn't my baby be upset too? We're in this together.'

'Oh!' Nelly clapped her hands to her face in obvious distress. 'Oh dear, no!'

The younger woman paid her no attention but glared across at the unseen Alex. 'Well, Alex? Aren't you going to say anything?'

'I've told you, you can stay as long as you like. There's plenty of room.'

'You could try and sound a *little* more welcoming.'

'What do you want from me? I'm happy to help, you know I am. But you've caught me by surprise. You turn up in this incoherent state, with barely any warning . . .' Alex was hesitant. 'And please remember, we already have a guest staying here. My tenant from Pixie Cottage.'

'So, get rid of the woman.'

'Thelma!'

It was Nelly who had exclaimed in horror, bless her. But Jennifer had heard enough. This must be Alex's girlfriend, heavy with his child and looking to him for help and support, which he was clearly unwilling to give. Quite naturally she was upset to find another woman in the house. No doubt she suspected Jennifer was a love rival.

Get rid of the woman.

Jennifer shrank back from the doorway, feeling a little sick. It wasn't true, of course, but a mental image of Raphael and Hannah as newly-weds struck at her mind like a viper and she couldn't seem to shake the bloody thought loose.

Oh yes, she knew all about love rivals.

Her first impulse was to go back upstairs as quietly as possible, repack her cases and slip away back to the cottage. She could put up with workmen tramping about for a week or two. She could put up with hammering and radio music and shouting. Even in the private sanctuary of her bedroom. Frankly, she would put up with anything rather than stay another moment where she wasn't wanted. Especially after hearing the venom in Thelma's voice.

'Can't you make an effort to control yourself, Thelma? Play nicely, for once?' Alex sounded irritable. 'It's only for a short while.'

'What do you mean, *play nicely*? I'm not in a mood for putting up with strangers, that's all. And who can blame me, after what I've been through?' Thelma rocked back and forth on the arm of the large blue sofa. 'Oh God, my back . . .'

Jennifer turned to go, and the woman must have caught her instinctive movement, because she glanced towards the door and said loudly, 'Is that your *guest* eavesdropping at the door? How wonderfully polite of her.'

'Thelma!'

Now it was Alex's turn to exclaim angrily.

Jennifer fled in horror.

She was five steps up the staircase to the first floor when she heard someone behind her, and spun around to find Alex looming over her, big as a bear. He looked as furious as one, too. He was dressed all in black now, as though he was planning to attend a funeral later. Hers, maybe. Black t-shirt, black jeans, and barefoot. He must have kicked his designer trainers off in the heat, she thought, trying not to stare down at his bare, tanned toes. He smelt of cut grass and spice and all things hot . . .

'I'm sorry about that,' he said, standing far too close to her. 'Will you come back down for a minute? I'd like to introduce you—'

She cut him off, recoiling at the thought. 'No, thank you. I've decided to go home. Back to Pixie Cottage.'

He blinked at this announcement, looking shocked.

'Please don't leave, Jennifer,' he said. 'I need you here. I can't deal with this. Not now, not with everything else . . .'

Everything else?

'I'm sorry, but this isn't going to work out.'

'You haven't given it a chance yet. I don't want you to leave. Neither does Nelly. She needs you.' He shot a look at her face, then twisted his mouth. There was a hard tinge of red along his cheekbones. Cheekbones that had women sighing in ecstasy all around the globe. '*I* need you.'

She was taken aback by his deferential tone. 'Really?'

'Absolutely.' He looked at her pleadingly. 'What can I say to persuade you? Is there anything I can do to make you happier here? Anything at all.'

Jennifer didn't know what to say.

'That's very kind, but I can't stay. All this . . .' She gestured at the house, its space-age glass atrium. 'It's a distraction from my work. I have a speech to write. For the opening of the Pethporro Folklore Festival.'

'The speech you were giving to the goat?'

Now it was her turn to redden. 'Yes.'

'So you've already written it?'

'Yes, but it's not finished. I need to tinker with it.'

'Tinker?'

'It's a technical term. You wouldn't understand.'

'What I understand,' Alex said, 'is that my grandmother is very sick and her time on this earth may be limited. You're a kind person, Jennifer. I can see it in your face.' He lowered his head close to hers, adding softly, 'All I'm asking from you is a few days out of your busy schedule. I can't get Nana to talk to me about her illness. But maybe she'd talk to *you*.'

Looking directly into his eyes, Jennifer found it difficult to think clearly. It must be some kind of absurd biological override, she thought hazily, struggling against a primal urge to drag him upstairs and encourage him to have his way with her. As though a man like Alex Delgardo would need any encouragement in bed, if that unfortunate woman downstairs was anything to go by. But getting hot and sweaty with a virtual stranger wasn't who she was, and she didn't plan on making a fool of herself over a man for the second time in twelve months. That would be too horrible and painful for words.

Then he smiled.

'Come back downstairs,' he said, and held out his hand to her.

Her breath whooshed out, and suddenly she couldn't remember how to get any of it back into her lungs.

He was the most baffling creature she had ever met. She had always prided herself on being an observant person, one who could see how other people operated and use that knowledge to stay out of trouble. But Alex Delgardo had her head spinning. Granite-hard one minute, melting the next. Brutal in his ways, then abruptly charming. She was never quite sure how authentic he was being; couldn't get a grip on the real Alex Delgardo.

She supposed it was the actor in him. The ability to play whatever role was required of him from minute to minute. Maybe there *was* no real Alex Delgardo. Maybe even Alex no longer knew who he was, not deep down.

Perhaps he was just an endless layer of masks, with no true face underneath.

'One day,' she said, working hard to ignore his hand. 'I can stay for one more day. Then I'll reassess my options.'

'Thank you.' She caught what looked worryingly like a flash of triumph in his eyes as he jerked his head. 'Now come and meet my visitor. Then you and Nelly can talk goats.'

'My favourite topic . . .'

Jennifer followed him back downstairs towards the living room. Huffing upstairs to pack her bags was still an option, one she could swiftly choose if things took a nasty turn. But it seemed easier to acquiesce for the moment.

Besides, she was intrigued by the odd dynamics of this household. Very few people had the power to surprise her. But Alex and Nelly had done so consistently, and that was worth a few more days, wasn't it? Or one day, at least. That was all she was willing to give him.

She had to admit to being curious about his girlfriend, anyway. Thelma was clearly very rude. Eavesdropping, indeed!

'You can't go, anyway,' he said at the bottom of the stairs.

'Says who?'

'Françoise left the back door open and I'm afraid your cat escaped,' he said, and made an apologetic face. 'Sorry. Thelma's arrival distracted me, and I forgot to mention it. You'll need to find him first.'

Jennifer stopped, aghast. 'Oh no, poor Ripper!' She turned back, determined to find her beloved cat at once. 'Sorry, but this has to wait. Cats can easily panic in new surroundings. And this place is so huge, all those big lawns, and goats everywhere . . . If he gets lost in your grounds, I may never get him back at all.' She tried to quell her rising sense of apprehension. 'He must be terrified.'

'I doubt it.'

'How could you possibly know that?' She was amazed by his air of calm. Plainly the man didn't know the first thing about looking after pets. 'Are you, or have you ever been, a lost cat?'

CHAPTER FOURTEEN

Alex Delgardo blinked and took a step back. She imagined nobody had ever asked him that particular question before.

'No,' he said slowly.

'Exactly what I thought. You have to get into the mindset of the animal before you can understand its logic.'

'I see.'

'Poor little mite's probably hiding in a bush somewhere, scared out of his wits.'

'Or on his way back to Pixie Cottage.'

'I hadn't thought of that,' she said frankly. 'Cats do that too, don't they? Like homing pigeons.' Jennifer suddenly realised she was chewing on a fingernail, something she hadn't done for years. Embarrassed, she stuck both hands behind her back to avoid further temptation. 'Okay, that settles it. I need to find Ripper. Before he gets himself well and truly lost.'

'Not right this minute, surely?' Alex gestured towards the living room door. It was still standing open and the room was silent. No doubt his girlfriend and grandmother were both listening to this exchange. 'There's no hurry. I'll drive you over to the cottage as soon as we've finished.'

'But Ripper might still be in the grounds.' She paused,

thinking hard. 'Or in the woods. He loves the woods. All those rabbits and voles . . .'

She was genuinely anxious now. What if she never saw Ripper again? It would be all her fault for deciding to bring the cat. She ought to have left the Siamese at Pixie Cottage, where at least he knew his surroundings. She could have walked back daily to feed and water him. This was what she got for being lazy. Her only friend in the whole world, and she had lost him . . .

'A familiar voice is all he needs,' she added. 'And maybe a can of tuna.'

'I wouldn't bother with the tuna. Françoise already tried to coax him back in with some scraps. As soon as she picked him up, I'm afraid Ripper lived up to his name.'

'Oh dear.' Somehow, her hands had crept out from behind her back. Jennifer started to chew on her fingernail again, but saw him watching and stopped herself. 'It's not his fault, honestly. Ripper's a rescue cat and he doesn't like strangers. They make him agitated.'

'I'd suggest he doesn't like anyone. Except possibly you.'

'We understand each other,' she said defensively.

'Why am I not surprised?' His sideways glance was dry, though not unkind. 'Luckily, we have an ample first-aid kit here, with plenty of plasters and antiseptic cream. I just hope her tetanus booster is up to date.'

'I'm so sorry. I hope she's okay.'

'Françoise gets butted by goats on a regular basis,' he said blithely. 'She'll survive a few scratches.' His smile became persuasive. 'Look, come and say hello. Five minutes, that's all. Then I'll help you find your cat.'

Thelma had gravitated to the sofa proper and was lying

in a foetal position, head at one end, bare feet drawn up on the blue cushions, having kicked off her high heels. She appeared to be dozing, but opened her eyes in undisguised irritation when Alex strode into the room and announced loudly, 'This is my house guest and tenant, Miss Bolitho. I do hope you're going to be on your best behaviour, Thelma.'

'Aren't I always?' Thelma's voice was arctic and far from welcoming. She looked Jennifer up and down with barely concealed hostility. 'Hello.'

It was all Jennifer could do not to turn around and walk straight back out of the room. She had a lost Siamese to find, after all. But she refused to descend to the same level of rudeness.

Alex spoke quickly before she could reply. 'Miss Bolitho, this is Thelma.' He paused, then added in a disparaging tone, 'My younger sister.'

'Oh.'

Jennifer, who had folded her arms defiantly across her chest, preparing for battle, if not outright war, immediately felt foolish. And maybe a little relieved. She had been fighting so much lately, and on so many fronts, and she had not really wanted to be plunged into yet another death-or-dishonour confrontation.

Thelma was his *sister*.

Not his lover.

Not the mother of his unborn child.

And now she could see the family resemblance between them: that bold nose, the narrow mouth and jutting chin. Not so flattering on Thelma, but certainly striking. And of course, her hair was dyed blonde.

The same headstrong defiance, too. Nature or nurture, she wondered?

That explained the barbed remarks the two of them had been throwing at each other ever since Thelma arrived. Siblings could be like that, couldn't they? Even step-siblings, in her case. She and Caroline had not been the best of friends while growing up. Once, she had hacked all the hair off Caro's Barbie dolls, and in retaliation her stepsister had poured a pot of glue over her head. It had taken days to wash out. But they still loved each other. It was the sharp, relentless banter of familiarity, not actual dislike.

'Better watch what you say,' he was telling Thelma, leaning over the sofa with obvious relish. 'She's a witch. She has the power to turn you into a toad.'

Thelma's eyes bulged.

'Now you're being ridiculous.' Jennifer ignored his mocking smile and stuck out a hand to the very pregnant Thelma. 'Hello, I'm Jennifer.' After a brief hesitation, Thelma reached up and shook her hand. Her grip was limp, her palm over-warm. But at least she had not refused to shake hands. 'What an interesting name. I don't think I've ever met a Thelma before.'

'Haven't you? My mother was mad, you see.'

'Sorry?'

'She was mad. So she gave me a mad name.'

Nelly made a protesting sound under her breath. 'Poor Sarah, I don't think we should talk about her like that. You should never speak ill of the dead. They can't defend themselves, for a start, and anyway, it's not good manners. Besides, my daughter was not mad. Just out of step with the rest of the world.'

Thelma made a huffing noise. 'Mum was bonkers. Let's not dress it up. She even put me to sleep in a drawer.' Thelma looked at Jennifer as though appealing to her. 'I mean, who does that? Only crazy people, right?'

Jennifer opened her mouth, then shut it again. She wondered if she was the one going mad. 'A drawer?'

'A bloody *drawer*. The same place people keep their socks and knickers and their white linen handkerchiefs.'

Alex had been leaning against the window frame, gazing out across the grounds, his back to the room. Now he glanced round. 'Pay no attention, Jennifer. She doesn't mean *recently*. My sister is talking about when she was a baby. Nearly three decades ago, in other words. Our mother was always moving about, and she didn't have enough money for a cot. Later, of course, she turned to Nana for help. But when we were babies, she used to lay us down in a drawer instead of a cot. Lined with a blanket for comfort.'

Jennifer was confused. 'If you were a baby at the time,' she said to Thelma, 'how do you know you slept in a drawer?'

'I told them,' Nelly admitted, and shook her head guiltily. 'I thought it was a charming story. But Thelma was outraged.'

Thelma put a hand to her prominent bump. 'Who wouldn't be? Keeping a baby in a drawer, for God's sake. My little angel won't get that kind of treatment.'

'Because you're loaded,' Alex pointed out, not unreasonably.

'That's the pot calling the kettle black.'

Jennifer started to realise that she was completely and jarringly out of place here. Alex and Thelma were both very wealthy. She suddenly wished she was back home at Pixie

Cottage, staring up at the damp patch on the wall and worrying about her bills.

Nelly seemed to sense her discomfort. 'It was a very common occurrence when I was young,' she explained to Jennifer. 'There was so much poverty, especially here in Cornwall. And times are still hard for many people today. All these cuts . . .'

Ignoring her, Thelma stiffened and sat upright against the cushions, her face blank. 'W-what's that? Can you hear a car coming?'

When Nelly began to say something, Thelma shook her head urgently and held up a hand for silence. Now even Jennifer could hear it. The sound of another car on the noisy gravel of the drive, moving dangerously fast.

'Oh my God. He's come for me.'

Jennifer looked at her in surprise. 'Who?'

'How the hell did he know where to find me? I didn't tell a soul I was coming here.' Thelma swung her legs off the sofa and scrabbled blindly for her discarded heels, her face pale now. Jennifer didn't understand what was going on but responded instinctively to the other woman's distress, crouching to help her gather her shoes and handbag. 'Stall him for me, will you, Alex? I . . . I can't face him. Not yet. I've got to find somewhere to hide . . .'

Alex's voice cut across her breathless words.

'It's not Stuart.'

But Thelma was already off the sofa, hopping about on the polished floorboards with one high heel on, trying to balance long enough to squeeze into the other one. Her foot was red and swollen, and looked very painful. 'Not Stuart?

Then who is it?' Her voice was sharp. 'Not that ginger-haired weasel lawyer of his? Graham Something.' She was breathing hard, her large chest heaving with indignation. 'Stuart's not sent him to threaten me, has he? Because I wouldn't put anything past him.'

'It's Brodie.'

'Oh.' The monosyllable slipped out like a sigh. Thelma stopped hopping angrily and subsided onto the sofa, still clutching the shoe Jennifer had given her. 'I thought Brodie was on holiday this month. Last time we spoke, he couldn't wait to escape. Said he was desperate for a break.'

Alex crooked a dark eyebrow at his sister. 'He cancelled his holiday.'

'Why?'

'You can't guess?'

Jennifer suspected they must be talking about their grandmother's mysterious illness, but covertly, given Nelly's presence in the room.

Suddenly, the front door banged open and everyone stiffened, listening. A moment later Brodie loped into the room, his face alight with some strong emotion. He seemed surprised to find Jennifer there, but said nothing, his gaze flashing straight to Thelma on the sofa.

'I was in town,' he said hoarsely, 'but I came back as soon as Alex rang. Are you okay? What happened?' He was talking directly to Thelma as though they were the only people in the room. 'Did he hit you again?'

Jennifer sucked in her breath.

Thelma said nothing, but her hand trembled visibly on top of her bump.

Her husband was a wife beater?

Nelly, who had retreated to the safety of an armchair when Thelma started hopping about, got up and floated out of the room without meeting anyone's eye. 'Tea,' she said vaguely, a flower still dangling from her fingers. 'And I must speak to Françoise about dinner. We'll be five now.'

Feeling decidedly in the way, Jennifer followed her out into the atrium. More than ever, she just wanted to return to the relative peace of Pixie Cottage.

Ripper, she thought belatedly, and headed off towards the kitchen after the vanishing figure of Nelly. But before she reached the door, she heard footsteps behind her.

It was Alex.

'Wait,' he said, reaching her. 'This is such a mess. I know I probably don't need to say this, but can you forget what you just heard?'

'Of course.'

'What you need to understand about my sister is—'

'I said it's fine. No need to explain.'

'I don't want you thinking—'

'Are you worried I'll ring *Hello* magazine or the tabloids, and sell all this juicy gossip for a few thousand quid?'

Alex stared at her, then gave a hoarse bark of laughter. Not humorous laughter. 'Actually, that hadn't even occurred to me.'

'Perhaps it should have done. I can't pretend to be an expert, but people pay a lot of money for that kind of privileged information about celebrities and their families. You should be more careful of your privacy.'

'I am, usually. Fiercely so. But this is different.' He studied her, his head tipped to one side. 'You're different.'

Now it was her turn to laugh. But she wasn't being funny, either. 'I would be flattered. Except I haven't forgotten what you said to me the last time I came here. Or the way you said it.' Hurt heaved in her chest, surprising her with its violence. She hadn't realised how strongly she felt about his cold dismissal that day. She had been cross at the time, and offended by his tone. But hurt? 'You were quite clear you didn't want me back on the premises.'

He nodded, looking away from her. 'That's true.'

'So what's changed?'

'You don't want to go there.' He seemed fascinated by a vast spider plant that had taken over the only shady corner of the atrium.

Now the hurt was like an iron band around her chest, tightening with every word he spoke, every look he refused to give her.

'I don't need to bother going there. I already understand what's changed. You've found a use for me.'

That spider plant must be a particular favourite of his, she thought bitterly; he could barely look away from it. 'That's pretty unfair.'

'I'd call it accurate.'

'I told you, it was a bad day.'

'Why?'

'If you must know,' he said, abruptly removing his gaze from the spider plant and fixing her with it instead, 'that day was the anniversary of somebody's death.'

Jennifer heard a slight tremor in his voice, and felt awful. 'I'm sorry.'

'Anyway, all you need to know is that it wasn't personal.

And you are different. I don't know how, but Nelly feels it too.' He paused. 'I just wanted to say . . . Thelma's marriage isn't a happy one. You could have worked that out for yourself. But the obvious solution – divorce – isn't one she seems willing to pursue.'

'But if her husband . . . If there's abuse . . .'

'I know.'

She didn't know what to say. Except 'I'm sorry' again.

'We've been in this situation a number of times now. She leaves him. Stuart somehow persuades her to return. Things are quiet for a while, then something occurs. Some emotional event, some catastrophe. And the cycle kicks off again.' Alex grimaced. 'I called her recently and made the mistake of mentioning my suspicions about Nelly. I thought it hadn't affected her that much. But now this.'

'Everyone deals with bad news differently.'

'I suppose so.' He shrugged. 'I've tried to intervene a few times, but Thelma's stubborn, like everyone in this family. Once she's made a decision, she never changes her mind. She won't listen to reason. Or to me. And this time she won't even listen to Nelly.'

It was so hot and bright under the glass roof of the atrium, she could hear her heart beating erratically. The massed green foliage made the air sultry, too, almost unbearably so. Jennifer watched a tiny green fly climb nimbly up the sheer wall of Alex's chest, and reached out to brush it off his black t-shirt. Her fingers tingled with sudden warning, as though his body was hot, and she jerked her hand back.

He caught his breath at the contact, glaring down at her hand.

Oops.

He hadn't liked that.

'Do you think she'll listen to me?' she asked, partly to cover her own confusion. *What the hell had just happened between them?* 'Is that what you wanted to ask? If I'd speak to Thelma, too?'

'I'm not sure how much good that would do, frankly.'

'Well, I can try. It certainly sounds like your sister needs a shoulder to cry on, at least. But I need to look for Ripper first.'

'Fine.' Alex studied her thoughtfully, as though something had just occurred to him. 'You know a lot about Cornwall, don't you? I suppose you speak fluent Cornish?'

'Not really, my Cornish is pretty rusty.'

'So you could do with a refresher course?'

She looked at him suspiciously. 'I suppose it wouldn't do me any harm to brush up. Why do you ask?'

'Nana's signed up to local Cornish language classes. Maybe you could go with her. It would be a perfect chance to build your friendship.'

The class Penny Jago was running in Pethporro, no doubt. One of Hannah Clitheroe's closest friends. Jennifer felt a faint shudder run through her at the thought of bumping into Hannah, or worse, having Penny report back to Hannah and Raphael that she'd seen her. That she had lost weight since their break-up. That she looked a little lost, perhaps.

But even worse would be having them all think she was hiding away, too humiliated to show her face after losing Raphael to another woman.

'Sounds like a plan,' she said, and forced a smile.

'Excellent. Nana will be so pleased when I tell her. I know she

wasn't keen on going to the class alone. But Celtic languages ...'
He grinned, his face transformed. 'So not my thing.'

'We can't all be brilliant linguists.'

'No, I'll leave that to you.' His eyes lit up with laughter.
'So, have you always lived here in Pethporro?'

'I've moved about a bit. It was good to come home, actually. To feel settled again.'

'Your parents live here?'

'It's complicated.'

'I know how that particular story goes.' Alex hesitated.
'And is there a ... I mean, are you seeing anyone at the
moment?' There must have been a flash of anger in her face,
because he looked away. 'Sorry, none of my business. Yet
again.'

She decided not to comment.

'I'll drive you back to the cottage,' he offered. 'In case the
cat's headed for home.'

'I'd rather walk.'

His eyes met hers. 'Of course you would,' he said.

And just like that, he turned with a faint smile and walked
away, leaving Jennifer startled, in a pool of sunshine.

Relieved to be alone at last, Jennifer walked outside and
stood looking across the lush, rolling green lawns towards
the woods. 'Ripper?' she called, shading her eyes against the
bright sun. 'Ripper? Here, Ripper!'

But there was no sign of the Siamese.

She turned on her heel, painstakingly checking everything in sight – lawns, bushes, trees, outbuildings – for a
glimpse of his glossy coat. But she couldn't see him anywhere.

Could the cat have disappeared into the woods, and be on his way home to Pixie Cottage?

Her phone buzzed in her pocket, and she drew it out.

A text from Caroline.

Hope you haven't forgotten our dinner meet-up this Thursday. Had no word yet about time. Bit worried. I'm bringing wine, yes?

When she called Caroline back, she got her answering service.

She hesitated.

Caroline would be agog with curiosity at the news that she was staying at Porro Park, and would immediately assume Jennifer was making a move on Alex, even though it was all perfectly innocent. She had intended to ask Caroline to meet her in town instead. But she couldn't cope with seeing her stepsister right now.

'Hey, Caro, it's me,' she said for the answering service. 'Erm, can we postpone dinner this week? Sorry to mess you about, but I'm . . . erm . . . snowed under with work. Give me a call back sometime and we'll rearrange.'

That should keep her at bay for a few days.

She continued across the lawn, calling for the cat, growing ever more concerned for his well-being. 'Ripper? Come on, Ripper!'

A loud whirring from above made her look up in alarm as a coastguard helicopter flew low over the house and gardens, light glinting off its distinctive red body. Birds shot up and the treetops bent; the high leafy branches, stirred by its passing, rustling loudly.

Someone must be in trouble along the coast or out to sea, she thought, watching it fly on over the woods.

Suddenly, with an unearthly yowl, Ripper shot out of the undergrowth and bounded towards her across the sunlit grass, all paws and rippling fur.

'Oh, Ripper,' she said, near breathless with relief, and stooped to gather him up. 'You had me so worried. Did the noisy helicopter scare you?'

For once, the skinny Siamese didn't resist being picked up, but began to purr at once, half closing his eyes, and she laughed at his beatific expression.

'You naughty boy!'

Now the helicopter had gone, the bright gardens at Porro Park were at peace again. As was she, soothed by the cat's return. Her relief at being reunited with Ripper was genuine and heartfelt, of course. But it was also tinged with an increased awareness of the attraction between her and Alex Delgardo. The longer she spent in his company, the harder it was to ignore it. And his question about possible boyfriends had shaken her.

Are you seeing anyone?

She had not known where to look. Apart from not at him.

'Okay, gorgeous, how about a tasty snack of tuna flakes?' With Ripper cradled in her arms, Jennifer began to retrace her steps to the house, though she would much rather be walking in the opposite direction and marching straight home to Pixie Cottage. 'And maybe a saucer of cream . . .?'

CHAPTER FIFTEEN

Just before seven o'clock the following evening, Alex revved up his silver Aston Martin and drove Jennifer and Nelly into Pethporro for their Cornish language class. Thelma had somehow squeezed into the back of the car too, chatting most of the way about possible names for her unborn child.

Nobody had mentioned the fact that Alex had turned up to supper the previous evening with heavily bandaged hands, so Jennifer didn't like to say anything either. But she was curious.

Watching his bandaged hands on the wheel, she turned to Thelma and whispered, 'What on earth did Alex do to his hands?'

But Thelma merely shrugged and looked away.

It seemed Jennifer was not to be let in on the secret, whatever it was. Had Alex burnt himself in the kitchen, perhaps? Or fallen while walking in the grounds and injured himself? She couldn't imagine either scenario, frankly.

The sun was still blazing down on their heads when they arrived in Pethporro, despite the fact that it was early evening. Alex dropped them right outside the town hall where the Cornish language classes were traditionally held, his expensive sports car turning heads, a few passers-by even stopping to gawp when they recognised the driver.

Jennifer was glad of her knee-length, sleeveless cotton dress in the heat, but watched Nelly with some concern. Her floaty blue dress was much longer, draping the floor as usual, and the old lady had sweat on her forehead as she climbed out of the front of his low-slung car.

'Here, Nana, give me your arm.' Alex came hurrying round to the passenger side. 'You can lean on me.'

But Nelly pushed aside her grandson's helping hand. 'I'm fine, Alex, please don't fuss.' She leant against the car, already out of breath, and made a face when he tried again to support her. 'Give me a minute, would you? It's this heat, that's all. Nothing wrong with me. I'll be better once we get inside.'

Alex exchanged a worried look with Jennifer, who was scrambling out of the Aston Martin on the other side. The open-top sports car was beautiful to look at, and purred along the main road like something out of a James Bond movie. But it was not the ideal vehicle to carry four people comfortably around bumpy Cornish lanes. Especially when one of them was heavy with child.

'I'll look after her,' she mouthed to him behind Nelly's back, and then bent to collect her bag from the back seat. It was unwieldy, containing a notepad, pens and her old Cornish dictionary, but she slung it determinedly over her shoulder.

'Have fun,' Thelma said drily, and laced her fingers together over her swelling bump. She had been crammed in next to Jennifer during the short but scarily fast drive into the centre of Pethporro, their shoulders and knees jostling at every sharp corner, wind whipping at their hair.

Alex helped a still-protesting Nelly up the steps into the town hall. 'I'll pick you up again at nine. Ring me if you need to escape any earlier.'

'Jenny and I will be fine, thank you,' Nelly told him firmly, reaching the top of the steps. 'You two have a lovely dinner. Just don't drink anything alcoholic.' She glanced back at Thelma darkly. 'Either of you.'

He and Thelma were going on to the tapas bar for an evening meal, and she and Nelly would have sandwiches when they got home, it had been decided. Alex had tried to persuade Nelly to have Françoise prepare them both a proper meal before going out, but his grandmother had stubbornly refused. 'Cheese and salad sandwiches is good enough for me,' Nelly had insisted back at the house, raising her eyebrows at Jennifer. 'What about you, Jenny?'

Jennifer had readily agreed.

She rather liked the way Nelly had started calling her Jenny. It was affectionate, as though she were one of the family, and almost made her feel young again. She had not been 'Jenny' to anyone except Caroline since primary school days.

But when Alex turned to leave them and said, 'Enjoy yourself, Nana. And you, *Jenny*,' with mocking emphasis, she rewarded him with a cold glare.

'Jennifer,' she corrected him.

Which made him laugh all the more. Damn him.

Alex headed back down the steps towards Thelma, who had climbed out too and was manoeuvring her bump cautiously into the front seat of the sports car.

'I'm surprised you're able to drive,' Jennifer called after him, 'with both hands bound up like an Egyptian mummy's.'

He raised his bandaged hands above his head and waved without looking round at her, then got into the silver Aston Martin and drove off with a roar of its powerful engine.

'What on earth did he do to hurt his hands, anyway?' she asked Nelly, feeling a little frustrated. 'Is it a secret? I do wish someone would tell me.'

Getting no response, Jennifer turned to find Nelly had disappeared, presumably having gone ahead without her.

So much for looking after her!

Hurrying into the town hall in pursuit, she was confronted by a colourful poster tacked to the noticeboard, decorated with cheerful-looking Cornish piskies: CORNISH LANGUAGE CLASSES. *Every Tuesday, 7–9pm, with Penny Jago. Meeting Room 2.* With a deep breath, Jennifer hoisted her heavy shoulder bag and shoved through the door into Meeting Room 2. There were three rows of seats facing a whiteboard and a fan spinning slowly on a side table to help cool the air.

Heads turned curiously at her entrance.

She checked every face looking in her direction, her heart thudding ominously. To her relief, there was no sign of Hannah Tregar, née Clitheroe.

Nor was Raphael there.

Not that she had expected to see *him* in a Cornish language class, of all places. Raphael was a farmer by trade. He was a rugged, well-built shepherd, not a linguist. But he took a lively interest in all things Cornish, and sat on the town council, so he might have decided to take a local language class.

Her thumping heart began to slow.

Nelly was seated on the back row, head down, scribbling something assiduously in her notepad. As though she had been there for hours.

It seemed everyone had turned up early tonight.

Except her.

Penny Jago, leaning over what looked like a register at the head of the class, straightened and stared at her in surprise.

'Hello.'

Penny's tone was not friendly.

'Sorry,' Jennifer said, more abruptly than she'd intended, and jumped when the door banged shut behind her. 'I . . . I thought the class started at seven.'

'It does,' Penny said, and glanced up at the wall clock behind her.

Everyone else looked up at the clock too. Accusingly. Then, like three rows of owls, their heads swivelled round to look back at Jennifer.

It was five past seven.

'Sorry,' Jennifer muttered again, and slid awkwardly into the seat next to Nelly. 'I didn't realise the time.' Her bag fell off her shoulder and her books fell out. As she lurched sideways to grab them, several pens also fell out. Her favourite pen skidded noisily across the wooden floor, coming to rest somewhere under an empty adjacent desk. '*Shit.*'

Oh God, had she said that out loud?

Straightening up, with a Cornish dictionary in hand, she knew at once that she had. Every face in the class rotated towards her again, silent and disapproving.

Including Nelly's.

'Shit,' Penny repeated expressionlessly, then picked up a green marker pen. Turning to the whiteboard, she wrote briskly – SHIT – then swapped the green marker pen for a black one and wrote a word beside it in Cornish Gaelic, *KAWGH*.

Looking over her shoulder at the class, she repeated the word 'Shit', then immediately added, '*Kawgh*.'

'*Kawgh*,' they all intoned dutifully.

Even Nelly.

'In this evening class, we use Cornish rather than English wherever possible,' Penny said, clearly directing her comment to the two newcomers at the back of the class. 'If you could try to bear that in mind.'

Jennifer, who had dropped onto her hands and knees to scrabble about for the escaped pen, felt her face go red.

Sh . . . Kawgh.

She resisted the urge to get comfy beneath the desk and not come out until everyone had gone home. That would be cowardly. Instead, she climbed back into her seat and focused on writing her name in capital letters and the title CORNISH LANGUAGE CLASSES across the top of a clean page in her notepad. At least they couldn't all still be looking at her, she thought, carefully dividing the page into two columns with the help of a ruler, Cornish on one side, English on the other, just as some of the others were doing.

It was an intermediate, rather than a beginners' class. But she would soon catch up; her Cornish was rusty, not nonexistent. She only hoped Nelly also knew enough Cornish to be able to follow what was going on.

Penny was saying something in Cornish and writing on the board again.

Absent-mindedly, she opened her Cornish dictionary to check one of the words on the handout someone had passed back to their row.

Nelly nudged her. 'Penny just asked you a question in Cornish,' she said, and jerked her chin towards the front of the class. 'Didn't you hear?'

'Sorry?'

She looked up to find everyone looking at her again. And Penny, waiting expectantly beside the whiteboard, where it seemed to say 'Where I live' in Cornish.

'Erm.' She frowned and dug deep into her memory of a previous class, several years ago now, and produced what was a garbled version of 'I live at Pixie Cottage'.

Not true, her conscience pricked at her. And she caught Nelly's eyebrows lifting and falling, but she stuck her chin out. No way was she telling this lot – not to mention Penny Jago, close friend to Hannah Tregar – that she was currently in residence at Porro Park, which everyone in Pethporro must know was currently the dwelling place of one Alex Delgardo, film star and reclusive millionaire.

Penny's mouth quirked in a lopsided smile. 'Thanks,' she said in perfectly fluent Cornish. 'So you live at Pixie Cottage?'

'Yes,' Jennifer said, more confidently. 'Near Porro Park.'

'That's interesting, Jennifer. Good to have you back in Pethporro.' Then she added in English, 'Unfortunately, I was only asking your name.'

'Oh.'

'Never mind,' Penny said. 'I'm sure it will all come back to you. Eventually.'

Jennifer squeezed her pen so hard the lid popped off and fell to the floor. This time, she didn't bother to bend and pick it up.

Penny looked at Nelly, repeating the same question.

Nelly licked her lips, frowned at the whiteboard with fierce concentration, and finally replied in eloquent Cornish.

'Very good,' Penny said, looking impressed. 'Well done.' Then she asked in Cornish again, 'And where do you live, Nelly?'

Nelly looked blank.

Penny wrote the question out in Cornish on the whiteboard, then tapped it with her marker pen, repeating herself in English.

'Ah, I can see now what you said.' Nelly sat up straight, nodding. 'I live at Porro Park.'

'Alex Delgardo's place?' Penny asked in English, and everyone turned to stare at them again. 'The film actor?'

'That's right. He's my grandson.'

Penny beamed at her. 'How wonderful. You must be very proud of him. So you're not that far from Jennifer, then?'

'Actually, she's staying with us at the moment,' Nelly said.

Penny gaped. 'With you and . . . *Alex Delgardo*?'

'It's a big house, we have plenty of room. And Alex insisted that she come to stay.' Nelly hesitated, looking confused by Jennifer's horrified little headshakes. Then she ploughed on awkwardly, 'Because of her damp problem.'

'Jennifer has a damp problem?'

'Only in her bedroom,' Nelly said. 'Though I'm sure it's nothing serious.'

'Nothing a handyman couldn't take care of, in other words?'

'Exactly.'

'I'm glad Alex was able to deal with it so promptly.' Penny gave a snort, her face alight with wicked laughter. 'These damp problems can be awfully . . . frustrating.'

Then Penny turned back to the whiteboard and began to scribble out a Cornish verb table, her shoulders shaking slightly as she wrote.

Jennifer looked at Nelly sideways, but couldn't bring herself to show her true feelings. The old lady didn't have a clue that she'd said anything that could be taken the wrong way. Besides, she didn't know the real reason why Jennifer was staying at Porro Park. And hopefully she never would.

'*What?*' Nelly mouthed at her.

'Your Cornish is excellent,' Jennifer whispered back with pained restraint. 'You've studied the language before, haven't you?'

'Goodness, years ago now. Before you were even born.' Nelly kept one cautious eye on the whiteboard as she began to copy out Penny's verb table.

'You haven't forgotten any of it,' Jennifer grimaced, also copying down the verb table in her notepad. 'Unlike me.'

'Nonsense, you did perfectly well. And your pronunciation is particularly good. Proper Cornish, as they say. Much better than mine.'

Jennifer laughed. 'But at least you were saying the right thing.'

Penny had started to explain the verb table to the class, but stopped abruptly at this exchange and whipped her head round to glare at them both. 'Ladies? Please keep private conversations to a minimum. So the whole class can hear what I'm saying.'

'Oops,' Nelly murmured.

'Sorry,' Jennifer said aloud, but smiled secretly at Nelly as soon as the teacher's back was turned, and was rewarded with a nudge from the old lady.

They worked in silence for the rest of the class, talking again only at the break, when thick slices of Cornish hevva cake were handed round and coffee was served from an insulated urn on a side table.

'It's been a long time since I've seen you in Pethporro,' Penny said in her ear, and laughed when Jennifer jumped. The woman had crept up behind her while she was pouring two plastic cupfuls of coffee for herself and Nelly. 'Sorry, did I startle you?'

Jennifer dabbed ineffectually at some spilled coffee with a paper napkin. 'Erm, no, I'm just a bit clumsy.'

'Here, let me.' Penny grabbed another napkin and helped, swiftly clearing up the spillage. 'I saw you're doing a talk at the folklore festival. On Cornish magic.'

'That's right.'

'Still writing the folklore books?'

'I'm just finishing a new one,' Jennifer said, replenishing the spilled coffee so both cups held equal amounts. 'That's why I need to brush up on my Cornish. A few old documents have been giving me a headache.'

'Show them to me. I'll translate them, no problem.'

Jennifer bristled instinctively, but managed a polite smile. She did need some help, after all. 'Thank you, that's very kind.'

Clearly sensing her distrust and unbothered by it, Penny grinned and helped herself to a large slice of hevva cake. 'You should both take a couple of slices,' she said, nodding to the cake tray. 'Traditional hevva cake. It's delicious, and there's plenty of it. I made it myself, fresh this morning.'

'Thank you, I'll come back for some in a minute,' Jennifer said, as polite as an ice pick, and scooped up the two coffee cups. 'I must take Nelly her coffee first.'

She looked round and hesitated, spotting Nelly deep in conversation with a bearded man with a single earring. He was dressed all in black, was probably in his sixties and looked rather like Gandalf, though rounder in the middle. Judging by his wild hand gestures, he was either describing how to bowl a cricket ball, or possibly cast a fishing line into a trout stream.

'Well, congratulations, anyway,' Penny said lightly.

'On what?'

'Wangling an invite to stay at Porro Park with Alex Delgardo.'

'Oh, that.' She grabbed a quick sip of her coffee to cover her confusion and bit back a cry as it scorched her mouth. 'It's nothing. He's just, erm, helping me out.'

'With your damp problem, yes.' Penny smiled. 'Sounds nasty.'

Jennifer glared at her, speechless.

CHAPTER SIXTEEN

The next morning, Jennifer dragged herself away from her folklore research books to help Nelly with the goats. She had not expected to enjoy herself, but it turned out to be great fun. All seven of them had congregated on the back lawn, bleating and shoving each other, impatient for their hay. Bundling the rough, scratchy hay into their metal manger, she talked to them while Nelly bent, checking the state of their hocks and hooves, one after the other. Jennifer was starting to learn their names, as well as their sneaky ways, and a handy email from her old friend Rekha about basic goat care was allowing her to at least *appear* expert, even if she wasn't.

There was Fruitcake, who loved snacks, and Bananas, with an odd yellow tinge to her short, hairy coat. Baby, of course, and sweet Hoppy, with a limping gait and cheerful disposition. Bananas was easy to remember, but she wasn't sure of all the others. She was doing her best to make friends with them though. For some reason, Nelly still had it in her head that her guest was a goat-whisperer; under the circumstances, it seemed better to play along than continue to try to disabuse her. It was a useful excuse for spending time with the old lady, which might otherwise have left her suspicious.

After all the goats had been fed and watered, she chased after Nelly, who was already wandering back towards the house.

'What now?' she asked cheerfully. 'Any more tasks for me?'

'Goodness, no,' Nelly said, looking blank. 'You're our guest, Jenny. And you have a book to write. I wouldn't dream of taking you away from your research.'

'Oh, the book can wait,' Jennifer said, wincing inwardly at the lie. 'I thought we could spend a bit more time together. Maybe bake a cake.'

'Cakes, for tea? Well, that's a lovely idea. I'm always trying to get Thelma to do some baking with me, but she's not really a kitchen person.'

'That's sad.'

Jennifer followed Nelly into the kitchen. To her secret relief, Françoise was nowhere to be seen. She found the stern housekeeper a little unnerving; she was convinced the Frenchwoman knew why she was there – and disapproved.

'Oh, I'm used to it now. I gave up on Thelma years ago. She actually prefers shop-bought cake. Can you imagine?' Nelly tied an apron around her own waist with practised fingers. 'So, are you any good at baking?'

'Absolute rubbish. But I'm willing to learn.'

'How marvellous of you.' Nelly gave her a broad grin and thrust a sturdy black and white cotton apron into her hands. 'Since Françoise has gone out shopping, you can be my assistant today.' Nelly washed her own hands and then pointed Jennifer towards the sink, too. 'Better wash your hands thoroughly with soap and hot water first. Hygiene is very important for goat-handlers.'

'Goat-handlers must be soap-handlers.'

'Exactly. And stop looking so worried. You don't need any special skills to help out in the kitchen.'

'You may change your mind when you see how bad I am at cooking.'

'Ah, but this isn't cooking. It's baking. A very different discipline.' Nelly bent to drag some cake tins out of a low cupboard. 'Besides, I'll teach you whatever you don't know.'

'Which is basically everything,' Jennifer muttered.

'What was that you said?'

'Nothing.' Jennifer washed and dried her hands as instructed, then presented herself meekly at the kitchen table, which was littered with baking equipment and ingredients in packets. She could see eggs, flour, sugar, cooking chocolate and walnuts, along with various other tubs and containers. 'Right, what should I do first?'

'First, you watch how it's done.'

'Fine by me.'

Jennifer stood by and watched as Nelly broke eggs into a large ceramic basin, showing her how to do it without wasting any of the egg white, then whisked them lightly. She poured flour into a weighing bowl and placed it on the scales, checking the exact amount required with her recipe book. Then Nelly opened the packet of walnut halves and told Jennifer to count out thirty. Which she did, assiduously.

'Right, thirty walnut halves.' Jennifer came back to the table with the nuts. 'What's next?'

'Take these lovely-smelling things.' Nelly handed her two

bars of cooking chocolate. 'Open the packets, separate the bars into squares and then check those cupboards for a bain-marie.'

'A ban-*what*?'

'Bain-marie.' Nelly spelled it out, and then chortled at her expression. 'Bless you, child. Don't you know what a bain-marie is?'

Jennifer pulled a face.

'It's a special pan I use for making custard or melting chocolate,' Nelly told her, watching her open the two packets of cooking chocolate. 'There's one in the lower cupboard. First, break these bars into squares. Then pop them into the bain-marie, bring a pan of water to the boil and place the bain-marie on top.'

Jennifer looked in the pan cupboard for this mysterious bain-marie. It turned out to be a smooth, shiny metal bowl with a long handle. The bain-marie located, she set to work cracking the bars into squares, then melting the chocolate squares over a pan on the stove. Meanwhile, Nelly mixed flour, sugar and eggs in a bowl cradled comfortably in the crook of her arm. The rich smell of chocolate, sugar and eggs soon filled the kitchen, making Jennifer inhale with dreamy pleasure, wishing she had grown up knowing more about baking. But of course, she always had her nose in a book rather than a mixing bowl. You couldn't do everything, and she had decided early on not to make the kitchen her home. Except when it came to mixing strange ingredients in a cauldron, that is.

'There now,' Nelly said, nodding at her with approval, 'you look homely with a wooden spoon in your hand.'

'Some might call that a backhanded compliment.'

Nelly wrinkled up her nose, baffled.

'I thought you were calling me a stirrer.' Jennifer laughed when Nelly rolled her eyes. 'To be honest, the last time I spent this long in a kitchen was two years ago, trying out recipes for a spell book I was writing.'

This admission was a little daring, for she and Nelly had not actually discussed anything occult since she'd moved in at the park. But she knew from Alex that his grandmother was no stranger to homely Cornish spell-working, at least.

But Nelly did not look offended. Instead she smiled. 'Recipes for a spell book? That sounds like it might be worth reading.'

'I've got a copy with me upstairs. Would you like it?'

Nelly beamed. 'That's very kind.'

'To be honest, I'd be more comfortable with a spell potion right now. This is all new . . .' Jennifer peered dubiously into the bain-marie. The chocolate had almost melted now. 'What exactly are we making?'

'Chocolate slices, and a coffee and walnut cake.'

'Mmm.' Jennifer grinned round at her. 'Much tastier than eye of newt.'

'Alex is a chocoholic.'

Jennifer could hardly believe it. 'He looks like such a health freak.'

'That's what his agent wants people to think. You know, his *movie fans*.' Nelly sat down and hummed to herself while she stirred the mixture. There was a smudge of flour on the tip of her nose, but she was smiling, blissfully unaware of it. She obviously loved talking about her talented grandson.

'But Alex has always loved chocolate. Ever since he was a little boy and he used to beg me to bake him chocolate cookies whenever he visited.'

'But he was a child then. Kids always have a sweet tooth.'

'People don't change, Jenny. Don't let anyone tell you different. What someone's like as a child, that's what they're like when they're older.' Nelly laughed. 'Take me, for instance. I was a proper tearaway as a child. Always in the wrong place at the wrong time, doing what I wasn't supposed to. But I wouldn't be told what was good for me. And that's not changed.'

Stirring the chocolate as it slowly transformed into a sleek pool of sweet-smelling liquid, Jennifer thought back over what Alex had told her. Perhaps this would be a good moment to talk to Nelly about her health. Certainly she was unlikely to get a better chance. But she felt awkward discussing something so personal with the older woman. Especially when she dared not risk blowing her cover.

She took a deep breath, trying to dissolve the nervous knot in her chest. 'Nelly, Alex mentioned that you ... That is, he said you hadn't been well recently.'

She paused, aware that Nelly's cheerful humming had stopped. Her stomach churned and she felt suddenly panicked. Had she gone too far? This was Nelly's private business, after all.

'Please don't think I'm interfering. It's nothing to do with me, of course.' Her voice sounded breathless to her own ears. 'But if you ever want to discuss it—'

'You're right,' Nelly said, a snap in her voice. 'It's nothing to do with you. Or with Alex, either. And I don't want to discuss my health. Not now, not ever.' She paused, without looking round. 'Do you hear?'

'Yes, absolutely.'

The door into the kitchen swung open and Alex came in backwards, holding a parcel in both bandaged hands. 'This just came for you, Nana,' he said cheerfully, and turned to find his grandmother glaring at him from her seat, tea towel slung over her shoulder, a terse look on her flour-streaked face. 'Erm, something wrong?'

'Yes, *you*,' Nelly said shortly. 'You're what's wrong.'

Alex's eyebrows shot up at her tone. He glanced from Nelly to Jennifer in alarm, then placed the brown cardboard parcel next to the kettle.

Carefully, he studied the table cluttered with baking equipment and then said, 'Did I forget to tell Françoise to buy eggs again?'

'*You*,' Nelly said, struggling to her feet and dragging the tea towel from her shoulder, 'have been telling people about my private business. *You*,' she continued, punctuating every other word with a flick of her floury tea towel, aimed at his chest, 'don't have the right to do that. I'll thank you not to go round telling all and sundry about my worries.'

'Sorry,' he said hurriedly, jerking back, out of range of her lethal tea towel. 'My bad.'

Nelly fumbled with the tea towel, dropping it on the floor and made a loud, exasperated huffing noise. Watching in consternation, Jennifer wondered whether she should retrieve the tea towel so the old lady could carry on attacking her grandson with it. But then Nelly returned to the table and grabbed the mixing bowl instead. Full of cake mix.

'Oh, no,' Alex said, taking another few steps backwards and coming up against the kitchen door. 'No, no, no.'

'You can't go round talking about other people behind their backs.' She flicked the wooden spoon at him, sending a lump of cake mix flying through the air to land on his chin with a distinct splat. Alex dabbed at his chin with a look of disbelief, but she had not finished. The spoon rose again. This time a large splodge of cake mix bounced off his chest, leaving a buttery stain on his expensive-looking white t-shirt, and dropped to the kitchen floor. 'Just because you're a big star, it doesn't mean you can do whatever you like and get away with it.' She was breathless now. 'You're not too old to be sent to your room, young man!'

Still cradling the mixing bowl against her chest, Nelly sank down and would have hit the floor if Alex hadn't darted forward to save her.

'Let me go!' Nelly moaned. 'You . . . traitor.'

But Alex ignored her command, hugging his grandmother, his bandaged hands reaching round her easily. Nelly seemed to have given up fighting and was breathing erratically, her thin body heaving in his arms.

Gingerly, he removed the mixing bowl from her failing grasp and passed it to Jennifer over Nelly's head. 'I didn't mean to make you so upset,' he said, eerily echoing Jennifer's own words earlier. 'You know how much I care about you. You're my nan, and you're not well. I only wanted to help.'

Nelly said nothing, but stamped on his foot. And not gently.

He winced and sought Jennifer's eyes over Nelly's bowed head. 'I got it wrong. Sorry. We won't mention it again.'

Jennifer suddenly felt horribly in the way. This was a

family matter, and it was time for her to leave. Not to hang around, looking awkward.

'I should go,' she mumbled, and began heading for the door.

'Bam marry, bam marry!' Nelly repeated croakily, her face pressed into Alex's chest. The stifled words were clearly an imperative, and not to be ignored. But what kind of order was this? 'Bam marry!'

Alex locked a startled gaze with Jennifer, who halted and bit her lip.

Bam marry!

Jennifer didn't know what to think. The words sounded vaguely Cornish. Surely the old lady wasn't trying to suggest that they should . . .?

He drew back slightly to look down at the bowed, white-haired head leaning on his chest. 'Sorry, Nana, I didn't quite catch that.' His voice was husky and suspicious. 'Did you say you want me to . . . to get married?'

Extricating herself from his buttery t-shirt, Nelly shook her head violently. Then puffed out, '*Bain-marie!*' in a cross tone. She pointed back at the stove, where a pan of water was still bubbling merrily away, the steel bain-marie nestled inside it, coated with liquid chocolate. 'That blasted chocolate will evaporate if you leave it on the heat any longer.'

Jennifer lurched back to rescue the hot pan, her heart thrumming with relief. At least, she thought it was relief. It was hard to tell when she felt so light-headed. 'Got it,' she said, lifting it off the heat. The bubbling chocolate subsided at once. 'That was close.'

Judging by the expression on Alex Delgardo's face, he thought so too.

CHAPTER SEVENTEEN

On Friday morning, unable to bear her inner turmoil any longer, Jennifer rang her stepsister. Caroline worked in healthcare. She might know what to do about Nelly's situation. That episode in the kitchen had convinced her that the old lady was indeed hiding something serious about her health. Something her grandson ought to be made more fully aware of. After all, even if it was cancer, as Alex feared, there could still be medical help available, if only Nelly would accept it. Perhaps even a second opinion.

The drawback was that contacting her nosy stepsister would mean admitting where she was. And facing all those inevitable questions.

But what choice did she have?

The call went straight to her answering service. Caroline was obviously busy with a patient, or possibly en route somewhere.

Jennifer texted her instead.

Just a heads-up. I'm staying at Porro Park for a few days.

After a short delay, her stepsister's reply popped up on her screen.

OMG. WTF? Tell me everything, NOW.

Jennifer grimaced.

Bit busy. Got a spare ticket for tonight's folklore festival. Want to come? We can talk after.

She was half expecting a refusal. Or at least a struggle. Caroline was uninterested in folklore, and looked on magic with vague amusement, though she had never made fun of Jennifer's interests. Or not to her face, anyway.

But to her surprise, Caroline texted back an acceptance almost immediately.

You kidding? Of course I'll come. I want all the gossip!

Slightly disturbed by that reply, Jennifer picked up her research book on Cornish piskies and headed down to the sunny atrium.

She had agreed to meet Nelly in the living room for a spot of knitting practice this morning. Of course, she'd left her own needles and a current knitting project at Pixie Cottage, not imagining she would need them while at Porro Park. But Nelly had insisted they sit and knit together today, claiming she would lend her needles and wool. And it would be useful, because there were some tricky techniques Jennifer still needed to master, and although online tutorial videos were brilliant, they were never as good as a hands-on teacher in the same room.

Nelly was sitting upright in one of the large living room armchairs, already hard at work, her knitting needles flashing at incredible speed. 'A Christmas jumper for Alex,' she said with a smile, and held up the piece she was working on, thick red wool threaded with a jolly green mistletoe pattern. 'I know it's early, but ... Well, I like to get ahead of myself when I have any time spare for knitting.'

'It looks marvellous.'

'Here.' Nelly stopped and indicated the large knitting bag beside her armchair. 'Help yourself to whatever you like. You could make a nice little table square with that ball of blue wool. It's left over from a scarf I made for Thelma in the spring. Not that she ever wears it. Prefers all that posh designer clobber, I guess.' She hesitated. 'Or I could show you that cross-stitch loop technique you were asking about.'

'Oh, yes please.'

Jennifer hunted out a pair of size eight needles, her personal favourites, and cast on some of the blue wool. It was thinner than the chunky yarns she was used to working with, but fine for a practice piece. Nelly watched and advised as she purled the reverse side, soon getting the hang of it.

'Not so difficult at all, is it?' Nelly asked, going back to the half-finished jumper, barely seeming to glance at the pattern on her knee but knowing instinctively where to pick up the stitches again.

Jennifer laughed. 'Not now you've shown me, no.'

Ten minutes later, her phone buzzed and she stopped knitting, rooting it out from her pocket. It was Caroline again.

Will the big Delgardo be there?

Jennifer peered across at Nelly, but luckily she was intent on her knitting. She read the brief text several times with a leaden sensation in the pit of her stomach. Was that really all Caroline could think about? Whether some celebrity would be in the next row to her at a local event? It was nothing short of infuriating.

She stabbed crossly at the on-screen keyboard with one fingertip.

Doubt it.

Caroline must have had a busy morning. It was a good twenty minutes before her phone buzzed again with another message.

No worries, I'll still be there. What time?

Relieved, Jennifer texted her stepsister all the details, dragged her fingers through her unruly ponytail, then got back to work on her knitting.

'Everything all right?' Nelly asked, looking concerned.

'Oh yes, absolutely.'

'Let me see what you've done so far, then.' Nelly smiled, examining her knitting. 'Hmm, not bad. The tension's a little slack here, though.' As though to prove her point, she poked a hole through one of the looser stitches. 'Oh dear.'

Jennifer bit her lip. 'Always my problem. I can never seem to get the tension right.'

'Here, watch me.'

Nelly took the blue knitting onto her own lap and showed her a few tricks to keep the tension more even throughout, and then took up her jumper again. For a while, they knitted together in a companionable silence.

So engrossed was she, in fact, that Jennifer didn't realise anyone was watching them until the living room door opened wider and a voice said, 'Hello?'

Alex stood in the doorway, his large frame dominating the space, but with the unexpected addition of a tatty old rope looped several times about his wrist, its frayed end dangling to the floor. It gave him the sinister air of an executioner.

Nelly looked up, startled. 'Oh, Alex . . . What's the matter?'

'Nothing serious. I just need a hand with something.' He

played the rope between his hands. 'I thought maybe Jennifer could help me.'

For once, Nelly did not smile at her favourite grandchild, which surprised Jennifer. Was she still angry at Alex for trying to find out more about her illness?

'She's too busy knitting,' Nelly said stiffly. 'Can't Thelma help you with whatever it is? Or Françoise?'

'Françoise is defrosting the chest freezer. And Thelma has gone back to bed for the day. Says she's got something called . . . Braxton Hiccups. I'm not sure what that is.'

Nelly stared at him, bemused. 'Hiccups?'

'Braxton Hicks,' Jennifer corrected him, laughing. 'They're like practice contractions. Most women feel them in the third trimester, I think.'

'Right.' He made a face. 'Goats, magic, now pregnant women. I didn't know you were an expert on babies, too.'

'I'm not, but my stepsister is. She's a midwife.' Jennifer smiled. 'Babies are all she talks about,' she added, exaggerating a little.

'Understandably.' His eyes narrowed on her face. 'Wait, is she the blonde from the tapas bar? Caroline Enys?'

'That's her,' she said.

'I remember.' He paused, his expression thoughtful. 'Anyway, Thelma's got these Braxton Hicks things. And apparently this means she can't help. Or do anything much, except clutch her stomach and moan. Which is what she's doing right now.'

'Do you need me to call the doctor for her?' Jennifer put down her knitting, struggling to ignore a ludicrous twinge of pique. How come he remembered Caroline so clearly?

Had she made a big impression on him? 'Or my stepsister, perhaps?'

'Personally, I doubt it's that serious. If I know Thelma, she's just trying to get out of her chores. Like she did when we were kids.'

'Chores? I thought she was a guest?'

Like me, she thought.

'Guests do chores in this house. Or they do when they also happen to be my sister.'

Nelly harrumphed. 'But *Jennifer* isn't your sister.'

He grinned, his face lighting up with humour. 'That's for sure. Still, I'm going to bend a rule and enlist her help anyway.' He raised his eyebrows at Jennifer. 'If you can tear yourself away from your knitting for half an hour, that is.'

'Only if Nelly doesn't mind . . .' She suddenly noticed that his bandages were gone. Curiosity got the better of her, and she asked mischievously, 'Your hands better now, then?'

He smiled, but said nothing.

There were yellowing bruises on the backs of both hands, and angry red scars across several of his knuckles. What on earth had he done to himself? And how had it happened?

Ignoring her interested stare, he waggled the rope at her. 'Well?'

'I told you, it's up to Nelly.'

Nelly hesitated, looking from her face to his, then said with obvious reluctance, 'You go off with Alex if you like, dear. I'll be fine here.' She bent her head to her knitting once more. 'I'm sure you'll have more fun with the goats than with me.'

'I don't know about that.' But Jennifer got up, unable to

resist the temptation to spend time with Alex Delgardo. He might be arrogant and high-handed, but he was also intriguing to her. Something in those keen eyes of his ... 'I can spare him five minutes, I suppose. He is my landlord.'

Alex headed for the doors that opened onto the lawn, and she followed him. It was sunny outside, so bright she almost wished she'd brought her sunglasses. Though maybe that was just because she wanted something to shield herself from his piercing gaze. He did seem to be looking at her very closely today. It was a little unnerving.

He pointed towards their new goat enclosure, where she could see several goats dutifully grazing and a few others butting the wire fencing as though determined to knock it down.

'Baby escaped again. I thought maybe you could help me catch her. Given your skills as a goat-whisperer.'

She ignored his crooked eyebrow and headed over the lawn towards the goats, straightening her crumpled summer dress, vaguely aware of her heart beating faster.

Stupid, stupid heart.

He was a good-looking man and he was flirting with her. So what?

The truth was, they were complete opposites in every way, and sexual attraction was overrated. Even if it did make her feel more alive whenever he walked into the room.

'Where might she be?' she asked.

'They're quite sociable, goats. There's a chance she may be hanging about the enclosure to be near her friends. That's where we should look first, anyway.'

'How did she get past the fence?'

'She wasn't in the enclosure. Nelly decided she was getting depressed in there and needed some exercise. So we tied her to a stake in the apple orchard.' He showed her the rope again with its frayed end. 'Only she seems to have eaten through her rope.'

'I didn't know goats could get depressed.'

'I thought you knew everything about goats?' He didn't wait for her to answer, but continued smoothly, 'We've been keeping her under lock and key for the past few days. Just while the workmen are at Pixie Cottage, fixing your damp issue. Didn't want her wandering over there and ending up in a concrete mixer. But she hates being confined.'

'It sounds like Baby needs to be walked.'

'Like a dog?'

'Why not? Better than keeping her tied to a rope all day. Especially when she can gnaw through it that easily. She's obviously a free spirit.'

Alex nodded, but said nothing. They walked in silence together for a while, reaching the fenced enclosure and then walking all the way round it in search of the lost goat.

There was no sign of Baby.

'Maybe she's gone back to the orchard,' she said at last, staring across the sunlit lawns towards the dappled shade of the apple trees.

He did not respond.

Glancing at him sideways, she was astonished to see a faint sheen of tears in his eyes.

Jennifer stopped. 'Alex?'

He ran a hand across his damp eyes. 'Sorry.' His voice was gruff. 'Pay no attention.'

'Don't be ridiculous. What's wrong?'

Alex grimaced. 'Something bad happened this morning.'

'Go on.'

'It turns out Nelly has a hospital appointment next week. She tried to hide it from me. But they rang this morning to change the time, and Françoise patched the call through to my office by mistake.' He stopped and swallowed hard, looking away. 'I asked who it was, and the woman on the other end said she was calling from the oncology department.'

Jennifer's heart winced. 'I'm so sorry.'

'That more or less confirms it. My grandmother has cancer. I asked the woman on the phone to give me details of her condition. But of course she refused, and rang off shortly after.' He cleared his throat. 'When I told Nana what happened, she got really angry. She wouldn't believe it was an accident. She told me again to stop interfering.' He rubbed his face again. 'I shouldn't be inflicting this on you.'

'It's okay to be upset. You care about your nan. So you want to know how to help.' Jennifer stepped away, suddenly uncomfortable. 'I'm going to see my stepsister tonight. She may have some advice on how to tackle this.' She caught an odd look on his face. 'Do you mind if I mention Nelly's illness to her? Caroline's very discreet, she won't tell Nelly she knows.'

'I think that's an excellent idea. Thank you.'

Their eyes met, and held.

In the awkward silence that followed, she unlooped the rope dangling from his wrist. 'Come on,' she said lightly. 'Let's find this goat.'

They began to walk across the lawns towards the bright

orchard. 'You sure this isn't interfering with your preparation?' he said, still sounding gruff. 'You've got that big thing tonight. Your speech at the folklore festival, isn't it?'

She was surprised he had remembered. 'That's right.' She glanced at her phone, ignoring an abrupt flutter of nerves. 'It's early yet, though. I don't need to be there until six.'

'You want a lift into town? No point us both driving in.'

They crossed the lush green grass, a few feet apart, walking at the same easy pace. She had partially unwound the rope from her shoulder and was toying with its frayed end, which smelt mustily of goat. It was as though they were bound together with a rope of their own, she thought, an invisible tether from her heart to his . . .

Suddenly, his words filtered through to her and she stopped, confused. 'Sorry, did you say you're going into town too?'

He stopped, looking back at her. 'To the festival, yes.'

'I don't understand. You've got a ticket for the folklore festival?'

'Two tickets, actually. Nana bought them.' His smile looked strained. 'I'm surprised she didn't mention it. She's very keen to go tonight. To hear your speech.'

'Oh.'

Alex removed the rope from her grasp. 'You're shredding the end of it,' he said gently when she protested. His smile became winning. A million-dollar smile, she thought. 'So will you let me drive you into town tonight?'

'I suppose so,' she said reluctantly, 'if we're all going.'

His brows rose at her tone. 'Look, you can go on your own if you prefer. It was just a suggestion. I don't want to force you to spend time in my company if you'd rather not.' When Jennifer said nothing, staring at him uncertainly, that famous smile of his became fixed. 'Boy, you really don't like me, do you?'

'It's not that.'

'Forget it. You can make your own way there.' Alex swung off, striding fast, the rope trailing behind him like a tail. There was a tense note in his voice. 'And I'll find the goat on my own. You go back to your knitting.'

Bloody hell.

She hadn't meant to, but somehow she had managed to offend him. Yet again. Maybe if she went after him and explained that she was merely nervous about tonight's festival . . .

But her feet refused to move. Because that wasn't entirely true, was it?

It was being with him she was nervous about.

Not her speech.

CHAPTER EIGHTEEN

The town hall in Pethporro was packed by the time Jennifer arrived, slightly later than intended and out of breath, carrying a box of her own books for the festival bookstall. She'd never seen it so busy.

She left Caroline's ticket with Nancy, the smiling helper on the door, who'd given birth only last winter, so knew her stepsister well.

'Don't worry,' Nancy said with a nod, putting the ticket in her money belt, 'I'll see Caroline gets it when she arrives.' She looked Jennifer up and down. 'You look amazing. Very witchy.'

Was that supposed to be a compliment?

'Thanks.'

In passing, Jennifer glanced at the large poster advertising tonight's opening event, and cringed inwardly at the glossy photograph she'd sent to the festival organisers. It made her look dark and forbidding, more Wicked Witch of the West than an expert on folklore and Cornish Wicca. But she supposed it might attract holidaymakers in search of an entertaining evening. She only hoped the audience wouldn't boo her when she got up to speak . . .

She elbowed her way past the crowded queue at the ticket booth and into the main hall, wishing she hadn't chosen to wear high heels tonight. Especially not such new heels, barely worn before. They were already starting to pinch her toes.

But sandals had not seemed dressy enough, given the special occasion, and her floaty white and green dress – bought at the Celtic Centre only last month – really deserved to be teamed with heels. Georgette had called the dress 'elvish' in design, a tightly moulded sheath from chest to hips, where it flared out in soft, dreamy layers of chiffon to just above her knees. It was like wearing a dress made of clouds. The dark green five-inch heels complemented the dress perfectly. But they didn't facilitate fast movement, particularly when the wearer was also carrying a heavy box.

'Need any help, Jennifer?'

It was Pete from the Celtic Centre, Georgette's partner. Standing on the stage at the front of the hall, he watched her struggling with the box.

'I'm fine, thanks,' she said breathlessly, and slid the box of books onto the far end of the bookstall.

'Okay.' Pete went back to tapping the microphones in turn, checking the town hall's sound system. 'Testing, testing.'

Others had been there before her, she realised. Ducky Blethering had left copies of her famed *Cornish Folklore Through the Ages*, a doorstop of a book with which Jennifer was thoroughly familiar. And there was a handful of other books, including a shiny new pamphlet on trees and plants in folklore which caught her attention. Sam Trevisty had been busy, she thought, turning the pamphlet over to examine the back cover. This might be one she wanted to buy for her private collection, she decided.

'All set?' Pete had snuck up behind her, taking her by surprise. He gave her a bear hug, his jewelled beard tickling her forehead, then spoke into the handheld microphone he was still clutching. His deep voice echoed around the hall, emerging from several different speakers at once. 'Ready for your big talk tonight?'

'As ready as I'll ever be.'

'That's the spirit.' Pete gave her a wink before clicking off the handheld microphone. As she started to unpack her books, he played about with the headset he was wearing, angling the adjustable mic nearer his mouth. 'Testing, testing, one, two, three.'

The sound crackled through the speakers, and then died.

'That doesn't sound good,' she said.

'Testing, testing.' But this time the speakers made no sound at all. Shaking his head, Pete removed the offending headset. 'That one's not working. I wonder if there's a loose connection?'

'Good luck.'

'Ditto.' Pete headed back to his sound desk near the podium and began fiddling with the settings, his deep voice rumbling into the headset again. 'Come in, Control.'

A petite, smiling woman in a severe black skirt suit and white blouse appeared by the stall. There was an orange badge pinned to her lapel that said Festival Helper, along with a smiley face icon. 'Hello, Jennifer.' She slid behind the table and began rearranging the books, evidently having been put in charge of the stall. 'I haven't seen you in ages.'

It was Bailey, Penny Jago's partner. A solicitor at Knutson's in Pethporro, she was always immaculately turned out. The opposite of her girlfriend, in fact; Penny was tall, and as willowy as a model, yet rarely wore anything even remotely formal. Hippyish clothing was the norm among the Cornish folklore community, of course.

Bailey looked decidedly out of place at this event.

Jennifer blinked, uneasily aware that Bailey must know all about her staying over at Alex Delgardo's place. No doubt it was the talk of Pethporro by now.

'Oh, hello, Bailey.' Somehow she managed a smile, though she wasn't sure whether Bailey was friend or foe. She and Penny were close friends with Hannah, after all. 'I didn't expect to see you here. H-how are you?'

'Just dandy, thanks.'

She recalled what Caroline had said about Bailey undergoing IVF treatment and wondered if it had been successful. The younger woman was certainly glowing, her wide eyes sparkling. Perhaps with that special euphoria reserved for women expecting a child.

'I saw Penny the other night. At the Cornish language class.'

'She told me.' *Of course she did*, Jennifer thought, but kept smiling. 'Penny will be here soon.' Bailey rifled through her float tin, head down, checking the amount of cash she'd brought. 'She's coming with some of our friends.'

Jennifer stiffened.

She's coming with some of our friends.

What did that mean?

'Caroline will be here tonight, too,' she said defensively.

The two women knew each other because of Bailey's IVF treatment. 'Though she seems to be late. I left a ticket for her on the door.'

Bailey said nothing, still counting under her breath.

More people were filtering through now from the ticket queue into the hall, looking for seats. The first few rows had been reserved for local VIPs and performers at the opening ceremony, including a local primary school whose choir would be singing Cornish folk tunes. For the first time Jennifer noticed a second poster for the event, set on an easel at the back of the hall, featuring an even larger, blown-up photograph of her and the other key speakers. The audience members had to shuffle past this poster as they filed into the hall, and she saw them pointing at the photograph and muttering.

'They got a witch on tonight. Wonder if she brought her broomstick?' one of the men said, his words echoing clearly across the hall. He was red-faced, wearing a flat cap and green wellies, despite the heat. His amply built female companion nodded in Jennifer's direction, saying in a thick Cornish accent, 'Aye, and there she is, over by them books. Don't look much like a witch, do she?'

Bailey stifled an obvious snort of laughter, closing the float tin. 'I see the farming community has arrived. This should be fun.'

Pete must have heard the remarks too, because he turned and grinned at her, putting his thumbs up. He bent back to his work.

Oh for goodness' sake . . .

Her novelty value did not last, thankfully. By the time

Jennifer had finished setting out her books for sale on the stall, with a list of prices and an honesty tub for cash, she was no longer the strangest person in the hall.

A group of druids came in together, men and women in long, flowing white robes, some green-trimmed, their two leaders bearing staffs decorated with twined strands of ivy and honeysuckle, rather like the wizard staffs Pete sold at the Celtic Centre. They caused a stir among the more staid audience members, who turned in their seats to stare at the odd sight. One of the older druids, a white-haired woman known as Guinevere – though her real name was Janet – waved at Jennifer in a friendly fashion and mouthed, 'Good luck!'

Jennifer waved back, and then gathered her handbag and speech together. There was no point putting it off any longer. The other key speakers were already at the front, talking to Pete, and the hall was almost full now.

'See you later,' she said to Bailey, who had been watching her surreptitiously ever since their conversation.

It seemed she was definitely an object of gossip in Pethporro, and not for all the usual reasons. Which made her deeply uncomfortable.

Reluctantly, Jennifer made her way up to the platform where the singing and speeches were to take place.

Ducky Blethering was already there, easily eighty years old but looking as spry as always, her grey hair swept up in an imposing bun. 'How are you?' she asked, gripping Jennifer's hand with alarming strength. 'I heard about that business over the Boxing Day pageant. If you ask me, you were very poorly treated.'

'Thank you.'

'I was laid up with gout over Christmas, otherwise I would have come into town and given *that man* a piece of my mind.'

She meant Raphael Tregar, of course.

'I'm over it now,' Jennifer said quickly, not wanting to go there. 'It's all in the past.'

'He was no loss to you.' Ducky lowered her voice. 'I saw he married that *furriner* in the end.'

Foreigner?

Jennifer was bemused. 'Sorry?'

'That Hannah's a Clitheroe by name. But in every other respect, she's an NC.' Ducky winked at her. 'Non-Cornish, you know? Born and bred in London, that's what I heard. But,' she added grudgingly, 'I suppose Trudy *was* her maternal grandmother. And back in the day, you didn't get many people more Cornish than Trudy Clitheroe. She was all for Cornish devolution, you know.'

'Self-government?'

'Of course. It's the only way forward for Cornwall. We've got a London rally planned for this autumn. There'll be a march up Whitehall, and a picket line with Cornish flags flying. I'll be taking a tent and sleeping bag in case I need to spend the night in the big smoke.' Ducky peered at her eagerly. 'Could I persuade you to join us?'

Luckily, Jennifer was spared from having to answer that. A sudden stir in the hall made them both turn, hearing gasps and whispers.

'Our newest Pethporro celebrity has arrived, I see,' Ducky said.

Among the last few people taking their seats was Alex

Delgardo, accompanied by Nelly. To her surprise, Nelly was walking with the aid of a stick, leaning heavily on Alex's arm as he helped her to a reserved seat on the front row.

At first, she was surprised to see them sitting in the reserved section, near their local MP, the Mayor and his wife and Dr Ashley, the museum curator. But the festival organisers could hardly have seated a big movie star like Alex Delgardo at the back. It would have looked insulting, not to mention opening him up to possible harassment by members of the general public. Though even on the front row, several people had already approached Alex with their programmes open and a pen at the ready, asking for his autograph.

Neither of them had spotted Jennifer yet. Which was a relief, as she felt decidedly awkward up here, in full view of everyone in the hall.

Huffing and puffing, Bettina finally arrived on stage, her old mentor, who had come to present an update on the rejuvenation of the Cornish language. People had been saying she was unwell, and now Jennifer could see that had not been an exaggeration. Bettina was only in her seventies, yet had brought her own oxygen canister with her, supported on a small trolley complete with mask and tubes. One of the festival helpers arranged it next to her seat.

Her heart flooding with joy, Jennifer hugged Bettina tight. 'I'm so happy to see you,' she said.

'Me too,' Bettina agreed, extricating herself carefully. 'Though don't break my ribs, dearie.'

'Sorry.'

But she kept grinning, unable to hide her pleasure. Bettina

was one of her favourite people in Cornwall, and the woman who'd set her on a path that had led eventually to a career in folklore and magical craft.

The oxygen canister was a worry, though.

'This looks serious,' she said, frowning over the tangle of plastic tubes.

'Emphysema.' Bettina sighed. 'Don't worry, I can cope without it for short periods. But I need the canister with me, just in case I get an attack of breathlessness.'

'You poor thing.'

'All my own fault. You take my advice, dearie, and don't keep birds.' Bettina was famous for her passion for small birds, even having a huge aviary built on to her small cottage to accommodate all her little feathered friends. 'Them canaries, them budgies . . . Beautiful little darlings, but the dust in the air is lethal.'

'What does your doctor say?'

'You know doctors. Always gloomy.' Bettina fell into a coughing fit, and grimaced when it was finally over. 'He says my lungs are on their way out, and there's nothing to be done.'

'Oh, no!'

Ducky had been listening to this, her lips pursed. 'Birds, my backside,' she told Bettina sharply, arms folded across her chest. 'It was those fifty years smoking nefarious substances that did for your lungs.'

'Good God, Ducky. You still alive?' Bettina raised thin, pencil-drawn eyebrows at the older woman. 'You can talk, anyway. You must have smoked enough *herbal cigarettes* in your time to put a small elephant to sleep.'

'At least I'm not *built* like an elephant, small or otherwise.'

There was not much love lost between the two old folklore experts, Jennifer recalled, and backed away awkwardly, caught in the middle of their spat.

Bettina's eyes flashed. She looked Ducky up and down. 'Your hair looks more like a stork's nest every time I see it. Something laying eggs in there?'

Not deigning to reply, Ducky merely contented herself with jerking her assigned chair – the middle one – out of the row, then dragging it past Bettina's seat and closer to the podium. It made a squeaking sound as the legs scraped across the wooden boards, nearly knocking over the oxygen canister as it passed.

Jennifer stared, bemused.

'Ducky, what on earth do you think you're doing, woman?' Bettina demanded, also watching this operation in disbelief.

'I'm speaking first, so I should be next to the podium. Not you.'

'You ... you put that chair back in its place.' Bettina began to cough exaggeratedly. 'You're ruining everything. Stop it, you old crone.'

'Make me, witch.'

'Oh!'

Bettina grabbed her oxygen mask and sucked on it violently, glaring at Ducky over the plastic rim.

'Erm, Bettina, are you okay?' Jennifer asked, wondering if she needed to go and find out if the organisers had a doctor standing by. 'Perhaps you should sit down. Here, let me help you.'

But Bettina merely waved her away impatiently. 'You stop

Duckface rearranging the furniture,' she managed to say, between snatched inhalations of oxygen, 'and I'll sit down.'

Catching the eye of the nearest festival helper, Jennifer beckoned the woman over. 'I think there's been a disagreement about who sits where,' she whispered in the helper's ear, and then decided to take that opportunity to slip away. 'I'll be right back. Just grabbing some water. Dry throat, you know. I expect we could all do with a glass.'

Behind her, Bettina gave off a furious shriek that would not have sounded out of place in her own aviary.

The two women might be sniping at each other, but they'd been rivals for ever, almost like warring sisters, and had more in common than most people might have realised, listening to them now. In fact, their sharp enmity reminded her of Alex and Thelma, the sparring she'd witnessed between brother and sister that came naturally in some families.

Probably best just to leave them to it, she decided.

The hall was almost full now. The wall clock told her it was almost half past six, the time when the festival was supposed to kick off. And she could see the Mayor approaching to make his opening remarks, shaking hands with people on his way to the stage.

At last, Caroline was there, making her way down the central aisle towards the front. There was a seat free on one row, and she ducked into it, looking stressed. She was clad in black leggings with a navy-blue top, hardly her usual elegant standards of dress. Come straight from a home visit, no doubt.

Properly nervous now, Jennifer felt a cold sweat break out

on her palms, despite the mounting heat. There was a table set to one side with a tray of glasses on it and two large jugs of iced water, condensation dripping down the glass. Picking up a jug, she sucked in a few deep breaths herself, and mentally recited a mantra for mindfulness while pouring three glasses of water in a row, one for each of them.

The mantra was just beginning to take effect, calming her nerves, when she became aware of someone striding purposefully down the hall, heading straight for the stage.

She looked up, surprised. Her hand shook, nearly dropping the jug.

It was Raphael Tregar.

CHAPTER NINETEEN

'Oh . . . crap.'

She had just poured water all over the table instead of into the last glass. The audience in the front row, near enough to hear the muttered expletive, gasped and stared. She reddened, dabbing ineffectually at the spillage with a napkin and hurriedly planning her retreat. Before she could escape, Raphael had climbed the short flight of steps onto the stage and stopped right in front of her.

'Hello, Jennifer.' The familiar voice was arresting, tugging at her senses. Everything she had ever felt for this man came rushing back at the sound, a flood of painful memories tangled up in hopeless, unrequited love. It made her heart hurt. 'Looks like you've had a bit of an accident there.' Raphael paused when she did not respond. He sounded almost sorry for her, which was awful. 'Need a hand?'

'I . . . No, it's . . .'

She couldn't look up at him. Couldn't even complete a sentence. The water was dripping off the edge of the table now, creating a tiny pool on the stage. A slip hazard. They would need a mop soon. Maybe a warning sign. One of those neon-yellow A-frames depicting a red crossed circle and a startled-looking man slipping on a wet patch. Her napkin was sodden, unable to contain any more water.

This was ridiculous.

'I've got this, it's fine.' She stopped dabbing and handed the soggy napkin to a festival helper, who had arrived with a bin and some more wipes. 'Thank you.'

Then she forced herself to raise her head and meet his ironic gaze.

Raphael Tregar.

'Hello.' It was a shock that she managed to sound almost calm. To anyone else listening, that word would have sounded perfectly ordinary. Not a quiver to be heard. But she knew he would have heard a thousand shades of uncertainty, longing and frustration behind it. 'Good to see you again.'

Raphael looked as dark and forbidding as ever, but with a gleam of amusement in his eyes. Not sorry for her at all, she realised. More as though he knew exactly how hard this encounter was for her. And didn't care.

But of course he didn't care.

This man had no reason to feel anything for her, except possibly disdain for what they had shared in the past. He was recently married. A new father, too, even if the child was not biologically his own. She remembered that grainy photograph in the local newspaper, the one that had left her eyes red and swollen from weeping for hours after spotting it. Raphael had seemed so happy outside St Juliot's Church, his smiling bride on his arm. He had looked complete. Like there was no room in his heart that wasn't filled by Hannah and her baby. How could it be otherwise?

Jennifer began to fumble the three glasses of water onto

a tray, meaning to carry them back to the other two speakers. Her hands were trembling, spilling yet more water on the now slick table. Pure nerves about the speech, she told herself. But she knew it to be a lie.

To her consternation, Raphael had not moved, and was watching her closely. It was like being under a microscope. 'Are you sure I can't help you with that?'

She hesitated, then said, 'Yes, thank you,' and let him take the tray from her hands. Their fingers touched, just the tips of his warm against her knuckles. Her breath whooshed out, and she felt hot and unsteady. Like it was happening all over again. The dark, mysterious spell of his presence casting its pall over her . . .

'W-where's Hannah?'

She tried to say the name so lightly, and yet it felt like a piece of lead on her tongue, weighing it down, making her voice thick and clumsy.

'Back home with the baby.' He straightened with the tray, seeming oblivious to the way her gaze followed him hungrily. 'Where to?'

Jennifer gestured to the row of chairs near the podium. Somehow, Ducky had been persuaded to return her chair to where it belonged and was seated next to Bettina, the two women deep in conversation. The Mayor was at the podium with Pete, being shown how to use the microphone headset.

He was not hers any more, if he ever had been.

He belonged to Hannah.

With a terrible sense of despair, she followed Raphael back to the others and watched as he offered water to Ducky and Bettina, who both refused, not bothering to hide their disapproval. Her fault, of course. Word had got around the Cornish folklore and witching community that he had clashed with Jennifer last year over the running of the Boxing Day pageant, making it impossible for her to stay on as pageant organiser. Then he had married the next woman in the job, Hannah Clitheroe.

She took her glass of water and sat down to study her typed-up speech, pretending not to know he was still there, watching her. But the words on the page were incomprehensible, a blur of letters and punctuation making no sense at all.

'I wanted to say,' Raphael began haltingly, 'how sorry I was to hear you'd been forced to leave Boscastle. That shouldn't have happened.'

He was referring to her previous landlady, who had served her with an eviction notice on discovering she was a witch. Even though Jennifer was more a theoretical witch than practising. But that distinction had been lost on the woman.

She stared blindly at the top sheet, belatedly realising it was upside-down and turning it the right way up. No wonder the words had seemed unreadable.

'You haven't had much luck recently, have you?' Raphael was saying, his voice nagging at her nerves.

Ducky tutted under her breath.

With a loud sniff, Bettina shook her head and sketched a common witching symbol against bad luck with her left hand. *Driving out the devil*, it was commonly called. Which was about right, Jennifer thought, wishing she had the nerve to make the sign herself. But she knew he had always distrusted that aspect of her nature. The intuitive side.

Ignoring the other two women, Raphael said softly, 'You probably wish I was somewhere else right now.'

She glared at him over the top sheet.

His mouth twitched in a wry grimace. 'Things haven't gone your way recently. But Hannah's plate is looking to be pretty full this Christmas. She's decided to take a year off work to spend time at home with baby Santos. So the position of pageant organiser is vacant again.'

Jennifer blinked.

'We'll be advertising the position,' he continued hurriedly, 'probably next month. But your experience and local knowledge would make you a strong candidate if you'd like to apply for the post.'

Her grip on the typed sheets of her talk loosened, and they fluttered to the floor, scattering everywhere. Raphael crouched at once to retrieve them for her, apologising as he had to reach through Ducky's legs for an errant sheet, much to the old lady's pretend shock.

'I hope you'll consider it, at least.' He handed her the speech, their eyes meeting as he added, 'I was sorry that things went wrong between us last time. Nobody's fault. That just happens sometimes. But it would be good to work with you again.'

She didn't know what to say.

Her body was suffering agonies, her brain in free fall. She had all but forgotten where she was and how many people in the audience must be watching this little exchange with curiosity. Her heart would not stop thumping like a wild animal enclosed in the cage of her ribs. Her mouth was dry, her breathing ragged. She didn't dare reach for a sip of water, though; her hands were trembling again and she would probably drop the glass, spilling it everywhere, like a fool.

'I thought I'd mention it anyway.' Raphael Tregar straightened with a nod and went to shake hands with the Mayor, a personal friend of his. 'Good luck,' he said heartily, and made his way off the stage.

It would be good to work with you again.

The Mayor began his opening remarks. The audience applauded. The druid contingent cheered and laughed at some carefully targeted joke. She stared wildly towards the back of the hall. Her sheets were in disarray, the pages out of sequence. She struggled to recall the order of the speakers. It was him, then Ducky, then Bettina, and she was due to finish up with her own talk.

The Mayor was going through the list of speakers. He indicated her. 'And lastly, we'll be hearing from a key local expert on Cornish folklore, Jennifer Bolitho, who has some intriguing facts for us, especially on the vexed question of Cornish piskies. Do they exist, or not? Though I think we all know the answer to that one, given what pests they can be.'

Everybody laughed.

She smiled automatically. But her mind was a blank as she bent her head, pretending to study the sheet in her hand. Cornish piskies, elves, black dogs, ghosts and ghouls. She knew nothing about any of them. All she could focus on was Raphael's ruggedly handsome face, the timbre of his voice tugging at her heart and the way their eyes had met just now, an explosion going off inside her body . . .

It would be good to work with you again.

He had changed since the last time they'd met, she thought. Then, he had been cold, almost an enemy. Now he was smiling, looking at her with friendship in his eyes.

Was he unhappy with Hannah already?

Impossible.

Raphael Tregar was head over heels in love with his wife. Her first glance at the picture of the newly-wedded pair outside St Juliot's Church had told her as much. That photograph in the newspaper had withered any last vestiges of hope inside her, leaving her in a dark, lonely place. So why on earth had he asked her to work with him again, to apply for the ill-fated post of Pethporro pageant organiser for a second time?

Had Hannah put him up to it?

Did the happy couple pity her, living on next to nothing in a damp, poky little cottage in the middle of nowhere, and now even having to rely on Alex Delgardo's hospitality while her place was fixed up?

What an appalling idea.

She could not seem to breathe properly, her lungs closing too soon, snatching at the air. Jennifer glanced longingly towards the oxygen canister at Bettina's knee, but could not focus on it. She rolled the speech up into a kind of paper cylinder and squeezed hard, tapping her knee with it. Her fingertips felt stiff and had begun to tingle. Even her chest hurt now, a dull, crushing ache spreading out like she was having a heart attack. Except she was far too young to be suffering a cardiac arrest . . .

What was wrong with her?

'Back in a . . . a minute,' she managed to whisper to Ducky, next to her, and got up, keeping low as she slipped away from centre stage as surreptitiously as possible.

There was a heavy red curtain covering the stage wings. Behind it was a door that led to the changing rooms. Jennifer knew the way, having given talks here before several times. Fumbling her way through the curtain folds, she got through the door and silently trod down a few wooden steps into the backstage area. There, she shut herself into the ladies' changing rooms. She groped for the light switch, dropping her speech on the floor, and then bent over, struggling to breathe. The room had no air con and was stiflingly hot. She could feel sweat forming on her forehead. It trickled down her back under the clinging chiffon dress.

Her lungs were in spasm. The air burnt her throat.

She stared down at her fingers. They were rigid now, unyielding, like pieces of wood on the ends of her hands. And were tinged slightly blue right at the tips.

Her ears started to buzz. Good grief, was she going to faint?

It didn't matter if she fainted. She was alone, so alone. Nobody would know, not even if she collapsed and died here, and nobody would care. To them, she was the Wicked Witch of the West . . .

Suddenly, she was being helped to sit on a chair in front of the brightly lit mirrors, a supportive arm about her waist. 'Relax, keep breathing, in and out. No, don't fight for air. Just let it happen.' Male hands cupped her face, enclosing her mouth like a warm mask. 'Take small breaths against my palm, don't try to breathe too deep.'

Jennifer sucked in a tiny amount of air, her chest heaving as she fought against the desire to gasp.

'Yes, that's the way. Now hold each breath for a few seconds, then exhale slowly.' His voice was soft in her ear. 'It's okay, Jenny. You're perfectly safe.'

Don't call me Jenny, she thought fiercely, eyes closed against the bright lights of the changing room mirrors.

She didn't know how long they stayed like that. Probably only a few minutes, but it could have been hours. Her heart, thumping erratically before, began to slow. She could breathe evenly again, her chest relaxing.

Finally, her mind focused on who he was, her unexpected helper. It certainly wasn't the man she'd hoped for: her ex-lover, the married man. Someone else's property now.

It was someone infinitely more dangerous.

Alex Delgardo.

'Better now?' he asked.

It was unlikely she would ever feel quite this mortified again. Slowly, she opened her eyes and looked at him over his cupped hands. 'Yes,' she said, hoping she didn't look as bad as she felt, though her hair was in her eyes and her mascara must be ruined. 'I'm sorry. I ... I don't know what happened.'

'You had a panic attack.'

'A ... a what?'

'It's called a panic attack. You can't breathe. You get light-headed. Your chest hurts. Your lips turn blue and your fingers—'

'Go stiff.'

'That's down to the lack of oxygen in your system. The body starts shutting down. The extremities are the first parts to suffer.' He drew back, lowering his hands, and watched her take a few tentative breaths on her own. 'The best way to counteract an attack is to keep a paper bag handy.'

'A paper bag?'

'For breathing into. It helps you regain control.' He sat back, releasing her. 'Unfortunately, I didn't have one with me tonight. That's why I cupped my hands round your mouth. Not as effective. But it worked.'

'Right.' She locked her gaze with his. His dark eyes were flecked with amber again, glinting in the light. Mesmerising. 'Thank you.'

'No problem.'

'You seem to know a lot about panic attacks.'

There was a long silence.

'That's because I get them too.' His voice was husky. 'Occasionally.'

She was shocked. 'Stage fright?'

'No.'

That surprised and confused her. She recalled how he had turned up swathed in bandages. Was he talking about that?

'Something else scares you, then?'

He said nothing for a moment, but held her gaze. Then said carefully, 'We should get you back out there. Your speech.'

'I can't give a speech now. Not after that.'

'Of course you can.'

She shook her head wildly, beginning to breathe too fast again. His smile was dry but sympathetic as he bent and retrieved her speech from the floor, pressing it back into her hands.

'The show must go on. Besides, you've been working on

that damn thing for weeks, haven't you?' When she stared, he nodded. 'So get out there and sock it to them.'

'They'll have seen me leave the stage. All of them. You saw, you came after me . . .' She gasped, realisation hitting her suddenly. 'Oh God, what must he be thinking?'

'Who?'

'I . . . It doesn't matter.'

She didn't want to tell him about Raphael. It was too humiliating.

'Up you get.'

His voice was curt now. He pulled her to a standing position. His warm hands straightened her dress, her hair, then brushed her cheek.

She looked at his mouth. But she did not dare move any closer. How could she? He was even more untouchable than Raphael Tregar. A man like Alex Delgardo could have any woman he wanted. She would be nothing but a temporary distraction from the stresses of his profession. And then he'd be gone, leaving her emptier and more alone than ever before. He would burn her up like a raging forest fire, like gasoline poured on dry brushwood and set alight . . .

'Go do your thing, witch woman.'

CHAPTER TWENTY

After the post-festival drinks, driving back in the warm dark, Jennifer found herself unable to account for what had happened backstage. It had felt like a dream moment, something unreal. But she knew it had happened, because Caroline had asked her later what on earth went on during her absence from the stage. An absence of less than ten minutes, apparently, though it had seemed endless at the time. She had not known how to answer her, and was still unsure herself.

Unfortunately, Caroline was not one to let things of that nature drop. Especially where men were concerned.

'You sure this is okay, me coming back with you to the big movie star's house?'

Beside her, Caroline turned the car stereo on, frowning when nothing happened. Her stepsister had helped herself liberally to the free booze on offer after the festival opener, and now sounded a bit tipsy. Jennifer was stone-cold sober, of course, as the designated driver, but she didn't mind that. It was better to keep her wits about her, having agreed to take Caroline back to the house.

'Stop calling him that.'

'Why? He's a big movie star and it's his house. Anyway, Alex Delgardo may not welcome a pleb like me turning up on his doorstep.'

'I told you, he's worried about Nelly. He thinks she may have cancer. I said you might be able to persuade her to open up.'

'I'm not forcing Nelly to do anything she doesn't want to do. That wouldn't be ethical.' Caroline was fiddling with the car stereo, head bent. 'Why won't your CD player work?'

'Broken.'

'Have you ever considered getting it fixed? Okay, radio it is.' She found a funky 1970s tune on the radio, and cranked up the volume until the Citroën was a mobile disco speeding through the darkness. 'Love these old hits.'

Jennifer tapped her fingers on the wheel to the insistent beat. She kept thinking of Raphael's bizarre invitation to reapply for the post of pageant director. His dark face swam before her eyes. What had his motivation been? He was married now, and happily. Why couldn't he see it was best for them to stay as far away from each other as possible?

'So, what happened backstage?' Caroline asked again, not letting it go.

Jennifer had been right. She had not given up.

'Nothing,' she said evasively.

'You said you felt ill.'

'I did.'

'You looked like you were going to be sick.' Caroline stifled a laugh and reached up, releasing her tidy chignon. 'Everyone stared when you got up and left the stage. It was hilarious. Bettina even tried to follow you, but she got tangled up in those tubes.'

'Oh, God.'

'Why did she have an oxygen canister with her tonight, anyway?'

'Emphysema.'

'All those birds, I guess.'

'So she claimed. Though Ducky accused her of being a weed addict.'

'Good old Ducky. Her talk was brilliant. And Bettina does have that bloody big greenhouse out the back. Oh God, my feet and ankles . . . I had such a long day at work.' Caroline slipped off her sturdy work shoes. With a sigh, she sat back and propped her bare feet up on the dashboard, cooling them in the rush of night air through the window. 'Come on, spill the beans. What's going on between you two?'

'Sorry?'

For a moment, she thought Caroline was talking about Raphael Tregar, and she cringed inwardly. But apparently *he* wasn't on her mind at all.

'You and the big Delgardo. You staggered off behind the curtain, clutching your chest and looking like a ghost. I thought Raphael might go after you. He half got up . . .'

'What?'

'Only Alex Delgardo jumped onto the stage and strode through the curtain without a second's hesitation, like he'd been sent back there to defuse a bomb.'

Which wasn't too far from the truth, Jennifer thought.

'So Raphael sat down again,' Caroline added.

Jennifer grimaced.

'Stop pretending nothing happened, Jenny. I can read you like a book, remember.' Her stepsister studied her profile curiously. 'What was he saying to you before the Mayor kicked off the event?'

'Delgardo?'

'Raphael Tregar.'

Jennifer took a corner rather too fast and had to slam the brakes on before they ended up in the ditch. These narrow Cornish lanes had to be respected, especially at night. She looked up at the velvety black sky, the sharp pinpoint of stars stretching ahead of them in the darkness. There was Venus, too, a brilliant glitter rising opposite the moon. The planet of love, beautiful and not to be trusted.

Briefly, her voice as flat and unemotional as she could make it, she outlined what Raphael had told her about the Pethporro pageant directorship.

Caroline swore. 'You're kidding me.'

'All true.'

'He's got a nerve, that man.'

'I have the feeling his wife put him up to it.'

Caroline swore again.

'No, I imagine she meant well.' Jennifer realised she was gripping the steering wheel like it was Hannah Tregar's throat. 'A peace offering of sorts.'

Her stepsister peered at her, and Jennifer was glad night had fallen across the Cornish coastline and her expression couldn't be seen clearly. 'I have to say, Jenny, you're taking this very calmly.' There was a speculative note in her voice. 'Almost too calmly.'

'I don't know what you mean.'

'Raphael spoke to you for three minutes and you went to pieces.'

'Don't exaggerate.'

'Yet Alex Delgardo got you back on stage in double-quick time. How did he manage that, exactly?'

Jennifer thought about the way he'd calmed her down, his gentle hands cupped about her mouth, his expertise . . . *A panic attack*, he'd called it. The memory nagged at her, and she had to admit to being bewildered. Then she remembered that Alex had said he suffered from them, and not due to stage fright.

But that made zero sense.

What could scare a big celebrity like Alex Delgardo enough to push him into a full-blown panic attack?

'Jenny?'

She slowed for the turn to Porro Park and was surprised to find the tall iron gates open. Usually, the gated entrance was operated by a key code, with an intercom for guests or deliveries. Tonight it had been left open. But of course – she had asked Alex before he left the festival event if she could bring Caroline back to his house, and why. No doubt Alex was as keen as she was to get Nelly seen by a healthcare professional.

'We're nearly there,' she said thankfully, turning down the long gravelled drive. Her whole body was quivering, both from the mental exhaustion of giving her speech and from the emotional roller coaster she'd ridden with two very different men that night. But she couldn't relax yet. She would have to drive Caroline home after she had spoken to Nelly. Bed seemed a long way off. 'Let's leave the interrogation for another day, yeah? It's Nelly who needs you tonight. Not me.'

Caroline sighed and dragged her bare feet down from the dashboard. 'So are you going to apply for the Pethporro pageant job?'

'No. Maybe.' She felt the flutter of fear in her chest again, and despised herself for it. 'I don't know. Ask me another time.'

'Oh my God, is that the house?' Caroline was leaning out of the window to see the vast glass and metal structure ahead, lit up in the darkness. 'It's incredible. You never said it was so modern. Delgardo's own design?'

'I believe he oversaw the renovations, yes.'

'The man's a genius.' Caroline closed her window, then turned on the internal light. She pulled down the visor to reveal the mirror and hurriedly tidied her ash-blonde hair, mussed by the wind, with her fingers. Her frown was uncertain. 'Should I put more lipstick on, do you think?'

'It's not a date, Caro.'

'I'm going to Alex Delgardo's house. Alex *Delgardo*!' Caroline pulled a striking pink lipstick out of her bag, applied it with a few expert strokes, then threw it back into her bag.

Alex must have been waiting in the hall for them, because as soon as Jennifer had parked in her usual spot, the front door opened and there he was, a dark outline against the brightly lit interior.

An outside light came on to illuminate the gravel drive. Caroline slipped her shoes back on, then drew her breath in sharply and fumbled for the door. 'It's now or never.'

'Stop stressing.'

'It's all right for you, dressed up like Galadriel,' Caroline muttered under her breath. 'I wish I'd worn a dress. Something knockout, like yours. Not these old leggings and dreadful clogs. But I came straight from work.'

'You look amazing,' Jennifer reassured her, sotto voce. They walked towards Alex Delgardo together, arm in arm, both taking their time over the uneven gravel, though her heels were killing her and she could not wait to kick them off. 'As always,' she added, with a touch of asperity. Caroline had been the man-magnet when they were teens, and Jennifer had struggled to keep up, in the end not bothering.

Suddenly, Jennifer was struck from behind by something hard and knobbly, and ended up pitching onto her face on the gravel drive.

As she toppled forward in the dark, Caroline let out a shriek beside her, twisting round. 'What the hell was that?' The pitch of her voice rose even higher. 'Oh, good grief, there's some kind of thing . . .'

'It's a goat,' Jennifer said, face down.

'A *what*?'

'A goat.' She raised her head, blinking, and checked gingerly to see if her dress had torn. 'I told you, they keep goats.'

'Oh God, I remember. Seven goats.' Caroline peered about herself cautiously. 'So there might be more of them out there . . . Argh, what's that?'

Caroline abruptly sped past her, pursued by Toby, the goat with the big ears, his insistent bleat low and terrifying. Her stepsister plunged up the steps and slammed into Alex's waiting arms.

'Welcome,' he said deeply, righting her.

CHAPTER TWENTY-ONE

Jennifer, still on her knees in the gravel where Toby had knocked into her, stared up at them both with sudden, burning resentment.

'Thank you,' Caroline said breathlessly, gazing at him and the house in wide-eyed awe. 'I mean, hello again, Mr Delgardo. Did I bang into you? I'm so sorry. That was very clumsy of me.' Her laugh was almost a girlish giggle, as though she had regressed from professional woman to schoolgirl in a matter of seconds. 'But there are goats out there, you know. Seven of them!'

Alex had a torch in his hand. When he shone it across the lawn, several four-legged shadows skipped past the bright beam and away into the darkness. No doubt the goats knew they had outstayed their welcome.

'Are you hurt?' he asked her, clicking off the beam.

'No, all good.' Caroline jerked a thumb over her shoulder without taking her eyes off the star's face. 'I think Jenny took a tumble, though. Sneaky little things, aren't they? The goats, I mean. They came right at us out of the dark. Nearly knocked me flying, too. But I can move fast when I need to.'

'So I noticed.' He was smiling, much to Jennifer's annoyance. She picked herself up and brushed gravel off her knees, apparently invisible now that Caroline was there. Which was so close to being the story of her life, she could have wept. 'Françoise was supposed to lock them in their enclosure before she left tonight. She must have forgotten.'

'Françoise?' Caroline frowned. 'Is that your goatherd, or something?'

'My housekeeper.'

'Oh, I should have known you'd have a housekeeper. Do you have a butler, too? And a valet?' Without waiting for an answer, Caroline peered past him into the house, her face vibrant with curiosity. 'Have you been waiting long for us to arrive? It wasn't my fault. There was a vast queue of punters all wanting signed copies of Jenny's books.'

'And there were drinks,' Jennifer said, sotto voce.

'It was a fascinating talk,' he said, turning to her. 'I meant to compliment you on it at the time, but you did seem swamped by your, er, admirers.'

With a smile, Alex stood aside to let them both enter the house. He'd changed since the town hall, wearing a white shirt, open at the neck and with short sleeves that clung to his tattooed biceps, coupled with faded blue jeans. To add to the casual look, he was barefoot. Yet again. Going about with no shoes on seemed to be his favourite thing, Jennifer thought, trying not to stare at his tanned feet.

The atrium, thick with lush, well-watered greenery, was empty, and the house was quiet. Too quiet.

'Where's Ripper?' Jennifer asked suspiciously, glancing about the place.

'I haven't seen him all evening.'

'He probably got himself shut in my room again. I did leave in a hurry earlier. Or he could be in the kitchen. Do you think Brodie might have fed him while we were out?'

'I doubt it. Brodie's gone to visit his parents.'

'Oh.'

'He'll be back tomorrow. Or should be.' Alex was studying Caroline with curious eyes. 'To what do we owe this pleasure?'

'Sorry to intrude, especially so late,' Caroline said quickly. 'I'm here to see Nelly. Is she about?'

'She was exhausted after tonight's excitement. I suggested she went straight to bed. So I'm afraid you've had a wasted trip.' He turned with obvious bemusement as Caroline peered eagerly into every open doorway along the atrium. 'But since you're here now, do make yourself at home.' His eyes met Jennifer's but she looked away at once, ridiculously shy. 'I can offer you wine or spirits, if you'd like a nightcap.'

'I'd love a nightcap,' Caroline said promptly.

Jennifer frowned. 'You've had enough.'

Caroline glared at her. 'That's for me to say, surely?'

'Whatever.' Jennifer wished her heart was not beating so loudly. 'But I won't have anything alcoholic, thanks. Not if Nelly's already gone up to bed.'

She was finding it hard to cope, standing so close to Alex, suddenly very aware of him physically. If only he hadn't followed her backstage tonight . . . Her lips were still tingling from where he'd cupped his hands around her mouth, helping her to breathe.

'On second thoughts, Caro,' she said huskily, her fist clenching her car keys, 'perhaps I'd better drive you home.'

'What? But we've only just arrived.' She pushed out her lower lip. 'And it's not so very late. I don't want to go home yet.'

Despite her fears about the plain blue top and leggings, Caroline actually looked lovely, ash-blonde hair tumbling about her shoulders. In an expensive gown, she would have been a perfect match for Alex Delgardo, as tall and willowy as any of his famous girlfriends.

Jennifer felt hot tears prick behind her eyelids. Which was simply ludicrous. There was nothing to cry about here. She was tired, she told herself. That was all.

And her feet hurt.

'But you only came to speak to Nelly, and she's in bed.'

'Then I could stay over and speak to her in the morning,' Caroline said swiftly, and threw a cajoling smile at her host. 'Couldn't I, Mr Delgardo?'

CHAPTER TWENTY-TWO

'Call me Alex,' he corrected her, his voice at its most charming, and Jennifer's hands tightened into fists.

'Thank you, *Alex*.' Caroline's smile was becoming more like the Cheshire Cat's by the moment. Though it was sadly unlikely she would disappear any time soon. 'I don't mind staying over.'

'What?' Jennifer stared at her.

'I can sleep on the sofa. Or the floor of your bedroom.' Caroline turned pleading eyes on Alex. 'You don't mind, do you?'

'Not at all,' he said smoothly. 'But there's no need for you to rough it. We have several guest rooms available.'

'Of course you do. It's such a huge place, isn't it? A mansion, really. All alone in the middle of the countryside, too, like something out of a Cornish folk tale.' Caroline studied the marble-floored atrium uncertainly. 'With a few modern twists.'

'Thank you,' he said, his smile wry. 'You're welcome to stay overnight, Caroline. If you're sure it wouldn't be inconvenient, work-wise. Jennifer told us how busy you are.'

'It's my day off tomorrow.'

Jennifer was bemused by this revelation. 'Is it?'

'Not technically. But I can ring in sick.'

'Caroline!'

'I'm owed time off, anyway. And I can feel a headache coming on. All those long speeches tonight, people droning on in Cornish . . . It always gives me a headache, that kind of thing.' She shrugged, ignoring Jennifer's disapproval, and then studiously crossed several marble squares without treading on the lines, so she could peek down a corridor that Jennifer thought probably led towards the garden room. Caroline had a thing about treading on the dividing lines between squares. Or rather, *not* treading on them. 'I'll have a chat with Nelly first thing, and go into work late. The midwifery team can manage without me for a couple of hours. Hardly anyone's pregnant at the moment, anyway.'

Alex's eyebrows shot up. 'Is that so?'

'Crazy, huh?' Caroline looked him up and down thoughtfully. 'Not enough kissing and cuddling going on in Pethporro, is there?'

His smile broadened. 'Now that's a shame.'

'I thought you didn't like too many visitors to the park,' Jennifer heard herself say, rattled by the banter sparking off between the two, and was rewarded with a surprised look from Alex. 'That is, the first time I came here you said—'

'That was before I knew you,' he interrupted. 'Or your sister.'

'Stepsister,' Jennifer and Caroline corrected him at the same time, sounding more like twins. *Demonic twins*, Jennifer thought, meeting Caroline's challenging gaze with a furious look of her own.

'I take it the "step" part is important to you both?' Alex seemed amused.

'Very,' they chanted in unison, then glared at each other again.

Oh, for goodness' sake.

Jennifer folded her arms tightly across her chest, wishing she hadn't brought Caroline home with her tonight. The talk with Nelly could have waited for another day. But the situation had felt so urgent earlier, she'd been unable to rest until something was done about it. Now, though, things seemed to be unravelling . . .

What was Caroline playing at, flirting with him so openly?

Alex laughed, looking from one to the other of them. 'I'll try to remember that.' Leading the way to the living room, he added over his shoulder, 'So, Caroline, if it's settled that you're staying overnight, how about that nightcap?'

While he led the way into the living room, Caroline pulled a most inelegant face at Jennifer, who stuck her tongue out in response just as he turned on the threshold, catching her in the act.

'Tut, tut, Jenny,' he said, 'such immature behaviour.'

Jennifer flushed.

Hurrying past them both into the living room, Caroline exclaimed, 'What a wonderful room. All these gorgeous sofas. Matching curtains, too. Who's the designer?' She fell back onto the four-seater sofa facing the big windows, bouncing and nestling against the cushions like a twelve-year-old. 'Mmm, comfortable, too.'

Hands in his pockets, Alex strolled towards the glass drinks cabinet. 'What can I get you both?'

'Nothing for me,' Jennifer said tightly.

'Why ever not?' Caroline gave her another sharp look. 'You heard Alex. I can stay overnight, no problem. You won't need to drive anywhere.'

Jennifer met her gaze. 'Maybe I've got a headache coming on, too.'

'Oh, pooh.' Caroline lay back against the sofa cushions and smiled eagerly up at Alex, who was still waiting by the drinks cabinet. 'What have you got to offer me?'

'Everything,' he said.

'I bet.'

Jennifer had heard enough. She strode to the door, which was difficult to manage in high heels. She nearly turned an ankle but carried on regardless. 'I'm going to change out of this preposterous outfit,' she muttered.

'Don't hurry back on my account,' Caroline called after her.

It was all she could do not to drag off one of her high heels and chuck it at her stepsister's head. Yet Caroline had done nothing wrong. There was no overt reason for her to feel so uneasy, or as though she were about to cry. Jennifer couldn't understand it. But there was an ache in her heart all the same.

Neither of them said anything, or tried to stop her, of course. But why would they? Now Alex and Caroline could be alone together.

How utterly perfect for them.

Jennifer came to a halt halfway across the echoing atrium, sick of hearing her heels clip-clop like one of Nelly's seven goats. She slipped off her shoes and tucked them under her arm with a sigh of relief before attempting the master stair-case. The marble flooring felt so cool on her hot, aching toes . . .

She heard a low-voiced exchange behind her, then Caroline's gurgling laughter.

They probably hadn't even noticed yet that she'd left the room. Too busy ogling each other in anticipation of tonight's flirtation fest, she thought grimly.

Nobody could blame Caroline for being drawn to him, of course.

Least of all her.

Alex Delgardo would be an impressive scalp to hang from any woman's belt. The biggest celebrity to hit Pethporro since Kate Winslet drove through once in an open-top sports car. Or so local rumour had it. Only two people had seen this fabled event, late one evening, and they'd both been slumped in the bus shelter at the time, clutching super-sized plastic bottles of cider.

Jennifer had reached the top of the stairs when there was a strange thudding behind her. Turning, she found Alex Delgardo bounding towards her, taking the stairs two at a time and grimacing oddly. She started to run along the landing towards her room, which was at the far end, but was easily overtaken by Alex.

She shrank back against the wall. 'W-what is it? What are you doing?'

'I could ask you the same thing.' He placed a hand on the wall beside her head, his tattooed bicep mere inches from her face. 'You bring a stranger back here and then walk away, leaving me alone with—'

'Caroline is not a stranger. She's my sister.'

'Stepsister,' he corrected her.

'Whatever.' Jennifer drew herself up, refusing to be intimidated by him. 'You seemed happy enough talking to her at the tapas bar. And she's here to talk to Nelly. I thought you'd be pleased about that.'

'I *am* pleased.'

'Yes, I rather thought you were.'

'What's that supposed to mean?' When she paused, he said, 'Come on, spit it out. I can see you're dying to.'

'I got the feeling you two wanted to be alone together. So I obliged.'

'I was being polite.'

'That was you being polite? No wonder you have a reputation for overacting.' She saw his eyes flash, and did not care that she'd needled him. He was the one who'd run after her like she was on fire. Which she probably was, if the heat in her cheeks was anything to go by. 'I'd hate to see you actually being *charming*. What would that look like, I wonder? Would clothes be removed?'

Now he was glaring at her. 'You think I fancy your sister? Sorry, your *step*sister?'

Frankly, she didn't know what to think. He was an actor, after all. Which was just another word for a pretender. Had he been pretending with Caroline? Was he pretending with her? Would she not be better just packing her bags and her cat and heading straight back to her mouldy cottage before she did something they would both regret?

'I think you like to play with people. Reel them in.'

'I see.' He was breathing quickly, his gaze darting about

her face like he was trying to read every micro-expression she could come up with to keep him at arm's length. 'Perhaps you should avoid thinking, then. It's likely to get you into trouble.'

'So what was with the whole chasing-me-up-the-stairs routine just now? You nearly scared the life out of me.'

'Maybe I don't like surprises.'

'You don't like surprises,' she repeated in tones of disbelief. 'All I did was leave the room.' His dark brows rose, and hers lifted too in automatic defiance. He was being flippant. It was hard not to become flippant too. 'What kind of surprises are we talking about here? Like me wanting to change out of this damn dress?'

His dark gaze dropped from her face to her dress, studying it. The clinging grey-green bodice first, then lower, to the smooth hips and the pale chiffon flare to her knees. And her slender bare feet, of course, coral-pink glitter varnish twinkling on each toenail. Just slotted in beside his own bare feet, which were much larger and somehow intrusively masculine.

For a moment, all she could hear was the erratic rhythm of her own heart. Then Alex lifted his head to meet her gaze, his lips twisted in a wry half-smile.

'I could help you with that, if you like,' he said.

Without a second's thought, her hand flashed up and she slapped his cheek.

Hard.

Alex stared down at her, dazed and astonished. His hand dropped from the wall, releasing her, and Jennifer ducked past him.

As she burst into her bedroom, a crazed Siamese rushed past her in a cream and brown blur, heading for the stairs.

'Ripper!' she cried in anguish.

But Alex was already lurching along the landing towards her, perhaps bent on revenge for the slap.

She ducked inside, pushed the bedroom door shut and turned the key in the lock. 'You asked for that,' she called through the door, then sank down against it, legs trembling.

CHAPTER TWENTY-THREE

I could help you with that, if you like.

She closed her eyes.

Of all the come-to-bed lines she had ever been fed, that was probably the cheesiest. It was also the most tempting.

She couldn't decide which of them was the bigger idiot. Him, for feeding her that line, or her, for wanting so desperately to say yes.

'Jennifer? I'm sorry,' He was keeping his voice low, thank goodness, though she had no doubt Caroline must be listening intently to their entire exchange from downstairs. 'I don't know why I said that.'

'Not much of an expert on the male psyche then, are you?' she said ironically.

'Enlighten me.'

Was he serious?

'Oh, go away,' she told him.

'Jennifer—'

'You're bothering me.'

'For God's sake, you make me sound like a . . . a . . .' He seemed to be casting about for an appropriate description of his behaviour, but failing to find anything that was both accurate and flattering.

'A sex pest?' She ignored his quick protest. 'Or were you suggesting you could help me with a fiddly zip or hard-to-reach buttons when you asked to help me take my clothes off? Because I can manage on my own, thanks.'

She dragged at her green chiffon dress, trying to wriggle out of it without undoing the zip at the back, not caring if it tore.

The fine material ripped.

'Shit.'

'You were saying?'

It sounded like he was right up against the door.

'I was saying, go away.' She came back to the door, raising her voice, no longer caring who heard. 'The dress is off now. So your services are surplus to requirements, Mr Delgardo.' She stepped out of the crumpled heap of green-and-white chiffon and stood there in her underwear, hands on hips. 'Better luck next time.'

'Honestly, what I said before ... It came out wrong.' He paused. 'I just wanted to say I was sorry, that's all.'

'So, you've said it. Now you can go back downstairs.'

'I'm going, don't worry.'

But she didn't hear him walking away.

'Alex?'

She stiffened at the sound of his name. It was Caroline, calling up the stairs in a soft voice, no doubt perplexed by his absence.

Jennifer was pretty perplexed herself. She found him sexy, but she didn't want to spend the night with him. That way madness lay. Their worlds clashed violently; they didn't just collide. He was a movie star, for goodness' sake, and she was . . . Well, she was a Cornish witch.

Hardly a match made in heaven.

So why wasn't she okay with the idea of him and her stepsister hitting it off?

'Alex? Are you up there?' It was obvious Caroline wasn't going to give up until he reappeared. 'Yoo-hoo! I need a refill. Is anyone coming back downstairs?'

'You'd better go back down to her,' Jennifer told him, frustrated, her head pounding, 'before she wakes everyone up.' She leant her forehead against the door, her voice suddenly muffled. 'You don't want that, trust me. Caro can get *really* loud when she's drunk. Like a factory klaxon.'

There was a short silence.

Part of her longed for him to stay there. To persist in trying to apologise. The perverse part that wanted something from Alex Delgardo she could never have.

But it seemed he was tired, too. Weary of the game they were playing. 'Goodnight, then,' he said flatly, and turned, walking away.

Jennifer listened to his footsteps receding downstairs, and Caroline's voice, silky with seductive pleasure, and could have howled with pain.

She just didn't know why.

Jennifer threw herself face down on her bed in her knickers and bra. She grabbed a pillow and pressed it over her head and ears, not wanting to hear anything from downstairs, not wanting even to think.

It took her all of five minutes to give in to the desire to know what the hell they were doing, struggle into her blue pyjamas and sneak downstairs on tiptoe.

The door to the living room was ajar.

She peered through the gap between the door and the frame. Alex was over by the drinks bottles, presumably mixing himself another nightcap. Caroline was sitting down, legs crossed, looking very come-hither. When he turned round, she patted the sofa cushions beside her. 'Sit down,' she said, almost purring, 'you look silly standing all the way over there.'

He barely hesitated before sitting down beside her. 'Fine, but it's getting late and I need to fix up a guest room for you.'

'What, *you*?' Caroline's eyes widened as she stared at him, incredulous. 'Are you going to make the bed up yourself? With sheets and a duvet?'

'If necessary.'

They're sitting so close together he might as well put his arm round her, Jennifer thought, almost grinding her teeth. Were their thighs touching?

'Don't you have a maid to do it for you?'

'It's their night off,' he said.

Caroline jabbed a finger at him, snorting with laughter. 'See, I knew you must have a sense of humour somewhere under all that stiff, Hollywood self-obsession.'

'I beg your . . . My *what*?'

'Otherwise why would Jennifer be bothering with you?' Caroline suddenly lurched towards him. Her fingers seemed to be playing with his shirt. 'You won't hurt her, will you?'

Her voice was husky. 'I love Jenny. I know it doesn't always show. We fight like cat and . . . Well, cat. But she's my stepsister. And I can see when she's struggling.'

'Struggling?' he repeated blankly.

Her hand dropped from his shirt. 'Because of *him*.' She was looking nervous now. *As well she might*, Jennifer thought, trying to hang onto her fury.

'Him?'

Caroline nodded, chewing on her lip.

'I see,' he said slowly. 'So there's a *him* in this situation.'

'Oh God, yes. Her perfect man.'

'Is that so?' He was almost drawling now. 'I had no idea she was actively involved with anyone, let alone a perfect man. And what is this man's name?'

'I'd rather not say.' Caroline's voice had dropped to a whisper, probably scared of being overheard. 'I mean, if Jenny hasn't mentioned him to you yet, I probably shouldn't—'

'Tall guy, dark hair, looks a bit rough around the edges? Like some West Country farmer out of a Thomas Hardy novel? I saw him at the festival tonight. He's the one who upset her, isn't he? Quit stalling and tell me who he is.'

Jennifer had heard enough.

Pushing the door open, she said coldly, 'Raphael. That's his name.'

Alex turned his head, his eyes widening as Jennifer walked into the room, barefoot and in her PJ shorts. Hardly her best look, but what the hell.

'Raphael Tregar.' Her eyes clashed with his, daring him to say anything. 'And yes, he broke my heart.'

CHAPTER TWENTY-FOUR

She ought to have stayed upstairs, of course.

Only when Alex studied her from head to foot, taking in her bare legs in the loose-fitting shorts, did she wish that she had reached for her dressing gown before coming downstairs. But she was way beyond caring now. *Let him stare*, Jennifer thought, raising her chin and meeting his gaze defiantly. She wasn't one of his wealthy friends with a designer negligee. She was an ordinary Cornishwoman, albeit one with a penchant for witchcraft, and she wasn't prepared to change either her appearance or her behaviour just to suit his notions of how a woman should look at bedtime.

Folding her arms across her chest, she waited for his sharp retort. There was bound to be one, after all. He always had a smart reply ready to go.

Alex Delgardo said nothing, though, merely staring back at her in silence. Especially at her legs, it appeared.

'What?' she said, challenging him with a toss of her head. She transferred her glare to Caroline. 'As for you, who said you could discuss my private life with a stranger?'

'A stranger?' Alex's brows shot up so high they almost

disappeared into his hairline. His gaze rose from her legs to her face at last. 'So *I'm* a stranger now. Thanks.'

'You're not one of my family. Not like Caroline. Who should have known better than to discuss my relationships behind my back.'

Caroline had a petulant flush to her cheeks now. 'I was only trying to help.'

'Oh, and there I was, thinking you were *gossiping*. Silly me.'

Alex stood up, and she backed away automatically. He set his fists on his hips, an odd gesture for a man his size, and gave her back that frustrated glare.

'We were *both* only trying to help,' he said.

She swallowed, not knowing what to say to that.

The odd thing was, she actually believed him.

A sudden crash from upstairs shocked all three of them into silence. Something – or someone – had just made contact with the floor above their heads. Loudly.

Alex stared upwards, then muttered, 'What the hell?' and ran from the room.

'Whose room is above us? Were we making too much noise?' Caroline whispered, staring at her in horror. They both listened to him thundering up the stairs. 'We must have disturbed someone up there. That's your fault, that is.' She shook her head. 'Coming down here, all guns blazing, behaving like a . . . a fishwife.'

A fishwife? With guns?

'I'm not sure whose room that is,' Jennifer said, pushing Caroline's mixed metaphors to one side. This was more important. 'But we need to find out. What if it's Nelly, trying to get our attention? Or falling out of bed?' She studied the ceiling, feeling horribly guilty now. 'Alex said his grand-mother went to bed early. Maybe she's been taken ill.'

'How can you not know whose room it is?'

'I don't go poking around the house, peering into other people's rooms. It's a bit rude. I'm a guest, and my room's on the other side of the house.' She pointed in the direction of the bedroom she had just left. 'I should have stayed upstairs. I knew this was a mistake.'

'Then why didn't you?'

They were both whispering frantically, though there was no point. Alex couldn't possibly hear them from upstairs.

'Because I knew you were talking about me, and I can't stand being talked about behind my back.'

'Ah, so you admit it.'

'Admit *what*?'

'That you were eavesdropping in the first place. Other-wise, logically, you would never have known we were talking about you behind your back.'

'What's your point?'

'That you *do* go poking around the house. And hearing no good of yourself, as eavesdroppers always do.'

Jennifer flashed her an awful look, but said nothing. What was there to say? Except a few mean things she might regret tomorrow. Then she froze.

'Jenny?'

It was Alex calling down the stairs, and he sounded frantic.

Caroline gripped her arm as they both started for the door. 'Oh God, something awful must have happened. I only hope it's not your fault.'

'*My* fault?'

'All the noise you made,' Caroline hissed after her. 'Raising your voice.'

'I swear, one of these days . . .'

Caroline had stopped in the doorway but gestured to her to keep going. She bit her lip, watching Jennifer cross the atrium. 'I'd better stay down here, okay? I don't want to stick my nose in where it's not wanted.'

'Your nose may be needed,' Jennifer told her flatly. 'Come with me.'

She hurried up to the first floor, with Caroline following a few steps behind, both of them holding onto the smooth polished rail of the banister. The imposing staircase, sweeping high above the greenery of the atrium floor, had never seemed so long a climb. Above their heads, she could see nothing but velvety darkness through the glass roof, the stars invisible. She wanted to stay calm – getting agitated wouldn't help whatever situation awaited them. But her heart was thumping hard and her palms were clammy.

She was afraid, she had to admit it. What would she find upstairs? Nelly collapsed on the floor? Was Caroline right – could this be her fault for making a scene so late at night?

'Is Caroline there?' Alex appeared in an open doorway, looking almost panicked. When he saw Caroline with her, he gestured to them both impatiently. 'In here,' he said shortly, and disappeared again.

Inside the bedroom two vast glass doors stood open onto a tiled balcony, lace curtains fluttering and swaying in a stiff night breeze coming from the sea. Dominating the room was a massive king-size bed strewn with snow-white pillows and rumpled sheets, the headboard and frame made of black leather. Above the bed was a mirrored ceiling, reflecting nothing but a sea of luxurious white cotton.

The bed's occupant was lying on the honey-coloured deep-pile fleece beside the bed, groaning and clutching at her large belly.

It wasn't Nelly.

Alex, down on one knee beside Thelma, bent his head to listen to her frantic complaint, then relayed the message over his shoulder. 'She says it hurts. That something's wrong, and the baby's not moving any more.' He swore under his breath. 'God, why did Brodie choose to take tonight off? I could really do with him here.'

Caroline immediately set to work. 'I'll examine her. You call an ambulance.'

'If only we had the helicopter here . . . But I wasn't comfortable using it any more, so I had Brodie fly it back to London.' Alex looked round at Jennifer, his face rigid. 'My fault again.'

'Don't worry about that now,' Jennifer said, trying to keep calm for his sake. 'You heard Caroline. Call an ambulance.'

He nodded, then hunted belatedly through his pockets for his mobile, still staring at his sister, and began to key the numbers in.

CHAPTER TWENTY-FIVE

It was dawn when Jennifer jerked awake, lying awkward and uncomfortable on a large sofa. Her body was stiff and unyielding, her bare feet cold. She had not had enough sleep; she could tell from the way her body responded to being awake: groggy and slightly nauseous. Whatever bad dream she'd been having fled, leaving her with a vague sense of anxiety.

Her eyes flickered open on a shadowy robed figure, swaying with arms raised in the air, as though performing some ritual dance.

For a moment, she had no idea what was happening or what she was doing there. Then her brain took in the ghostly images and fed them through some kind of internal processor. Full of dread, she had watched the ambulance pull away in the early hours, silent but with blue lights flashing.

Then she had closed the curtains and curled up on the sofa, unwilling to go upstairs to bed and miss Alex's return from the hospital.

That was the last thing she remembered.

Now someone had entered the living room and was opening the curtains to let in the soft morning light.

'No word yet?'

It was Nelly.

Alex's grandmother had emerged from her bedroom when the paramedics arrived, but seemed too upset to do much but wring her hands and keep asking Thelma if she was all right. So Caroline had taken charge and steered the old lady back to bed, sending Jennifer to make Nelly a calming cup of valerian tea so she could get some sleep. 'No point everyone being awake,' she'd said coolly, and Jennifer had obeyed without argument.

She'd never been so glad to have her stepsister on hand. Caroline had known precisely what to say on the phone to the emergency services, and had briefed the arriving paramedics on the pregnant woman's condition, even accompanying Thelma in the ambulance. 'You can follow in your car,' she told a grim-faced Alex, who had insisted on going to the hospital too. 'Thelma will need a familiar face once we're there. Someone to hold her hand and fetch her drinks. Hospital waits can be gruelling.'

Alex had squeezed his sister's hand as she was helped into the ambulance. 'I'll get you transferred to a private hospital, don't worry.'

'I don't need a private hospital.' Thelma's voice had been faint, her skin greyish, her forehead wet with perspiration. 'Just someone to tell me what's wrong.'

The paramedics had assured her she would be in good hands, then Caroline had climbed in beside her and the double doors had closed.

Car keys in hand, Alex had turned to her, his eyes uncertain. 'You'll wait with Nelly? Keep an eye on her for me?'

'Of course.' She had touched his hand. 'Go, be with your sister.'

Her phone had been lying beside the sofa all night.

Now, pushing fatigue aside, Jennifer forced herself into a sitting position, then reached for her phone. 'Morning,' she said, and found her voice rusty, her tongue dry. *Dehydration*, she thought, and longed for a cup of tea. But she needed to check her phone first. 'I'm sorry. I didn't mean to fall asleep, only close my eyes.'

'Nonsense, you'll be no good to anyone if you're too exhausted to stand up.' Nelly came to stand over her, clad in her floor-length white nightie, long hair that had been loose last night now tied in a single plait and draped over one shoulder. 'You look done in,' she said, then asked less certainly, 'Thelma and the baby . . . Any word from the hospital yet?'

Jennifer, unlocking her phone, found a text message. Instantly relieved, she read it out with a smile. 'This came at three from Alex. *Arrived safely at hospital. Thelma and baby stable, but doctor keeping her in for tests.*'

'That doesn't sound too bad.'

'Definitely not.'

Nelly smiled. 'I'll make us some tea.'

'Sounds marvellous. But you should let me make it.'

'Don't be silly. You're our guest. And besides,' Nelly added, wandering through the atrium towards the kitchen, 'you always make my tea too weak.'

Jennifer grinned.

The goats were already gathered outside the kitchen window, eager for their breakfast snacks. She waved at Baby, who tilted her narrow head and baaed needily.

'Great greedy lumps,' Nelly said, flapping a hand at them through the window. 'You can wait. We humans get our tea first. Then I'll sort you out some cream crackers, how's that?'

Jennifer came in and pulled open the fridge door, helping herself to a yoghurt. She sat down at the table and smiled at Nelly, who was pouring them both two mugs of tea from the pot.

Her phone buzzed. It was a new text message.

'Oh.'

Nelly stared, putting down the pot. 'What is it? What does Alex say?'

'It's another text. But this one's from Caroline, my stepsister. You may remember her from last night.'

'I'm not in my dotage. Of course I remember her. Lovely blonde girl who was helping Thelma with the pain.'

Jennifer nodded. 'Caroline's a midwife. She went with Thelma in the ambulance.'

'So, what does her message say?'

'Erm ...' Jennifer licked dry lips and read out Caroline's text. '*Suspected placental abruption. Doctors discussing emergency C-section. More news soon.*'

'Oh my God.'

Nelly sat down heavily, staring at nothing.

'I'm sure it will be fine. It's a really good hospital, and they have a superb maternity unit there.'

Nelly did not look convinced. 'Thelma must be so frightened, poor pet.'

'Alex is with her.'

'So why hasn't he rung home?'

'I imagine he didn't want to wake you.'

'But I *am* bloody well awake.' Nelly thumped her fist on the kitchen table, making Jennifer jump. 'This is my granddaughter and my first great-grandchild we're talking about. I should be kept properly informed about what's going on. Not left in the dark, wondering what on earth's happening, like I don't matter. Like I'm a stranger.'

'You're not supposed to use your mobile inside the hospital, that's probably why we've had so little news. Or maybe it's been a long wait. Hospitals are so busy these days.'

Nelly harrumphed, covering the pot with a tea cosy shaped like a goat's head. 'I suppose so. Though it still doesn't make it right.'

'I'll see what I can find out.' Speedily texting back, Jennifer thanked Caroline for the latest update, then asked how Thelma was coping. *Nelly is desperate for news*, she added, then hit send.

'Thank you,' Nelly said, watching this process with interest.

Jennifer finished her yoghurt and drank her tea, suddenly aware this might be an ideal opportunity to get Nelly to open up about her own health problems. They were alone, waiting for news from the hospital. It felt like a time for simple truths. But she remembered the dreadful scene last time she'd tried talking to Nelly about her diagnosis, and she didn't fancy a rerun of that. Though perhaps if she came at it sideways ...

'At least this way,' she said gently, 'you may get to meet your great-grandchild early.'

Nelly stared at her dangerously. Her fingers crooked

around the mug handle, as though planning to chuck the hot tea in her direction. 'What are you trying to say?'

'Nothing,' Jennifer said quickly, poised to duck.

But Nelly did not throw her drink at Jennifer's head. Instead, she lifted the mug to her lips and took a cautious sip.

'Well,' she grumbled.

'I only meant it could be a blessing in disguise,' Jennifer continued, her heart thumping, 'if both mum and baby come out of this in good health.'

'That's one way of looking at it.'

'I know you don't want to discuss your own health problems.'

'What gave it away?'

Awkwardly, Jennifer pressed on. 'But don't you think it's time you took Alex and Thelma into your confidence? You could have lost your granddaughter last night. Some things are more important than pride.'

'Pride?'

'You don't want to look dependent on anyone. I know exactly how that feels.' Jennifer made a face. 'I've spent the past six months avoiding everyone I know, pushing my own family away, biting people's heads off when they ask how I am. But sometimes you have to accept that you need other people.'

'I don't,' Nelly said stiffly.

'And they need you,' she added. 'Alex and Thelma may be grown up now. But they still love and need you in their lives. Even if that means sharing your bad news.'

Nelly's face crumpled.

Hurriedly, Jennifer got up and gave her a tight hug. 'I'm

sorry,' she said at once, realising with horror that Nelly was crying. 'I didn't want to upset you.'

'No, you meant to make me see sense.' Nelly waved away her apology. She sniffed loudly, dragging a cotton handkerchief out of her voluminous nightie. 'And you're right, I know you are. Alex and Thelma should be told what ... what's been happening.' She blew her nose. 'I just don't know how.'

'So, tell me first,' Jennifer suggested, 'and then, if you like, I can tell them.'

'No,' Nelly said abruptly, pushing her away and sitting upright again. 'I would like to tell you. I need to tell someone, or I'll ... I'll burst. But only if you promise me you'll never tell anyone else.'

'Not even Alex?'

'Especially not Alex.' Nelly shot her a sharp look, her eyes still brimming with tears. 'He's had a tough time this past year. The horrors he's been through ... Well, you wouldn't understand. But I've had to watch him suffer, and it's nearly broken my heart, not being able to help, except to be there for him.' She dabbed at her eyes, then shoved her damp hanky back into the depths of her nightie. 'The last thing I want is to hurt the poor boy more, just as he's coming out of that bad time.'

Jennifer frowned, not understanding. *The horrors he's been through ...*

What on earth did she mean?

'Anyway,' Nelly continued, her voice growing stronger, 'if you promise not to repeat what I say, and especially not to Alex, then I'll tell you what's wrong.'

Troubled, Jennifer pushed her questions about Alex aside. For now, Nelly's problems had to take precedence over his issues.

'Go on,' she said.

'I've got cancer.' Nelly's voice croaked, stumbling over the awful words, then she cleared her throat. 'Ovarian cancer. Stage four. That means it's metastasised to my lungs and liver. Not much point in surgery now, that's what the oncologist told me. It could kill me.'

'Oh, Nelly.'

'There are other things we could do, according to the consultant. New therapies, trial medications. But there'd always be side effects, and frankly, it's too much of a faff at my age.' Nelly spoke for a few moments about how she had discovered her illness, and the information she had been given about possible treatments and palliative care, all of which she had declined. Then she glared at her, as though daring Jennifer to say anything to contradict her decision. 'I'm nearly ninety years old. Too old for playing silly buggers. I'd rather take my chances with the cancer. See how long I've got left.'

'I'm so sorry.'

'What are you apologising for? Hardly your fault, is it?' Nelly sounded cross. But her lower lip quivered, which made Jennifer cry, though she had been trying to hold back the tears. 'My own stupid fault, that's what it is. I knew something was wrong. But I don't like doctors and hospitals. All that fuss. The endless questions and form-filling, and waiting about in rooms full of germs. So I did nothing about it. By the time things got really bad, and I forced myself to book a check-up with the doctor, it was too late.' She looked up and saw a tear rolling down Jennifer's cheek. 'Now what are you crying for? I'm an old lady. I've had my time on this earth. There's no need for tears.'

'Are you in pain?'

'I wasn't. But lately ...' Nelly grimaced. 'I suppose it's made me a bit cranky. I've never been one for moodiness. Raising my voice, all that. But these past few weeks, the pain's been getting a little more than I can bear. And I seem to be snapping at everyone in sight. Including you.' She gave Jennifer an embarrassed half-smile. 'I'm sorry.'

'Like you said, no need to apologise. You're going through something appalling here. I can't even begin to imagine how you must be feeling.'

'You don't want to imagine it,' Nelly said.

'Can I at least persuade you to go back to the oncologist, or even to the local doctors here? They could prescribe you pain relief medication, I'm sure.'

'I'm happy taking valerian tea, and a few old Cornish potions. I'm sure you understand what I mean. I'd prefer to go the natural way, if I can. Not zonked out on morphine.'

'That's your decision, of course. But it may get harder. And you need to talk to Alex and Thelma about this. To involve them in your care.'

'Why?'

'Because they're your family and they love you deeply. And Alex is going out of his mind with worry. He knows something's wrong, but you won't let him in.' She reached across the table and put a hand on top of Nelly's. 'There's no harm accepting help. Some people don't have any family to fall back on. But you do. All you have to do is tell them.'

'I suppose you're right. But I hate it. As soon as it's common knowledge, everything will change. People will start interfering in my business. Telling me what to do.' Nelly dashed away another tear of her own, the gesture impatient. 'Being *kind*.'

'Is that so unbearable?'

'Yes!'

'People are only kind because they care.' Jennifer was struggling, not sure what to say. She wished she had never agreed to spy on Nelly for Alex. Now she knew this terrible secret, and couldn't even tell him. 'You don't have to go through this on your own, Nelly. There's another way.'

'To do what? Die gracefully?'

'Please, let me tell Alex.' She felt terrible inside. 'It's not fair that I know this, and your own grandson doesn't.'

'No, absolutely not. You mustn't say a word. You promised!'

'Yes, I promised.'

Jennifer clamped a hand over her mouth. She couldn't say another word, she was so choked up.

Nelly shook her head forcefully and squeezed Jennifer's hand, though she herself was crying, too. 'No more tears, I won't allow it.'

'Sorry, I . . . don't think . . . I can help it.'

'For heaven's sake, look at us. A right couple of leaky taps.' Nelly drew her large handkerchief out again and blew her nose on it. 'You're right, of course. And I don't want to do this alone. Otherwise I would never have agreed to come and live here with Alex, in this great barn of a house.'

'You don't love it here?'

'Love it?' Nelly looked at her, seeming bewildered. 'It's more like a conservatory than a house. With a swimming pool in it. And an exercise room. The boy's mad.'

Jennifer laughed through her tears. 'It is a strange design. I can't disagree with you there. But the goats like it.'

'The goats are ecstatic here. All this land, the orchard, plenty of grazing.' Nelly made a face. 'I'm not complaining. Alex is a dear, sweet boy. A man, really. But he still seems like a boy to me. And since his accident . . .'

'Accident?'

'The hotel bombing. Didn't he tell you?'

The hotel bombing.

Jennifer stared. Her heart thumped erratically. 'I heard about it on the news when it happened, but not in any detail. And he's never mentioned it to me.' She frowned, trying to recall the facts. 'There was a terrorist incident near where he was filming. A bomb went off.'

'Yes, in a hotel. A friend's party.' Nelly shook her head mournfully. 'It was dreadful. Really unspeakable.'

The horrors he's been through . . .

Was this what she had meant earlier? Jennifer waited to hear more, but in vain. It seemed Nelly had come to the end of that story, and nothing else would be forthcoming.

'Alex must have been devastated,' she said.

'Yes.'

'I imagine that's why he's down here instead of in Holly-wood. It's a good place to get away from the outside world.' She frowned, thinking back. 'Has he taken on any film roles since then?'

'Oh, I don't know about that.' Nelly looked away, her

expression suddenly evasive. A few wisps of hair had worked loose from her plait, white strands brushing her cheek. 'I wonder what's happening at the hospital,' she muttered, dragging one thin strand into her mouth and sucking on it. 'Why haven't they let us know yet? It's been ages.'

'I'm sure they'll be in touch as soon as they have something to tell us. Caroline will text me. Or Alex may ring. These things can be very complicated.'

Jennifer finished her tea in silence. But she was remembering the way Alex had spoken to her so coldly the first day they'd met, his badly grazed hands, the way he had helped her backstage, understanding almost instinctively that she was having a panic attack, plus his occasionally strange and distant behaviour . . .

'Tell me what really happened to Alex,' she said softly, pushing her mug aside. 'What made him the way he is? Was it the hotel bombing?'

'Alex wouldn't like it if I told you.'

'I swear on my life,' Jennifer met her troubled gaze, 'I'll keep anything you say to myself. I won't tell him you said a word. I won't tell anyone, in fact.'

'But it's a secret. I don't want to break a confidence.'

'Even if it means helping him to get better? And it's not that much of a secret, surely? It was all over the news when it happened.'

'Oh yes, the actual *bombing*.' Nelly looked confused. 'But I'm talking about what happened afterwards. Once he and Brodie finally got out of hospital.'

'He and ... Brodie?' A shock ran through her at these words. 'So Brodie was with him when the hotel was bombed?'

'Of course, poor boy. That's how he lost his leg.'

'Oh, my God.'

Her mobile rang shrilly in the silence that followed, and they both stared at it. Jennifer swallowed, and picked up the phone with shaking hands.

CHAPTER TWENTY-SIX

'Hello?'

'It's Alex.' He sounded exhausted, his voice croaky. 'Sorry about the early call. I thought it might be better to call your mobile than the landline. Is my grandmother awake yet?'

'Yes, she's here with me.'

'Put her on, would you?' He hesitated, then added huskily, 'Please.'

Wordlessly, she passed the phone to Nelly.

'Hello?' Nelly put the phone to her ear. Her eyes widened as she listened. 'Alex, darling, slow down ... What's happened? How is Thelma? And the baby?'

After that, Nelly said nothing more, but sat with a hand clamped over her mouth as she listened to his update, looking horrified at times, relieved at others.

Finally, the old lady nodded, seeming to come back to life. 'Of course,' she said more clearly, and looked across the table at Jennifer. 'Are you able to drive me to the hospital?' When Jennifer nodded, Nelly handed the phone back to her. 'He wants to speak to you, dear.' Then she got up and stood in the middle of the kitchen, staring at nothing.

Alex said hoarsely, 'Jenny?'

'Yes, I'm here.'

'The baby was born by emergency Caesarean section about half an hour ago. It's a boy. Premature, but the doctor says he'll live.'

'Thank God.'

'Thelma's not in a good way, though. She's lost a lot of blood. Placental abruption. Did Caroline tell you?'

'Yes, she texted a few hours ago.'

'They're saying if they can't stop the bleeding . . . Well, I'd be grateful if you could bring Nana to the hospital in Truro at once.'

'Of course.'

'Can you get here as quickly as possible? Are you okay to drive? Will you be safe?'

'Don't worry, I managed to grab some sleep.'

'Good.' He paused. 'I need to ring Brodie, too, let him know what's happened. He'll want to cut short his visit to his parents, I expect.'

Jennifer nodded, recalling how close Brodie and Thelma had seemed. He would be shocked, no doubt, to hear of her emergency Caesarean.

'And her husband?'

'Stuart.' He made a frustrated sound under his breath. 'Yes, I don't particularly want to speak to him, but it's unavoidable. Just before they took her into the operating room, Thelma asked me not to inform him about the birth. She doesn't want her husband to track her and the baby down.' He sighed. 'But in all conscience, I can't keep Stuart in the dark. Not given the dangerous nature of her condition.'

'That can't have been an easy decision.'

'No.' There was a short silence, then, his voice full of emotion, Alex said, 'Look after Nana for me, Jenny,' and rang off.

Not given the dangerous nature of her condition.

He'd said Thelma had lost a great deal of blood already, but the doctors couldn't seem to stop the bleeding.

Was it possible his sister might die?

Jennifer looked up to find Nelly standing by the sink, crying into her hanky again. Her heart squeezed in anguish. She hurried over, mobile in hand. 'Please don't cry. I'm sure everything's going to be fine. Alex says they're both in good hands.' But she could see Nelly did not believe her. 'I'll get out of these pyjamas and drive you to Truro straight away. That's better than waiting around here for news, isn't it?'

'Yes, thank you.'

'It won't take me long to get ready. You should probably go and change too.' When Nelly did not move, she forced a smile. 'Unless you want to swan about Cornwall in your nightie? That will give the tourists something to stare at.'

'Get changed?' Nelly plucked at her long white nightie, only then seeming to realise what she was wearing. 'Oh yes, that's a good idea.'

Nelly drifted away upstairs, drying her eyes.

Mobile in hand, Jennifer stood alone in the middle of the kitchen, staring at the blank screen. She felt in limbo, her thoughts jumbled and elsewhere – inside Alex Delgardo's head as he dealt with his family's misfortunes. He had sounded so distraught on the phone. And now she knew the most awful secret about his grandmother, but couldn't even share it with him. She had made a promise to Nelly.

CHAPTER TWENTY-SEVEN

'He's perfect.'

'What did you expect?' Jennifer whispered back, though she was not quite sure why they were whispering.

'I don't know.' Alex still sounded stunned. He ran a hand through his unkempt hair. 'He's been through such a traumatic birth.'

Thelma's newborn son lay in his incubator in the neonatal intensive care unit, being kept warm under a heating lamp. He was fast asleep and unlikely to wake.

All the same, they kept their voices down out of respect. There were other babies nearby in the unit, and at least one mother slumped in a chair, asleep despite the time of day. Day and night became curiously blurred for new parents, Caroline often said, due to a newborn's total lack of appreciation for circadian rhythms.

Thelma's condition had stabilised by the time Jennifer and Nelly arrived at the hospital, though apparently the consultant had come close to suggesting a hysterectomy to save her life. His sister might be out of immediate danger, as Alex had told them with obvious relief, but she didn't look too good either. For now, she needed to rest and let her body recover.

Currently, Thelma was asleep in a private room, with Nelly watching over her.

The baby had to stay in the NICU, however. 'Caroline says birth is always traumatic for the baby,' Jennifer told him. 'Even with a Caesarean section. It's the end of everything they thought they knew about life.'

'But the start of something new.'

'New, yes. But also bright and unpleasantly noisy.' Jennifer stretched and yawned behind her hand. 'Sorry, I'm zonked. I need to get back to bed.'

Although she had slept, her body knew it needed more than a few hours to function at maximum capacity. She had no idea how Alex was still on his feet, having not slept at all. Years of unearthly hours as an actor, she supposed, followed by riotous all-night parties. Either that, or he had the constitution of a god.

Alex turned away from the door into the intensive care unit. Slowly, he looked her up and down. 'Me too,' he said huskily. 'Thanks for bringing Nana here. It was a lot to ask.'

'What nonsense,' she said briskly, only realising, on seeing his quick grin, that she sounded like his grandmother.

'It was a long way to drive after a difficult night.' He checked his phone, then glanced guiltily at the NO MOBILE PHONES sign on the wall and put it away again. 'Nana shouldn't be left with Thelma much longer. She's been in there two hours. She'll be exhausted.'

'Amazing, isn't she? Made of iron, that woman.'

'I only wish she were.'

Jennifer belatedly remembered how sick his grandmother was. It was hard to keep her illness in mind; Nelly had the energy and purpose of a woman half her age, bless her. Alex still didn't know what was wrong with her. He had his suspicions, of course. But not the truth. Stage four ovarian cancer. It was the worst news possible. And a burden weighing her down, given how badly Alex wanted to know the extent of his grandmother's illness.

She wanted to blurt out what she knew, before it was too late.

But how could she?

Nelly had made her promise faithfully not to tell anyone, and she could not betray her new friend . . .

'I'll collect Nelly,' he was saying wearily, 'then head back to Pethporro with her. You coming too?'

Jennifer rummaged in her pocket for her car keys. 'I guess so, yes,' she said, and smothered another yawn. It seemed his fatigue was catching.

Two female nurses, presumably coming on shift, bustled out of the lift, chatting and laughing. At the sight of Alex Delgardo, they fell silent, staring, then giggled as they walked past.

'Hello, Mr Delgardo,' one nurse said bravely, and they were both rewarded by Alex's warm, magnetic smile.

That charismatic sex appeal . . .

He could switch it on – and off – like a headlight beam, Jennifer thought resentfully, and looked away, embarrassed by her sudden stab of jealousy, listening as he said a few words to the two nurses, who then walked on, still giggling, faces flushed and wreathed in smiles, positively glowing from his attention.

'You're dead on your feet.' Alex frowned, holding out his

hand for her car keys. 'Give me those keys. I can arrange for someone to drive your car back to Pethporro. Come home with me instead. It'll be safer.'

'You can't be safe to drive either. You haven't slept at all.'

He smiled, taking her keys, and swivelled on his heel, heading back towards the security doors into the maternity ward. 'Who says I'm driving?' he threw over his shoulder.

Jennifer followed at a slow pace, thoroughly confused. And not just by what he had said, but by herself. Her feelings for him were all jumbled up inside, piled one on top of each other, crazy, chaotic, impossible.

She had to get away from him, she knew that. Yet she kept finding him close. And it was physical, not just emotional. She was hot, burning up for him, her desire like a solar flare constantly in danger of bursting out of her tongue and fingertips; she could barely control herself these days.

But she had to push it away, didn't she?

She couldn't let this insanity win. Not after the damage her feelings for Raphael Tregar had done to her heart. Like wildfire, he'd left her dead and smouldering inside, ruined and broken. She couldn't go through that hell again.

When she reached Thelma's private room, Alex was already crouched beside the bed, talking in low, urgent tones to his grandmother, who had been watching Thelma while she slept.

He did not look round when she entered, but Jennifer got the feeling they had been discussing her. Nelly half turned, shooting her a quick, furtive glance from under her brows, nodding as she continued with their conversation.

Jennifer stayed by the door, not wanting to intrude on a family conference. Thelma was still unconscious, it seemed, her eyelids closed, hands limp by her sides. She lay sedated and comatose in her hospital bed, perhaps not even aware that she had given birth. She was hooked up to a drip, wires from various monitors protruding from under her covers. Apart from a quick trip to the loo and to visit her newborn great-grandson – cooing over his tiny hands and wrinkled face under the yellow knitted cap – Nelly had not moved from Thelma's bedside the entire time.

Now, getting up at last from the plastic seat, Nelly stumbled and would have fallen if Alex hadn't caught her.

'Silly me,' she mumbled, but her words were slurred.

'Nana?'

Jennifer helped him seat Nelly again. The old lady felt surprisingly heavy, her limbs floppy and uncoordinated. She frowned, worried. 'Alex, I think she needs a doctor.'

'Nonsense,' Nelly managed to say, trying to push them away, but it was clear she was seriously unwell. Her eyelids flickered shut, then open again, her eyes rolling up as though she were fainting.

'I'll look after her,' Jennifer told Alex urgently. 'You go, find a doctor.'

Alex nodded, but she could see he was reluctant to leave his grandmother.

'Hurry, please,' she told him, and he left, calling up and down the corridor outside, 'Hello? We need a doctor in here, urgently!'

Nelly's eyes were mostly showing white now. She lolled in the chair, one leg at an odd angle, her mouth slightly open as she gasped, 'I'm ... fine.' Her hand flapped at nothing. 'Just need ... a lie-down.'

'Don't worry, I've got you,' Jennifer said, though she was increasingly struggling with Nelly's weight. She crouched to support the old lady better, afraid she might slip off the chair and hurt herself on the hard floor. 'Alex has gone to fetch a doctor.'

'I don't want ... bloody doctors!'

Jennifer felt sick with anxiety. 'You have to tell someone about your condition,' she whispered in Nelly's ear. 'Please, let me tell Alex. You need proper care.'

But she was not sure Nelly could hear her any more.

A moment later, Alex returned with a doctor and nurse in tow. Jennifer stepped back as the nurse checked Nelly's pulse and spoke to her, getting only a few incoherent mutterings by way of a reply.

She had never felt more helpless.

'I'm Dr Fletcher.' Briskly, the doctor introduced himself to Alex. 'Does your grandmother have any pre-existing medical conditions?'

'I don't know, I'm sorry. She's been unwell lately, I know that.' Alex was frantic. 'But she's refusing to tell anyone what's wrong.'

'I know what's wrong with her,' Jennifer said miserably.

Alex turned, staring at her.

On the chair, Nelly gave a feeble groan. 'No, no ...'

'I have to tell them. Don't you see that?' Jennifer barely recognised her own voice, it sounded so strained. 'I'm sorry, Nelly. I don't want to break my promise to you. But I can't just stand by and watch you die.'

The doctor looked at her keenly. Swiftly, Jennifer explained Nelly's diagnosis of stage four ovarian cancer and how, so far, she had been avoiding medical care. 'She told me it's no use getting treatment at her age. Not when her cancer's so far gone. That she just wants to go naturally, in her own way.'

Alex's eyes widened as she spoke. 'How long have you known this?' he said as she finished, his voice deep and shaken. 'And when were you planning on telling me?'

But she couldn't bear to say anything, merely shaking her head. 'Later.'

'Alex?' Nelly croaked.

He bent and put an arm around Nelly's shoulders, supporting her on the chair. 'It's okay, Nana, I'm here.' More nurses arrived, and he glanced round at Jennifer with a distracted expression. 'Where's Caroline? I thought she was getting coffee. That was over an hour ago. We could do with her advice.'

'I don't know.' Jennifer fumbled for her phone and found a text from Caroline. She scanned it and blinked. 'Oh hell, I missed this. Caroline's been called into work on emergency cover. But she'll be here as soon as she can. I'll call her once we know what's going on.'

The doctor straightened, looking directly at Alex. 'We'll need to admit your grandmother at once, I'm afraid.'

They were moving Nelly onto the floor now, having failed to keep her upright on the chair. She was placed carefully on her side and kept warm with a blanket, her face waxy and pale. After a low-voiced conference with another doctor, Dr Fletcher sent one of the nurses to fetch a trolley bed for Nelly.

'Perhaps you could go through the paperwork for her admission, Mr Delgardo,' he said, 'and bring in some night-clothes and personal items?'

'Of course.' Alex looked grim, his mouth tight. 'Is it the cancer?'

'The cancer?' His tone was surprised. Dr Fletcher shook his head. 'That seems unlikely. I'd guess your grandmother has suffered a stroke.'

'A *stroke*?' Alex sounded aghast.

'Her symptoms would appear to fit that diagnosis, yes. To be one hundred per cent sure, we'll need to do tests. A brain scan, for instance, and blood tests. Once she's stable.'

Alex seemed speechless.

'But your sister should be awake soon.' Dr Fletcher checked the bleeping monitors, picking up Thelma's chart and casting a swift glance down the top sheet. 'This all looks good. She's obviously a fighter.'

'Yes,' Alex said huskily.

An orderly came in, pushing a freshly made-up trolley bed, and Jennifer stepped back as the hospital staff eased Nelly up onto the bed and wheeled her from the room. Clearly torn between his sister and his grandmother, Alex stood in the doorway, staring after the disappearing trolley bed as it headed for the lift.

'I should go with her,' he said, but his gaze kept straying back to Thelma.

Jennifer said, 'You heard the doctor – Thelma's a fighter. If your grandmother has had a stroke, that's a critical situation. You need to be with her.'

'Yes.' His face cleared, purpose returning to his voice. He

squared his shoulders, suddenly a straight-backed soldier again. 'Though I still wish I could transfer Nana to a private hospital.'

'Why can't you?'

'I tried to persuade her to join my healthcare plan when she first moved in with me. But she refused point-blank. She's a huge believer in the NHS.' Still he hesitated in the doorway. 'Will you stay with Thelma for me, then?'

'Of course.'

She drew the plastic chair up to his sister's bed, tired and only too willing to sit down. It had been a bloody long twenty-four hours.

'Jennifer?' She looked round, surprised by the harsh tone in his voice. 'You never answered my question from before. I thought we had an agreement. How long had you known about Nana's cancer diagnosis before finally deciding to share it with me?'

He was angry. And she could not blame him, given the circumstances. He must think she had been hiding the truth from him all along.

Jennifer wished she could sit him down and reassure him. Explain how it had all happened so quickly. But there was no time now. Not when his grandmother could die at any moment. Better that he went off hating her than wasting any more precious moments away from his nan's bedside.

'Later,' she repeated firmly. 'We'll talk about it later, okay?'

Alex nodded, and left the room after one last glance at his sister. But she had seen the terrible accusation in his face, and knew he had not forgiven her.

CHAPTER TWENTY-EIGHT

It was late afternoon before Jennifer headed for the special care ward where Nelly was being treated, and peeked round the open double doors.

Alex sat beside Nelly as she lay unmoving in the hospital bed, his back stiffly upright, his sombre gaze fixed on her grey, heavily lined face. The old lady had been wired up to monitors which beeped intermittently, the noise only slightly reassuring, given her almost complete stillness, her chest rising and falling very gently. The curtains had been pulled partially round the bed while a young nurse checked Nelly's vital signs, clipboard in hand.

Jennifer crept forward as quietly as possible, for there were other patients in nearby beds and she didn't want to disturb anyone.

'Hello,' she whispered, and his head turned.

There was a quick flash of pain in his face, and she knew he had neither forgotten nor forgiven what he must see as her betrayal. 'Have you come from Thelma?' When she nodded, he searched her face. 'How is she?'

'Much better. She woke up some time ago and asked for coffee immediately. A whole jug of coffee, to be precise.'

'Sounds like Thelma.'

'She didn't get any, but a nurse brought her a wheelchair and she's gone to visit the baby in the intensive care unit. She wants to see you.'

'I expect she wants an update on Nana's condition. What did you tell her?'

'The bare minimum. I thought it best not to alarm her.'

'Thank you.' Alex stood up and stretched wearily. 'God, I could murder a strong coffee myself.'

The nurse looked round then, and said in a low voice, 'You should take yourself back home, Mr Delgardo.' She hung her clipboard on the end of Nelly's bed, studying them both with undisguised disapproval. 'Get some sleep. No point sitting here for hours on end.'

'Yes,' he said, grabbing his jacket and stifling a yawn. 'I suppose you're right.'

'We'll ring if there's any change.'

'Thank you.' He smiled at the nurse, and Jennifer saw the young woman's face light up, delighted by his attention. *Amazing what a difference a smile can make*, she thought. Especially from a good-looking celebrity like Alex. 'For everything,' he added softly, and the nurse actually blushed.

They walked across the hospital complex together, stopping briefly for black coffee from a machine, which he knocked back in a few thirsty gulps.

'Want a hot drink?' Alex was poised to put more coins in the machine. His voice was strained and distant, and there was a chill in the air between them. It was upsetting to think he somehow blamed her for what had happened with Nelly earlier. But explanations could wait until after they'd seen Thelma and her newborn baby. A busy hospital was hardly the best place for that kind of fraught conversation.

'No thanks,' she said.

He shrugged, and stifled another yawn behind his hand. 'Suit yourself.'

That young nurse was right, Jennifer thought, studying him covertly. Alex had bloodshot eyes and was clearly in desperate need of sleep. Not to mention a hot shower and a shave, judging by his dishevelled hair and the heavy stubble around his mouth and jaw.

'What did the doctors say about Nelly's condition?'

'That it was a stroke, and a serious one,' he said shortly, crumpling up the disposable coffee cup and stuffing it into a recycling bin. 'That we shouldn't hold out hope of a full recovery. Maybe not even a partial one.' He swallowed. 'Given her frail condition, the consultant said she could go at any minute.'

'Oh, Alex.' She touched his arm. 'I'm so sorry.'

Glancing down at her hand, his eyes suddenly brimmed with tears. He moved off at once, as though to hide his distress, and her hand fell back to her side.

'Thank you,' he said thickly, striding towards the maternity wing. She almost had to run to keep up with him, taking two steps to every one of his. 'But I believe in Nelly,' he threw back at her, his voice curt. 'She's a fighter, too, like Thelma. I only wish I'd known sooner about her condition.'

They found Thelma in the neonatal intensive care unit, sitting in a wheelchair beside an incubator, intent on her newborn son, who lay asleep inside under the warming lamps.

'Good to see you awake at last.' With a forced grin, Alex bent to kiss Thelma on the forehead. 'I see someone's got the right idea, sleeping it off.' He straightened, studying the baby. 'How's he doing?'

'He'll survive. Just needs plenty of TLC.'

Jennifer couldn't take her eyes off the baby. His eyes were closed in sleep, his face flushed, tiny fists clenched on either side of his head. In an oversized nappy and with his head warmed by a knitted woollen hat, the baby looked fragile and vulnerable. It took her breath away, realising how close he had come to not making it.

'And here you are already, giving it to him in spadefuls. I love the knitted hat. Very haute couture.' Alex pushed his hands into his pockets, his gaze shifting back to his sister. 'Shouldn't you be resting, though, sis? Not that I'm criticising. But you're not exactly in top form yourself.'

'Resting? Are you kidding?' Thelma's voice rose. 'I couldn't lie in that bloody bed a minute longer, wondering where you were and what was happening. At least here I can do something useful. I kept asking the nurses, but nobody was able to tell me a single thing about Nana, except she'd had a stroke. And your mobile was turned off.'

'Sorry. Hospital regulations.'

'Whatever.' Thelma made a face. 'Anyway, that's why I asked what's-her-name . . .'

'Jennifer,' he growled.

'Yes, Jennifer.' She glanced in Jennifer's direction unapologetically. 'That's why I asked her to bring you to see me.' Thelma's voice cracked. 'If you must know, I've been worried sick about Nana.'

'Honestly, I'm sorry about that.' Alex put his arm around Thelma's shoulders. 'It wasn't deliberate. I thought you'd be asleep, that's all.'

Jennifer saw genuine contrition in his face. Tears pricked at her eyes, and she felt suddenly awkward, intruding on this private moment between brother and sister.

'How could anyone sleep with all this going on?' Thelma searched his face with a nervous air. 'So? How is Nana?'

'Critical but stable. She's on the special care ward at the moment, but she'll be going into a private room once she's out of danger.' From his lack of detail, Jennifer guessed he had decided not to share their grandmother's cancer diagnosis with her yet. That wasn't something his sister needed to hear right now. Thelma had enough to worry about with her premature baby. 'I'm going back to Porro Park to fetch some of her things, so she feels more at home when she comes round.'

'What a good idea,' Thelma said quickly. 'I've made a list of things I want too. Can you do a sweep of my bedroom while you're at it?'

'Me?'

Her face stiffened. 'Beneath you to find my hairbrush and slippers, is it?'

'No, I just meant ...' Alex struggled for the words to express how exhausted and helpless he felt right now, and gave up. 'Okay, I'll see what I can do.'

'Give me the list,' Jennifer said, and held out her hand. 'I'll get what you need.'

He looked round at her in silent gratitude.

'Fine, it's back in my room.' Thelma was staring hungrily

at her baby again. 'Come here and meet your nephew, Alex. Isn't he just the most gorgeous thing you've ever seen?'

'Not as gorgeous as you,' Alex said promptly, and his sister laughed.

'Take some photos of us together,' she ordered him, turning her head to smile beatifically at her child. She wriggled a hand through a porthole cut in the transparent sides of the special care incubator to stroke the baby's cheek. 'Try to get us both in the shot, would you? Nana's missing all this. She'll need the photos for when she's awake.'

He took out his smartphone and obeyed, snapping off a slew of impromptu shots of mother and baby. 'You shouldn't even be out of bed,' he told her.

'I'm in a wheelchair.'

'All the same.'

'Can I see those photos?' He held out the phone and Thelma groaned. 'I really must redo my roots. Hang on a tick . . .' She tidied her hair, then sat up straight and smiled for the camera, showing perfect white teeth. 'Take some for Instagram, would you? Try not to show my big wobbly belly.' Afterwards, she sagged back into her chair with a weary laugh. 'Oh my God, I'm knackered. I wonder if they deliver espressos here. If I don't get caffeine soon, I'm going to die.'

Alex put his phone away. 'Have you thought of a name for him?'

'I have a list, but it's back at the house. I wasn't preparing to name a baby today.' Her face closed up, suddenly defensive. 'Have you told Stuart?'

'I left a message on his answering service when you were first admitted. Then another one when . . .' He fell silent.

'When it looked like I was going to croak?' Thelma nodded to Jennifer. 'Yes, I heard all about my near descent into Hades. I don't remember much about it, frankly. One minute I was writhing in agony, the next someone was putting a mask over my face, and then nothing.' She bit her lip. 'Did Stuart reply?'

'Not yet.'

She drew a shaky breath. 'Bastard.'

'That doesn't mean anything. He may not have got the message yet. You know what Stuart's like, always on the move. Or maybe he's on his way here, and hasn't had time to reply. It must be a good five hours on the train from London. More, if he's decided to drive.'

'I don't want to see him.'

'Thelma . . .'

'I'm serious, Alex.'

'Look, I'll leave you to think about it. I've got to whisk Jennifer home and collect Nana's things. Yes, and yours too.' He gave her a smile. 'Don't worry, I haven't forgotten about your hairbrush.'

'And my list of baby names if you can find it. Thanks, sweetie.' Thelma narrowed her eyes as he bent to kiss her cheek. 'Is something wrong?' she asked abruptly, glancing from him to Jennifer. 'You both look odd. As if there's something you're not telling me.'

Jennifer felt her stomach clench. She did not know what to say.

'Of course not,' Alex began with a casual air, then stopped, seeing his sister's raised eyebrows. Awkwardly, he shoved both hands deep in his pockets. 'I should have known there was no point trying to hide it from you. It's Nana.' He grimaced. 'Look, I'm afraid it's bad news. And I'm not talking about the stroke.'

Thelma's eyes widened with sudden apprehension.

'Go on,' she whispered.

It was nearly six o'clock when they finally left the hospital. The sun was still bright and hot; it was another of those long, unrelentingly sunny days. The kind that made it hard to believe anyone could be sick or dying in such glorious weather.

Alex stopped outside the maternity wing and lifted his face to the heat. For a moment he stood silently, eyes closed, ignoring the bustle of people and traffic around them in the busy hospital car park. Then his eyes snapped open at the sound of voices and he turned round, just in time to have his photograph taken by a burly man with a professional-looking camera around his neck.

Jennifer felt sure she must have been in the shot too.

It wasn't a comfortable thought.

'He's over here!' The photographer took another few dozen shots of them both as Jennifer stared in astonishment, his flash going off, presumably to ensure a good shot of their celebrity target. 'It's Delgardo all right. With some woman.'

'We need to get out of here,' Alex said urgently, turning his back on the man. He started to walk away with long strides, Jennifer hurrying beside him to keep up.

'You've got my car keys,' she told him.

'Don't worry about that. I made some calls earlier. Sorted

it all out.' He glanced at her, his face unreadable. 'How are you with heights?'

'Sorry?'

The photographer had run around ahead of them, right out into the road, and was snapping more pictures.

A woman was with him now, holding out a microphone wired up to an iPad, by the look of it. 'Alex, Alex, over here,' she called out, pushing the mic towards them. 'Is it true your love child has just been born by Caesarean section? That he's fighting for his life in there? Are you worried he may not make it, Alex?'

To Jennifer's amazement, Alex grabbed her hand and performed an abrupt about-turn, doubling back towards the entrance to the maternity wing.

But there were more reporters bundling out of the doors, their eyes lighting up at the sight of their prey. They swarmed towards Alex and Jennifer, more cameras raised in their direction, more insulting questions being thrown at him.

Jennifer felt awful on his behalf.

'Why don't you go away?' She shielded her face with her bag. 'What are you even doing here? This is a hospital. Have some respect.'

'We had a tip-off Alex Delgardo was here.' The reporter who had spoken shoved a mic under her nose, demanding, 'What's your name, love? Are you Alex's latest? How do you feel about him having a baby with another woman?'

Incensed, she glared at the man. 'How dare you? Get your facts straight, at least. That's his sister in there. Not his girlfriend.'

A great roar went up from the crowd at this, and the hubbub of voices soared. Several of the reporters clamped mobiles to their ears and started shouting her words down the phone to whoever was on the other end.

Alex shot her a furious look.

'Sorry,' she said, realising she had just made a colossal mistake.

Thankfully, at that moment a limousine with discreetly blacked-out windows drew up at the kerb. The driver, wearing a peaked cap and uniform, got out and ran round to open the back door.

'Mr Delgardo,' he said, inclining his head to Alex. He stared at the press, clearly unnerved. 'I hope I didn't keep you waiting. Traffic's quite heavy.'

'Just get us out of here, all right?' Alex took Jennifer's elbow and guided her towards the open door. 'After you.'

'I've never been in a limo before.'

'There's a first time for everything. Better hurry up before we get mobbed.'

A small crowd of onlookers had gathered outside the door of the maternity department, staring at Alex. Several had taken their phones out and were filming him, no doubt for their social media accounts.

Filming both of us, she thought with sudden apprehension, and dived into the back seat of the limo, her head turned away from the cameras.

Alex climbed into the limousine beside her and the chauffeur shut the door, hurrying back to the driver's side. Through the blacked-out windows, Jennifer saw the reporters turn away, losing interest now their prey was safely out of reach. But they had got the story they'd come looking for, she felt certain of that.

If only she'd stayed calm and ignored the provocation.

As the limousine pulled sharply away from the kerb, Jennifer leant back in her seat, exhausted and depressed. The cream leather upholstery was cool against her back, the air conditioning a miracle after the stifling heat outside.

'Champagne, sir?' Over the intercom, the driver's voice was oddly intrusive in the enclosed space. 'There's a bottle chilling in the cabinet. And strawberries.'

Alex hit the intercom again. 'Thank you. Just drive.'

'Very good, sir.'

He clicked off the intercom.

'I'm sorry,' Jennifer said, feeling like an idiot.

'Forget about it.'

'They were just so rude. I thought it would help if—'

'It never helps.'

'I see that now.' Her cheeks were hot with shame. 'I should have kept my mouth shut. Like you did.'

'It doesn't matter. It's done now.'

She could have kicked herself. But he was right. It was done now, and she couldn't take it back. She only hoped Thelma wouldn't hate her even more than she did already.

'I'm sorry about Nelly, too. But there's still hope. Isn't there?'

'I doubt it.' His head was turned away, staring out of the window as the limousine joined the evening traffic outside the hospital grounds.

'I like Nelly . . .' Her voice broke. 'She . . . I . . .'

Tears brimmed in her eyes, blurring her vision, then

tumbled down her cheeks. *Damn it!* she thought, clenching her fists by her sides. She hated crying.

'I'm so sorry,' she somehow managed to say through her tears. 'I wasn't trying to hide the truth from you earlier. Nelly only told me about her diagnosis before we drove out to the hospital.'

He said nothing, which made her feel even worse.

'I should have told you straight away. But I didn't get a chance. Everything was happening so fast. Then she collapsed, and—'

'Jennifer,' he said hoarsely, interrupting her.

With an effort, she lifted her head.

Their eyes met.

Alex made a rough noise under his breath, then abruptly leant forward and put his lips against hers.

Shocked to the core, she nearly pushed him away. Alex Delgardo didn't want *her*. Not really, not deep down. This was less about her, and more about him needing someone to take his mind off what just happened at the hospital. About a desperate need for physical comfort and reassurance amid the terrible awareness that he was about to lose his beloved grandmother and there was nothing he could do about it.

She ought to say no, maybe even slap his face again.

But perhaps she needed a little comforting too.

Just one kiss, at least.

Pure human instinct took over. Her arms went around his neck, and then Jennifer was touching and kissing him back, eyes closed against the bitter reality of her world.

CHAPTER TWENTY-NINE

Jennifer did not know why she had given in to what was clearly brain fever and returned his kiss. But, oh goodness, there was no going back now. She was kissing him. Alex Delgardo. In a limousine with blacked-out windows, like something out of a Hollywood film. She had secretly imagined this moment, lying in bed at night on her own, but nothing could have prepared her for the reality. As soon as their mouths had touched, her nervous system went into overdrive, tiny electric shocks sparking everywhere in her body, her skin alive with intense awareness, her breathing rapid, heart thudding under her ribs like she'd been running too fast.

His large hands framed her face, and he kissed her deeply.

She trembled against him, utterly lost to reason and a sense of her surroundings, consumed by a need she had not felt in years. Not even with . . .

Raphael.

This wasn't Raphael Tregar.

'Jenny,' he said, and kissed her throat, repeating her name in a voice that suggested he felt the same, as though he were drowning. 'Oh God, what are we doing?'

'Good question,' she mumbled, eyes still closed.

One of his hands pushed under her top, finding her breast, and she gasped. It ought to have been funny. Being felt up by a celeb in the back of a limo. A story to tell Caro later in a whispered, giggling conversation in some pub. Except she wasn't laughing. And neither was he. They were both in deadly earnest.

A rhythmic buzzing against her hip recalled her to sanity.

'I ...' Swallowing, she forced her eyes open. They were inches apart. Alex looked intent, his own eyes still closed, his breathing shallow. 'I think that's your phone.'

His eyes snapped open and he stared back at her, a hard colour running up his face. He said nothing. But his hand stopped its slow exploration, then reluctantly withdrew.

Alex answered his mobile, head turned away, looking out of the window. 'Yes?' His tone was curt. He listened for a moment without saying anything, then said, 'Understood,' and ended the call as abruptly as he had begun it.

While he was on the phone, Jennifer had scooted back over to her own side of the seat, tidied her hair and pulled down her top, which was sadly rucked up. She noted him furtively doing the same after the call ended, his dark hair slightly dishevelled where she must have clutched it at one stage, dragging him closer.

She was in pain, too.

But this wasn't going to solve anything. Nelly's care was what they should be focused on right now. Not each other.

Alex shoved his phone back into his pocket and turned towards her, still flushed but seemingly back under control.

'Well,' he said awkwardly.

'Forget it.'

'Sir?' The chauffeur had turned on the intercom. If he was aware of what they'd been doing in the back, there was no hint of it in his smooth, respectful voice. 'We're only a couple of minutes out. I thought you might like to know.'

Alex hit the intercom button again. 'Thank you.' Then he sat back and closed his eyes again as though nothing had happened.

But a kiss was just that, she told herself. A kiss. Their lips had met briefly, followed by a spot of groping and heavy breathing. Nothing the average teenager wouldn't have done in the back of a car, and fairly unremarkable as sexual encounters went.

Of course, Jennifer had felt like her insides were boiling and the top of her head was about to be blown off in some volcanic-style eruption. But she was a single woman living alone, and – petting Ripper aside – kisses of any kind were scarce, let alone kisses like *that*.

Belatedly, the chauffeur's words filtered through to her brain.

'Hold on . . .' Jennifer sat up and stared out of the car window, uncomprehending. 'We can't be home already. We only left Truro about ten minutes ago.'

'Well spotted.'

The limousine slowed almost to a halt, and then turned down a bumpy dirt track marked PRIVATE AIRFIELD.

'What on earth . . .?' She looked round to find him unfastening his seat belt. 'Alex, what are we doing here?'

There were buildings ahead. An aircraft hangar of some

kind, the tin roof battered and loose in places. The limousine bowled over an uneven stretch of grassy track towards the nearest building, then skewed to a halt beside the open hangar doors. Inside were several light aircraft, a couple of men in overalls wandering about. Both men glanced towards the limousine with curious expressions, but did not stop what they were doing to investigate.

'Don't tell me you're a pilot and we're going up in one of those tiny planes?' Jennifer tried to sound calm, but her insides were churning at the thought. 'Is that why you asked if I'm okay with heights?'

'Not entirely.'

She didn't know what that meant, but she was nervous. The chauffeur had opened the door on her side and was waiting patiently for her to get out. 'Miss?' he said, looking in at her.

Unless she wanted to make a scene, it seemed she had little choice. Not looking at him, Jennifer swung her legs out of the limousine and straightened, turning her face to the warmth of the evening sun. Her legs felt decidedly shaky, she realised, taking a few steps away from the car. And not just at the idea of flying.

Alex spoke briefly to the chauffeur, then led her in through the hangar doorway while the uniformed man got back into the car and bounced away over the grassy track. It was cool out of the sun. Alex turned aside to check his phone, his dark head bent in fierce concentration. Jennifer shivered, standing alone, and watched the limo's faint dust trail slowly peter out as it reached the main road and turned off.

In the skies towards the north coast, a black dot appeared. Soon she caught the distant whirr of rotating blades.

'There's our ride,' Alex said, putting his phone away. He stepped out from the hangar and pointed up at the enlarging dot. His face looked pale. 'Ever been in one of those?'

She could see now that it was a helicopter. A small black civilian helicopter with a white logo on the side. And she was apparently going up in *that*?

'Never,' she said flatly, and wondered if it was too late to run after the limo driver.

'Another first, then.' Alex met her nervous gaze, unsmiling. To her surprise, he did not look exactly enthused himself. 'You didn't say how you are with heights.'

'I'll let you know once I've experienced some. I've never even been on a plane, let alone a helicopter. The highest I've been off the ground was sunbathing on the school roof during the holidays.'

The whirling blades grew louder as the helicopter began to descend, a deep and constant *thwack-thwack-thwack* that filled the still evening air. She could even see the pilot now, a face peering down at them through the cockpit window. He looked vaguely familiar, but her brain refused to function properly, pushing the thought away.

Any minute now, the helicopter would land to collect them, and then would presumably take off again, only this time with her inside.

Oh, good grief.

A sudden terror swamped her, and she took a step backwards, shaking her head in absolute refusal. 'Sorry, no way.'

'If you can manage a broomstick . . .'

Jennifer shot him a fulminating look. 'Seriously?'

'Trust me, this is the quickest way home. And it's perfectly safe.'

'I'd rather walk.'

'No, you wouldn't.' But she noticed Alex was also looking nervous as he steered her forward. 'Please don't be difficult,' he said, his words terse in her ear. 'I need you to help me collect the things on the list, then fly back to the hospital as soon as possible. I have to be there for Nana when she wakes up.'

'Well, since you put it like that . . .' Trees in a nearby field bent and swayed in the fierce wind whisked up by the helicopter's descent. 'Okay, I'll do it,' she said grimly. 'But don't blame me if I throw up on you.'

'I consider myself quite easy-going, but I draw the line at people vomiting on me.' He raised his voice. 'Assuming I don't throw up first, that is.'

'You don't like helicopters either?'

'It's a long story.'

Something in his voice made her turn and look up at him curiously. 'I like long stories, remember? You could tell me on the journey. Keep my mind off the long drop to the ground.'

'Maybe another time,' he said, a distant look on his face.

There was some mystery there. But what?

He held out his hand. 'Follow me and keep your head down. Unless you fancy re-enacting a scene from the French Revolution.'

'Sorry?'

'The guillotine.' He cut an imaginary line across his throat.

'Basically, you don't want to lose your head. He'll touch down in a moment. But the blades won't stop rotating.'

Jennifer took his hand, though she was far from eager to leave the ground. 'Why not?' She had to shout to make herself heard now.

'Because he'll be taking off again as soon as we're on board.'

Together they ran across the grassy expanse of the private airfield, over a tarmacked runway and into a large field adjacent to an area marked out as a helipad. The grass was short and dry, scorched brown in patches by the long, hot summer they'd had.

He'll be taking off again as soon as we're on board.

She felt dizzy already.

By the time they got there, the helicopter had touched down, the air churning madly, making the trees sway. Close up, she could see the pilot more clearly, a fair-haired man wearing a helmet and headset with a microphone angled beside his mouth.

Brodie!

He waved them on board, smiling sadly at her. No doubt he too was distressed by the news about Nelly. 'Hello,' he mouthed at her, his voice inaudible above the sound of the rotating blades.

She was pleased to see Brodie again, but not even remotely reassured. Her heart thumping wildly, her palms sweating, Jennifer clambered into the helicopter behind the pilot's seat.

Was it too late to refuse?

She'd never felt the urge to fly anywhere; she hated the idea of flying, and had avoided it all her life.

Now she was inside a helicopter, near deafened by the unearthly roar of its blades, and fumbling with some kind of unfathomable harness. Was this her safety belt? It looked more like something used to tether a mad goat. She banged two pieces of metal pointlessly together and felt like crying.

Alex bundled in beside her and shut the door, which softened the din from the blades. 'Like this,' he yelled in her ear, showing her how to clip her safety belt in place, then shouted, 'Back in the air!' to Brodie, and jerked upwards with his thumb to reinforce the message.

Before she'd even settled properly into her seat, the world gave a sickening lurch and they were rising from the airfield, leaving her stomach somewhere below.

'You'll be fine,' Alex growled in her ear, no doubt seeing her face whiten. 'I've done hundreds of hours in choppers like this. It's a doddle.'

'A doddle. Right.'

Alex ignored her, talking to Brodie now via the mouthpiece, his expression intent. He seemed at home in the swaying helicopter, though she noticed how rigidly he sat, clutching the pilot's seat back with whitened knuckles, his body language tense despite all those 'hundreds of hours' of flight experience.

She herself was feeling less scared now. The sun was low on the horizon in the west, imbuing fields and hills with the most rapturous glow, the ocean shining endlessly into the distance, dazzling blue-gold as it reflected the light. From so high up, everything below looked tiny; vehicles queuing on the busy Atlantic Highway were like toy cars, towns and villages passing in a blur of thatched roofs and winding lanes.

And the patchwork of green fields as far as she could see across Cornwall and into Devon was breathtaking in its complexity.

Suddenly the helicopter banked, taking her by surprise.

'Ouch!' Having banged her head against the window, she righted herself, leaning too far the other way and bashing into Alex instead. 'Oops!'

His hand shot out to support her as she bounced about. The helicopter had shifted direction, she realised, and was now heading north along the coast towards Pethporro. Alex looked out of the other window, nodding sombrely and saying something into the mouthpiece that sounded like 'coats'. Or, possibly, 'goats'.

She glanced down at his hand, which had somehow slipped from her shoulder to her hip, and felt a prickling flush in her face. The warmth from his hand, nestled against her hip, was burning through her clothes to her skin, setting her alight all over again.

Was she now a 'sure thing' for him?

If they'd been in a car, not a helicopter, she would have demanded he stop and let her out. But that was impossible; the shadow of the helicopter was racing beneath them over the cliffs and rolling Atlantic waves.

Alex had noticed her discomfort at last. He shifted his hand, then angled the mouthpiece away, shouting, 'Brodie says the goats are missing Nelly,' at her.

'Poor things.'

'They're not eating.'

'I'll take them some crackers once we get home,' she yelled back.

Home.

Except it wasn't her home. It was his, and she wasn't even a bona fide guest there. She was his tenant.

Yes, they'd had a mad kiss in the back of his limo. But as soon as Nelly was out of hospital – she would not consider any alternative to that scenario – and Thelma had decided where she and the baby would be living, Alex Delgardo would be off back to Hollywood or London or New York, or wherever he was filming next.

Movie stars don't settle in Cornwall, she thought grimly, staring out of the window. Celebrities might visit the country for a few months, looking for peace and quiet. But eventually they all returned to their glamorous lives and forgot about the ordinary people they'd left behind in the sticks.

She had to protect herself.

Protect her heart.

The helicopter dipped, beginning its descent. As promised, the trip had taken no time at all. Ahead, she could see the familiar dark green woodlands around Pixie Cottage and then the broad lawns of the park. The trees below danced about in the helicopter's noisy wake, leafy tops thrashing from side to side.

A few ghostly white figures skipped into the apple orchard, looking panicked.

Nelly's goats.

'I wonder if the workmen have fixed up the cottage yet,' she said loudly, as Brodie set the helicopter down on the lawn. 'I should call Caroline tonight and get back to my own place. I don't seem to have done much work recently, and my book won't write itself.'

He didn't reply.

CHAPTER THIRTY

A week after returning from the hospital, Jennifer drove down the coast to the port of Boscastle, where she was booked for an open-air storytelling session as part of a tourist event. She arrived an hour early and nipped into the Museum of Witchcraft, one of her favourite haunts. A few people nodded to her in passing; folklorists like herself and adherents of the magical arts. One woman even stopped for a quick chat about an invitation-only event later in the year, where they needed a storyteller.

Much to her relief, nobody mentioned the recent press coverage, or the speculations that she was Alex's girlfriend. It had been a shock to see her own face leering out of the national newspapers or on the internet, snapped side by side with Alex. HERO DELGARDO SAVES THE DAY had been the headline in one sensationalist gossip mag, where it was speculated that only Alex's quick actions had saved the lives of his sister and nephew.

She had moved back to Pixie Cottage the day after her return from Truro. It had seemed like the only thing to do, now Nelly was in hospital. And the workmen had done a good job. Her bedroom had been fully replastered and repainted, and was now cosy and comfortable.

She had slept deeply on her first night home, curled up tight in her own bed at last, a relieved Ripper purring and kneading at the pillows.

But her dreams had been full of Alex.

It seemed she could escape him physically, but not mentally. And judging from the ache in her heart whenever she stared out at the brilliant sunshine, or lay reading in the bee-filled garden, emotional escape too was impossible.

The museum always had a calming influence on her nerves. She loved to wander through its dark, maze-like rooms, peering into cabinets at mystical objects and flicking through old books. Especially now, when everything else in her life seemed to have gone wrong. It took her mind off Alex Delgardo, if only for a few happy hours.

Afterwards, she slipped into the sunny National Trust café next door, and enjoyed a black coffee and cheesy scone while making notes about a Cornish folk tale she was working on for her new book. Yet she couldn't seem to engage her interest, her notes lacklustre, her brain unable to make the leap of comprehension between one idea and the next.

She strolled through hot sunshine to the famous harbour instead, like one of the many tourists, and stared down at the bright, glittering waters.

Last winter, coming out of the Museum of Witchcraft, she had suddenly found herself face-to-face with Raphael Tregar – and Hannah Clitheroe. She'd seen the way Raphael looked at Hannah that day and had known instantly that for her, it was over. But of course it had taken months to give up all hope of getting him back.

Even now she felt the old aching sense of loss, and wondered if she would ever truly get over him. If she'd be able to look Raphael Tregar in the face again and not yearn for what she could never have.

By the time she had made her way back to the centre of the village, a large crowd had already gathered for the open-air event. There were morris dancers knocking sticks and whirling about in their traditional raggedy outfits, faces painted in garish colours to entertain the tourists. At a guess, she estimated there must be several hundred people there, crammed onto the narrow streets or watching from nearby beer gardens.

Jennifer too watched the dancing for a while, and took a few photographs. Then she ducked into the ladies' toilets at the Cobweb Inn to change into her costume.

'And now for our storyteller!'

On cue, she stepped out into the rough circle made by the ring of spectators, wrapped in her long cloak and with her hair dressed with flowers and ribbons.

The crowd erupted, some whistling, others clapping and stamping their feet. The din was tremendous, quite nerve-racking. Her heart was thudding as she raised her arms wide and turned in a slow circle, a gesture invoking the magic territory of the story. She would never get used to so much attention – it still left her mouth dry, all the applause and the people staring.

But when she opened her mouth to begin her tale, the nerves always seemed to slip away and the storytelling took over . . .

'Once upon a time,' she began loudly, thrilled by how the crowd hushed at the sound of her voice, 'there was a merry-maid who looked after the harbour at Padstow. It was a harbour much like this one at Boscastle, only far deeper in those days, one of the few places along the northern coast where large ships could find safe anchor.'

'What's a merry-maid?' someone called out, and Jennifer turned, smiling at the boy who had spoken.

'I'm glad you asked that question, friend. A merry-maid is an old Cornish term for a mermaid, a woman who lives under the sea like a fish, yet breathes air, the same as humans.'

She swung her cloak in a wide sweep as she walked around the edge of the circle, catching eyes in the crowd, making sure everyone could hear her clearly.

'The merry-maid of Padstow kept a clean harbour, and was much respected by the Cornish. But she was a lonely soul, and it was not long before one of the fishermen of Padstow, named Ralph, caught her eye.'

'*Eye, eye!*' one of the Morris dancers quipped, and everyone laughed.

'Every day, he saw the merry-maid alone on a rock, combing her long golden hair and singing. So he began dropping anchor near the rock and listening to her song. His friends in the fishing fleet warned him to stop his ears against her unearthly voice, saying it would come to no good.' Jennifer paused for effect. 'But Ralph was smitten.

'Soon, the merry-maid coaxed him out of his boat to

swim with her on long, warm evenings, or to sit beside her on the rock, learning the strange words to her song. In fact, Ralph became so enamoured of this merry-maid, he took her home, wrapping her shining tail in a long cloak like this one,' and here she swirled the cloak about her ankles, laughing when the crowd cooed and applauded, 'so his parents would not suspect her true form.

'But when winter came, Ralph no longer saw the merry-maid. He forgot about her lovely song and her golden hair, and fell in love with a human woman instead.

'When spring came, and Ralph's boat sailed past her without stopping, the merry-maid became distraught. Her song grew louder and more discordant as the weeks passed. But Ralph paid her no heed, his mind on his lovely bride-to-be. In her despair, the merry-maid neglected her duties to the harbour, and it silted up with sand, so larger ships could no longer stop there. She dragged on the nets of passing fishing vessels until they ran aground, and tried to lure sailors to their deaths on the rocks along the coast.

'Eventually, one fisherman grew so angry he took a crossbow and shot the merry-maid, leaving her terribly wounded. She cursed Padstow harbour and all fishermen before disappearing beneath the waves. And that might be where her story ends, but for one curious thing.

'Ralph married his beloved, and took his new bride out in his boat. Nobody knows how – maybe a summer storm arose, or there was an argument between the two – but his wife fell overboard and was never seen again.'

'Sounds like foul play to me!' a woman shouted from a nearby beer garden, and was nudged by her giggling friends.

'Maybe.' Jennifer threw her arms wide in a dramatic gesture. 'But from that day on, at dawn or twilight, the fishermen of Padstow claim to have seen two figures on that rock, not one ... Two merry-maids, sitting companionably side by side, combing out their golden hair and singing unearthly songs of the sea.'

At least some people ended up happy in these old stories, Jennifer thought, bowing low as the crowd applauded.

But at what cost?

About three weeks after the birth of Thelma's child, as Jennifer turned out the downstairs lights in the cottage and began heading upstairs to bed, she was startled by a knock at the front door.

It was nearly midnight and pitch-black outside.

There had been no sound of a car, nor any light. The air was warm and still, the night electric with tension. Cornwall lay wrapped under a spell of hot weather that had not broken for weeks, except for the odd summer shower.

Whoever it was had come on foot through the woods.

Standing at the base of the stairs, one hand on the wooden newel post, Jennifer looked back at the closed door. She was still in her short, sleeveless summer dress, but was on her way up to change into her PJs. She'd been working hard all evening and had just downed a stiff gin and tonic to help her settle.

Now her senses were prickling.

The knock came again, more insistent. Then a familiar voice growled through the letter box, half annoyed, half amused, 'I know you're in there, Jenny. Come on, open up.'

It was Alex.

Opening the cottage door, she peered out at him. He was dressed all in black, which didn't help her see him against the pitch darkness outside. 'It's gone midnight,' she pointed out with pretend impatience, hoping it would mask her excitement at seeing him again. His ego didn't need inflating any further. 'What do you want, Alex?'

'I thought witches lived for the night-time?'

'Not this witch.'

Alex looked her up and down, taking in the short yellow summer dress. 'Cocoa and an early night with the cat instead? Very cosy.'

'Gin, actually.'

'Better and better.' He stepped neatly aside as Ripper, who had pricked up his ears at the first knock, slipped past them into the night. Turning to watch the cat disappear into the shadows, he called out, 'Happy hunting, Ripper.'

Then he turned and smiled at her. A dangerous smile, she thought warily.

'May I come in?' he asked.

'Will you go away if I say no?'

'Try it and see.'

Oh, bloody hell.

She left the door open for him and went to pour herself a nightcap. It was unlikely she'd get much sleep now anyway. Her head would be buzzing with Delgardo for hours.

'What a good idea,' he said huskily, suddenly at her elbow.

'God, you made me jump!'

'Twitchy little thing, aren't you?' He raised his eyebrows at her furious expression. 'Difficult evening?'

'You have no idea.'

'I wouldn't bet on that. Any chance of a G and T for me?'

She slopped some gin into a glass and pushed it towards him. 'Help yourself to tonic.'

'Thank you so much,' he said, all politeness.

'What are you doing here, Alex? You haven't been in touch for ages.'

Well, several days, at any rate. Not since his last update on the hospital situation, when he'd telephoned to say Thelma was home at Porro Park, though her baby would have to stay in the hospital for another fortnight at least, and Nelly appeared to be on the mend.

He didn't reply, handing her the bottle of tonic.

She added a healthy dose to her own gin. She didn't want to get drunk. Then a sudden, terrible thought struck her and she glanced at him sideways, her eyes widening.

'It's not Nelly, is it? Is that why you're here?'

'I am here because of Nana, yes.' With a brief smile, Alex clinked his glass against hers. 'She's finally out of hospital.'

She stared. 'Nelly's *home*?'

'Brodie and I brought her back yesterday. Didn't you hear the chopper?'

She had indeed heard the helicopter rising noisily into the air the day before, and even caught a glimpse of it returning later, the leafy trees bending in its wake. But she'd thought nothing much about the sighting. Alex's helicopter had been in use several times a week recently, no doubt ferrying him to and from the hospital at Truro, saving him the lengthy road journey between there and North Cornwall.

'Yes, but I didn't realise what it meant.' She drank a silent toast to the old lady, who had survived a serious stroke against the odds. Hanging on by her toenails, Caroline had put it after she'd popped into the hospital to visit Nelly last week. It seemed her tenacity had won out. 'That's marvellous. How is she?'

His smile faded. 'As well as can be expected.'

Jennifer waited, seeing him struggle for words and knowing he had more to say. Her heart sank. There was bad news coming.

'I persuaded Nana to have some more tests done while she was at Truro,' he said slowly. 'She tried to resist but we talked her round, me and Thelma. And it's worse than we thought. Her cancer is so widespread now, the consultant thinks she may . . .' Alex's voice had thickened, and he stopped abruptly, taking a gulp of gin before continuing. 'He's given her a few weeks. That's all she's got left. Three bloody weeks.'

'Oh no, poor Nelly.' Tears sprang quickly to her eyes, but she knew it wouldn't help him if she shed them. Her heart broke for them all, though. It didn't necessarily make things easier to know the end in advance. Sometimes it actually made things worse, because then life became about counting down the days and hours, about marking 'last times' for every activity. 'Is there nothing they can do to give her more time?'

'There's a new drug trial, but she's too old to qualify.'

'Alex, I'm so sorry.'

'It didn't sound like a good fit, anyway. Nasty side effects. None of us wants that for her. Not at this stage.' Rubbing his chin as he nodded, not meeting her eyes, it was clear Alex was struggling to contain the depth of his grief. 'I've finally got her to accept an offer of pain management, though. That's something. We brought home a whole pharmacy of drugs from the hospital, with Nana complaining all the way about hating pills and how she prefers nature's remedies. But at least I was able to leave her sleeping peacefully before I walked over to see you.'

He grimaced. 'Turns out she's been in absolute agony for weeks, but kept quiet about it. That's why she refused to tell anyone how sick she was, apparently. Because she didn't want . . .' Again, he choked. 'Didn't want to *make a fuss.*'

Her heart cracked for both of them. God, life was so unfair.

'That sounds like Nelly.'

His mouth twitched. 'Stubborn as an ox, my old nan.'

'She's not the only one.'

He downed half his gin in one swallow, then gave her a suspicious look. 'Come on then, out with it.'

'Sorry?'

'I sense a biting remark on its way.' He grimaced. 'But nothing I don't deserve. I didn't treat you very fairly at the hospital, did I?'

She fell silent.

'It was the shock of hearing you tell that doctor about Nelly's diagnosis . . . That she was dying. I lost my mind for a short while there. But I realise now you weren't hiding it from me. It was Nelly herself who'd done that, not you.' He cleared his throat. 'I behaved badly. I'm sorry.'

'It doesn't matter now.' Jennifer looked away, feeling awkward. In the silence that followed, she heard the ticking of the mantel clock and the faint cry of a hunting owl outside in the woods. She became suddenly aware of the lateness of the hour, and that they were completely alone together in the little cottage. 'But you didn't walk all the way here just to tell me about Nelly,' she added softly. 'Did you?'

When he didn't reply, his face stiff and unreadable, Jennifer turned away, her heart thumping. Okay, so maybe she was wrong. Maybe Nelly *was* the only reason he'd come here tonight, for a shoulder to cry on, and the rest of her guesswork – that Alex felt the same about her as she did about him – was pure fantasy on her part.

It was tempting to pour herself another generous measure of gin, only with rather less tonic this time. But she didn't trust herself enough to drink heavily in his company. Not with the kisses they'd shared in the limousine still playing on an endless loop in her head. Not mere kisses, either. There had been hands involved . . .

Talk about madness. This man was completely out of her league. Even if anything did happen between them, there was no way it would last for very long. He would go jetting back to Hollywood soon enough, and she would be left broken-hearted.

She stumbled back towards the door, half tripping over a stack of local newspapers. Sodding gin. Or maybe she hadn't drunk enough of the stuff.

If he stayed much longer, she was going to make an idiot of herself.

'It's late,' she said, in as dignified a tone as she could manage. 'Perhaps you should go.'

'Jenny,' he said, catching her by the arm as she passed and pulling her towards him. 'You're right,' he said huskily. 'That wasn't the only reason I came over tonight.'

CHAPTER THIRTY-ONE

'I came to invite you to a party at Porro Park,' he said, releasing her arm, and she stared into his eyes blankly, taken entirely by surprise.

'A party?' she repeated.

'It's Nelly's ninetieth birthday next weekend. She doesn't know yet, so please don't mention it to her, but I'm marking the occasion with a surprise gathering. Friends, family and special guests.' He was smiling, but she could hear despair in his voice. And she could guess why. Nelly only had a few weeks left. This party was being thrown not so much to celebrate her ninetieth birthday, she realised, as to let the old lady go out on a high. Then he shocked her by asking, 'Will you come?'

'*Me?*'

'Of course.' This time his smile was genuine. 'Nana's really taken you to her heart. I know she'd want you to be there.'

She blinked. 'Are you sure? She didn't seem very happy that I broke my promise to her and told the doctor about her diagnosis. And in your hearing, too.'

'She wasn't hugely ecstatic about that, no,' he admitted. 'But when she came round, in the hospital, she herself admitted that she'd been wrong to hide it from us for so long.' His voice softened. 'Besides, if you don't come to the party, you'll never find out if she's forgiven you or not.'

Jennifer met his eyes, smiling shyly, and then wished she hadn't. There was so much emotion there, she didn't think she could bear it. Not when it seemed to echo what was going on inside her, too.

'Th-thank you,' she stammered, not knowing where to look. 'I'd love to be there. It's very kind of you to ask.'

'Not at all, you'd be missed if you didn't come.' He seemed to relax a little. Mission accomplished, perhaps. Finishing his gin, he put the glass down next to hers. 'Well, thanks for the drink.' There was another awkward silence. They were really very good at them, she thought. No conversation between them escaped without at least one long, prickling silence. 'You were on your way up to bed, weren't you? I'd better go, leave you to it.'

She drew a sharp breath, suddenly overwhelmed by the most appalling sense of loneliness. *Don't go*, she wanted to cry. But somehow she kept silent and dared not even look at him, her lips pressed hard together, her fists clenched at her side.

'Unless you want me to stay?' he added softly.

Her heart rate accelerated at those words. Stupid, stupid heart.

Do I want him to stay?

Her whole being screamed, *yes*.

But she couldn't make her mouth and tongue work to say the word. Because she was still afraid. For God's sake, what if she was reading this all wrong? What if he didn't mean it the way she thought he did? What if he meant stay for another drink? Stay for a chat? Not stay to make love, to kiss and wrap their arms around each other, to hold fast to that heat in the dark night . . .

'I don't want your pity—' he began in a low voice.

'You think that's what this is?' she interrupted him, her frank gaze lifting to his face, her tone suddenly fierce. 'Pity?'

'What happened in the limo—'

'That wasn't pity either. And nor is this.' She took his hand and pulled it to her cheek, which was warm and flushed. Her skin tingled at the electric contact between them, skin to skin, and she knew he could feel it too, from the way his eyes slowly widened, his intent gaze searching her face. 'Are you blind?'

'I'm beginning to wonder,' he muttered.

'We shouldn't, of course,' she said in the same breath, then half laughed, not elaborating on that statement. This was madness. It couldn't end except with goodbye. How could it? He had his world, she had hers. There was no half-way territory for them to inhabit, except for a few incredible hours perhaps in the privacy of a bed. Her eyes devoured him instead, pushing logic aside. 'But I don't think I can help myself.'

'Good, because neither can I.'

Alex pulled her close, his body strong and graceful as a dancer's. And she wanted to dance with him, to whirl him about the floor and let him whirl her too.

'Jenny . . .'

There was that agony in his face again.

'What is it?' she whispered, daring to brush her fingers down his cheek. 'Look, I know you're hurting. I can see pain in you every time you move, hear it every time you speak. And it's not just about Nelly, is it? It's something else.'

He didn't answer, but buried his face in her throat instead, kissing her hair, his warm lips tickling her skin. It was maddeningly sensual. But of course it was, she told herself impatiently. He was Alex Delgardo, world-famous film star; he knew all the moves. He'd probably kissed dozens of women into adoring compliance.

And left them all.

His hands moulded her against him.

'Jenny,' he repeated hoarsely, as though his grasp of vocabulary had stopped at her name. 'Jenny . . .'

But there was that catch in his breath again, a tiny, barely perceptible hitch that told her, under the smiles and kisses, Alex Delgardo was suffering.

'Alex, please . . . Whatever it is, you can trust me.'

'I want to kiss you,' he whispered back. 'I want to take you to bed.'

She shivered, closing her eyes, and their lips met.

The shock of contact between their mouths sparked up and down her spine, a white-hot flash that left her nerves jangling.

One kiss, she promised herself. Then she would say goodnight.

But her starving body had other plans. Greedy, uncontrollable plans. The more Alex kissed her, the more impossible it became for her to call a halt. Truth was, she wanted him, she was hungry for him, and she'd ceased to worry about whether this would last and she would end up on her own again afterwards.

Sod afterwards. This was for tonight. One magical night only. That was what she told herself anyway, pushing all the other problematic concerns to the back of her mind and kissing him back.

Her skin was soon prickling and running with heat, her hands moving over him too, urging him closer. It was compulsive. She couldn't stop herself and she no longer cared if this was a mistake.

I want to take you to bed.

Though he was edging her nearer to the sofa, in fact, not upstairs to bed. And as soon as the backs of her knees collided with its soft edge, she buckled and collapsed backwards, with him on top of her. To her surprise, Alex seemed prepared for the fall, supporting his weight on his hands as he moved over her, their legs entangled, knees bumping.

'Sorry.' He teased her lower lip between his teeth. 'Did I hurt you?'

'No,' she gasped.

Hungrily, he pulled one of the shoulder straps down on her summer dress. Then the other. Then dragged her bra down and set his lips to her exposed breasts.

'Oh God.' Her face burnt. 'Yes.'

A few minutes and some heated kisses later, her dress was removed and tossed somewhere across the room. Impatient to see him naked too, she tried to drag his tight-fitting black t-shirt over his head, failed spectacularly, and watched while he helped her wrestle it off, his whole body leaning back.

As he threw the t-shirt aside and turned back to her, Jennifer stared up at him aghast, shocked into silence.

His chest and upper abdomen were horribly scarred. Something had happened to him, something violent and appalling. Scars criss-crossed his muscular torso and dipped towards his flat belly, tough snakes that ridged and coiled, ending in tapering reddish-pink networks, like the burning touch of a flail.

'Oh, Alex,' she whispered, and set a fingertip to one of the long, angry scars, tracing it down his ribs. 'These are ... They look so painful. Do they hurt?'

She did not recall ever having seen these scars in any of his films, and he usually did at least one bare-chested scene in his action movies. Which meant his injuries must have been incurred since his last screen appearance. At the hotel bombing?

Was this why he had stopped acting?

Alex smiled grimly and captured her hand, jerking it up to his lips. 'I'll tell you about them another time. But not tonight, okay?'

He kissed her palm, the delicate brush of his tongue there undeniably erotic. Jennifer sucked in her breath. The scars on his torso had shocked her, but when he touched her like that, it was hard to focus on anything but the nagging ache inside.

'Do the scars make a difference, Jenny?' There was a note of uncertainty in his voice. His eyes met hers with sudden intensity. 'To this?'

She understood his fear then, and shook her head. 'Of course not.'

'Good.' Alex stroked her hand down his ruined chest and abdomen, and even lower, making her gasp. 'Because I'm in the mood to make love, not talk. How about you?'

Jennifer awoke with a start, her heart thumping. It was pitch-dark in her little cottage and someone was shouting.

'My fault, my fault!'

What the hell?

Hazily, still lost in her dream, Jennifer scrabbled up against her pillows, staring at the figure by the window. The man was a dark mass, slamming both fists into the wall, and his head too, by the sound of it. Shouting and sobbing now.

Alex.

'My bloody fault, mine, mine, mine . . .'

She was naked, she realised, looking down at herself with a shock. He had kissed her, and things had quickly spiralled out of control. Everything had felt rushed and intense, tinged with desperation. Later, they'd gone upstairs and made love again in her single bed, more slowly, and eventually fallen asleep in each other's arms, sweaty and exhausted.

Now Alex was out of bed again and trying to demolish the cottage with his bare fists. She had no idea why, nor what had occurred to make him leap up and start yelling at nobody with so much fury it made her heart hurt.

Jennifer swung out of bed, not wearing a stitch, and stumbled unsteadily towards him in the dark, unsure of her reception and not wanting a fist in her face.

'Alex?'

He kept yelling and sobbing as though she weren't there. Or he hadn't heard her. Was he sleepwalking?

Snapping on the desk lamp, she studied him by its pale light. His face was tortured but closed in and unaware, as though he were still asleep, caught in some nightmare. Yet his eyes were open. Wild and wide open, staring past her in horror. Where was he?

Her gaze was drawn back to the scars on his torso.

Cruel, vivid scars.

He smashed a hand against the wall again, shouting something about not being able to breathe, then struggled with the window catch, as though planning to hurl himself out.

She tried again, this time more urgent. 'Alex?'

When he still didn't respond, focused on his task, she reached out to touch his bare shoulder. He whirled at once, swearing and knocking her hand away. 'Tell me why! Why them . . . and not me?' The words became a pure howl. He crashed to his knees, weeping, inconsolable. 'Why not *me*?'

'I don't know,' she said helplessly.

Crouching to his level, she touched his face, his throat, his ruined chest. And she didn't know. She was unsure exactly what he was talking about. But she could guess.

The hotel bombing.

Nelly had mentioned it, and indeed she recalled reading about it at the time, shocked by some of the graphic coverage on television and across social media. The carnage left behind by a suicide bomber. Footage that should never have been made public. That must be where he'd got the scars. And the pain he kept returning to, the hurt she had seen in his face.

Why not me?

'Are you talking about the bombing?' she asked gently. 'The hotel? But that wasn't your fault, Alex.'

He groaned, but said nothing. She was still not sure he could hear her.

His skin was cold and clammy, his breathing fast and shallow. Jennifer recalled the breathless horror she'd felt backstage at the town hall, caught in the grip of what he'd called a panic attack, and wondered if this was one of them. Were they night terrors? Or an anxiety hangover from trauma? Whatever the correct diagnosis, she could see that the past was haunting him. Jennifer ached to be able to help him. But this was beyond her skill.

The shouting and crashing about phase seemed to be over, at least. Alex was rocking silently back and forth now, hunched up like a child, arms wrapped around himself.

Self-comforting.

'You're hurt,' she said. 'I mean, *really* hurt. You're bleeding,' she added softly, and put a fingertip to one clenched fist, where the skin was grazed across his knuckles, showing red.

'Why not *me*?' he groaned, still not looking at her. 'Oh God, why not *me*?'

Jennifer stroked his cheek, hoping the gesture would penetrate his bewildered senses where language on its own did not seem to be having much impact.

But he wasn't even aware of her presence.

Abandoning all hope of trying to get through to him, she ran downstairs to find her mobile. Typically, it was nowhere to be seen. Their clothes were strewn everywhere. Breathless and unsettled, she crawled about until she found her phone on the floor beside the sofa, under his trampled t-shirt. The battery was low but there was enough power to make a call.

Flicking through her contacts list, she found the one Brodie had given her when she moved up to Porro Park, 'in case of emergencies'. She rang his mobile number, hoping Brodie wouldn't mind being woken at nearly four o'clock in the morning.

He answered on the third ring, sounding unfazed by her call. 'Hello, Jennifer.'

'I'm sorry to wake you up,' she began tentatively, but Brodie interrupted her, his voice crisp and urgent.

'I wasn't asleep. What is it?'

'It's Alex.'

'So I guessed. What's happened?'

CHAPTER THIRTY-TWO

Jennifer sat for a moment after the call had ended, listening to the hoarse mutterings and thuds from the room above. Her hands were trembling and she felt nauseous. *I'm in shock*, she thought. But Alex was in a far worse state, and he still needed her. She dragged on her clothes in a haphazard fashion and hurried back upstairs, feeling more together now that she had called for back-up and was no longer starkers.

'I've rung Brodie,' she announced, walking into the bedroom.

Alex was still where she'd left him, down on his haunches against the wall, naked and beautiful, even with the scars. His face was ravaged with fear, his eyes squeezed hard shut.

'Brodie,' he whispered, and his eyes opened, though he did not look up at her. He repeated the name several times, like a talisman against bad luck. 'Brodie, Brodie.'

This was progress of a kind; at least he seemed more aware of his surroundings now. 'Come on,' she said firmly, 'let me help you to the bathroom. You don't want Brodie to find you like this, do you?'

Taking his hands, she tried to drag him upright again. Alex resisted, grunting under his breath, his full weight pulling back against hers. Her hands slipped helplessly over his bulging biceps, one tattooed with a crowned serpent, as she struggled to get the huge man upright.

He was so strong and heavy!

'How about a shower?' she said. 'Cold water should wake you up, even if nothing else can. One, two ... three!'

On three, she tugged hard.

Alex lurched to his feet and returned to full consciousness as he swayed there, turning a confused, groggy look on her.

'Jenny? What ... what's going on?'

She hugged him, hugely relieved to have him back and speaking normally. 'I think you were sleepwalking.' She was glad it was over. But it was clear Alex had some serious issues, and she wasn't sure how she felt about that. Not after what she had seen tonight. 'Or sleep-*bashing*.'

He blinked, staring down at his grazed knuckles. 'Shit.'

'You should see the wall.'

'Oh God, not again.' Alex turned as though to survey the damage. But the newly repainted wall was relatively unscathed, just a few scratch marks and a small dent near the window frame. All the same, he groaned in contrition, leaning his forehead against the wall as though exhausted by what he'd been through. 'I'm sorry, Jenny. So sorry.'

Not again.

What did that mean?

She touched his shoulder. 'You don't need to apologise. But you could explain.'

'I can't talk about it.' He set her to one side, gently but with absolute conviction. 'I'm sorry you had to see me like this. But talking isn't going to help. Trust me, I've tried that.'

He glanced down at his scarred torso, swore under his breath and then stumbled across the bedroom. 'Where are my clothes? I need to go.'

'Brodie's on his way.'

'What?'

She took a step back at the anger in his voice. 'Hey, you were out of it. Shouting like a maniac, smashing yourself against the wall. I thought you might jump out of the window. What did you expect me to do?'

He lurched towards the bed and grabbed at the top sheet. Ripping it off the bed, he wound it raggedly around his shoulders, concealing his chest and abdomen. 'Maybe give me the benefit of the doubt first?'

'Alex, what on earth is this about? Talk to me, please.' She pushed a hand through her hair, losing patience with the way he kept rejecting her. 'However bad it is, I'm not going to judge you.'

He gave a bitter laugh. 'You have no idea.'

'Actually, Nelly told me about the bombing. She said you weren't responsible for what happened.'

'Nana wasn't there. And neither were you.'

'So tell me what happened.'

'I can't.' His chin sank onto his chest. The despair and grief in his voice tore her apart. 'It *was* my fault, Jenny, can't you see that? Mine, all mine.'

'Alex, you have to stop blaming yourself like this. It's simply not logical. You're not psychic. You couldn't possibly have known what would happen that night.'

'Oh yes, I could.' His gaze lifted slowly to her face, becoming dangerous. 'We'd had warnings. We'd been told there were extremists active in the area. I ignored all that. I just wanted to enjoy myself.' She heard the disgust and self-loathing in his voice. 'To have *fun*.'

Alex turned away, one end of his sheet trailing behind him across the floor. His shoulders were tense, arms wrapped around himself.

'Let me get your clothes,' she said, sensing how awkward he felt, standing there in nothing but a sheet.

She ran downstairs and collected his things. When she took them back up, Alex dressed slowly, his hands fumbling, his back turned.

She wished he felt able to face her. But she understood.

A car was approaching fast along the tree-lined road that led to Pixie Cottage. Headlights flashed across the freshly painted white walls of her bedroom.

'Brodie,' she said.

The ache in her heart was almost unbearable.

'Look,' he said suddenly, his head still bent, 'this isn't working. I don't think we should see each other any more.'

Jennifer could hardly breathe, staring at him.

'But I need you to do one last thing for me,' he added, his voice hoarse. 'Make sure you come to Nelly's party, would you? To say goodbye.'

She could hardly speak, her vision blurred with tears. 'Of course.'

'And bring Caroline. Nana wants to thank her for helping Thelma.'

Brodie had arrived; she heard him banging on the front door below. He shouted through the door too, his voice urgent and breathless. 'Alex? You up there?'

'Yeah,' Alex shouted back, 'I'll be right down.'

So that's that, she thought, watching as he left without another word to her. They had made love, and then Alex had dismissed her from his mind as yet another complication he couldn't afford in his already troubled life.

It was Raphael all over again.

CHAPTER THIRTY-THREE

Caroline picked her up at seven on the evening of the party so they could drive round to the house together, though Jennifer had insisted she could walk through the woods perfectly well. 'Not in that dress,' her stepsister said tartly, on seeing her outfit, 'or those heels.' And it was true that Jennifer felt rather overdressed for what was mostly going to be a family affair. But she had heard whispers that the Mayor had been invited, and possibly some celebs, too, and had feared the jeans and sparkly top she had originally planned to wear would make her look ridiculous.

So she'd dragged out of the wardrobe an old silver dress dating from her reed-thin university days. It now hugged her fuller figure, not to mention being insanely short as well as low-cut at the front. This she coupled with a pair of black-and-chrome stilettos that could easily double as murder weapons if required. She'd had the heels for ages, too, and had only given them one outing before tonight. Which, if memory served, had left her nearly crippled for days afterwards. But the stilettos matched the dress.

Nonetheless, Jennifer had hesitated, peering dubiously at her reflection in the bathroom mirror. Would she look like a strippergram in this skimpy, spangly get-up, tottering up the drive at Porro Park?

But Caroline had grinned with appreciation, seeing her at the doorstep of the cottage. 'You'll do,' was all she said, but given that she usually exclaimed in horror at Jennifer's dress sense, she'd clearly struck the right note.

Naturally, Caroline herself had turned up looking like she was attending the Oscars, all red velvet and plunging bodice, dripping with jewels.

'How the hell did you afford that dress on an NHS salary?' was Jennifer's first incredulous thought, which she voiced as she slid into the car.

'I didn't,' Caroline said smoothly, flicking back her perfect loose blonde waves with an air of pure Hollywood indifference. 'I borrowed it. I found this fabulous online clothes-hire store. I have to return it within three days. They even do the dry-cleaning.'

'Still expensive though, I bet.'

'God, yes.' Caroline sighed. 'But so bloody worth it. Don't you think?'

'I guess.'

'It's incredibly hot, though. Not exactly right for a summer party.'

'You can always take it off,' Jennifer said.

'For the right man, definitely.'

Jennifer laughed.

'Party time!' Caroline put her car in gear, her voice high with excitement. 'Here's to an evening of champagne and canapés.'

Jennifer clung to the door handle as the small car lurched

forward, boxes of latex gloves and midwifery kits sliding noisily around on the back seat, and tried again to suppress the flutter of crazy nerves in the pit of her stomach. She'd been suffering from attacks of breathlessness all day, her skin alternately sweating, then cold and clammy. In fact, she'd been a nervous wreck ever since Brodie had driven round to the cottage a few days ago, delivering two invitations for Nelly's birthday party in sleek, gold-embossed white envelopes.

One for her, one for Caroline.

She had drawn the printed invitation out of its envelope, catching a hint of perfume as she did so, and read it in silence. It was perfect: simply but beautifully written. And poignant enough to melt the hardest of hearts.

Dearest friend, you are invited to share in our party celebrations at Porro Park to mark Nelly's 90th Birthday.

Then two lines of poetry below.

Because the birthday of my life
Is come, my love is come to me
— Christina Rossetti

Tears had pricked at her eyes, and Jennifer had bitten her lip to avoid letting those hot emotions spill out in front of her visitor.

'Is there someone you want to bring with you?' Brodie had asked casually, seeing her studying the 'Plus One' written with a flourish next to her name.

She wondered who had handwritten all the guests' names on the invitation cards. It must have taken ages. Thelma? Brodie? Or possibly Alex himself?

She traced the 'Plus One' with one fingertip.

'Erm, maybe. I'm not sure.'

Brodie had searched her face, clearly not deceived by this evasive response. 'I know he can be hard work at times,' he said quietly, 'but dig a little deeper, and you may be surprised by what you find.'

'Excuse me?'

But Brodie had not elaborated on this cryptic piece of advice, merely heading back to his car and adding over his shoulder, 'Nelly's not well enough to receive visitors at the moment. But she's been asking after you every day since she came home. So I hope you won't miss the party, yeah?'

Jennifer had stood there, watching his car pull away and struggling against a helpless sense of being manipulated. Her hands had twitched on the white gold-embossed envelopes, and on a momentary impulse she had nearly torn the damn invitations in half. But she knew Caroline would never forgive her if she did that. And would never go on her own without Jennifer.

Plus, there was Nelly to consider.

She badly wanted to see the old lady again, to say sorry for having broken such a solemn promise only hours after making it.

She could only hope Nelly had forgiven her by now. But even if she hadn't, it was still important that Jennifer got the chance to explain.

She also wanted to say her goodbyes, and sit next to this

stubborn, free-spirited woman, who seemed to carry what Jennifer needed to know and to hand that knowledge to her at just the right time. There was so little time left for Nelly, and it felt wrong to avoid visiting her simply because she didn't want to bump into Alex.

So she'd called Caroline, and endured her stepsister shrieking with delight down the phone for a full ten minutes, and then sat down afterwards to make a birthday present for Nelly. It had taken several days to finish, but she'd been determined to get it right. Now the present was wrapped in a brightly coloured cloth bag, resting on her lap.

Caroline paused at a junction and glanced down at the bag. 'What's that?'

'Nelly's present.'

Caroline pulled out onto the main road, waving cheerily and shouting, 'Sorry!' as she nearly collided with a tractor lumbering along in the opposite direction. The tractor driver, a young man, made a rude gesture but kept going.

'I'm giving her a woollen scarf,' Caroline said, quickly checking her mirror. Not for traffic behind them, it seemed, but in case her make-up was smeared. She pursed her lips, ran a careful fingertip under each kohl-lined eye, then looked back at the road, apparently satisfied with her reflection. Which of course she would be. Her make-up was as immaculate as ever. 'One of my own hand-knitted jobbies.'

'In this heat?'

Jennifer wound down her window and looked out at the wide expanse of cloudless blue sky. It was already getting on for early evening, yet the weather was still warm and sunny. The tangled Cornish verges along the lane were abuzz with bees and insects, the hedgerows alive with bright butterflies. She watched a cabbage white flutter past her window, its wings light and airy, and hated the fact that Nelly's summer was about to be cut short by a terrible disease. Though if there was no way round it, glorious sunshine was better than rain and gloom for her final days, she decided unhappily.

Why did life have to be so bloody unfair?

'The scarf is for the goats.' Caroline sounded defensive. 'I thought that small, cross-eyed goat—'

'Baby,' Jennifer supplied.

'That's the one. I thought Baby might look cute in a pink scarf.'

'Oh.' Jennifer smiled mistily. 'What a lovely idea.'

'What about you? What did you get her?'

Jennifer hesitated, wrapping protective hands around the cloth bag on her lap. 'It's . . . a secret,' she said at last.

Caroline laughed. 'Something witchy, is it?'

'Nelly will understand.'

'Maybe.' Her stepsister took the next corner at her usual speed and then slammed on the brakes, staring ahead in wide-eyed astonishment. 'Oh, good grief. Will you look at that?' She stopped dead, her breath quickening. 'Now what do I do?'

The approach to Porro Park was crowded, with cars and vans everywhere, parked higgledy-piggledy on the grass verges or blocking the road near the gate. People were standing in groups or talking excitedly into their phones. Reporters or merely curious onlookers? There were cameras there, too, tracking the long line of limousines approaching the property from the main road to the north.

Someone had tipped off the press about Nelly's party.

As they watched, a private helicopter circled overhead. Heads turned at the roar of its passing, then it dropped down behind the tall trees that marked the boundaries of the park. Photographers raced to the fence to get shots of the new arrivals, but the trees made them invisible. Some major celebrity arriving by air, presumably. Apparently, Alex had wanted to limit guests to locals only, but word of Nelly's ninetieth birthday had reached a number of his friends in the film industry, and they'd asked to come to the party, to catch up with Alex again and also to wish his much-loved grandmother a happy birthday.

'What are we waiting for?' Jennifer asked Caroline, who had simply halted in the middle of the road, staring with her mouth open. 'Keep driving.'

'There's security on the gate.'

Sure enough, there were several burly guards in uniform on duty at the gate. One man had an Alsatian dog on a leash and was walking the animal round every vehicle before allowing it inside the grounds. The dog was panting and straining at its lead as though eager to take a bite out of someone. Probably the heat, driving him crazy.

'So what?' Jennifer waved the invitations at her. 'We're guests, remember? They have to let us in.'

Caroline seemed to snap out of her trance. 'Yes, of course. Sorry, I just . . . It's still hard to believe we're a part of this . . .'

'Circus?'

'Huge media event, I was going to say.' But Caroline smiled, putting the car back into gear. 'Come on, let's do this. Like you said, it's not like we're gatecrashing.' She threaded her way slowly through the crowd of reporters and photographers, some of whom turned, peering into the car and even snapping a few pictures of them. Presumably in case they might be newsworthy guests. 'Oh my God, they're taking photos of us.' She checked her reflection in the mirror again as Jennifer hurriedly closed her window. 'We could be in the next issue of *Hello*. I knew I should have worn more eye make-up.'

'Are you kidding? You're wearing enough for both of us.'

Caroline shot her a look, but slotted neatly into the entrance queue behind a cream stretch limousine with blacked-out windows.

'I wonder who's in that car,' she whispered.

'Someone who's going to fall madly in love with you tonight,' Jennifer said promptly, 'marry you and take you away from all this.'

'Sounds good.' Caroline was grinning. 'But what would all my pregnant patients do if I left Pethporro?'

'Cross their legs.'

Once they had been shown where to park, they followed other newly arrived guests along a specially laid walkway to the house. The walkway had an arched roof covered in some creamy silken fabric to shade them from the heat; it rustled deliciously overhead, flapping in an occasional sea breeze.

As they trod carefully past the orchard, a few steps behind a man who looked suspiciously like Brad Pitt, four or five goats danced past, collar bells jangling crazily, pursued by a very tall middle-aged woman in shorts and vest top, scrawny arms and legs flailing, long grey hair flying out behind, her eyes wild and focused on her prey.

'Who the hell is that?' Caroline demanded, stopping

dead. Her voice echoed down the length of the covered walkway, and the Brad Pitt lookalike stopped too, gazing round to see what had attracted her attention.

'Hi!' the woman called, waving cheerfully at them before disappearing further into the sun-drenched orchard.

'I think that was . . . Lizzie.'

Jennifer, who had turned to watch the strange figure until she was out of sight, now felt as though her head had been removed and then replaced the wrong way round.

She spun back towards Caroline, nearly toppling over in her too-high stilettos. 'Oops.' Her stepsister steadied her, clucking in disapproval. 'Sorry. It's these bloody shoes.' She paused. 'Do you remember Lizzie?'

The Brad Pitt lookalike gave the now-empty orchard one last bemused look, then continued on towards the house, jingling change in his right pocket.

'One of old Trudy Clitheroe's waifs and strays?' Caroline made a face, though she was watching the man in the tuxedo. 'How could I forget? She was such an eccentric . . . Living in a van in the middle of a field. But what on earth is she doing at Nelly's party?'

'Herding goats, apparently.'

Caroline sighed, seeming to dismiss the mad vision from her mind. 'Do you think that really was Brad Pitt?'

'Not unless he's grown a few inches since his last film.'

'Damn.' Caroline linked arms with her as they walked up to the house. Loud music could be heard from both the back lawns and the interior of the house, accompanied by a ripple of laughter and the sound of people mingling. 'Good-looking though, wasn't he?'

'Not bad.'

'Maybe he's Brad Pitt's stunt double.'

'You're obsessed.'

'I'm *single*, that's what I am,' Caroline hissed.

'So am I.'

'Huh, that's a total fib.' Caroline laughed at her bewildered expression. 'Don't worry, I'm not judging. I just wish you'd told me you were seriously interested in Delgardo. If I'd known, I'd never have flirted with him after the festival that night.' She hesitated. 'And I'm sorry, by the way.'

'What for?'

Her stepsister wriggled on her arm. 'Oh, something and nothing.'

'Caro,' she said warningly.

'I bent his ear about you, that's all. At his house that night. You two disappeared upstairs, and then he came down looking a bit . . . well, forlorn. I told him to do the right thing and ask you out properly.'

'Oh, my God.'

'Though I also said that if he wasn't interested in you, I was totally available for dinner or drinks or . . . anything, really.'

'You are so embarrassing. I can't believe it.'

'But then later, I was sorry for hassling him like that. About you, I mean. It's obvious he's had a hard time recently and isn't ready for dating.' Caroline peered at her curiously. 'Did he ever tell you what the problem is?'

'Apart from the fact that he got blown up,' Jennifer said flatly, 'no.'

'That hotel bombing? But that was yonks ago.' Her stepsister shrugged. 'Still, he must be feeling better now. Cheetham was trending on Twitter this morning. The word is, they're making another of those action films of his. So our big celebrity may not be hanging around Pethporro for much longer.'

Jennifer kept walking, her face rigid, but it felt as though someone had punched her in the stomach. Alex hadn't mentioned anything about a new Cheetham film deal.

But then, why would he? She was his tenant, not his friend. Worse still, she was a tenant he'd *slept with*. He wasn't likely to tell her he might be leaving Cornwall soon, not when his imminent departure might make her clingy, or driven to talk to the media about their affair.

'Hey, sis, you okay?' Caroline's voice softened, becoming sympathetic. 'I'm sorry if I spoke out of turn.' She tutted. 'I take it Alex didn't tell you about the new film?'

Jennifer couldn't look at Caroline, knowing her face must be flushed, pain showing in her eyes. Inside, she was screaming. She hated how vulnerable he had made her feel. If it had been a meaningless fling with her handsome landlord, she could have laughed this off. Seen the funny side of his behaviour. But she hadn't gone to bed with Alex Delgardo on a whim. She'd gone to bed with him because she had fallen in love. With the man, not the world-famous actor. But she was a fool if she couldn't see that they were, and always had been, one and the same. And why should *she* be the exception to the rule, the one who would move him to love her back?

Alex had shown her what he thought she wanted to see. But ultimately, he was indifferent to her. And soon he would be gone.

'No, he never said a word.'

CHAPTER THIRTY-FOUR

The house was even more packed than the road outside. Only not with the media this time, but with catering staff and crowds of guests in suits and evening wear, the latter enjoying the Cornish sunshine as they listened to a folk band playing on the lawn. Trays of champagne flutes were circulating, and tables of refreshments had been set out at intervals, with chocolate fountains and platters of artfully arranged canapés. Some of the guests were household names from the world of film and television, and others were local dignitaries like the Mayor and the museum curator, and the MP for their constituency.

Françoise approached them in her stern black uniform, her arms full of presents, many wrapped in silver and gold with massive bows. Behind her trailed two young lads in black trousers and short-sleeved shirts, equally laden down with presents. '*Bonsoir*, mesdames. Is that a birthday present for Nelly?' she asked Caroline, nodding to the present she was clutching. 'I'll take it. She's not well enough to open them all tonight, unfortunately. So we're collecting her presents and putting them safely to one side for her.'

Caroline handed over her present to one of the lads.

'How about yours?' Françoise looked at Jennifer pointedly.

She pulled the bag closer. 'I'd prefer to give this to Nelly in person.'

Françoise pursed her lips and shrugged, saying, '*Bien*,' before moving on to the next guest.

Jennifer looked around but could not see Alex anywhere in the crowd. Was it possible that Caroline was right? Was he planning to jet off soon and make another action film? No, she couldn't believe it. He would never leave Nelly, even if it meant putting his career on hold a little while longer. Or was that just her, being biased? 'Pinch me,' Caroline whispered, pointing towards a handsome black man in a white tuxedo, standing alone under a marquee, looking vaguely bored. 'Isn't that . . .?'

'Yes.'

'I think I may faint.'

'That would be silly, because then you'd miss talking to him.'

'*Me?*' Caroline's voice became a squeak. Her eyes widened at the same time, fixing on him hungrily. 'Talk to *him*?'

'Why shouldn't you talk to him? You're a person, he's a person. And you're far better-looking than he is.' When Caroline shook her head, Jennifer shoved her from behind. 'Go on, hurry up. Before someone else nabs him. I know he's your hero.'

'Oh. My. God.' Caroline had flushed as pink as the champagne she was drinking, but she wove a little unsteadily through the crowd and smiled up at her idol, who promptly smiled back and began a conversation.

Her job done, Jennifer finished her glass of champagne,

trying to pretend she was not as nervous as a teenager at her first disco. *Why shouldn't you talk to him? You're a person, he's a person.* If only she could take her own advice.

She glanced idly about the crowded lawns, wondering if, among the many groups of guests, there was anyone here she knew. More than expected, she realised. There were plenty of locals here, people who knew Nelly, including students from the Cornish language class, one of whom nodded back with a smile when she waved at them. Penny and her partner Bailey were here, too, sitting on a bench in the shade of a vast oak, giggling and feeding each other chocolate-coated marshmallows.

Lizzie was good friends with Penny Jago, of course. She wondered if that was why Lizzie was here tonight. That would make sense. Though why she was chasing goats through the orchard was beyond her skills as an amateur detective.

The guy in the tux was whispering something in Caroline's ear; her cheeks had gone completely pink, a perma-grin curving her lips. *She's in heaven*, Jennifer thought, happy for her.

'Love at first sight, by the look of it,' a deep voice said casually at her elbow. 'You may not see your sister for the rest of the evening.'

Startled, Jennifer nearly dropped her champagne flute, her fingers suddenly nerveless.

It was Alex, of course, standing mere inches away.

'Hello, Jenny.' He plucked the empty glass from her hand and gave it to a passing waiter. 'Can I offer you another glass of champagne?'

'No, thank you.'

Jennifer looked at him, her face a stiff mask, and struggled to hide the hurt she was feeling.

Maybe she had no right to stake a claim on him, but she couldn't help it. She was cut up about Alex's betrayal: this film role he had apparently accepted without mentioning to her that he would be leaving any day. The only thing she could control was not letting him see how much he had hurt her.

'I'm glad you decided to come tonight.' He paused, his mouth twisting. His gaze met hers, some inner turmoil there too, though he had spoken lightly enough. 'Nana's inside the house. She wants to see you.'

Alex was wearing a black tuxedo, immaculately cut, with polished black shoes and a gold ring on his finger that she had never seen before. His dark hair had been styled; even his stubble was sharp and designer-perfect. She thought he had never looked more devastatingly attractive. Nor more distant and unfamiliar.

'I ... I have to talk to Caroline,' she muttered, but he caught her by the arm before she could escape.

'Will you come inside and talk to Nana first?' he pressed her. 'Please, she'll be hurt if you don't. This party is for her, remember.' He glanced down at the bag she was carrying. 'Is that a birthday present? Come and give it to her yourself.'

She followed him into the house, reluctant to spend too much time in his company, but equally unwilling to let Nelly down.

She still owed his grandmother an apology, after all.

The bright atrium was packed with guests drinking champagne and chatting noisily. It was hard to get through the crowd, not least because Alex stopped several times to introduce her to friends of his, famous actors whose faces she knew from the big screen, and a big-name director who had flown in specially from Los Angeles that morning.

Jennifer shook their hands in a daze, smiling and laughing in all the right places but feeling horribly out of her depth.

'I can find Nelly on my own,' she told Alex, stopping in desperation as he threaded a path through the busy atrium to the living room. 'Honestly, I'm fine. You should go back to your friends.'

He turned, a flash in his eyes that could have been anger. 'My *friends*? So you're not my friend now?'

'They obviously want to talk to you, not me.'

'But I want to talk to *you*.'

They were standing close together in the ridiculous crush of people, the overheated atrium hotter than ever, the noise level so intense they were practically shouting at each other just to be heard. Jennifer tried to shift through the crowd, to escape his fierce stare. His arm snaked round her waist, pulling her back towards him. She gasped, a shock of awareness pulsing through her at his touch.

'Alex? How are you, darling?'

A willowy brunette had greeted him in a smoky, arresting voice, her face familiar, too – another actress, no doubt – forcing Alex to stop and speak to her.

Darling?

'Patsy, thank you for coming.'

'Delighted to be here, Alex.' The woman was purring, her smile almost triumphant, no doubt for having stolen his attention from Jennifer. 'We all love your wonderful grand-mother. Do you remember that time you flew Nelly out to watch us filming *Western Edge*?' The woman gurgled with laughter. 'She sat up late one night, telling everyone their fortunes. She knew I'd divorce Andy before I'd even married him. A real demon with the tarot cards. Does she still do readings?'

He released Jennifer, turning to kiss the woman on the cheek, but there was frustration in his face.

'No, she's not been well recently.'

'That's too bad.'

Free at last, Jennifer twisted on her heel to get away from him, smiling at people as she pushed and apologised, squeez-ing through the crush. She suspected he wouldn't even notice she had gone. Not with the slinky brunette in her figure-hugging dress regaling him about some Netflix series she was due to appear in.

A real demon with the tarot cards.

Perhaps she ought to have asked Nelly to read the cards for her, not Georgette at the Celtic Centre. But she would have been baring her soul and her romantic inclinations to Alex's grandmother, and she wasn't sure how comfortable she felt about that.

Besides, Jennifer would be asking about Alex Delgardo now, not Raphael Tregar. And that was definitely not a sub-ject she wanted to broach.

She only managed a few steps before Alex caught up with her again.

'Jennifer, for God's sake . . . Stop running from me, would you?' He stepped in front of her, instantly dominating the space, and then bent his head to her ear so as not to be over-heard by those around them. The warm intimacy of his breath on her neck left her shivering. 'After you've seen Nelly, we need to talk. Alone.'

'Seriously? I thought we were done.'

'What?'

'You've got a short memory,' she hissed, not wanting any-one else to know her personal business. 'At the cottage the other night.'

Alex had the grace to look embarrassed. 'I wasn't think-ing straight. I was half out of my mind.'

He urged her on through the noisy press of the crowd, one hand steering her forward, the other shaking hands with people as he passed. *A born multitasker,* she thought, try-ing to avoid twinges of jealousy at the way the women looked at him, like he was something to eat.

'So when are you heading back to the States?' she asked.

'Sorry?'

'You're due to start work on another film soon, aren't you? I just assumed they'd be shooting it in America.'

Alex stopped again, staring at her. 'You need to stop believing everything you read online,' he began, but was interrupted by someone else calling his name.

They had reached the doorway into the living room, which was blocked by numerous people chatting, with barely any room to move in or out.

'Alex, fantastic to see you again.' A portly man with a sweaty face put a hand on his shoulder, then pumped Alex's hand up and down, his accent American. 'Great party, man. Great people here, I love it. Thanks for the invite. And I can see why you like this part of England. One hell of a location. This whole place, it's so quaint, like one of those Jane Austen sets. I expected to be met by a horse and carriage at the airport. Ever thought of filming here?'

'No,' Alex said bluntly.

'That's great.' The man wiped his glistening forehead with a handkerchief, then said urgently, his tone businesslike, 'Listen, I'm so pleased you've decided to consider a new Cheetham film. And this new script, it's totally right for you. Can we talk privately about it? Maybe we could do lunch before I fly back.'

Alex muttered something evasive, his expression hunted.

So it was true.

Despite his protests before, he *was* leaving England.

Desperate to escape, her heart jerking in a spasm of pain, Jennifer slipped silently away before he could stop her, and peered round the door into the living room.

The first person she saw was Thelma. Far from being left shattered by her emergency C-section, Thelma looked superglam tonight, rocking high black heels with a wide-skirted gold-and-black dress, her freshly dyed blonde hair flowing loose and burnished down her back.

Jennifer edged past a huge man in a kilt who was blocking her view. 'Excuse me.'

Now she could see the room more clearly.

Nelly was stretched out on the sofa, clad in a dressing gown despite the heat, surrounded by party guests and half-unwrapped presents.

She looked frail and unwell. Jennifer was speechless with distress. Nelly's skin was as white as paper, her lips pale, too, with dark blueish rings under her eyes as though she hadn't had a proper night's sleep in weeks. Yet she was wearing a sequinned party dress under her dressing gown, and there was a spark about her, a resilient laughter in Nelly's face as she listened to Brodie, who seemed to be unwrapping presents on her behalf and describing each one in detail.

Brodie caught sight of her and lifted a hand in welcome. 'Over here, Jennifer,' he said clearly, his voice cutting through the hubbub of conversation. There was relief in his face. 'Nelly's been asking for you all evening.'

Jennifer hesitated, looking down at Nelly, suddenly uncertain of her welcome. 'Nelly, I hope you don't mind me coming tonight. Just tell me if you want me to leave, and I will.'

'Leave?' Nelly repeated faintly.

'Because of what happened at the hospital.' Jennifer kept her voice low, not wanting anyone else to overhear. 'I'm sorry. I promised not to tell anyone about your illness. And then—'

'Oh, don't be so daft.' Nelly flapped a hand at her. 'I've forgotten about all that. Anyway, you were right. Alex and Thelma deserved to know. And now they do, thanks to you.' Her smile was a blessing. 'Come and kiss me.'

Hugely relieved, she bent over Nelly, kissed her on the cheek, then looked about for somewhere to sit. It was a big room, but all the seats around Nelly's sofa were taken. People stared back at her awkwardly. She didn't know any of them.

'Give us a few minutes, guys,' Brodie said to them, his gaze on her face.

The seats were all slowly vacated, people moving off, glasses in hand. Brodie dragged a chair forward for her and Jennifer sat on it, not knowing what to say but aware of Nelly's sharp eyes watching her.

'Can I fetch you a glass of champagne, Jennifer?' Brodie asked.

Shyly, she murmured her assent.

'Nelly?'

Nelly winked up at him, saying something about iced water.

Then they were alone.

'Now, child, what's all this nonsense?' Nelly nodded to her face, frowning. 'I hope you're not blubbing over me.'

Jennifer hadn't even realised she was crying.

CHAPTER THIRTY-FIVE

Tears rolling down her cheeks, Jennifer was suddenly aware that Alex had walked into the room. She shot him a quick look over her shoulder, unable to help herself.

He was standing in the doorway, casually sexy in his black tuxedo, twisting the gold ring on his finger. Not surprisingly, he was being ogled by several other women in the room, including a tall, glamorous beauty in a near-transparent wraparound skirt and skimpy top. Jennifer recognised her as someone vaguely famous; a celebrity from the world of television, perhaps.

But Alex seemed oblivious to their stares, looking directly over at Jennifer.

At once, she bent her head, hiding from that too-clever gaze, perched like a bird on the edge of the chair. She was embarrassed by her tears, and didn't want him to know she was upset. He might want to talk, but she didn't think she could bear that. Not when she still felt so fragile. It was easier just to shut him out of her consciousness.

Except Nelly blew her cover.

'Come on now, Jenny, there's no sense crying,' Nelly said loudly. She held out a limp hand and nodded approvingly when Jennifer took it. 'Let me tell you a secret. I'm happy to go. Well, not happy. But not fighting it any more.'

Suddenly, Alex was there too, leaning over the sofa to listen.

Jenny bit her lip hard and dared not look at him for fear she would lose control and begin sobbing uncontrollably. As it was, her chest was heaving, and her vision had blurred to streaks, eyes brimming.

'Alex, you need to hear this too.' Nelly smiled up at her grandson, including him in the conversation. 'I'm ninety years old, and to be honest, I'm in a lot of pain. More pain than I let on to the doctors, because they'd only fuss. The pills help, of course. But nothing ever quite numbs it completely. I'd rather hang on until I'm a hundred, get my telegram. Who wouldn't? But it's better to know when it's time, and go out on your own terms.'

'Nana,' Alex said, his voice heavy.

'You're a fine young man, Alex,' his grandmother said, and let go of Jennifer's hand to pat his. 'I couldn't wish for better grandchildren than you and Thelma. And now I have a great-grandson too. Isn't life marvellous?'

Alex nodded and cleared his throat, then said, 'Nana, we're cutting your birthday cake soon.' His voice sounded gruff as he struggled with his emotions. 'Are you well enough to get up for that, do you think?'

'If you and Brodie help me, maybe.'

'Wait,' Jennifer said, and hurriedly held out the bag she'd been clutching on her lap. 'Before you go, this is for you, Nelly.'

She opened the bag and withdrew a smooth round white

stone about the size of her palm, with a carved pattern on the upper side, picked out in black paint. The pattern, as most people agreed, looked like an ancient labyrinth, or a tree with many concentric circles spreading outwards.

'I made it myself,' she said quietly. 'It's a Tír na nÓg stone. The symbol of the Otherworld. A spirit guide for you.'

Nana took the stone, staring down at it. Tears formed in her own eyes. Then she said in a trembling voice, 'Oh, my dear.'

'For the journey.'

'I understand.' Nana's hand closed around the stone. She nodded, looking deeply moved. 'Thank you.'

'No,' Jennifer said quietly, 'thank you, Nelly. Coming here this summer, meeting you . . . it's changed my life.'

'Has it really?' Nelly searched her face, then glanced up at Alex. There was a sadness in her eyes that was not for herself. 'Well, I'm glad of that, at least.' She slipped the Tír na nÓg stone into the pocket of her dressing gown, and said more cheerfully, 'Tell me one of your stories, Jenny. Just a quick one, for my birthday. I think I'd like a story to round off the day.'

Jennifer wiped away a tear and nodded.

'Once upon a time, further up the north coast in Morwenstow,' she began, in a voice that started as a whisper and grew steadily stronger as the old lady settled to listen, 'there was a beautiful nymph called Tamara. Having been born in a nasty dark hole in the ground, she loved to run about in the sunlight. She had two admirers, named Tavy and Taw, both of them giants, and so strong and handsome, she couldn't choose between them.'

'Ah.' Nelly smiled, clearly recognising the story. 'Go on.'

'Her parents warned her against consorting with giants, but Tamara was headstrong and refused to listen. The three of them roamed the wild moors together, day and night, quite to the despair of her father.' Jennifer unconsciously raised her voice, aware that the hubbub of conversation in the room had died away and the party guests around them had fallen silent. From outside in the grounds, she could still hear music coming from the entertainment tent, but the room itself was quiet. 'One day, her father chased her across the high moors to give her an ultimatum: *come home with me at once, Tamara, or never come home again.*'

Alex leant against the wall a few feet away, arms folded, his gaze intent on her face as he listened to the story.

'When Tamara laughed in his face, her father was furious. He put a curse on her, that she should regret her wicked behaviour and weep salt tears for ever. In that instant, Tamara began to weep, and was transformed into a river, flowing away from him towards the sea.'

'Oh, what a foolish man,' Nelly muttered, shaking her head.

'And her two admirers?' Alex raised his eyebrows. 'What happened to them?'

'When the handsome young giants saw what had happened to their beloved,' she said, 'they wept for days until they too turned into rivers, desperate to be joined with Tamara. Tavy ran across the moors under the silvery moonlight until at last he found her, and mingled with her wide waters. But it's said that Taw lost his way in the dark, and to this day runs sorrowfully in the wrong direction, weeping as he seeks his lost love.' Her gaze moved back to Alex as she reached the end of her story, finding him rapt. 'And that is how the West Country came to have three great rivers, the Tamar, the Tavy and the Taw.'

The applause startled her, for in her mind she had been telling the story only to Nelly and Alex. But others had gathered around the sofa while she was speaking, and now she turned to them too, smiling but a little shy.

'That was a lovely story, my dear.' Nelly sighed, and then put a hand to her chest as though in pain. But she seemed pleased. 'Quite perfect.'

Brodie appeared at the end of the sofa, smiling. 'Ready for your birthday cake, Nelly?'

'I'm always ready for cake. Even if I didn't bake this one myself.' Nelly sat up with an effort. 'Give me a hand, boys.'

Together, the two men lifted Nelly from the sofa and supported her across the room to the doors standing open onto the lawn. People had been gathering outside for some time, and began to clap as she appeared on the threshold, lit up by the rays of the setting sun.

'Goodness,' Nelly said, breathless, and stepped outside into the evening.

Jennifer held back, dabbing ineffectually at her damp cheeks as the tears continued to flow. How could she not cry?

On the lawn outside, a large table had been set aside for the birthday cake, which was a vast affair made of seven iced tiers, decorated with intricate iced flowers and marzipan fruits. There were no candles, but the number 90 had been drawn elaborately on the cake in pink and blue icing. Françoise was waiting beside the cake with a woman that Jennifer took to be her girlfriend, a brunette dressed simply but beautifully in a blue knee-length dress.

Nelly laughed in delight at the astonishing confection, then accepted the silver cake knife from Françoise. She set it into the thick, creamy icing with a shaking grip while everyone applauded and cheered.

Alex began to sing 'Happy Birthday', and by the second repetition everyone else had joined in, the sound of several hundred voices swelling to fill the evening air.

Jennifer sang too, with a quivering voice, and wished her heart was not squeezing in pain for the old lady.

The cut Nelly made in the cake was not deep, but it was symbolic. When she fell back, looking exhausted, the white-aproned caterers took over, cutting the first slice of cake and setting it on a delicate bone china plate for Nelly. Françoise held the plate for her while Nelly tottered between Brodie and Alex to a padded lounger at the side of the lawn.

'Here you go, Nana.' Alex handed her the slice of birthday cake with a fork. 'Happy ninetieth birthday.'

'Thank you, it does look delicious,' Nelly said, but Jennifer noticed she didn't touch the cake, leaving the plate on her lap as she peered past her grandson at the crowds of partygoers. 'But where's Thelma? She should be here too.'

'I'll find her, if you like,' Brodie said.

'Would you, dear?' Nelly smiled faintly at him. 'It's nice, having all these famous faces around the place. I think I saw James Bond over there. Or whatever the actor's name is these days.' She put a hand to her chest again, sighing breathlessly, as she had done earlier. 'But it's my birthday, and I want my family around me.'

'Of course.'

Jennifer watched Brodie head off back into the house,

and Alex sit down beside his grandmother. Then she turned away, deliberately distancing herself from the festivities. This was a private moment for the family and close friends. And she still felt a bit like an interloper, especially after Alex's coolness. Her heart winced at the memory of that night, but she pushed it aside, putting on a brave smile.

Today was all about Nelly. Not her own stupid problems.

Françoise was bustling about, overseeing the cutting-up of the cake for the rest of the party guests. She spotted Jennifer standing alone and beckoned her over, surprisingly friendly for once. There was even something slightly sinister about her smile. But perhaps that was because it was so rarely seen, Jennifer thought.

'Have some birthday cake,' Françoise said coolly, handing over a fork and a plate with a slice of dainty cake on it.

'Thank you.'

'And may I introduce you to my partner, Marie?' Françoise turned to the well-dressed brunette beside her. 'Marie, this is Jennifer, the lady who has been so helpful during Nelly's illness. Especially with the goats.'

'Ah, 'ow nice.' Marie smiled at her pleasantly, her French accent very pronounced. 'Ze goat woman.'

'That's me, the goat woman.' Jennifer laughed, glad of the excuse not to cry for once, and saw both women look at her blankly. Hurriedly, she held out her hand instead and Marie shook it. 'Pleased to meet you,' she added more sombrely.

'Have you seen ze baby?' Marie asked her.

'Baby?'

Françoise pointed across the lawn to where Thelma stood, a baby cradled in her arms. It couldn't be her own son, of course. Baby Joseph, named after his great-grandfather, was still in the neonatal unit, recuperating from his premature birth. Caroline had told her earlier that Thelma, by all accounts a zealous new mother, had to be persuaded to leave his side for a few hours to attend her grandmother's party. Besides, this baby had to be at least six months old, by her guess.

'Whose baby is that?' Jennifer asked, puzzled.

Françoise shrugged, turning back to her task of handing out plates of cake.

'*Je ne sais pas,*' Marie said, and gave her a helpless smile. 'I don't know. But he is a pretty baby, *n'est-ce pas?*'

Taking the slice of birthday cake with her, Jennifer drifted back towards the little gathering around Nelly's padded lounger. She carefully insinuated herself slightly behind Brodie, so she didn't feel as though she were pushing in but could still hear what was being said, and tucked into the cake. It was meltingly delicious, exactly as it looked.

The baby was indeed very pretty, and almost certainly male, judging by his jaunty blue cap and sailor suit.

'Look at this little darling,' Thelma was saying, holding out the wide-eyed, gurgling baby to her brother. 'Do you want to hold him?'

'I'll pass, thanks,' Alex said drily.

'He's only a baby. He won't bite.' Thelma showed the baby to Nelly instead. 'Here, Nana, this is baby Santos, Hannah Tregar's baby. She's here with her husband. She let me hold him, because she knows they won't let me bring Joseph home from the hospital yet.'

Hannah Tregar's baby.

Hearing these words, Jennifer felt a great rush of pain and almost physically recoiled, only curbing the impulse with an enormous effort.

'What a beautiful child,' Nelly was saying. She tickled the child under his chubby chin and the baby gazed back at her with huge, solemn eyes.

'Ah, here's his mother now,' Thelma said, not bothering to hide her disappointment, and everyone turned to look. 'I was wondering where she'd got to.'

As if nothing worse could happen that evening, it did: Hannah Tregar came striding across the lawn with Raphael in tow. They were hand in hand, and looked deeply in love with each other. Just as they had done in their wedding photograph in the newspaper. The one that had caused Jennifer so much anguish and heartache.

Jennifer could not help herself; she looked straight at Raphael, sensing his head turning as he recognised her.

Their eyes met.

She waited for the inevitable shock she always felt on meeting Raphael's gaze, a sensation not unlike being hit over the head with a cricket bat, or so she liked to imagine, for it tended to leave her dizzy and momentarily unable to speak.

Only it didn't happen. Their eyes met, and then ... nothing.

Perplexed, Jennifer continued to stare at Raphael Tregar, and was uncomfortably aware of Alex looking from him to her, his expression stark.

'He's a little cherub,' Nelly added indulgently as Thelma cuddled the baby again. 'And Santos is a lovely name. Quite unusual.'

'Thank you so much, I'm his mum,' Hannah said promptly, stopping beside Thelma with a proud grin. She flicked back her blonde hair, still as bouncy and smiling as Jennifer remembered from Christmas. Though for some reason her mannerisms seemed less annoying now. 'You must be Nelly,' she said, bending to shake the old lady's hand. 'I'm sorry I haven't had a chance to say hello before. Raphael's been making me traipse all over the place. Your grounds are simply enormous, aren't they?'

'Don't blame me,' Nelly said at once, nodding towards Alex. 'Blame my grandson. He found this place for us.'

'Oh, I'm not complaining. Porro Park is totally gorgeous, I love it. But I'm afraid my husband's got an unhealthy obsession with goats at the moment, and you have a whole orchard full of them. Plus, we saw our good friend Lizzie over there, and she and my husband could talk for Cornwall. Especially when it comes to livestock.' Hannah paused for breath at last, bestowing a broad smile on Nelly. 'Anyway, happy birthday!'

'Thank you.'

'You want Santos back?' Thelma said, handing the squirming bundle over with a last look of regret. 'He's so sweet. And that olive complexion . . . He'll be a heartbreaker when he grows up.'

'Like his dad, then. Whose name was also Santos.' Hannah looked at her sadly. 'My boyfriend died soon after I realised I was going to have his baby.'

'That's awful,' Thelma said, biting her lip.

'Yes, it still hurts.' Hannah brushed a finger down her son's flushed cheek. 'We're flying out to Greece soon. So his grandparents can meet little Santos.' She paused, chagrin in her eyes, no doubt having seen the expression on Thelma's face. 'But you must be missing your own baby. You'll have Joseph home with you soon, I'm sure.'

'Definitely.' Thelma made a determined face. 'Even if I have to steal him from the hospital.'

'She's kidding,' Alex said quickly.

'Only partly,' Thelma said, and then hesitated. 'Hannah, do you know my brother, Alex?'

Jennifer held her breath, still hiding behind Brodie.

Not Alex, she was thinking fiercely.

You got Raphael. You're not getting Alex, too.

'Hello,' Hannah said with a touch of uncertainty, looking him up and down, as though she was measuring him against her current husband. 'So *you're* Thelma's brother.'

'For my sins.' He thrust out a hand. 'Alex Delgardo.'

Hannah laughed as they shook hands. 'I know who you are. Raphael mentioned he'd met you at the folklore festival. Only very briefly, but still . . . We don't get many movie stars in Pethporro. It was quite a grand occasion for him.'

'Hannah,' Raphael said, a warning note in his voice, though he shook Alex's hand pleasantly enough. 'Hello again.'

'Sorry, am I embarrassing you?' Hannah laughed, looking round with her restless gaze. Her smile faltered as she spotted Jennifer hiding behind Brodie's shoulder. But she kept talking. 'It's wonderful to be at Porro Park, Mr Delgardo, thank you so much for the invitation.'

'Please, call me Alex.'

'That's very kind.' Hannah Tregar's gaze slipped back to

Jennifer's face. 'Well,' she finished lamely, 'we'd better go and see if we can drag Lizzie away from your goats. I believe we're giving her a lift home.'

'No need, darling, she's right over there,' Raphael said, slipping an arm around his wife's waist. He smiled broadly as he nodded to Alex. 'Delgardo. Good to see you again. When's the next Cheetham film out?'

'No idea,' Alex said coolly.

Raphael raised his eyebrows but did not pursue the topic. 'What a fantastic party this has been. We particularly loved the folk singers. Very Cornish. We may grab them for the Boxing Day pageant if they're free.' He nodded to Nelly too. 'Happy birthday. I hope you're having fun.'

Nelly stirred. 'Boxing Day pageant?'

'That's right.' Raphael became enthusiastic. 'Hannah organised it last year. There's a costume procession through the town, with floats and traditional characters like the 'Obby 'Oss and the Lord of Misrule, followed by a torchlit party on the foreshore afterwards.' He smiled indulgently down at Nelly. 'You'd enjoy it, I'm sure. So, I hope to see you all there on Boxing Day.'

Alex started forward angrily, then stopped himself. But the look he threw Raphael was far from friendly.

Nelly's face was stricken. Her time would have run out long before Christmas.

Jennifer could have throttled Raphael for saying something so insensitive.

Raphael couldn't be expected to know, of course. All the same, she saw Alex clench his fists as though barely suppressing an urge to punch the farmer on his prominent nose, and suddenly realised that she wouldn't care if he did. In fact, she might even join him.

Now, at long last, she felt it again. That cricket-bat-round-the-head sensation. A stunning blow that left her ears ringing, her legs unsteady.

She didn't much care if Raphael got punched in the face.

She didn't care full stop.

She wasn't in love with Raphael any more.

CHAPTER THIRTY-SIX

Oblivious to the consternation he had caused, Raphael turned, deliberately seeking out Jennifer with that authoritarian gaze of his. She froze, not having realised he'd seen her lurking there. He still had his arm around his wife's waist, his love for Hannah open and undeniable.

But at least now she no longer cared about that. He could love Hannah to hell and back, it made no difference to Jennifer.

She didn't love him.

And what a relief it is, she thought, with a rush of elation, to be able to step back from all that angst and burning resentment and see them as just another married couple.

It was all she could do not to shout it exultantly in his face.

I don't love you any more.

Though the real question vexing her was, why not?

What had changed?

'Jennifer,' Raphael said crisply, 'I'm glad to have this chance to speak to you again. Have you given any more thought to what we discussed at the festival?'

'Erm, not really,' she said, her attention elsewhere.

Why was she no longer in love with Raphael? There was

only one realistic answer to that question, and Jennifer felt sick just thinking about it. No; it couldn't be true. It was too horrific. Talk about out of the frying pan and into the fire.

Oh God, it was because she was in love with Alex Delgardo. She loved Alex.

Her head swam with the awful realisation of her own stupidity, her hands clammy, her face hot. She had just repeated the exact same mistake she had made with Raphael, only it was a thousand times worse. How the hell was she going to get out of this mess?

It had all been so different when she fell in love with Raphael. She hadn't been expecting to feel anything for the laconic farmer with his habitual flat cap, and so failed to recognise the signs quickly enough. In fact, she was no longer sure that what she'd felt had been love. It had *felt* like love, of course, and burnt her to the bone for months.

But looking back, the frenzy she had felt for Raphael seemed like a weak shadow of this deeper, all-consuming love for Alex.

'We've started advertising for the position of pageant director,' Raphael was saying. 'You've got a three-week window to apply. I hope you'll consider it. We could do with someone of your expertise on the job. As you can see, Hannah's rather busy at the moment so can't take on the extra work.' Smiling, Raphael drew his wife and her child closer, the meaning behind that intimate gesture not lost on her. Or on Alex, she guessed, who was still studying them both with that unreadable look on his face. 'Take a look at the Pethporro website – all the details are there. Or I can email them to you.'

She managed some kind of non-committal reply, not really aware of what she was saying, and then she caught Alex's eye. He was looking directly at her now, furious.

Her nerve broke.

Jennifer muttered, 'Excuse me, would you?' She headed blindly back to the house, blundering into Penny and Bailey, who were just coming out. 'Sorry.'

'Hey, you okay?' Penny called after her.

She didn't reply, desperate to find somewhere quiet to hide while she recovered. But the living room and atrium were so crowded, she couldn't push through the other guests quickly enough.

Giving up, she stood with head bent, one hand clamped over her mouth as she tried to remember what Alex had told her about deep breathing.

Several people asked if she was feeling unwell, but she just waved them away. The pain in her chest steadily increased and her fingertips began to tingle through lack of oxygen. Groping forward a few more steps through the crowd, she wondered if she could make it to the kitchen without being noticed. A glass of cold water might help . . .

'Jennifer?' A hand touched her shoulder. 'I think we need to talk.'

It was Hannah Tregar.

Oh God, what now?

Raphael's wife had left her baby with her husband, presumably, and come charging after her for some kind of showdown.

'What do you want?' Jennifer said, backing unsteadily into someone who grunted and said angrily, 'Watch out!'

Apologising to the elderly gentleman whose foot she'd inadvertently crushed with her stiletto, she felt her temper rise and turned to meet Hannah's blunt gaze. 'Leave me alone, will you?'

'There's no need to be rude,' Hannah said sharply, raising her eyebrows. 'Look, I know what you're thinking.'

'I doubt it.'

'You think I stole Raphael from you. But we both know that's not true. Raphael didn't love you. He never loved you. You just misread the signs.'

'Thanks for clearing that up.'

'I just want you to know we don't hold grudges. And you should absolutely take that job as pageant director. It's perfect for you, and you don't need to worry that I'll make life difficult for you, because I won't.' Hannah frowned, studying her. 'You don't look too good. Are you feeling okay?'

'I'm fine.'

Hannah seemed unconvinced. She turned, looking through the crowd of guests. 'Let me call someone for you. Your sister, maybe.'

Raphael appeared, walking easily, the blue-clad baby in his arms, the crowd seeming to melt away before his tall figure. *Parenthood suits him*, Jennifer thought, noting the faint smile curving his lips. *No*, she corrected herself. *It completes him.*

'Raphael,' Hannah called to her husband, her voice clear above the chattering guests and the sound of folk music floating in from outside. 'Quick, over here. I don't think Jennifer's feeling very well.'

'No, I . . .' Jennifer backed away unsteadily as Raphael

approached, and banged into someone behind her yet again. Today was all going wrong. 'Sorry, sorry, sorry.'

She turned, feeling like death, and found herself looking into Alex Delgardo's serious gaze. Her heart did a little jerk and her breath came back in a rush.

'Oh,' was all she could say.

'There you are,' Alex said coolly. 'I've been looking for you everywhere.'

He bent and kissed Jennifer on the mouth. Right there, in front of everyone. Like it was the most normal thing in the world.

Like they were a couple.

Ears buzzing, pulse thundering, Jennifer became aware of the noisy atrium quietening around them. *Everyone must be staring at us*, she thought feverishly. But there was no way to escape, and perhaps she did not want to. He was holding her by the shoulders, his grip almost a caress, his mouth moving persuasively against hers, and her brain could no longer make a pathway between one thought and another.

Alex pulled back slightly and bent to whisper in her ear, a hint of laughter in his voice. 'Don't let them get to you.'

Slowly, she opened her eyes. 'W-what?'

'I won't stand by while you get bullied under my own roof, Jenny.' He released her, straightening. 'Now, don't forget to breathe.' His smile was dry as she sucked air into her lungs. 'That's it. You okay?'

She was no longer struggling for breath. But she stared up at him, stricken.

Alex hadn't kissed her because he felt anything for her. He

only kissed her to demonstrate to Raphael and Hannah that she wasn't a lonely loser with no friends. Except she was *exactly* that. Because surely the kiss had been pure make-believe. Just another Oscar-worthy performance by the great Alex Delgardo.

'What the hell . . .?' His head jerked round.

There was a man somewhere in the atrium, shouting Alex's name.

The party guests, who had stared in amused astonishment as he kissed her, fell back as someone came shoving through the crowd towards them.

'Found you at last, Delgardo!' It was a man she had never seen before, a red-faced, balding man in his late thirties with a vicious scowl and a strong Cockney accent. 'You're mistaken if you think a few overfed flunkeys are going to keep me out. Or those bloody goats you keep running wild out there. Twice I nearly stepped in the most disgusting . . .'

The man stopped and cleared his throat, hearing the sound of muffled laughter all around him. 'The point is, I've got a legal right to be here, see? And I took the precaution of bringing my lawyer this time. So you'd better watch what you say.' He jerked his head to indicate a ginger-haired man in a suit behind him, perspiring and carrying a briefcase. 'Now, where's my *wife*?'

Alex had folded his arms, listening to this tirade. 'Hello, Stuart,' he said calmly, then glanced down. 'Oh dear. Is that goat shit on your shoes?'

Stuart.

Suddenly, Jennifer understood. This was Thelma's estranged husband, who must have taken advantage of the party to force an entrance. And his 'weasel' of a lawyer, as Thelma had once described him.

'*What?*' Stuart looked down too, horrified, then grimaced. His polished black shoes were clean, barely a speck of mud on them. 'Ha, ha, very funny. I want to speak to Thelma, do you understand? She can't keep me from my son. I know my rights.'

'Your son's not here.'

'Don't give me that bullshit, Delgardo. I saw my wife from the gate, holding a baby. She was right there on the lawn.'

'Never considering it might not have been your son she was holding?'

Stuart gave an incredulous laugh. 'Oh yes, very likely. So whose baby is it, then?'

Raphael stepped forward, towering over Stuart. 'Mine,' he said shortly, his brows drawn tight, making it obvious he didn't like Stuart or his lawyer.

'Oh.' Stuart looked Raphael up and down, then shrugged and looked back at Alex. His expression was less certain now, though. 'I still want to speak to her. I know she's here, you can't deny *that*. We've got unfinished business.' He sniffed. 'For starters, there's a joint bank account she's cleared out without my permission. I want all that money back, or else.'

Brodie came limping through the rapt guests, out of breath and looking furious. Behind him came three security men. 'Sorry, Alex. He got past me.'

'Well, what did you expect? That I'd be outrun by a one-legged man?' Stuart laughed, and then took a hurried step back when Brodie squared up to him. 'Here, you watch it. No violence. My lawyer's taking notes.'

His lawyer, who had been standing there clutching his

briefcase, looked embarrassed and began to fumble in his pockets as though hunting for a pen.

'You're not wanted at this party, and you certainly weren't invited,' Brodie said, keeping his voice low, standing almost chest-to-chest with Thelma's husband. 'Now get out before you're thrown out.'

'Brought those three lads to back you up, did you? Because you're not man enough to throw me out on your own?'

Brodie tensed.

'Don't rise to his bait,' Alex said warningly.

Brodie looked round at Alex, frustration in every line of his body.

Without warning, Stuart suddenly shoved him and Brodie stumbled backwards, nearly colliding with a young girl, but throwing himself sideways to avoid her. Not surprisingly, he lost his balance and pitched over, knocking into a waiter, who also wobbled briefly and then dropped a full tray of champagne glasses.

'You bastard!'

Alex's fist came swinging out and caught Stuart full in the face.

Stuart crumpled to his knees, grabbing at his nose. Blood trickled out from between his fingers and he swore thickly. Then he glared up at Alex and hissed, 'You are so going to pay for this,' though the words were barely coherent.

Thelma, who had been peering round Raphael's back, shouted at her husband, 'Get out of here, Stuart! I'm glad he hit you. Getting a taste of your own medicine for once.' Then she clasped a hand to her mouth and burst into tears. 'You ... great ... bully.'

'Don't distress yourself, my dear. Your husband is just leaving.' Nelly hobbled slowly out of the living room, leaning on a stick, Caroline at her elbow. Everyone shuffled out of her way, staring as she passed. 'Brodie,' she said, just as he got back to his feet and started dusting himself down, 'would you take Thelma to the kitchen, please? My grand-daughter looks as if she could do with a nice cup of tea.'

Brodie nodded grimly and led Thelma away.

It was silent in the atrium.

Nelly limped to where Stuart was still on his knees, a spatter of blood below him on the marbled floor, and looked down at him with an expression of icy disapproval. 'I never liked you, Stuart. There's something about you that reminds me of frogspawn.'

'Frogspawn?' Stuart repeated blankly, holding his nose.

'Thick and glutinous. But Thelma loved you, so I said nothing. However, she doesn't love you any more, and she wants you to leave. So off you hop, there's a good frog.' When Stuart started to say something, Nelly held up a shaking hand. Her voice grew higher. 'No, not another word. This is my birthday party and I don't want you here. Is that clear?'

Alex dragged Stuart to his feet and thrust him towards the main entrance. 'You heard my grandmother. Get out and don't come back.'

'But I've been *assaulted*.'

'Self-defence,' Raphael said sharply, stepping in front of Alex as though taking charge of the situation. 'I saw the whole thing, and so did everyone else here. You're trespassing on private property. You were asked to leave. But rather than do that, you attacked a member of staff, forcing Mr

Delgardo to take action. If you try to make a criminal case out of this, you'll be facing serious charges of your own.' He gave Stuart's lawyer a quelling look. 'And I'm sure your lawyer will advise you along those same lines.'

The lawyer opened his mouth, then shut it again.

Stuart staggered towards the door, fuming. 'Don't just stand there, you fat useless idiot,' he told his lawyer. 'Do something, Graham.'

The lawyer fumbled with his camera phone and snapped a few pictures of Stuart, his face and shirt sticky with blood.

'I've had enough of this nonsense.' Alex nodded to the three burly security men, who plunged forward eagerly. 'See these clowns off the premises. And if they give you any trouble, call the police.'

The guests in the atrium had slowly begun to disperse, some saying their goodbyes to Alex and wishing Nelly a happy birthday again as they left, no doubt sensing the party would soon be over. Others had followed the security men outside, perhaps hoping to enjoy the spectacle of Stuart and his lawyer being manhandled into a vehicle and out through the gates. The atrium was almost empty, and cooler now the sun was going down.

Jennifer took one look at Nelly's face, her pallor and sunken eyes, and put out a hand. 'Let's get you back to the sofa,' she said urgently, and saw Alex turn at once, hearing the anxiety in her voice.

Between the two of them, they supported her as she walked inside to the big sofa in the living room. Nelly collapsed backwards onto the cushions, closing her eyes and muttering something under her breath. Caroline, who had been watching their progress, went to fetch her a glass of iced water.

'I'm calling my doctor out,' Alex said, watching in concern. 'My private doctor this time. There must be something he can do.'

Nelly muttered to him under her breath.

Alex knelt beside her, taking his grandmother's hand. His face was tense with worry. 'Sorry, Nana, I didn't catch that. What did you say?'

Her eyes fluttered open, and she gave him a weary smile. 'I don't want a doctor. I'm tired, that's all.' She peered past him at Jennifer, and then whispered, 'You two young people go and enjoy yourselves. Let me sleep.'

CHAPTER THIRTY-SEVEN

Jennifer was anxious about the deterioration in Nelly's condition. She had never seen her so frail. But she thought some quiet time on the sofa, with just family and close friends around, would help to restore the old lady's energy. It had been a long day and Nelly was seriously ill, her health bolstered by a whole host of medications designed mostly to reduce her suffering. Not surprising, then, that she was looking so weak and unlike her usual ebullient self.

Jennifer grimaced. She was strung out herself, her body still tingling. From that very public kiss, though, not the panic attack that had preceded it.

The Delgardo effect, she thought drily.

Besides Raphael, whose shocked expression had burnt itself eternally onto her retina, how many other people had seen them locked in that unexpected clinch? Several dozen, at least. Maybe more. And how many of those were likely to share that moment on social media tonight?

She had spotted a few camera phones waving in the air when she'd surfaced, but her brain had been reeling at the time. It was only now, following the traumatic scene with Stuart – a fight that would certainly make it into the world's press – that she was beginning to worry about the potential damage.

'Try to get some rest, Nana.' Alex pulled up a chair next to Nelly, then glanced at Caroline, who had returned with water and was now plumping the cushions behind her head. 'Sorry, are you able to find Thelma for me? She's probably in the kitchen with Brodie.'

Caroline smiled at him warmly. 'Of course.'

Soundlessly, Jennifer left the room, slipping out through the wide-open doors into the evening air.

The sun was setting, the house and gardens lit up with golden light, and there was a distinctly cooler feel to the evening now. She shivered, wrapping her arms around herself, but kept walking. Better to be outside than in. It wasn't as though she could be of any help to Nelly, and with all this confused buzzing in her head, she needed time alone to think.

Bending to pick up some wine glasses abandoned on the lawn, Jennifer was gently chastised by one of the catering staff, who waved her away, saying it was their job to clear up, not hers. So she wandered across the lawn, tired and a little unsteady on her heels after several glasses of fine champagne. The folk band were packing up, and though there were still a few tuxedo-clad celebrities lounging in the marquee with bottles and cigarettes, it was clear the party was over.

'Jenny.'

She turned, overwhelmed as always by Alex's physical presence. He loomed over her, the hard lines of his face tinged gold by the sunset. 'Alex?' She felt almost angry with him, which was irrational. 'Why are you out here? Nelly needs you.'

'Thelma's sitting with her. She's practically asleep, anyway.' He pushed his mobile into his trouser pocket. 'I've called my private medical service. Someone should be here to look at her within the hour.'

'She probably just needs to rest.'

He took a deep breath, his powerful chest rising under the silk shirt. 'That's what Caroline said, too.'

'Caroline's usually right.'

There was a distant jingle of goat bells somewhere under the trees, and they both glanced over instinctively in the direction of the sound.

'I meant to say,' she continued awkwardly, 'I saw someone I know out with the goats earlier. Her name's Lizzie.' Jennifer hesitated, recalling the grey-haired woman she had seen earlier chasing through the orchard. 'She's—'

'Gifted with goats, or so I'm told. You know her?'

'Everyone knows Lizzie.'

'We needed someone to look after the goats full-time. One of Nana's new friends recommended her. Penny Jago, the one who runs the Cornish language classes in Pethporro.' He hesitated. 'You still going to those classes?'

'I haven't had time. I'm up against a deadline with my book.'

Alex said nothing, his expression brooding as he studied her.

Jennifer felt light-headed, suddenly too intensely aware of him. She dared not meet his eyes, though she felt his gaze intent on her face.

He had kissed her before out of kindness, or perhaps driven by some knee-jerk male rivalry, knowing that Raphael Tregar was watching them. She tried to block it out, but kept remembering his lips on hers, the restless excitement spiralling inside her again. He was standing so close now, she could smell the tangy scent of his aftershave and, beneath it, his own masculine scent.

Desperately, she cast about for something to distract him. To distract them both. 'Is Raphael Tregar still here?'

'Missing your ex already?' Alex made a face, seeing her embarrassment, but then added savagely, 'If you must know, Tregar just left. Him, his wife and her baby.' When she didn't make a comment, he pressed on, his tone growing harsher. 'Those two make a nice couple. Perfectly suited, I'd say.'

She closed her eyes, feeling sick.

'It's obvious why he chose her over you,' he continued, his voice ragged. 'Hannah Tregar's a stunner. And she provides the perfect light for his shade. All that blonde hair, those big baby blues.'

'For God's sake . . .'

'Don't keep holding a torch for him, Jenny.' He bared his teeth. 'You're worth more than him. More than that.'

Her face burning with shame, she turned away, desperate to escape his cruel words, and stumbled over an empty champagne bottle the caterers must have missed.

Alex caught her and dragged her close, spinning her round to face him. She swayed against him on her stilettos, unsteady and off-balance.

'He may not need your darkness, but I do,' he said thickly, staring down at her. His hunger was naked, undisguised.

'Christ, Jenny, when are you going to forget him? Look at me. I'm right here.'

She pushed at his chest, eyes blinded with tears. They seemed to come so easily, these days. It had been a summer of tears, and she was tired of crying.

'I thought you were finished with me. That night at the cottage . . .'

'I told you, I wasn't thinking straight.'

'But you're not even planning to stay in Cornwall.'

He was frowning. 'What?'

'Don't pretend you don't know what I'm talking about. That man you were speaking to before about a film deal—'

'Jeff. The executive producer on the last Cheetham film.'

'You've agreed to make a new one.'

He hesitated. 'I haven't signed anything yet.'

'It's only a matter of time though, right?'

He did not deny it.

Jennifer drew herself up, unable to listen to her heart when her head was yelling so loudly. This was crunch time, and she knew it. Things were getting serious between them. Too serious. How could she commit to a man who might not be around much in the future? She had always known their worlds were too different for the relationship to work. This hint of a possible film deal merely confirmed her fears.

'Look,' she said more calmly, 'you should absolutely make another Cheetham film. Of course you must. It's the best decision for your career.'

He searched her face. 'But . . .'

'But I can't start a relationship with you. I can't live like this.'

'Like what?'

'Never knowing how long it'll be before you're bored with life in the sticks and want to head for Hollywood again,' she said grimly. 'I know you only came back here to look after Nelly.'

'That wasn't the only reason.'

'I also remember what you said to me at the cottage. That it was over. That it wasn't going to work.' She raised her chin. 'You may claim you weren't thinking straight, but you haven't tried to take those words back.'

He released her, groaning and running a hand through his short hair. 'Listen, there's something else I need to tell you. Something ... hard. I haven't been entirely straight with you—'

An anguished cry from the house interrupted him.

Alex stiffened, turning his head.

Thelma lurched through the open doors onto the lawn, looking anxiously around the gardens, her face white with shock. 'Alex? Where are you?' When his sister saw him, she called across the lawn, 'Alex, come quickly.' Her voice was breathless, her words garbled. 'It's Nana. I can't get her to wake up.'

CHAPTER THIRTY-EIGHT

Nelly looked so peaceful lying there on the sofa, her face smoothed out, oddly younger now, her eyes closed. She looked exactly as though she had nodded off while her guests left the party, and might wake soon, refreshed and ready for another eventful year in her long life.

But Jennifer could see that Nelly was not asleep. She was deathly pale, and there was an unnatural stillness about the old lady, her chest unmoving, her lips slightly parted as though on a last breath.

'Nana?' Alex fell to his knees beside her, his voice cracking. 'Nana, please . . .'

Thelma stood by helplessly, her hands covering her face. 'Is she . . .? Oh God, I can't bear this. I only stepped out for a few minutes, I didn't know . . .' She gave a little moan. 'Please tell me she's not dead.'

But Alex did not answer.

The door was pushed wider, and Brodie and Caroline came into the room together. Caroline was flushed; perhaps even a little tipsy. Brodie looked sober and intent.

'What's going on?' Brodie stopped and stared at Nelly.

Caroline half bumped into him and stopped too. Despite

her air of inebriation, she seemed to take in the situation at a single glance. 'Nelly?' she said, suddenly and reassuringly professional. 'Nelly, can you hear me?'

She stepped past Alex's kneeling figure and took hold of the old lady's wrist between fingers and thumb, her head cocked to one side.

Everyone waited in silence as she felt for a pulse. But after only a few seconds, she laid Nelly's arm gently back by her side and straightened, her expression apologetic.

'I'm so sorry,' Caroline said in a hushed voice, looking first at Alex, and then at Thelma, who was now sobbing. 'I'm afraid she's gone.'

Brodie put his arm around Thelma's shoulders, and she sagged against him gratefully.

Alex said nothing, kneeling beside his grandmother. He had taken her hand and was pressing it against his cheek, head bowed.

'Oh, Alex,' Jennifer burst out, instantly in tears. 'I'm so, so sorry.'

Still Alex was silent.

Jennifer wrapped her arms around herself, stunned, chilled. *Nelly was gone*. The awful realisation thrummed through her whole body, and she didn't want to face it. Full of remorse, not wanting to intrude on their grief, she stepped away a short distance, wiping away a fat, rolling tear.

Behind her, a few party guests, who must have wandered in from the gardens to see what all the shouting was about, discreetly made their way out again. One pulled the lawn doors shut behind them, and for a moment the room was silent except for Thelma's ragged sobs.

The clock on the mantelpiece chimed a quarter past nine. Almost sunset.

'I'd better make some calls,' Caroline was telling Alex and Thelma. 'You two stay here, be with her for a while. Let me inform the authorities for you.' She put a hand on Alex's shoulder, then repeated softly, 'I'm so sorry.'

Jennifer wished she could be as comforting as her stepsister, that she too knew what to say, what to do. But what was there to say, except repeat that she was sorry?

'Oh, Nana,' Thelma moaned. 'No one was here,' she said in a high, shaking voice, looking round at them all. 'None of us was with her at the end.'

Jennifer said nothing. She couldn't. She felt numb inside, unable to take her eyes off Nelly. Only a short while ago, they had been laughing and joking with the old lady, giving her presents and birthday cake.

How could this have happened?

Guilt swamped her, a crushing weight on her chest. She bit her lip so hard she could taste blood in her mouth. *Had* anyone been with Nelly at the end, or was Thelma right? The thought tormented her. She and Alex had been so preoccupied with their own concerns, they had not even thought to check on Nelly. And while they were outside in the late sun, sniping at each other, the old lady had closed her eyes and slipped away . . .

Could this be her fault?

Caroline seemed to read her mind. Swiftly, she led her to the other side of the room, where the others wouldn't overhear their conversation.

'Stop blaming yourself, Jenny,' she said sternly.

'I wasn't there when she died. None of us was.' The tears ran freely down her cheeks. 'I . . . I was outside. With Alex.'

'There was nothing anyone could have done, even if she'd been found sooner,' her stepsister said bluntly, meeting her eyes. 'Nelly was a very sick woman. We all knew her condition was terminal, how little time she had left. And she'd chosen not to be resuscitated, anyway. Going like this, without any pain . . . It's a blessing, trust me.'

'But alone . . .'

'Sometimes people wait until they're alone before letting go. It's quite common, and not your fault.' But she gave Jennifer a tight hug all the same, and it was clear from her voice that she was shaken, too. 'If it's any consolation, I doubt Nelly knew anything about it. She went in her sleep.'

It's a blessing.

Jennifer tried to focus on that thought, but it was hard.

'Stay strong, sis.' Caroline released her with a sad smile. 'I have to make those calls. Her death needs to be reported. I won't be long.'

Her stepsister hurried out into the hall. Jennifer didn't know what to do, feeling like she didn't belong there. Alex and Thelma were both kneeling beside Nelly now, their heads bowed over the still body.

'I'll start seeing to the funeral arrangements straight away.' Brodie's voice was hoarse. He had tears in his eyes too. 'That is, if you'd like me to? If I'm overstepping the mark, Alex, just tell me.'

Alex stood up slowly. He took Brodie's hand and squeezed it. 'You're my best friend, Brodie. You can't overstep a mark that doesn't exist.' His voice was muffled. 'My head's in a mess right now. Thank you, I really appreciate your help.'

He glanced round and saw Jennifer standing there, alone at the back of the room. Their eyes met. He had been crying, his face wet. For those few seconds, she saw terrible, unspeakable sorrow in his face, and the same guilt she was feeling.

Then he looked away.

'Family only, I think,' Alex added. 'Let's keep this private.'

'Whatever you say.' Brodie embraced him.

Jennifer felt everything inside her collapse. She groped for the doors onto the lawn and stumbled outside. The blood-orange sunset was full in her eyes. Blinking, she raised her arm against the light. The music had finally stopped and the only people in the marquee now were hired staff, wandering about with bin bags, clearing up the party detritus and dismantling tables.

Closing the door behind her as quietly as possible, Jennifer stood for a moment, trying to compose herself. What was that quotation from Christina Rossetti on the invitation card?

> *Because the birthday of my life*
> *Is come, my love is come to me.*

Oh, Nelly, she thought, and wept again as she slipped off her stilettos and crossed the dew-damp lawns barefoot, making for home. *Safe journey, my friend. Safe journey.*

CHAPTER THIRTY-NINE

'It's not that I don't like it,' Caroline said, eyeing her own reflection dubiously, then shooting a quick smile at the hairdresser, who was looking aggrieved. 'It's just, I'm wondering if I should have gone more extreme.'

Jennifer glanced her way. It was true that her stepsister's new hairstyle was more of a trim than a cut, with some layering to add interest. But it did suit her face shape. Plus, her natural ash-blonde colour looked as stunning as ever.

But that wasn't really what Caroline was getting at.

'Like me, you mean?' Jennifer said, paying at the desk with her debit card.

'Of course not. Did I say that? Though, now you mention it . . .' Her stepsister raised her eyebrows, studying Jennifer's hair with fresh disbelief. 'I still can't believe you decided to have it all lopped off. You look like a Marine.'

'Don't exaggerate, it's not that severe.'

Besides, she thought, *it's done now. No going back.*

Though it was definitely strange, turning her head from side to side and not feeling the full weight of her hair any more. There were mirrors everywhere in the only hair salon in Pethporro, the snappily named Cornish Cutz, so she ducked her head to study herself again. Just to be sure she hadn't made the biggest mistake of her life. Or rather, her *second* biggest, according to Caroline.

But no, she still loved it.

Her new look.

The long, thick ponytail was gone, and in its place was a different woman entirely, with ultra-short, razor-cut dark hair that framed an elfin face, showing off high cheekbones and the slant of her eyes.

'I look like a Cornish pisky,' Jennifer said, a little ruefully. But she smiled at her surprising new reflection. 'It's perfect, though. I was sick of all that bloody hair. Like being Rapunzel.' Her mouth twisted. 'Only without the prince.'

'There was a prince,' Caroline said pointedly. 'But you dumped him.'

'You can't dump someone you're not having a relationship with.'

'Whatever.'

'I think it looks very nice,' the blonde hairdresser said suddenly, butting into their cryptic conversation. She didn't look much older than twenty. 'It's very fashionable, short hair.'

'If it gets much shorter, she won't have anything left,' Caroline shot back, but subsided at a glare from Jennifer.

Jennifer left a tip for the girl, who had done a great job on her hair. In her opinion, at any rate. 'Thanks,' she said, and headed for the door.

The sunshine was bright, but not as warm as it had been over the past month, a lively salt breeze blowing in off the Atlantic. Jennifer shivered, walking with Caroline on the shady side of the street, and wished she'd brought a jacket out with her today. It was the tail end of summer, the weather practically autumnal now, and most of the seasonal visitors had disappeared, leaving the car parks emptier and some of the tourist shops and cafés already closed until next year.

Pethporro had felt quieter and more intimate this past week.

More like home.

Her stepsister peered at her sideways. 'Tell me to mind my own business, but—'

'Mind your own business.'

'But,' Caroline repeated patiently, 'you haven't been yourself lately. Not since . . . Well, not since Nelly died.'

'Please, don't.'

'This haircut. It's extreme, but I think it's probably a good idea. All this moping about in your little cottage is downright unhealthy. You need to start doing new things again. Meeting new people.'

'Oh, God . . .'

'There's a really nice guy who works at the hospital. The minor injuries unit. I could set you up with him for a drink. I'm seeing this new bloke, Charlie. He's a librarian. Anyway, we could have a foursome one night.'

'I beg your pardon?'

'I mean, a double date. Go to the cinema together, or for a meal. Somewhere nice. Just the four of us.' Caroline smiled at her winningly. 'What do you say?'

'Caro—'

'You can't keep pining for him. It's ridiculous.'

'I'm not pining for anyone. I don't even know who you're talking about.' Jennifer felt herself blush under her stepsister's scrutiny. 'Anyway, I'm happy not dating anyone right now. A simple life, that's all I want.'

'I don't like you living alone in that cottage,' Caroline said flatly.

'Why?'

'Because you're bloody depressed.'

Shocked, Jennifer stopped dead and let go of her arm. 'Sorry?'

'Take a proper look in the mirror sometime. You're not yourself, Jenny. You look like a ghost. Yes, the hair's nice. But you're pale, and you've lost so much weight. You're not happy, admit it.'

Jennifer opened her mouth crossly to deny it, to explain that she was perfectly happy, thanks. But the words wouldn't come.

Was she depressed?

She was lonely at Pixie Cottage, that was for sure. But who wouldn't be, with only Ripper for company most days, staring at the dark woods and knowing he would never come walking out of those trees again?

'I don't believe it,' Caroline whispered, staring over Jennifer's shoulder. 'Will you look at who that is.'

Warily, Jennifer turned to look.

And her heart leapt.

It was Brodie.

He was standing on the other side of Pethporro high street, a bag clutched to his chest, staring back at them as though he couldn't believe his eyes either.

Jennifer struggled to hide her consternation. If Brodie was in town, maybe Alex was too. She didn't think she could bear to see him again. The wound was still too raw.

'Well, well. How very odd,' Caroline said quietly. 'I thought they all left Cornwall after the funeral. That's what everyone has been saying. That Alex signed up for a new Cheetham film and flew out to America almost immediately.'

'I'm pretty sure he did, yes. It was in *Hello.*'

She saw Caroline study her curiously, but said nothing further. She was done with pretending she didn't read the celebrity mags.

Brodie waited for a car to pass before hurrying across the narrow road. 'Hey,' he said, his eyes skimming Caroline's slim figure without expression, and then turned to Jennifer with a smile. 'You cut your hair. I like it. It suits you.'

'Thanks.'

'How are you?'

'I'm great,' she said automatically, and saw Caroline's mouth twitch.

'Yeah, she's just dandy,' Caroline said ironically.

He glanced at Caroline again, a little frown jerking his brows together.

'And how are you, Caroline?'

'I'm just dandy too. How about you? And Alex and Thelma?' Caroline's brittle tone softened. 'How are they bearing up? It's been hard for them, I expect. Losing Nelly so suddenly.'

He nodded, his eyes serious. 'I haven't seen much of Thelma lately, to be honest. She's got a place in London now, she and the baby. But Alex . . .' He stopped, looking directly at Jennifer. 'I'm glad I ran into you today. I was going to drive round to the cottage tonight, see if I could catch you at home. In fact, I've been trying to get hold of you for several weeks.' He paused. 'Didn't you get any of my texts?'

She felt awful. 'Yes, but . . . I didn't think there was much point replying. To be honest, I didn't want to stir things up again.'

Caroline glared at her silently.

Jennifer hadn't told her about Brodie's texts, and she did feel a little guilty about that. Though it was nobody's business but her own.

Brodie nodded. 'I can appreciate that. But as a personal favour, would you come back to Porro Park with me?'

'Right now?'

'Right now,' he repeated. 'Alex is there, packing up the place. Throwing things into boxes. He's planning to sell the whole estate, including your cottage. We're moving back to Hollywood.'

I knew it, I just knew it, she thought, with a stab to the heart, and recalled having prophesied exactly that scenario the last time they were together. Her triumph felt small and bitter now, though, like a bad taste in her mouth.

'What about Nelly's goats?'

'We've found them a refuge. Not far from Pethporro.'

'For all seven?'

His mouth quirked. 'In return for a generous donation, yes. Someone's bringing an animal transport van to pick them up tomorrow afternoon.' He hesitated. 'In fact, I think you may know her. It's Lizzie. She's helping out at the refuge now, apparently. Raphael Tregar recommended her to me. She's coming with Penny Jago – you remember her, I'm sure. The woman who runs the Cornish language classes. She's another of the refuge volunteers.'

'Yes, I know Lizzie and Penny.'

'So will you come back with me?' When she didn't reply, simply staring back at him in silence, Brodie made a face. 'Please, just come and talk to him. Five minutes.'

'Why, Brodie?' Her insides were twisted up with hurt. The last person she wanted to see was Alex. She had just got back to some semblance of normality. 'I've got nothing to say to him. If he sells the cottage along with the estate, fine. The next owner can either let me stay on or throw me out. Either way, I'll deal with that situation when I get there.'

'No one's going to throw you out of Pixie Cottage. I'll make sure that's understood.'

'Then why should I come back with you?'

'Because I'm worried about Alex,' Brodie said flatly. He stuck his hands in his jeans pockets, looking unhappy. 'Worried sick.'

'I don't understand.'

'Yes, you do.'

She looked away, saying nothing.

'Just come and talk to him before he leaves.' Brodie lowered his voice. 'Look, I don't know exactly what happened between the two of you. But I do know he hasn't been the same since.'

Jennifer groaned. 'We're not right for each other, Brodie.'

'Says who?'

'Says me.' She shrugged, not wanting to go into details. 'Anyway, it was one night, that's all. And even that didn't end well.'

'Alex knows that. Give him a chance to explain.'

'I don't need an explanation. It would never work between us.' She folded her arms, glaring at him, frustration rising. 'Pethporro is where I belong, and out there, in La La Land, under the bright lights, that's where Alex belongs. I know you mean well, and that you're trying to help. But our worlds are just too . . . well, too different.

'I'm sorry, I really am,' she added apologetically, 'but the answer's no.'

Brodie looked at her in despair. But he didn't argue.

Was she doing the right thing?

It hurt, not seeing him.

Not knowing.

But it was better to hurt like this now, she told herself, than to be left in pieces later, unable to recover from a love affair that was doomed from the start.

Jennifer nodded to Caroline before she was tempted to change her mind. 'Come on, let's go. It's half-day closing, and I need to grab some shopping before I go home.' She threw Brodie a wan smile over her shoulder as they walked away. 'Goodbye, Brodie. And good luck with it all.'

Caroline looked back at him a few times too, then studied her face, frowning. Once they were out of earshot, she said, 'Jenny, are you absolutely, one hundred per cent sure that was the right decision?'

'Yes, why?'

'Oh, no particular reason.' She gave Jennifer a lopsided smile. 'Except that you're my sister, and I know when you're telling someone a complete and utter whopper.'

'Stepsister,' Jennifer corrected her automatically.

'No, my *sister*.' Squeezing her arm, Caroline hugged her close. 'My very silly, impulsive, totally mad and delusional sister.'

CHAPTER FORTY

Holding a complex yoga pose on the mat in her bedroom next morning, in search of an elusive inner peace, Jennifer heard a gentle tinkling sound – a bell? – and seconds later, an all-too-familiar bleating. She unrolled from her pose, not without difficulty, and stumbled to the window in disbelief.

Baby stood in the garden below, chomping on the stringy remains of the old runner bean crop. There was a tatty length of rope trailing away behind her like a lead.

Had Baby broken free from a tether and run all the way through the woods like that? It was lucky she hadn't got hooked up on something and injured herself.

'Talk about déjà vu,' Jennifer said, sighing.

She gazed down at the incorrigible creature, looked back at her yoga mat and shook her head. There had been little hope of achieving inner peace anyway. But the goat's arrival made it official.

Brodie had said that Lizzie and Penny would be coming this afternoon to take Nelly's goats to an animal refuge. Which meant she had two options.

She could ignore the goat grazing cheerfully in her

vegetable garden and wait until Baby either wandered away on her own or somebody came in search of her.

Or she could lead Baby back to Porro Park . . .

Slowly, still trying to dissuade herself from doing anything about the goat's presence, she pulled on her jeans and a hoody before going downstairs to find her shoes.

If she didn't lead Baby back to Porro Park, Lizzie and Penny might give up trying to find the missing seventh goat and take the others without her.

That would be disastrous for Baby.

She dared not acknowledge the secret desire, bumping around at the back of her mind, to see Alex Delgardo again before he left Cornwall for ever. It was humiliating to admit that she was still lonely, of course. That seeing him again, even for a few minutes, would light up the world for her, a world that had grown rather drab and colourless. But she couldn't deny that she wanted to go to Porro Park one last time, despite what she had told Brodie yesterday, and despite what common sense was telling her.

But perhaps Alex wasn't even at the house. He might have left already. Packed up and flown in the night, now that there was nothing to keep him here.

That didn't stop her from hoping, though.

'Hello, you silly thing.' She approached the goat and made a quick grab for the rope, twisting it round her wrist for added security. 'That old runner bean plant doesn't look very appetising. Why don't you let me take you home instead?'

Baby did not resist, greeting her like an old friend.

She headed into the woods with the goat, listening to the rustle of branches, the leaves above them turning delicious shades of red and gold, Baby constantly nuzzling at her hip as though hoping to find cream crackers in her hoody pocket. But all she had in there was a tissue.

'Who's meant to be looking after you?' she asked the goat, who didn't reply, unsurprisingly. 'Whoever it is, they're not doing a great job.'

Baby bleated, her tone plaintive.

'Poor thing.' She tugged on the goat's silky ears, and then patted Baby's rump as she danced in a circle around her. 'You're missing Nelly, aren't you? Yes, so am I.' Then she felt a little tearful, and had to stop and blow her nose. 'But what good does it do, crying all the time? All I get is a red nose.'

The goat frisked about her playfully, kicking up her hooves and twisting the rope around them until they were almost tied up together.

'Oh, Baby,' she said, groaning, and bent to unpick the knot her frolicking had created. 'Look what you've done now.'

While her head was bent, someone stepped out of the trees on the path ahead, and when she glanced up, the sunlight slanting through the branches dazzled her, so she didn't immediately realise who it was.

'Need a hand with that?'

She straightened, her heart thumping.

It was Alex.

He was standing a few feet away, staring intently at her short hair. His own hair looked wet and heavy, slicked back as though he'd recently come from the shower, and his white t-shirt clung to his body, his jeans sitting low on his hips.

She stared back, unashamedly devouring every inch of his body with her eyes while hating herself for her weakness. He looked gorgeous and magnificently brooding, and she couldn't pretend any longer.

She was still in love with him.

And even as she finally admitted that to herself, accepting her own stupidity, she realised that she had never felt lonelier or more unhappy.

She met his eyes as he came up to her, and saw nothing in his face but his own natural intensity: the movie star charisma that had left her almost dazed the first time they met. Brodie had said he was worried about Alex. *Worried sick*. But she couldn't see anything wrong with him, except for a slight pallor. He'd lost weight, though, she realised, noting how loose his jeans were. Which made two of them.

'Not much good with knots, are you? Here, let me.' She dropped the knot without a word and Alex took over, untwisting the rope, nudging the goat aside as Baby tried to interfere. 'She probably ran off because she sensed what was coming.'

'Sorry?'

'Lizzie and Penny are due up at the house after lunch.' He did not look at her, though the knot was undone. 'Brodie told me he saw you in town yesterday, that he'd mentioned Nelly's goats will be going to an animal refuge. Not what I'd like, obviously, but . . . There'll be nobody here soon. Françoise has been feeding the herd in our absence, but once I sell the house, she and Marie will be coming to join me.'

She felt numb. 'In America?'

'Yes.' He paused. 'Would that bother you?'

For a moment, there was prickling silence. The question sat there between them like a malignant toad that might at any second transform itself into a prince.

Would that bother you?

Yes, her heart screamed at him.

But her frightened lips would not say the word. Because saying yes would mean she cared. More than cared. That she loved him. And then he would leave anyway, and the humiliation would be more than she could stand.

'No,' she blurted out.

His brows twitched together at her tone.

She pointed at the goat, who had managed to grab a mouthful of deadly nightshade from a nearby patch. 'No, Baby,' she added, hurriedly qualifying her remark, 'don't eat that! It's bad for you.' She swallowed. 'Very, very bad.'

Alex bent to wrench the deadly nightshade from Baby's stubborn jaws. 'Damn.' He chucked the torn leaves aside. 'I think she got some.'

'I don't think a small amount will kill her,' she said as the goat defiantly chewed what remained of her poisonous spoils. 'But it might give her an upset stomach. And her milk may suffer.'

He looked worried. 'Sure?'

'Pretty much. Most goats know to avoid the stuff, though. But not this pea brain. Better not give her so much slack, in case she grabs more.' She nodded to the rope he'd looped comfortably about his wrist, then frowned. 'Come to think of it, why does Baby have a rope attached to her collar, anyway? Was she tied up at the house and got away?'

'Erm . . .' He raised his eyebrows, studying the rope, and then the goat, seeming lost for words.

A sudden realisation struck her.

'*You* put the rope on her. You deliberately brought her

to the cottage this morning, didn't you? And left her in my garden.' She stared at him when he didn't respond. 'Alex?'

He made a face. 'Guilty as charged.'

'But why?'

'I don't know.' He bent his head, a hard tinge of colour along his cheekbones. 'For old times' sake? I mean, isn't this where you came in?' His smile looked forced. 'Stage right, with a goat?'

'You could have rung me. Texted, even.'

'I didn't know how. Not after . . .' He looked at her, almost pleadingly. 'Everything went wrong. The way I spoke to you at the party, and then Nana . . .'

His voice broke on that word.

'I'm so sorry about Nelly,' she told him, moved by the tears in his eyes. 'Your grandmother was a very special woman. A woman after my own heart. I miss our witchy chats,' she half smiled, 'and our baking marathons.' She paused when he didn't respond, feeling wretched. He couldn't even bear to look at her. 'I sent you and Thelma a card.'

'Yes, we got that. Thank you.' His voice still clogged, he cleared his throat. 'After the funeral, I kept meaning to ring you. To drop by the cottage one afternoon. But there were so many things that needed to be done. You know how it is.'

Yes, she knew how it was. Selling up, moving away . . .

For old times' sake, he had said. But he couldn't wait to get rid of her, that was the sad truth. Whatever Brodie was worried about, it was nothing she could help with. Now Nelly had gone, she wasn't a part of his world any more. This remote spot in the wilds of Cornwall might be her place, but it had never been his. He was just passing through Peth-porro on his way to somewhere else. To some*one* better.

She stuck her chin out.

'Now you've got your goat back, I'd better leave you to your packing,' she said, turning away.

'You cut your hair.'

Jennifer stopped and looked back at him, taken aback. Hesitant, she put a hand to her radically short crop. It still felt strange not to have all that hair everywhere, falling in her face, tumbling over her shoulders.

Did he approve? Did he hate it? And why the hell did she care?

'I think a goat ate it while I was asleep.'

His eyes flicked to her face, but he did not smile at her joke. 'It's sexy.'

She didn't know where to look.

'Thanks,' she said brightly, and began to back away. 'Well, goodbye.'

'Going back to your lonely cottage?'

'That's right,' she said, then added impulsively, desperate to show him she had moved on with her life, 'except I won't be alone for much longer.'

'Is that so?' His jaw clenched, his eyes turning as cold as the Atlantic. 'Okay, I'll bite. What's his name?'

Alex Delgardo, she thought grimly. 'I mean, I've taken a job.'

'Job?' He frowned. 'What job?'

Jennifer considered telling him to mind his own bloody business. But getting angry would only indicate that she felt something for him.

'Directing the Pethporro Boxing Day pageant. I put my

application in, exactly as Raphael suggested I should, and was given an interview. I heard back from him this morning – I got it.' Her smile was brisk and forced. 'I start next week, taking over from Hannah. She's offered to share her files on last year's pageant, so it shouldn't be too much work.'

His brows rose steeply. 'Hannah Tregar? I thought you hated her.'

'Hate's a strong word.'

His brows remained where they were.

'It hurt when he chose Hannah over me.' She saw his incredulous look, and made a face. 'Yes, okay, it hurt a lot. And for a long time, too. But I've put all that behind me. I need a job, and this one is perfect.'

'Right.' His lip curled. 'As pageant director, I'm guessing Raphael Tregar will be your boss, so you'll be seeing a lot of him. Maybe some brainstorming sessions at the cottage. Late into the evening.' His contemptuous tone stung her. 'But of course, that wouldn't have been a factor in your decision.'

Jennifer felt a furious heat in her face. 'Oddly enough, it wasn't.'

'Whatever,' he drawled.

Fury whipped through her. How dared he pass judgement on her? 'At least Raphael wasn't my *landlord* when he started sleeping with me.'

'What's that supposed to mean?'

She said nothing.

Alex dragged Baby away from the patch of deadly night-shade again, ignoring her high, crotchety bleat. 'Are you claiming I took advantage of you? That I used my position to ... That you only slept with me because ...' His words tailed off, his eyes stormy as he snatched several deep, shaking breaths as though trying to control himself.

Jennifer opened her mouth, then shut it again. The stupid thought had flashed through her head for a mere second, that was all. And she had thrown it at him with all her force, grateful for the sudden, unexpected ammunition. Only it had blown up in her own face now. And she didn't know how to take it back.

She shook her head wordlessly, wishing the dreadful words unsaid.

'Do you really believe that, Jennifer? That I took advantage of you that night?' His voice was like stone now, hard and unyielding. 'Tell the truth.'

'No,' she whispered.

'I can't hear you.'

'No,' she almost shouted, aware that the world had blurred. 'No, damn you.' She did not want to cry. Never again. She was sick of tears. 'It wasn't like that.'

He nodded curtly. 'Thank you.'

Then, to her horror, Alex turned and strode back towards Porro Park without another word, his back very straight, Baby skipping along beside him.

CHAPTER FORTY-ONE

I'll never see him again, Jennifer thought, watching him disappear through a sheen of tears.

It was for the best. How could it not be?

Alex had his world. She had hers. And there was no overlap between the two, except this one place, this wild and leafy Cornish wood where they had been happy for a time.

But nothing lasts for ever. Not even love. She'd proved that with Raphael.

I'll never see him again.

She had to get home, back to her safe little bolthole in the middle of nowhere, before the violent torrent of emotion that she knew was on its way burst out into soul-racking sobs. Jennifer took one unsteady step backwards on the woodland path, retreating to her cottage. Then another.

I'll never see him again.

To finish like this, though, on an insult, on a misunderstanding . . .

The pain was intolerable.

Jennifer drew a deep breath and plunged after him, calling his name wildly as she ran. He didn't slow down or turn his head, though he must have heard her.

'Alex, stop! For God's sake . . . I didn't mean it.' She caught up with him at last and grabbed his arm, sobbing breathlessly, 'I'm sorry, okay? That wasn't how it happened, and I never thought that, and I have no idea why I even said it. Except that I'm an idiot.'

Alex stared down at her, his face like sculpted wood, his mouth tight.

He dropped Baby's rope and the mischievous goat danced merrily away, hunting for more forbidden plants to forage, the loose rope trailing after her. Luckily there didn't seem to be anything poisonous in the vicinity.

'Alex?'

He jerked a hand to his cheek, rubbing it with the briefest and most impatient of gestures, and she suddenly realised he was crying. She met his eyes, and they were bleak, desolate.

'I'm sorry,' she whispered.

He nodded, then looked pointedly down at her hand on his bare forearm. When she released him, he started to walk away again.

'I can't breathe without you, you know,' she said after him clearly.

He turned, staring.

'That's how it feels, anyway. I wake in the night and it's like I'm suffocating. It hurts here,' she tapped her chest, 'so badly, I want to die. My head aches like I'm constantly underwater. I can't sleep, or if I do, I have nightmares. I can't eat.' She grimaced. 'Though I can drink, no problem. And all because of you, Alex Delgardo.'

Slowly, he came back towards her.

'But I'm sick of feeling like that,' she added before he could say anything. 'I'm sick of crying my eyes out over you. I'm sick of it all. The pointlessness. The waste of energy.' Jennifer threw her hands up in a gesture of hopelessness. 'I fell in love with you, Alex. But so what? I'll get over it. I got over Raphael, I can get over you.'

His face suddenly seemed to light up. 'You *fell* in love with me?' he repeated, watching her closely. 'Past tense?'

She shrugged, unwilling to open herself to any more hurt.

'Okay, if you're so over him,' he said, speaking very quickly, 'why take that job? You'll be working alongside Tregar, won't you?'

'Probably.'

'Seeing him most days, speaking to him, spending time with him?'

'I'll mostly be working from home.'

He stopped in front of her, his expression uncertain. 'But he'll be in regular contact with you. Phone calls, emails.'

'Yes,' she said huskily.

'Why do that to yourself? This is a man who rejected you, who chose another woman over you, who left you miserable and ready to retreat from the world.' When she began to protest, he shook his head. 'That's why you chose to rent Pixie Cottage, isn't it? Because you needed to turn your back on the world. To find a place where nobody could watch you hurting.'

Her mouth twisted at the pathetic way he made her sound, but she did not bother to deny it. She *had* been pathetic. And might be again, if she couldn't kick this gnawing pain in her heart. But that was the nature of unrequited love.

'So why put yourself through that kind of daily punishment? Are you absolutely sure you're not fooling yourself, that part of you doesn't need to see Raphael again? To be a part of his life again, even if only in a professional capacity this time?' He thrust his hands into his jeans pockets, rocking on his heels as he studied her, the look in his face suddenly calculating. 'I mean, you're an intelligent, educated woman. You don't need to settle for this kind of torture. You could have any job you want.'

'You don't know much about the North Cornwall job market, do you?'

'Okay. Then let *me* give you a job.'

Her throat closed up. 'What?'

'I'm serious.' His eyes were intent on her face. 'Come to Los Angeles. Travel the world with me. Just say the word.'

'Is that how you solve a problem in your world? Throw money at it?' She shook her head, backing away again. 'Now you really are crossing a line.' Her voice cracked. 'Landlord, lover, employer ... What next?'

'That isn't what I meant. Don't twist this out of context.'

'You want me,' she burst out, and saw his face harden. Then redden, his gaze sliding away, his breath quickening. 'Don't you?'

Alex struggled for a moment, not looking at her. Then nodded abruptly without saying anything.

'So how is this any different from me taking a job with Raphael?'

His dark eyes flashed back to her face, their depths suddenly restless and turbulent again. 'What are you saying?

That you lied before? That you do still love him?' His voice roughened. 'Because if so—'

'Do you love me, Alex?'

He stared, caught off guard, and said nothing. But there was guilt in his face.

'I'm glad we straightened that out,' she said breathlessly, vibrating with pain. 'This conversation is over. Goodbye.'

Now it was her turn to walk away, though every step was excruciating, as though she were treading on broken glass.

But at the end of this walk of shame was Pixie Cottage, her sanctuary, her safe haven. There, she could throw herself into her work for the next few months. Make phone calls, write emails and scribble on Post-it notes, planning the Boxing Day pageant. And probably weep herself into a coma at the end of every day with a large glass in her hand.

She had misread the look in his eyes, after all. Alex Delgardo didn't love her. He wanted her, but that was as far as it went for him. No love, no commitment.

'Jenny!'

She hadn't even heard him behind her. Suddenly he was there, spinning her round, his arms tight about her, his mouth on her hair, her cheek, her lips . . .

'Please don't go,' he muttered into her throat. 'You got me, okay?'

'Got you?'

'I love you, Jennifer Bolitho. I'm crazy about you.'

She pushed him away a little and stared into his face, speechless. He did not appear to be acting. So maybe she *had* misheard him. There could be no other explanation.

'S-sorry?' she croaked.

'I'm in love with you. Isn't that what you wanted to hear?' Alex groaned. 'I thought it was just a summer thing. That if I pushed you away, the feeling would go too. But I was wrong. I pushed you away and it nearly killed me. Like you, I haven't been able to sleep for weeks, or eat properly, or make any decisions about my career. I've been driving Brodie mad.' He bent his head towards her, his gaze fixed on her mouth. 'I'm a complete wreck, Jenny. And you're the only one who can fix me.'

Was he telling the truth? But he must be. Why would he lie?

She let him kiss her again, her senses swimming, then turned her head aside. 'Wait, I don't understand. Why not just tell me how you felt?'

He looked away. 'Because I was broken.' He was not trying to hide his suffering any longer, his face stark. 'I would have been no good to you. You were just coming out of that hell with Tregar, and I thought . . . well, you witnessed my night terrors first-hand. And there were other episodes, things I'm not proud of.'

'Your bandaged hands.'

He nodded. 'It was the day Ripper disappeared. Nana said she might have seen him heading for the orchard, so I went to check it out. A helicopter flew overhead, very low, close to the treetops.'

'I heard it too.'

'The sun was in my eyes, blinding me. And the helicopter blades, they were so loud, almost deafening . . .' He stared at nothing, obviously lost in the memory. 'I had a flashback. To the night of the bombing, you know?'

'Oh, God,' she whispered, horrified for him.

'I totally lost it. Started flailing about, screaming, shouting. Nearly demolished a drystone wall with my bare hands, apparently. Brodie found me before I'd done myself any serious damage, thank God. He got my head straight again, sorted me out with some meds for the anxiety.' He grimaced. 'I don't know what I'd have done without Brodie this past year. Killed myself, probably.'

'Please don't say that,' she said urgently.

'I'm sorry, but it's important you know all this before taking me on. Because there's a chance it's always going to be there, waiting for me.' He took a step back, releasing her, his face serious now. 'Do you remember the first day we met?'

'Of course I do.'

'That was the anniversary of the bombing. A really tough day. I was just about holding it together, for Nana's sake. But then I got a call from one of the other survivors, who was on the verge of a breakdown, and it brought everything back to me.'

She felt so guilty, remembering that first meeting. 'Nelly did tell me you'd had some bad news. I wish I'd known the truth. I thought—'

'That I was an arrogant bastard?' His smile was humourless. 'But how could you have known? I kept all that quiet, out of the papers. I didn't want it to touch Nana. She had enough on her plate with her illness.' He closed his eyes briefly, as though remembering. 'But after Nana died, I made a decision. I've been back in therapy. I've been taking it more seriously this time, keeping up with the meds, really committing myself to understanding what happened to me.

You see, the bombing at the hotel left me an emotional wreck. I looked fine on the surface, I could just about function. But inside I was shot to hell.'

'Post-traumatic stress disorder?'

'That's it, exactly. PTSD. I wasn't in a position to love anyone, not when I couldn't even love myself.' He had tears in his eyes again. 'After I met you, Jenny, that's when things started to change. I couldn't stop thinking about you. I knew you were special, right from the start. To be honest, it was a shock. I didn't expect to come to Cornwall and find someone like you. Someone honest and straightforward, and yet so different, too. Like you'd come from another planet. Your stories . . .'

'I didn't think you liked them. Or me.'

'Quite the opposite. You are so wise, Jenny. You see everything.'

She wished that were true.

'Tell me what happened the night of the bombing, Alex. The whole truth this time. And don't leave anything out.'

CHAPTER FORTY-TWO

Alex hesitated for a moment, looking back at her, turmoil in his face. Then he slowly nodded. 'I have to tell you sometime, so I suppose it might as well be now. But it's not pleasant.' He stepped away, putting a little distance between them. His breathing had increased, as though under stress. 'It was my fault she died, you see.' His voice trembled, and then broke as he added, 'My fault Brodie lost his leg. It was the worst night of my life. You didn't see them. The victims. The blood, the carnage . . .'

It was my fault she died.

'You said . . . she. Who are you talking about?'

He ran a hand over his face. 'Her name was Paula. One of the film crew. She was happily married, even had a son back home. She showed me photos of him during the car ride to the party. Cute kid, about three or four years old. I remember how proud she was that he was already learning to read.' He groaned. 'One minute she was fine, walking across the hotel lobby behind us. Next thing I knew, she was dead.' He was gazing fixedly at nothing, his face pale, eyes wide and dark with horror. 'Blown to pieces.'

'That's awful.' She swallowed. 'But not your fault, Alex.'

'Of course it was my fault.'

'You didn't bomb the place. You weren't the terrorist.'

'But I knew Paula didn't really want to be there. She'd told me about some friend of hers who owned the hotel, and was hosting a private party there. We'd been in the desert for weeks, and I was bored. I insisted that we go, and Paula probably didn't know how to say no to me. I was the big star, Alex Delgardo. People didn't say no to *me*.'

'Were you and her . . .?'

'God, no.' He stared at her, aghast. 'What do you take me for? She loved her husband, we were just colleagues. The poor bastard. I could barely face him at the funeral. If I hadn't been so full of my own importance, Paula would still be alive, and as for Brodie . . .'

'Brodie doesn't blame you.'

'Then he should. Some nights when I fall asleep, I see her face.' His breathing quickened, his voice suddenly hoarse. 'She's smiling, looking down at her phone. She says something like, *hang on, guys, I need to make a call*. Halfway across the hotel lobby, heading for the lifts. I stop to talk to someone. A boy who's asked for my autograph. We're talking films, you know. Me and Brodie and this boy, just having a laugh, and then . . . *boom*.' Alex flinched, his whole body ducking as though reliving the event. 'When I came to, it was dark and I was lying under rubble. There were flames, smoke . . . The place was on fire. When I got to my hands and knees, I tried to see what had happened to Paula and Brodie. But there were bodies everywhere. People screaming. It was like being in hell.'

'Oh God,' Jennifer whispered, shaking her head.

'I'd been hit by flying shrapnel. Right here in my chest. Brodie was so badly hurt, I thought he wasn't going to make it. They tried, but they couldn't save his leg.' He began rubbing at his chest with a circular motion, staring at nothing. 'There was no sign of Paula. Later, in the hospital, I found out she'd died. They had to do DNA tests to be sure it was her body they'd found. That was how bad it was.' He took a shuddering breath. 'Since then, I've been prey to ... flashbacks. Episodes, where I'm back there, in the smoke and the carnage.'

She put a hand on his arm. 'I'm so sorry.'

He closed his eyes.

She understood better now what he had been suffering, and wanted to kiss him. To comfort him, if she could. But she dared not. Not until all her questions had been answered.

'God, Alex. I wish you'd told me this before.'

'I wasn't ready to talk about it. To be honest, I didn't think I *could* talk about it. Until this summer, it was all locked in here. Under the scars.' He tapped his chest. 'Then I met you, and something clicked inside. I was able to feel again, for the first time since the bombing. But I was terrified you'd see right to the heart of me, to what I'd become. So I behaved badly, tried to pretend I wasn't interested.'

'You should have taken a chance on me, not pushed me away. Especially after Nelly died.' She swallowed. 'Do you know how much that hurt?'

He grimaced. 'I've got a pretty good idea.'

'It confirmed everything I'd thought about you.'

'That I'm an idiot?'

'No.' She couldn't smile. Pain was eating away at her,

destroying her oxygen. 'That you're a big movie star, and I don't belong in your world.'

'Not true,' he said huskily, catching her by the shoulders. 'Look at me, please. I'm just a man. Like any other man. And at that point, with Nana gone, my head was all over the place. I wasn't sure I'd ever recover enough to be worth a damn to you,' he said, then added reluctantly, 'Once the funeral was over, I wanted to end it all.'

She stared at him in shocked silence.

'I know, I'm ashamed of that now,' he said. 'But that was why I made plans to leave Cornwall. You deserve better than me, Jenny. I didn't want to burden you with that horror.'

'You don't ever need to be ashamed of what you've suffered, Alex. The world hurt you, so you closed off from it. I know exactly how that feels.' She stroked his rough, stubbly cheek, and sucked in her breath when he nuzzled against her palm. 'But if you love me, don't ever think that way again. Please.'

He closed his eyes. 'I'm climbing out of that hole now. Honestly.'

'But not *fixed*, you said.'

'There are no certainties with PTSD. No quick cures. That's why I pushed you away.' He swallowed compulsively. 'I felt unworthy of you. Half a man.'

'Don't.'

'I came back here this week to empty the place out. Sell the estate. Pixie Cottage, too. With you as a sitting tenant, of course.'

Her eyes widened, watching him. 'And now?'

'Now that I know there's hope,' he said, kissing her palm,

and then pulling her close against him, 'I'm willing to do whatever you tell me to in order to keep you in my life.'

'We could take therapy together. So I can understand better. Help you recover.'

Alex leant in fast and kissed her hard on the lips. Her whole body responded, her legs oddly boneless as she clung to him, her nervous system on overdrive. When he finally lifted his head again, he was smiling.

'Yes,' he said urgently, 'if that's what it takes. And I'll drop the idea of moving back to Hollywood. I want to be with you.'

'God, no, you mustn't give up your career.' His damp hair had flopped over his forehead, and she pushed the stray locks tenderly back. 'You don't have to give anything up for me. You already have me, Alex.'

'I do?'

'Didn't I already say so?'

'You used the past tense,' he pointed out.

'Okay, at first, I *fell* in love with you. The sexy film star, the supportive brother, the caring grandson.' She met his eyes. 'But now I *love* you, Alex. Not for who you are, or what you do, but for the way you changed me just by coming into my life.' Slowly, she traced his lips with her fingers, and felt him draw breath. 'When we met, I was in a bad place too. I was lonely, but it was a self-imposed loneliness. I was hurting, and desperate to keep the world at bay. Just like you.'

He nodded his understanding.

'I don't love Raphael any more. I want you to know that. It's taken a long time, but . . . My stories helped.'

'Your stories?' He frowned. 'They've helped you too?'

'Those old Cornish folk tales are about love and loss. Mostly loss, to be honest. And if there's one thing they've taught me, it's that life is short. Too short to waste time pining after someone who doesn't give a stuff about you.' She smiled sadly. 'Sometimes, your heart is right in front of you. But you end up following a fantasy instead and getting lost on the way. That's what happened to me with Raphael.'

'I'm not Tregar. I love you, and I'll never hurt you. That's a promise.'

She bit her lip, tears brimming in her eyes.

'And I'll never ask you to stay here,' she promised him in return. 'Acting is your life, and if Hollywood is where you need to be, then you must go there.'

'I'm glad to hear you say that.' His mouth quirked. 'I want to do another Cheetham film. They're fun. But I could always wriggle out of it.'

'Don't you dare. I want you to be happy, not chained to my side.' Her heart was singing with joy. She couldn't help smiling at his generosity. 'Since we seem to be negotiating our relationship here, is there anything you'd like *me* to give up for *you*?' Her eyes teased him. 'The pageant job, maybe?'

He bared his teeth. 'Tregar had better keep his hands to himself.'

'Raphael is too busy with Hannah and the baby to look at me. And even if he did, I wouldn't be interested. Besides, I'm not that needy any more. That's what I meant when I said you'd changed me, Alex. Just getting to know you has opened up a whole new way of thinking and feeling for me. It's going to be a challenge, not wishing you home with me the whole time. But it's what I need right now. To love with open hands. Not to hold on so tight.'

'If you're positive that's what you want . . .' He stroked her cheek, his gaze troubled. 'I don't ever want you to feel lonely again. Because I know exactly what that's like. To be with people constantly, yet feel unhappy and alone inside.' His voice softened. 'I remember the first time I came to visit you at Pixie Cottage. You looked beaten and withdrawn. But defiant with it, too. Like you'd bite any man who was stupid enough to get too close.'

'It didn't put you off though.'

'I like a challenge.' He grinned. 'And I liked that you weren't star-struck. Most women are falling over me within five seconds.'

'Oh, wonderful.'

'Trust me, it can be wearing, that kind of mindless adulation. But you were different. Even unhappy, you were still your own person. And marvellously eccentric.'

She laughed. 'Well, I can't give up the pageant job. I'm looking forward to the hard work. But is there anything else you'd like me to change? Should I throw away my broomstick, perhaps? Or my jar of newt eyes?'

'Don't you dare. I love that you're a witch,' he growled. 'I look forward to strange-smelling potions in the kitchen. It'll remind me of Nana.'

'Ripper, then?'

'That damn Siamese cat . . . No, you love him. As if you'd ever part with Ripper, anyway.' He shook his head. 'Seriously, you need him. I'm often away filming for weeks at a time, and though Brodie and I have plans to set up a film company down here, that could be a few years off. It won't always be practical for you to come with me when I'm filming on location. You'll have your books to write, and Ripper will be good company for you.'

'Until we have a baby.'

His eyes widened, fixed on her face. 'Are we having a baby?'

'Not imminently.'

His relief was tinged with excitement. 'But that offer's on the table, I take it?'

'Only if you want it.'

'Of course I want it. God, more than anything. To love you, to settle down with you, to start a family. I just thought . . . You're so independent, I didn't know you'd be interested. I swear to you, I'm going to make this relationship work.'

'We'll *both* make it work.' She took his hand and held it against her thudding heart. 'Together. As a couple.'

He gave a strangled whoop. 'Jennifer Bolitho, I love you!' His eyes narrowed on her face. 'But only if you're sure about this. I may be over the worst, but I could still relapse, my therapist said. Even with meds, things could get messy.'

'I can deal.'

'I'll remind you of that next time I'm smashing a hole in your bedroom wall.'

'That's not going to happen.'

'You can't possibly know—'

'It's not going to happen,' she repeated.

Alex smiled at last, the most relaxed she had ever seen him. 'Thank you for believing in me, my love.' She blushed at those words, and he bent to kiss her hand, his lips warm on her skin. 'I wish Nana were here to see this.'

'Me too. I really miss her.' A sudden thought struck her, and she gasped. 'Hold on, what about Nelly's goats? We can't let them go. We have to keep them at Porro Park.'

Alex blinked. 'We're going to have goats now? As well as babies?'

'Babies, *plural*?'

'Sorry, I got carried away.'

Jennifer laughed at his humour, but shook her head. 'Quit joking around and be serious for a minute. I've just realised something important.'

'Go on, darling.'

Darling . . .

It took her a few confused seconds of hot-cheeked pleasure to recover from that word, too. She decided she could get used to him calling her lovely names.

'You and me, Alex, looking after her goats together . . . It's exactly what Nelly would have wanted.' She gasped. 'In fact, I wouldn't be surprised if your grandmother hadn't planned all this from the very first day I turned up here, towing Baby.' She thought of Nelly's strange appearance in the shrubbery at Porro Park, and the way she had practically dragged Jennifer back to the house with her. 'It's like she put a spell on us.'

'That wouldn't surprise me. That's why Nana liked you so much, I'm sure. Two witches together.' He glanced over his shoulder at the escaped goat, who was tearing at a patch of faded nettles. 'Look, Lizzie and Penny will be here soon to pick up the goats. It does seem a shame to let them go to an animal sanctuary when they could stay here with us. Maybe we could walk up to the house together and apologise, tell them I've changed my mind.' He hesitated, meeting her eyes. 'If you're absolutely sure that all this – you, me, the goats – is what you want?'

'I've never been more sure of anything in my entire life.' Jennifer held out her hand and Alex took it without hesitating. Their fingers laced together, and they smiled at each other.

'Come on, then,' he said. 'Let's go and rescue some goats.'

Discover more from Beth Good . . .

A gorgeous Christmas romance

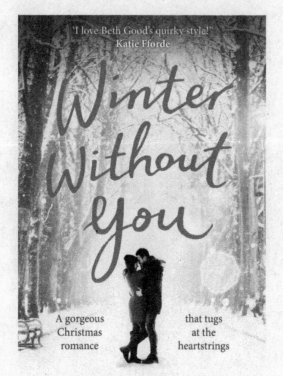

Winter Without You

A gorgeous
Christmas
romance

that tugs
at the
heartstrings

BETH GOOD